STARS
COLLIDE

OTHER TITLES BY RACHEL LACEY

Ms. Right Series

Read Between the Lines

No Rings Attached

STARS
COLLIDE

a novel

RACHEL LACEY

Text copyright © 2023 by Rachel Bates
All rights reserved.

Published by Montlake, Seattle

www.apub.com

Amazon, the Amazon logo, and Montlake are trademarks of Amazon.com, Inc., or its affiliates.

ISBN-13: 9781662509117 (paperback)
ISBN-13: 9781662509124 (digital)

Cover design by Faceout Studio, Jeff Miller
Cover illustration by Carolina Melis
Cover image: © Polina Tomtosova / Shutterstock

Printed in the United States of America

STARS
COLLIDE

CHAPTER ONE

Eden Sands was not "good." Over the course of her career, she'd been called many things. Beautiful. Arrogant. Talented. Rude. Generous. Cold. Hot. Difficult. Iconic. So many polarizing adjectives, but never "good." Good meant mediocre, and that was something she'd never be.

Eden stared at her reflection in the mirrored wall before her, imagining the arena full of her peers that she'd be performing for on Sunday. She wrapped her fingers around the microphone stand as the opening notes of "Alone" began to play. Onstage, she was invincible. Offstage, well . . . the past year had been a humbling experience in a multitude of ways.

"I didn't know," she sang, "how lonely it could be. A room full of people, yet no one sees me."

The Grammy Awards were just days away. Eden closed her eyes and imagined the heat of the spotlight, the roar of the crowd, the electricity that raced down her spine every time she took the stage. God, she hoped she'd be going home with one of those gold gramophones. After the year she'd had, she deserved a win. That yearning in the pit of her stomach said she *needed* it.

This performance had to make a statement. It had to show the world she was back . . . not that she'd gone anywhere, at least not intentionally. She was stronger than ever, and this performance had to prove it. Her manager, Stella Pascual, sat in the corner, observing Eden's rehearsal. Hopefully, Eden was about to wow her.

Eden opened her eyes, meeting her reflection unflinchingly. "I'm alone, but I'm not," she sang.

As the music swelled around her, she slid the microphone from its stand and stepped back, careful to hit the orange-taped mark on the stage with her boot. She turned and stalked toward the rear of the room, which had been marked to the exact specifications of the Grammy stage. A felt-covered contraption awaited her, decorated to look like a flower-laden hilltop. Eden spun with the music. She performed a few well-choreographed moves, swaying her hips in a way that would flare the skirt she'd be wearing on Sunday.

Then she turned and climbed carefully to the top of the hill. Multicolored lights shone overhead, transforming the stage into a lush field. Eden brought the microphone to her lips for the pivotal line that was her personal favorite. "I'm never truly alone, because I have myself to keep me company."

The music changed, and the field disappeared, replaced with glittering stones. She stepped forward onto her mark, allowing the felt beneath her feet to be snatched away, completing the transformation of the stage.

The hard, pounding beat of her most recent single, "Never Too Late," filled the room. She lifted the microphone and began to sing, moving in time with the beat. She sang an abbreviated version of the song to fit the Grammys' time requirements, ending with one hand punched toward the sky.

Sweat trickled down her back, and a blister throbbed under the ball of her left foot. Adrenaline coursed through her veins, and a wide smile stretched her lips. She slid her thumb over the base of the microphone, flipping the power button.

Her manager stood from the folding chair where she'd been watching Eden rehearse. Stella was a petite Filipino American woman, her long black hair pulled back today in a sleek ponytail. She crossed the room to stand in front of Eden.

"What did you think?" Eden asked.

"It was good," Stella said.

Eden ground her teeth. Not that word! Her Grammy performance couldn't be "good." She had to be exceptional. She needed to deliver a performance that everyone would be talking about the next day.

Reviewers had used phrases like "good but uninspired" to describe her most recent album. One had commented that she sounded "as if she were boring even herself." Another had called her "tired." Truthfully, she was exhausted. She'd poured her heart and soul into her music for twenty years, and yet here she was. Album sales were down. Her upcoming tour hadn't sold out. Her star was beginning to fade, which was infuriating.

She might be tired to her bones, but music was what got her out of bed every morning. It fueled her, and she was desperate to polish herself off and reclaim her place at the top.

"It was better than good," she protested.

Stella leveled her with a look that said, "You don't really believe that." And deep down, Eden knew she was right.

Eden huffed. "What do you suggest, then?" Because Stella never would have started this conversation if she didn't have an idea in mind. And as much as Eden didn't want to hear it, Stella's advice was usually spot on.

Stella's brown eyes gleamed. "Let's bring in a guest partway through your performance and make 'Never Too Late' a duet."

"I'm not a huge fan of duets." Eden frowned. Duets meant giving up partial control over her performance, which left room for mistakes. "And who would even agree to do it on such short notice?"

"The Grammys are known for pairing up performers for unexpected duets during the live broadcast," Stella said. "Viewers love it, and I have the perfect person in mind. If I'm right, she'll jump at the chance."

"She? Who?"

"Anna Moss," Stella said. "She's got the number one song on the pop charts right now, and a lot of people think she was robbed of the Best New Artist award last year."

"I know who she is." Eden knew the bubbly young pop star all too well. They'd never met, but Anna's music had been impossible to escape this year. Her new single, "Love Me, Love You," was annoyingly catchy enough that even Eden couldn't get the song out of her head. Anna herself was perky and blonde, smiled way too much, and wore blindingly colorful clothing.

"She's attending the ceremony. In fact, you're up for several of the same awards."

"I know that too." Eden kept her expression neutral because she also knew sales for Anna's new album had eclipsed her own.

"She's a huge fan of yours," Stella said. "She probably already knows the words to 'Never Too Late,' and I bet she'd be thrilled to perform it with you on the Grammy stage."

Eden pressed her lips together. She didn't want to perform with Anna Moss. It irritated the hell out of her that Anna was having a bigger year than she was, that performing with her could give Eden a boost. She was Eden Sands, for crying out loud! "Let me think about it."

"Don't think for too long. If you don't snap her up, someone else very well might."

Eden made a noncommittal sound. "I'll let you know tomorrow morning."

Thirty minutes later, Eden stepped outside into the LA sunshine, flanked by the head of her security detail, Taylor, and her assistant,

Paris. She inhaled the crisp air, grateful for Southern California's mild winters. Eden had been alerted earlier about the crowd waiting outside, so she had her stage smile in place as she began walking toward the car that would take her home.

"Eden! Eden!" The air filled with the sound of people screaming and shouting, all vying for her attention. When she turned toward them, she could hardly see their faces past all the cell phones being thrust in her direction. A few fans actually had their backs to her, taking selfies with her in the background.

And her smile widened, because her fans were *here*, despite her sales slump. Eden signed various photos and T-shirts and posed for selfies while Taylor helped maintain her personal space. Eden enjoyed interacting with her fans. Without them, she wouldn't have a career, but sometimes they got way too handsy. They grabbed and groped and tried to hug her, and she didn't particularly like being touched by strangers.

As she greeted the fans, Taylor and Paris kept her moving forward, and within a few minutes, she was safely in the back seat of the SUV. Taylor took her usual seat in front with the driver, while Paris sat next to Eden.

"Tomorrow's schedule is updated on your calendar," Paris said as she buckled her seat belt.

"Thank you," Eden told her assistant gratefully.

"You bet." Paris pulled out her phone and started tapping away, working her magic to keep Eden's life running smoothly.

Idly, Eden stared out the window, watching the colorful buildings and palm trees that lined the route from the rehearsal studio in Burbank to her condo in Marina del Rey. Her mind whirled with frustration, and her body buzzed with the leftover adrenaline from a full day of rehearsals.

She realized she was humming along with the radio a moment before she recognized the song. It was Anna Moss's latest single.

"That song will be the death of me," Eden muttered under her breath. Her foot tapped restlessly as the irritatingly catchy song she couldn't seem to escape filled the interior of the car. And maybe she hadn't said it as quietly as she thought she had, because her driver pressed a button on the radio, and the music changed.

When the car arrived at her building, she thanked her driver, said good night to Taylor and Paris, and stood, grateful for the private entrance that allowed her to go inside without fanfare. Thanks to that private entrance, the paparazzi had mostly left her alone at home since she'd moved here, which was a huge upgrade, although the condo itself was a downgrade from the Santa Monica home she'd shared with Zach.

The doorman held the door open for her with a smile. "Evening, Ms. Sands."

"Good evening, Marco. Thank you." She returned his smile as she stepped inside. The sound of trickling water greeted her, courtesy of the waterfall feature on the back wall. Ordinarily, she found it soothing, but right now, it made her long for a shower.

She punched the glossy gold button for the elevator, shifting restlessly as she waited for it to arrive. A duet with Anna Moss. That was absurd. Eden didn't need the young pop sensation to boost her own popularity, or at least . . . she shouldn't.

The elevator door opened with a brisk ding. She stepped inside and rode to the fifteenth floor, then let herself into her condo. Once she'd locked the door behind herself and reengaged the alarm, she let out a long sigh. A faint floral scent lingered in the air, reminding her that her cleaning service had been in earlier. The surfaces sparkled as brightly as the building itself, built not long before Eden bought this unit last year.

A new start for her postdivorce life. Another sigh threatened, but this time she swallowed it, annoyed by her own mood. Evenings were the hardest since the divorce. What did a person do for so many hours without someone to talk to? She missed having someone to laugh with as she watched mindless reality television, someone to sit across the table from at dinnertime. Unlike most people, Eden couldn't simply go out, not without calling a member of her security team to accompany her, and where was the fun in that?

She headed to the kitchen to pour herself a glass of water and then sat on the sofa in the living room to tab through a day's worth of messages on her phone. There weren't many. It was alarming, really, to realize how few friends she had without Zach in her life.

One of her notifications was for an entertainment podcast she followed, which had released a new episode discussing Grammy predictions. She clicked play, taking a drink of water as the hosts engaged in their usual banter.

"All right, folks, let's get right to it," the first host, a woman named Tarin, said. "We're all dying to know who this year's big Grammy winners will be. Let's start out with industry heavyweight Eden Sands. We all love her, am I right?"

"Hey, I'll be the first to admit that I rocked out to 'Daydreamer' when I was a teenager," the other host, Nicole, said with a laugh.

Eden rolled her eyes at the reference to her first number one hit. If she'd known then how many times she'd end up performing that song, maybe she wouldn't have been so quick to record it. That wasn't really true, though. She was grateful for every moment of her career.

"But the critical reaction to Eden's latest album has been tepid at best," Tarin continued.

"I hate to say it, but even I was disappointed," Nicole said. "Eden seems to have lost some of her passion this year. Maybe it has to do with her divorce from Zachary Tomlin?"

Eden flinched. Yes, the divorce had hurt—*still* hurt—but her talent wasn't dependent on having a man in her life, dammit.

"I'm sure that didn't help," Tarin agreed. "But there were a few albums this year that I did love, and I expect both of these ladies to take home multiple Grammys this weekend."

"Let me guess. You're talking about Sasha Sol and Anna Moss."

"That's exactly right, Nicole. Sasha's had quite a year, and her album *On the Rocks* is arguably the most deserving to win Album of the Year."

"I agree. Sasha could end up walking away with all the major awards on Sunday night. But let's not forget about Anna Moss. She's considered a long shot, but her sophomore album, *Simply Myself*, was the soundtrack to our summer, and she just might be the surprise star of the night."

Eden stopped the playback. She put down her phone and closed her eyes. The weight of everything she'd just heard pressed her into the cushion beneath her, forcing the air from her lungs. Stella was right. Anna might be just the right person to shake up Eden's Grammy performance. With a groan, she picked up her phone again, this time to call her manager.

"Eden, hi," Stella answered breathlessly. The sound of conversation echoed over the line behind her.

"Sorry if I called at a bad time."

"We're about to sit down to dinner, but I wouldn't have answered if I couldn't talk," Stella told her.

"I won't keep you, then. I just wanted to let you know that I'm in. I'll do the duet with Anna Moss."

CHAPTER TWO

Anna sucked in a deep breath. She held it as she counted to five in her head, and then she exhaled slowly. She was still new enough in this industry that she was easily starstruck, so her nerves were hardly unexpected. But this . . . this was maybe the most nerve-racking thing she'd ever done.

"Ready?" Kyrie asked, giving Anna an assessing look. Kyrie McIntosh had been Anna's assistant for several years and was someone she now considered a friend as well. She kept Anna organized and on time and made her laugh. Today, Kyrie's brown hair was tinged with blue, but tomorrow, who knew? It might be orange.

"Nothing in my teeth?" Anna made a face at Kyrie, baring her teeth.

Kyrie rolled her eyes, giving Anna a gentle nudge. "You look fine. Stop stalling."

"But . . ." Anna sucked in another deep breath. She worked hard to contain her inner fangirl when she attended industry events, but right now, she was about to meet her idol. She was about to rehearse for a Grammy performance with her idol, and her inner fangirl was *screaming*. Her inner fangirl was about to faint.

"I know you're a little bit in love with her, but she's just a woman, and right now she's waiting to rehearse with you." Kyrie made a shooing motion with her hands.

"Eden Sands isn't *just* a woman. She's an icon. A legend." Anna was determined to make a good first impression, hopefully even impress her.

Kyrie peeked through the doorway into the rehearsal space. "And she looks impatient. Get your ass in there."

"Oh God." Anna's voice sounded like she'd inhaled helium. Eden looked impatient? But Anna was ten minutes early. How early had Eden gotten here? She peered over Kyrie's shoulder, and sure enough, there was Eden. She stood in the middle of the room, talking to a Black woman, one foot tapping restlessly against the stage.

Anna's stomach tingled, because oh wow, she was really about to meet her idol. Even from a distance, Eden had a presence about her, something that made her difficult to look away from. That tingling sensation intensified.

"Go on in and introduce yourself," Kyrie urged.

"Okay, okay, I'm going." Anna stepped through the doorway.

"Knock her socks off," Kyrie called from behind her.

Under other circumstances, she would have flipped Kyrie off in retaliation for the jab, but right now, Anna was having trouble with basic functions like walking. Her knees shook, and she felt like she'd just drunk an extra fizzy soda . . . like her entire body was carbonated.

Eden watched her approach, her expression impossible to read. She was dressed all in black, a silky blouse tucked into formfitting jeans and knee-high leather boots. Her dark-brown hair was down, cascading over her shoulders in glossy waves, and those bright-blue eyes Anna had admired in countless photos were fixed on her with laser-sharp intensity.

Everything about Eden's stance said, "I'm a star, and I know it." This was the woman whose music Anna had listened to on repeat throughout her teens, the woman she'd fantasized about back when she was coming to terms with her sexuality. And now they were going to sing a duet together.

At the Grammy Awards.

Anna's knees almost gave out, but somehow she kept walking. Up close, Eden was tall, too, standing a few inches over Anna's five foot five.

Anna drew in another steadying breath, composing herself as she extended her hand. "Anna Moss. It's an honor to meet you, Ms. Sands."

Eden took it and shook. Her fingers were cool against Anna's, and her grip was firm. "Please call me Eden."

"Eden." Anna was pleased with how steady her voice sounded. She might be a raging fangirl, but she was also a professional, and first impressions were so important. "I hope you don't mind me saying that you've been an inspiration to me. I have so much respect for you, and I'm a huge fan of your music."

"I don't think anyone would mind hearing that." Eden smiled, but it was the kind of smile Anna had seen her give in interviews: appreciative but distant. Impersonal. "Thank you."

"You're welcome."

"So, I'm told you already know the words to the song?"

Anna nodded enthusiastically, holding up her phone. "Your assistant sent over a file last night showing the lyric split for the duet, so yes, I'm ready."

"Perfect. Let's get started, then." Eden turned and walked to the center of the stage, placing one hand on the microphone stand.

Anna looked around for a moment in panic. What was she supposed to do? The last thing she wanted was to look like an amateur in front of Eden Sands.

The woman Eden had been talking to when Anna walked in approached. "I'm Lora, the choreographer."

"Nice to meet you, Lora," Anna said, shaking her hand.

"Likewise," Lora said. "Eden will begin with 'Alone,' then segue into 'Never Too Late,' where you'll join her. Your portion of the performance is relatively unchoreographed. You'll enter from stage right when I give your cue and walk slowly toward Eden, meeting on this mark." Lora gestured to a section of orange tape on the stage. "As the chorus begins."

Anna followed as Lora led her through a quick run-through of the blocking for her performance. Then she was handed a microphone, and . . . this was really happening. It had been surreal enough when Anna was nominated alongside Eden for several Grammy Awards. Performing with her was something Anna hadn't even thought to fantasize about.

Her fingers trembled as she gripped the microphone. *Be cool, Anna.* She took her place offstage with Lora. The opening notes of "Alone" filled the room, and Anna watched transfixed as Eden began to sing. Her voice was rich and powerful, drawing Anna into the song. She'd seen Eden in concert before, but this was different . . . so much more intimate. That tingling sensation in Anna's stomach was back.

Eden strode to the rear of the stage, climbing a felt-covered hill as "Never Too Late" began. Lora turned to Anna. She counted down from five with her fingers and then pointed toward the stage.

Anna stepped out, microphone in hand, heart lodged somewhere in her esophagus.

"Your face is all I see," Eden sang. "Close my eyes, and you're free."

Anna lifted her microphone. "It's never too late for love. Never too late for second chances." Her voice filled the room, her natural soprano coming in higher than Eden's alto, and maybe she was projecting, but their voices seemed to complement each other nicely.

They walked toward each other as they sang, alternating lines during the verse. It was smooth . . . too smooth? Anna fought her natural urge to shake things up, following the blocking Lora had shown her. She and Eden faced each other to sing the final line together. Eden seemed to look right through Anna, her gaze distant. "Never too late for love."

As the music faded away, various staff and crew swarmed the stage, including Kyrie and Lora. Their expressions ranged from pleased to pensive, but no one looked wowed, confirming the nagging feeling Anna hadn't wanted to acknowledge. When she glanced at Eden, her jaw was clenched as if she knew it too.

"What did you think?" Eden asked. Her expression was neutral, but a challenge gleamed in her eyes, one Anna wasn't sure how to read. Did Eden want her to speak the truth or lie to protect Eden's ego? Anna's response might make or break Eden's opinion of her. That much was terrifyingly clear.

"Um." Anna passed the microphone from her left hand to her right as she weighed her answer. An idea had begun to take shape in her mind, a way to shake up their performance, but it would mean scrapping almost everything Eden and her team had put together so far. Did she dare? Then again, she hadn't made it this far by playing it safe. "Well, I thought it was *good* . . ."

A muscle beside Eden's right eye twitched.

Anna lifted her chin. No going back now. "But I did have a somewhat crazy idea for how we could shake up our duet that might really get people talking on Grammy night, if you want to hear it?"

Eden slow-blinked, her expression hardening subtly beneath the polite veneer. Anna felt the shift like being blasted with arctic air, and fuck, had she really just suggested she knew better than Eden Sands? She was *such* an idiot.

"Tell me." Eden feigned disinterest to cover her annoyance that Anna wanted to make changes to the performance. Until this moment, Anna had been exactly what Eden expected. Young, enthusiastic, and obviously starstruck by Eden, although she'd held her own during their rehearsal.

Anna had on red athletic pants and a black tank top with a rainbow across the front, her blonde hair in a high ponytail. She met Eden's gaze unflinchingly, and Eden felt a surge of irrational anger that Anna had so easily voiced what Eden had been too afraid to acknowledge. She could barely remember a time when she'd been that fearless.

"This hill reminds me of the music video for 'Daydreamer.'" Anna pointed to the felt-covered structure behind them.

That wasn't even remotely where Eden might have expected her to take this conversation, and now Eden was at a loss. She gave Anna a look that said, "Go on."

"It got me thinking," Anna continued. "What if we performed 'After Midnight' together instead of 'Never Too Late'?"

"Why 'After Midnight'?" It was the title track off Eden's latest album and had been a moderately successful single last fall, but she failed to see its relevance to their performance.

"Because it's about how you become a slightly different person after midnight, right?" Anna said. "You're more free to be yourself late at night when no one's watching. What if we make a twist on that so the 'after midnight' parts of the song represent a younger version of you instead? 'Daydreamer' is the song that first made you a star, and in the video for it, you wore a green dress embellished with flowers and a blonde wig. It's iconic. Everyone recognizes that look. What if I wear a similar dress for our duet? And I've already got blonde hair. I can represent past Eden, and our duet will be like you're singing to a younger version of yourself."

"You're the younger version of me?" Eden tried to keep her tone neutral, but she wasn't sure she succeeded. The gall of this girl to insinuate she was the next Eden Sands!

"No," Anna said quickly, for the first time looking as if she regretted starting this conversation. "I would never compare myself to you. You're a legend, and I'm . . . I'm just the woman lucky enough to share the stage with you on Sunday night."

"Your idea would involve a new song arrangement and wardrobe for you. Those things cost time and money, and the performance is in four days," Eden pointed out. It was the truth, and yet Anna's concept held water. It might even be great, as much as Eden hated to admit it.

"You're right." Anna took a step back. "It was a silly idea. I'm sorry I brought it up."

"It's not silly. Never let anyone convince you that your ideas aren't valid, Anna." Eden didn't care for Anna's bubblegum persona, but she'd been a teen pop star once, afraid to be a nuisance, eager to live up to everyone's expectations, even at the expense of her own well-being. She knew how devastating it felt to be told her ideas weren't good enough.

Anna looked at her, her expression a mixture of adoration and confusion. Eden wasn't sure what to make of her. Anna was acting like a starry-eyed fangirl one moment and calling Eden out the next. The dichotomy was oddly fascinating.

"It's a good idea," Eden admitted. In fact, Anna's concept for Eden to sing to a younger version of herself might make their performance the one everyone would be talking about, and wasn't that the reason Eden had brought her on board in the first place?

"You think so?" Anna asked, sounding slightly breathless. It was impressive the way she clearly looked up to Eden yet still wasn't afraid to go toe to toe with her. That took guts. Anna could sing too.

Eden nodded. "Let's see what the team thinks."

A smile slowly bloomed across Anna's face. "Really?"

"Yes." Eden led the way toward where Stella stood near the soundboard, talking to Lora. If they gave their blessing, Eden was willing to give this a chance. It was innovative, *different*, the kind of thing viewers would love on Grammy night.

"Anna, this is my manager, Stella Pascual, and I think you've already met our choreographer, Lora Headley." Eden made introductions and then gestured for Anna to explain her idea to them.

Anna related her performance concept to Stella and Lora, embellishing slightly on the way she'd first described it to Eden. Either her confidence had grown, or she'd had a chance to think it through in more detail now. When she finished, Eden could tell by the looks on Stella's and Lora's faces that they were on board.

"That's a *big* change," Lora said. "And we're already behind schedule by turning Eden's performance into a duet."

"It's a big change, but I love it," Stella said. "Anna, your wardrobe should be relatively easy to adjust, right?"

Anna nodded. "Yes, my stylist is still pulling options, so I could definitely have her switch gears and look for a green dress similar to what Eden wore in the 'Daydreamer' video."

"Perfect. Do you two want to work out the lyric split on your own?" Stella asked.

Eden stifled a sigh. "We can do that."

"I'll find Paris and have her print out a few copies of the lyrics for you to work off of." Stella turned and walked away.

Anna stared at Eden with wide eyes. "Wow. We're really doing this."

"Looks like we are. Why don't you talk to your assistant about the wardrobe change and then meet me in the break room?" Eden pointed to the doorway.

"You got it." Anna bounced away toward the blue-haired woman she'd arrived with. Okay, she walked, but there was a definite flounce in her step that had Eden fighting a smile.

She'd underestimated Anna. Perhaps she'd judged her by the colorful way she dressed, or worse, she might have even judged her based on the way the media portrayed her. Eden of all people ought to know better. She'd allowed herself to be poisoned by her own bitterness. She hated that she needed Anna's popularity to give her own a boost, but that wasn't Anna's fault.

This was on Eden, and she was going to fix her attitude, starting now.

"I think this last line should be yours." Anna tapped the paper in front of her. They'd highlighted and discarded several drafts as they worked out who would sing what. Eden had been surprisingly patient and cooperative. In fact, she seemed more relaxed overall than she had been when Anna first arrived that morning.

"But the last line is clearly the younger version of me." Eden turned her head to meet Anna's gaze. She had this intense way of looking at Anna that made her want to squirm . . . or blush. Sometimes both.

Anna was doing her damndest not to let her insecurities show, to hold her own beside her idol, although her nerves were shredded at this point. "But it's the last line," she countered. "It's your song, your performance, and I think if you sing this line, it could sound like you're reclaiming your younger self. You're still her. I'll just kind of fade away in the background."

Eden looked pensive for a moment, then nodded. "I like it, but you shouldn't fade away at the end. This is your performance too."

"I can pop back out afterward to wave to the crowd or whatever, but the end of the song should be yours."

"All right. Are we ready to start rehearsing?" Eden asked.

Anna popped to her feet. "I'm ready. Let's do this."

Eden stood with the smooth grace of a dancer, although Anna knew she'd never been one. As a result of having been a fan for so many years, she knew a lot more about Eden than she probably should. Perhaps Eden's elegance came from a lifetime of being in front of the cameras, her every move watched and critiqued.

Anna had been young when she got her start, too, but not as young as Eden. Anna was twenty-two when she was signed to play a nerdy teen witch on *Hex High*, the show that made her B-list famous. She had been twenty-five when she left the show to pursue her music career.

Eden had been just sixteen when she released her first album, which meant she'd been famous for more than half her life. Twenty years in the spotlight was a long time. Anna couldn't even imagine. The spotlight had been aimed in her direction for only a few years, and already she felt its burn.

It was getting harder for her to go out in public without being recognized, although she hadn't completely lost her anonymity yet. She wasn't complaining, though, because she was living her dream, writing and performing queer songs for her increasingly diverse fan base.

Now if only she could get the world to see her as an adult and take her seriously as an artist. She was so tired of being called bubbly and cute. Anna had never won a major award or received critical acclaim for her music. It would mean the world to her to win a Grammy on Sunday night, tangible evidence that she had the talent to succeed. That she belonged here.

She'd definitely cry if she won, probably sleep with her Grammy beside her bed. Yes, she knew awards were arbitrary. Many legendary artists were chronically snubbed, but she'd been practicing her acceptance speech since she was a little girl. She wanted a Grammy more than anything.

As Eden led the way toward the stage, Anna was struck again by her beauty. She walked with such poise, such presence. Eden owned every room she entered. Even her clothes were elegant. Her silk blouse shimmered in the light, and her jeans hugged her curves like they were made for her. Eden had a great ass.

And Anna was totally checking her out right now. She rushed to catch up, then caught Eden's eye to give her a quick smile. Eden returned it, and this smile looked softer and more natural than the one Anna had received when they first met.

Eden climbed to the top of the makeshift hill. "I'll start up here like I've just finished singing 'Alone.' Ready?"

Anna nodded.

Eden switched on her microphone and lifted it. "Smile for the camera. Perfect makeup, perfect hair."

Anna felt all the fine hair on her body stand on end at the sound of Eden's voice filling the room without musical accompaniment. This was a *moment*. She wanted to pinch herself. Anna listened in awe as Eden sang the first verse of the song.

"But after midnight . . . ," Eden crooned.

Anna was so mesmerized by her voice that she nearly missed her cue. She fumbled to turn on her microphone and walked out from behind the structure. "I let my hair down. After midnight, I'm not afraid to be a clown."

Lora held up a hand, and Anna stopped singing. "Let's tweak your entrance a bit."

Anna nodded. Lora tested a few variations of Anna's entrance, finally deciding she would emerge from behind the hill in a puff of stage smoke.

"Eden, after you sing your last line, you're going to give Anna a hug, as if you're embracing your younger self," Lora said. "Anna, you'll rest your head on her shoulder. We're going for a tender moment to end the performance."

It was a beautiful concept, but when the time came, Anna found herself flustered all over again about touching Eden. Mostly, she'd managed well today. Singing a duet with her idol? No problem. She was a professional. But cuddling up to the woman she'd fantasized about as a teenager? *Hoo boy.*

Carefully, Anna leaned in and rested her face against the soft silk of Eden's blouse. She smelled vaguely like roses, and Anna could feel the warmth of her skin through the thin fabric. Eden's bra strap was beneath her cheek, and the soft swell of her breast pressed against Anna's neck.

Eden's arms came around her, holding her gently, almost delicately, and Anna forgot how to breathe. Her heart gave a strange little double beat, and *oh no*, this was not a platonic reaction to a hug. This wasn't hero worship either. Anna probably shouldn't be surprised to feel the stirring of attraction. After all, Eden was gorgeous and exactly Anna's type. She'd always gone for older, powerful women.

For a warm moment, she was in Eden's arms, and then it was over. Anna straightened. Eden turned to speak to Lora, completely unaffected. Of course she hadn't felt anything. As far as Anna knew, Eden was straight, and even if she wasn't, she was unlikely to lust over Anna after all her fangirling earlier. They weren't exactly peers.

Lora clapped her hands. "Wonderful, ladies. Let's try it again from the top."

They ran through the song again. It went much smoother this time, and Anna was able to enjoy being part of the performance, not merely trying to hold her own beside Eden. They practiced the duet several more times, fine-tuning vocals and blocking, before they called it a day.

"I'll see you tomorrow." She smiled at Eden as they prepared to head out.

"You will. Goodbye, Anna." Eden breezed toward the door, flanked by her entourage, and Anna could only watch in starry-eyed wonder. *What a day.*

CHAPTER THREE

Anna reached for her sunglasses as she and Kyrie headed for the door. Her stomach growled. She was starving. And exhausted, the kind of tired she usually felt after a full day of press, the kind of tired that came from being "on" for hours on end. Rehearsing with Eden had been amazing, but it had also taken a lot out of her.

Anna could hardly wait to get home. She wanted to sit and savor her favorite moments from the day, to remember the thrill of Eden smiling at her and how their voices sounded when they harmonized together. Actually, she wanted to gush about it with her best friend.

Hopefully Zoe was around. Anna and her former *Hex High* costar owned a duplex together in Montecito Heights. It was the perfect BFF arrangement, as far as Anna was concerned. They each had their own space, but they could still pop by and see each other whenever they wanted. Hollywood could be oddly isolating at times, and she was so glad to have Zoe nearby.

Kyrie held the door open for her as they stepped into the parking lot behind the studio. The buzz of a large group of people reached Anna's ears a moment before she saw them. Eden was still here, surrounded by fans and even a few paparazzi. The fans were squealing and chattering as they shoved cell phones in her face and offered things to be autographed while the paparazzi snapped photos and shouted questions.

Before Anna could react, she felt a hand on her shoulder.

"Let's go back inside," a woman's voice said. "Quickly."

Anna turned to find herself facing Eden's manager, Stella Pascual, and her own manager, David Rukundo. What in the world was he doing here? Then Stella was ushering Anna and Kyrie back inside the studio.

"Wasn't expecting that," Kyrie said once the door had closed behind them.

Stella chuckled. "Eden's been rehearsing here all week, and word has gotten out."

"I didn't know you were here," Anna said to David.

He grinned, looking dapper as ever in a pale-blue suit that beautifully offset his mahogany skin. "Surprise. I stopped by to meet with Stella. We were discussing how best to promote your Grammy performance, but we didn't realize you and Eden would finish before we did."

"Oh," Anna said, not quite following. "Was there something you wanted to go over with us before we left?"

"More like we didn't want you and Eden to be photographed together just yet," Stella said. She looked tiny next to David's towering presence, and yet it was clear she was in control of the conversation. "We'd like to drum up as much hype as possible for this performance by teasing a surprise guest on Eden's social media."

"So I shouldn't mention it at all?" Anna's stomach dropped. That sounded like a good strategy for Eden, but why couldn't Anna use this opportunity to generate some hype for herself too?

"You're going to give a few coded hints on your social media," David said. "Stella and I drafted up some ideas, but we're open to your input as well. I've sent you an email."

"Okay," Anna said. That made sense, but she still wished she'd gotten to be part of the decision-making process.

"Sometimes a bit of secrecy can go a long way toward building buzz," Stella said, and if she said so, it must be true, because Stella Pascual was a legend in this business.

"Some of your fans may put two and two together between your hints and Eden saying she'll have a special guest for her Grammy performance, and that's okay. It adds to the buzz," David said. "We'll play coy, keep teasing, and hopefully your fans will all tune in on Sunday to see if they guessed correctly."

"They'll be salivating to know whether they got it right, whether two of their favorite pop stars will be taking the stage together for the first time," Stella said with a slightly devilish twinkle in her eye. "It will be amazing publicity for you both."

"Well, okay." Anna wasn't used to this kind of thing, but she was starting to warm to the idea. Plus, David was on board, and she trusted his judgment implicitly.

"So we couldn't blow the surprise by letting them snap photos of you leaving Eden's rehearsal space today," Stella said.

"Right," Anna agreed. "How will I leave, then?"

Stella waved a hand toward the door. "Oh, just give it another five minutes or so. As soon as Eden leaves, the fans will clear out. No reason to hang around since they have no idea there's another celebrity in here."

Anna nodded her agreement, but she was vaguely disappointed she couldn't greet the fans herself or share photos from her day on social media. She wanted to own this moment the way Eden had. It would all be worth it when she stepped onto the Grammy stage on Sunday, though.

Soon, she and Kyrie were on their way home. They made a quick stop to pick up burgers and shakes from Honeybee, Anna's favorite vegan burger place. She ordered herself a classic burger with extra pickles, then added burgers for Kyrie and Zoe. Three chocolate shakes and an extra order of fries completed the order.

Sure enough, Zoe was waiting on their shared back patio with a beer in hand when they arrived, her dark hair pulled up in a high ponytail. Anna waved at her through the window as she unlocked her front door, revealing a gray striped cat on the welcome mat, glaring at her.

"Hey, Nelle," Anna said as she stepped around her cat.

"I come in peace," Kyrie said jokingly, giving Nelle a wide berth. Nelle's razor-sharp claws were the stuff of legend in Anna's house. No one messed with her cat. Nelle swiped at Kyrie's leg, and she yelped, jumping sideways.

"Be nice," Anna chastised, not that it did any good. Nelle did as she pleased, which usually involved terrorizing Anna's guests for her own entertainment. Anna walked through the living room and opened the door to the patio. She and Kyrie stepped outside, leaving Nelle in the house.

Zoe pointed at Anna with her beer. "I need to hear absolutely everything about your day."

"That's good, because I definitely need to share." Anna sprawled in the chair beside her and handed her a Honeybee bag and a shake.

"Ugh, you realize these aren't as good as real burgers, right?" Zoe asked as she accepted the bag. "But they're still pretty good. Thanks."

"I think they're as good as real burgers." Kyrie shrugged as she settled into a chair and pulled out her burger.

"Okay, tell me everything," Zoe said. "Did Eden live up to your wildly inflated expectations?"

And then some . . . "Yes," Anna said as she unwrapped her burger. Her stomach growled as its savory scent reached her. "She's . . . intimidating, for sure, but she was polite. And my *God*, hearing her sing in such close quarters totally gave me chills."

Kyrie smiled wickedly. "And then you—in one of the ballsiest moves I've ever seen—told her you had a better idea for the performance and challenged her to throw out practically everything she'd been working on."

24

Zoe's mouth fell open, revealing several partially chewed french fries. "You did *not!*"

"I didn't tell her mine was *better*," Anna protested.

"Um, you basically did," Kyrie said.

Zoe leaned forward in her chair. "And how did she react?"

"For a minute, I definitely thought she was going to bite my head off, but she agreed to hear me out."

"And then Eden and her team decided to use Anna's idea, which means she's a total badass," Kyrie added.

"That is beyond badass," Zoe said, eyes wide. "This baby pop star is all grown up and giving performance advice to Eden fucking Sands!"

"Shush," Anna admonished, cheeks warm as she took another bite of her burger.

"Wait a minute." Zoe straightened, giving her an impish look. "Isn't Eden your celebrity free pass? I mean, not that you're seeing anyone to *need* a free pass, and as far as I know she's straight, but . . . isn't she?"

Anna's cheeks went from warm to flaming hot, because yes. One tipsy evening back in her *Hex High* days, when Anna and Zoe were still nobodies, Anna had declared that Eden topped the list of celebrities she'd get a free pass from her significant other to hook up with if the opportunity ever presented itself. "Celebrity free passes aren't meant to be taken seriously."

"Of course not, but did you want to jump her bones when you met her today?" Zoe still looked entirely too gleeful about the whole thing.

Anna shook her head. "I was mostly just focused on not making a fool of myself in front of her, and honestly a celebrity crush is more of a fantasy anyway, isn't it?"

"I don't know . . . is it?" Zoe grinned. "You're the one who met her celebrity free pass today, so you tell me."

"A fantasy," Anna said, pleased that she sounded certain, because there had been that one moment when they hugged . . . "Eden is someone I look up to, and luckily she didn't crush my fangirl heart when we met. We get to perform together at the Grammys, which is a dream come true, but it's strictly professional."

Zoe nodded. "You two will be the hit of the night. I'm calling it now. This is going to be your breakout moment, Anna."

Eden held her left arm above her head as Zelda, her stylist, painstakingly stitched the seam over the zipper that ran down the side of her dress, hiding it from view. Her condo was a flurry of activity—the busiest it had been in months—and while she sometimes found award-show prep tedious or even unpleasant, today she welcomed it.

Her home was full of people for a change, and it filled something inside her that she'd only peripherally realized was empty: the need for human contact outside of work. Although technically, this was still work.

"Almost finished," Zelda said as her hand wove back and forth against Eden's side. She'd long ago quit fearing an inadvertent prick from a needle. Zelda's hands were unfailingly steady.

"No rush," Eden told her. They were right on schedule, although her shoulder was beginning to ache from the awkward position. She'd always found these moments that people imagined to be the most glamorous parts of celebrity to be the least glamorous in reality. Red carpet prep was wearisome, but at least she was wearing a comfortable dress tonight.

In an hour, she'd walk the red carpet by herself for the first time in years. The thought of not having Zach at her side made that empty feeling come back. She'd get through it, though, and Paris would be with her, so she wouldn't be entirely alone.

"There." Zelda stood, surveying Eden's gown with a critical eye. "Spin for me, darling."

Obediently, Eden turned around while Zelda tugged and prodded at various seams and tucks before she finally proclaimed that she was finished.

"Gorgeous," Stella said as she materialized at Eden's side. "I wish you could wear this color for every red carpet. Really makes your eyes pop."

"I do love blue." Eden surveyed herself in the mirror. The gown was a rich sapphire velvet, strapless and formfitting to her hips, with a slit along her left thigh and an asymmetrical skirt that swirled to her ankles. Classic enough that she shouldn't make any worst-dressed lists tonight, but possibly too simple to land her on the best-dressed list either.

Eden was playing it safe, both with her dress and with her life these days. She'd always been one to color inside the lines, but she was especially wary of making any missteps this year. Her hair and makeup team moved in to touch her up now that Zelda had finished with the dress. Then she was accessorized with a diamond-and-sapphire jewelry set.

Last, she sat and slipped into her silver rhinestone-studded heels. As beautiful as they were, they hurt like hell, and she wanted to spend as little time in them as possible.

"All right, let's get a few snaps for your social media before you ruffle anything." Paris stepped in with her cell phone. She wore a floor-length black satin dress that matched her black-rimmed glasses, and her dark hair was twisted up in a no-nonsense bun. "Stylish yet practical" perfectly described Eden's assistant.

She smiled as Paris started taking pictures, positioning herself so that the dress parted, exposing most of her left leg. She kept one hand on the fabric, bunching it between her fingers because she wasn't on the red carpet yet and she wanted to have a little fun with it.

"Perfect," Paris said. "Now take a few selfies for me, and I'll post everything while we're riding over."

Eden accepted the phone and took a series of selfies, her expression ranging from pouty to goofy. She often took a variety and then let Paris

27

decide which ones to post. They used to only share posed shots, but Paris had been the one to notice that Eden's fans got extra excited for selfies. Maybe they liked the less formal nature of them or the fact that Eden had taken the photos herself, but her selfies always got the most likes.

They were Eden's favorite, too, a way to connect with her fans.

Paris quickly drafted a post and showed it to Eden for her approval. Eden had access to all her accounts on her phone but rarely posted to them herself or even opened the apps. Paris was responsible for at least 90 percent of Eden's social media presence.

Ten minutes later, Eden, Paris, and Taylor were on their way out the door. Taylor wore a stylish black suit, her short brown hair slicked back in the front with gel. She looked more like she belonged on a fashion runway than Eden's protection for the evening.

"That's a great look on you," Eden told her.

Taylor grinned, shoving her hands into the front pockets of her pants. "Thank you."

Eden picked up her bag and a wrap to keep herself warm during the ride. It was the first week of February, and although the weather in Los Angeles was relatively mild, it was still too cold to stand outside comfortably in a sleeveless dress. She, Taylor, and Paris rode down in the elevator and went out through the back, where her car was waiting.

After a thirty-minute drive followed by an even longer wait in the drop-off line for the red carpet, they finally arrived. Taylor exited the vehicle first. Paris took Eden's shawl and clutch and touched up her lipstick yet again. As Eden stood from the car, Paris helped her smooth the creases from the front of her dress.

The routine was second nature for them by now. Paris had worked as her assistant for five years, and Taylor had headed her security team for almost as long. They had attended countless awards shows together in that time.

Eden stepped onto the red carpet, entering a sea of camera flashes and shouts of "Over here, Eden!" and "Turn to the right!" and "Look to your left!" She was as obedient as possible, smiling endlessly as she turned from side to side so they could photograph her from every angle, including the back. They always wanted a pose that showed the back of the dress.

Her stomach churned with preshow anxiety, which was amplified by how badly she needed a win tonight. But she refused to let it show, not with dozens of lenses aimed her way, their blinding flashes exposing her every flaw.

Every few minutes, she'd move forward so the next group of photographers could get their shots. A cold breeze gusted against her, and she shivered. Thank goodness the fabric of her dress was thick enough to hide her nipples, because she was freezing. Glancing to her left, she spotted Max Briner about five spots behind her on the carpet. Should she have invited him to perform with her instead of Anna?

"Eden, over here!"

Her cheeks hurt from smiling.

"What can we expect from your performance tonight?" someone shouted.

"Something expected and something *un*expected," she replied, the response she'd rehearsed with Stella earlier.

She turned to the right and saw Sasha Sol a few spots down from her, wearing a dress as red as the carpet beneath her feet. Her skin was a warm brown, and she wore her hair in box braids that tumbled over her shoulders. She looked stunning, and if Eden had to guess, Sasha would be taking home several awards tonight. Eden had always been impressed with Sasha's music, and her latest album was her best yet.

Sasha stepped forward to speak to a reporter, revealing Anna a little bit farther down the carpet. She had on a knee-length hot-pink dress with a blue-and-yellow-striped sash, as brightly colored as her personality. Anna turned to the side, showing off the back of the dress. The sash was knotted in an elaborate bow that almost looked like the wings of a butterfly.

As Eden watched, Anna spun to face her. Her smile was radiant, and even from a distance, Eden could see the way her makeup shimmered from the strobe effect of the cameras. *Wow.* Although her outfit wasn't Eden's taste, she had to admit that Anna cleaned up nicely. This was the first time Eden had seen her out of her usual athletic wear, and the transformation was impressive. Anna was a knockout.

"Eden! Eden, over here!"

Dammit. She'd gotten so distracted by Anna that she'd lost focus. She turned to face the press, keeping her smile in place.

"Can you give us a hint about who'll be joining you during your performance tonight?"

"Well . . ." Eden darted another quick glance at Anna—pink was *definitely* her color—before looking over her shoulder in Max's direction. "I can confirm that person is on the red carpet with me tonight."

"Is it Max Briner?" someone shouted. The din of questions, combined with the camera flashes, was wearing on her nerves. She was ready to go inside.

She gave the reporter a coy look. "You'll have to wait and see."

CHAPTER FOUR

"Anna, are you hoping to win your first Grammy tonight?"

Anna placed a hand on her waist, cocking her hip for the cameras. "Winning a Grammy would be a dream come true, but I'm not exaggerating when I say it's an honor just to be here."

That was the truth. As badly as she wanted a Grammy, Anna intended to enjoy every moment of this night, regardless of whether she won. Performing on the Grammy stage was a big freaking deal, never mind performing alongside her idol. This would be one of the biggest moments of her career so far, and while she was pretty sure she appeared calm and confident on the outside, internally she was completely freaking out.

As Anna turned to the side, she noticed Eden a little farther down the red carpet. She had on a sapphire-blue velvet gown that made Anna's brain combust on sight. Eden took a step forward, giving her a glimpse of the slit that revealed her left thigh. Holy *shit*.

"Anna, tell us about your dress."

She dragged her gaze back to the row of reporters in front of her. "It's by Lavoie, one of my favorite new designers."

"Are those the colors of the pansexual flag?" a young woman with a microphone asked.

Anna beamed at her. "Good eye. Yes, they are."

"I love that," the reporter responded enthusiastically. "Thank you for being so open about your sexuality."

"Just being true to myself," Anna replied. She knew she was lucky to live in a time when she could be out and proud like this, and she was honored to do what she could to further normalize queer people living their best lives.

As Anna reached the end of the red carpet, Kyrie appeared at her side, wearing a simple white dress. The tips of her hair were a mixture of pink and blue today to complement Anna's dress while also serving as a subtle nod to her own flag as a transgender woman.

Anna and Kyrie headed for the entrance to the arena. Butterflies fluttered in Anna's stomach as she climbed the steps toward the main entrance.

"Well, well. Fancy seeing you here."

Anna's butterflies promptly died, settling into a heavy weight in the pit of her stomach. Slowly, she turned to face the last person she wanted to see tonight, or any night. "Camille, hi."

Camille Dupont looked unfairly gorgeous in her champagne-colored gown. Her blonde hair was swept into an elegant updo, and her smile oozed charm, but Anna had learned long ago that looks could be deceiving where Camille was concerned. "Don't you look darling tonight?" Camille reached out to touch the sash of Anna's dress.

She took an involuntary step back. "You look nice too."

"And who's this?" Camille looked at Kyrie as that all-too-familiar glint of jealousy flared in her eyes.

"This is Kyrie, my assistant," Anna explained. "You've met."

"Kyrie." Camille nodded. "That's right. Of course."

"Hi," Kyrie said with a polite nod.

"I think your hair was . . . purple, perhaps?" She waved a hand as if the color of Kyrie's hair was insignificant before focusing her gaze on Anna again. "Who are you here with tonight?"

"Just Kyrie." Anna nearly flinched at the breathlessness in her voice. She'd always been helpless to resist the power of Camille's presence. It was the reason she'd gone back to her time and time again, even when she knew their relationship had run its course, that Camille was controlling and manipulative and that Anna hated the way she felt when they were together.

"Three nominations tonight, Anna. Not bad." There was pride in Camille's voice now, and Anna involuntarily basked in it. "Shame you weren't invited to perform."

Anna clasped her hands in front of herself. "Maybe next year."

Camille's gaze slid over Anna's dress in a way that would have once lit her on fire. She was pretty proud of herself that it didn't have the same effect now. Then Camille's expression changed to one of distaste. She tsked. "Are you wearing . . . a pan flag?"

Anna wished the ground would open up and swallow her whole. She'd been so proud of her dress a few minutes ago, but as she saw herself through Camille's cultured eyes, she felt foolish. Anna was only too aware that she didn't have the respect of her peers yet. She was still seen as the star of a silly teen show, not as a serious artist. She should have worn a different dress.

"I think her dress is beautiful."

The unexpected voice had the effect of touching a live wire. Anna jumped, electricity firing through her system as she turned to find Eden standing a few feet away, watching with an inscrutable expression. Talk about beautiful . . .

Camille turned toward Eden, surprise written all over her face. "Ms. Sands, what an honor." She extended an elegant hand. "Camille Dupont."

Eden accepted her hand, but she did it with an air that had Anna quaking in her shoes. Where had that haughty attitude come from? Eden looked at Camille as if she were the least important person she'd ever met, when in fact she was a renowned vocal coach. Anna had been humbled to be accepted as one of Camille's students as a fledgling singer.

Eden gave Camille's hand a quick shake before turning to Anna. Immediately, her expression softened. "See you inside?"

Stunned, Anna could only nod.

Eden breezed past them, headed up the steps into the theater. Paris followed in her wake, carrying a blue clutch and wrap that matched Eden's dress. She gave Anna a quick wave as she passed. Eden's bodyguard walked beside Paris, looking smashing in a black suit.

"Eden Sands?" Camille said. "You *have* moved up in the world, darling."

"It's been a big year for me, career-wise."

"I know you tend to latch on to powerful women, but trust me when I say, she is *way* out of your league." Camille nodded her head in the direction Eden had gone.

Anna's cheeks scalded. "I . . . I don't . . ."

Kyrie touched her shoulder. "We need to go inside."

"Perhaps I'll see you at one of the after-parties?" Camille asked.

Anna managed a brittle smile. "Perhaps."

Two hours later, Anna slipped out of her dressing room, feeling as if she might have left some of her vital organs behind, because she couldn't seem to breathe properly. She was about to perform in front of twenty thousand of her peers, not to mention the millions of people watching from home, and . . .

She was going to pass out.

Kyrie closed the door to the dressing room behind them. "You okay?"

"No," Anna whispered. "This is . . . big. It's so big, Kyrie. What if I fuck up? What if I forget all the words?"

"That's what the teleprompter is for," Eden said behind her.

Anna's heart lurched into her throat, and she flushed with embarrassment that Eden had heard her freak out. "Right," she managed.

Eden was dressed for her performance in a silver gown that was embellished with so many sequins and crystals she seemed to shimmer. Once the stage lights caught her, she would glow. She was a star. A legend. And Anna was . . . not.

Way out of your league. Camille's words echoed in her ears.

"This is your first Grammy performance?" Eden asked.

Anna could only nod.

"My advice: Don't look at the audience. Look at me or at the cameras. It's less intimidating that way."

"Thank you," Anna said. Not that looking at Eden was any less intimidating, although Anna had gotten a little more comfortable around her over the last few days. Eden had been easier to work with than she'd anticipated, but they'd kept things professional the whole time they were rehearsing. All work, no friendly chitchat.

"They did a great job with your dress," Eden said. "I don't think anyone will miss the context."

"Yeah." Anna looked down at her green dress, embellished with brightly colored silk flowers. It was almost an exact re-creation of the dress Eden had worn in her "Daydreamer" music video.

"Speaking of that dress . . ." Paris stepped forward, holding up her cell phone. "Let me grab a few quick photos of you two together before you get out there."

Anna stepped closer to Eden, and they wrapped an arm around each other to pose for Paris. Eden leaned closer, her cheek pressed against Anna's as she held the phone overhead and snapped several photos. Anna's inner fangirl rejoiced. Her teenage self would never have believed this moment could happen.

Warm tingles traveled up her spine, causing warning bells to clang in her head. Now that Anna had gotten to know the woman behind the celebrity she'd admired for so long, her fangirl crush was becoming a real-life attraction, and . . . this was not good. If she'd learned anything from her time with Camille, it was that lusting after a mentor only led to heartbreak.

A member of the arena crew approached, gesturing for them to follow him.

"All right, that's our cue," Paris said. "Good luck out there, ladies."

"You got this." Kyrie gave Anna's shoulder a squeeze.

She nodded, not trusting herself to speak, but surprisingly, she felt calmer now than she had when she first left her dressing room. Anna had already lost the award for best music video—the only award she'd been favored to win—so now she just had to make it through this performance, and then she could relax and enjoy the rest of the night.

Sasha Sol was tonight's big winner so far, and Anna was thrilled for her. She had met Sasha before the ceremony began, and she was a total sweetheart and so talented. Anna was a big fan of her music.

As the live broadcast went into a commercial break, Anna and Eden were rushed into position by members of the crew. Anna sat on the stool that had been placed for her behind the hill, hiding her from view. Around her, the stage buzzed with activity. Briefly, she wished she could watch Eden deliver the first half of her performance, but at least she could watch the replay later.

"Ten seconds!" a voice called.

The activity around her briefly intensified, and then everything went quiet as the show returned from the commercial break. She listened as Eden was introduced, and then the opening bars of "Alone" began to play. Sitting with her back against the structure that housed the band, Anna felt the vibrations of the music all the way to her bones.

She closed her eyes, absorbing it, losing herself in the beauty of Eden's voice and the electricity that filled the room. It was one of the most intense things Anna had ever experienced, being onstage yet hidden from the audience. As she listened to Eden sing, her nerves melted away. Anna was one with the music.

"I'm never alone, because I have myself to keep me company." Eden delivered the final line, her voice heavy with emotion.

Anna's heart clenched. Did Eden really feel that way? Was she alone when the spotlight didn't shine on her? The music changed, and Anna leaned forward as the felt hilltop was stripped away, revealing the band. Eden stood overhead now, but Anna didn't dare look up. She couldn't let anything break her concentration this close to her entrance.

The opening beats of "After Midnight" pulsed around her, and Anna turned her microphone on. She pressed her hands against her thighs, ready to spring to her feet. Eden sang the opening verse, and Anna could hear the crowd clapping along to the beat. The energy in the room made the fine hairs on her arms stand at attention. With a hiss, stage smoke burst from the structure behind her.

"But after midnight . . ." Eden's voice reached her.

Anna lurched to her feet, eyes on the red tape marking her way through the smoke now billowing thick around her. She stepped onto the main stage, where a spotlight engulfed her, and the crowd roared with surprise.

"I let my hair down. After midnight, I'm not afraid to be a clown." Anna's voice sounded clear and strong, and luckily for her, the stage lights were so blinding she couldn't see the audience, even if she'd wanted to. She spun so that her skirt flared around her, then danced her way over to Eden as they alternated lines through the chorus.

Eden stood before her, looking like an actual celestial being, not merely a star. Her dress sparked beneath the stage lights, glinting and shimmering and dazzling Anna until she nearly *did* forget the words to the song. For a moment, she was lost, staring helplessly at Eden as an arena full of industry heavyweights looked on.

Eden gave her a reassuring smile, dipping her head in the smallest of nods. *You've got this.* Anna received the message loud and clear, and suddenly, she did.

"I'm a little bit more wild. I *am* my inner child. I haven't taken off my rose-colored glasses," Anna sang, tugging at imaginary glasses.

Eden held her gaze as the music swelled, her expression anguished. Then she turned her face toward the camera. "I don't daydream anymore."

Her voice was heavy with emotion, and *damn*, she had some acting chops. They'd tweaked the lyrics of the song to suit the theme of this performance, and Anna could hear the crowd buzzing in response.

Anna angled herself slightly toward the camera, which was on a boom that swung overhead, allowing the network to get its close-up for the people watching at home. Her gaze slid past it to the audience beyond. The stage lights had shifted, and now she saw so many faces she recognized, really intimidating faces. Holy shit.

She wrenched her gaze back to Eden. They circled each other as they sang, sparring back and forth as Eden wrestled with the demons of her younger self. Anna had never seen anything as mesmerizing as the way the stage lights glittered on Eden's silver dress.

And then that rhinestone-studded dress was against Anna's cheek as Eden embraced her inner child. When Anna straightened from the hug, her earring snagged on one of the crystals, yanking her back against Eden's chest. She was stuck. Before she could panic, her earring broke, freeing her.

Anna spun to stand with her back against Eden's, melting into the background as Eden delivered the final line of the song.

"After midnight, I'm free."

The crowd began to whistle and applaud, the noise again making those hairs on Anna's arms rise. Eden squeezed her hand, Anna's cue to step beside her.

"Thank you so much!" Eden called to the crowd.

"Thank you," Anna echoed, tears blurring her vision as she saw a few people in the audience get to their feet. It seemed to happen in slow motion: people in tuxedos and ball gowns, people Anna looked up to, industry legends, standing and clapping for *her*.

Well, for Eden, probably. For both of them, maybe. And then Eden pulled her in for a hug. Anna was grinning like an idiot, and Eden still smelled like rose petals, and she was definitely having an out-of-body experience right now.

If this was what heaven felt like, Anna never wanted to return to earth.

CHAPTER FIVE

Eden smiled, ignoring the camera in her face, as the woman onstage read out the nominees for Record of the Year. If she lost this one, she'd be going home empty handed, which wasn't the end of the world, but after the year she'd had, it kind of felt like it.

"The nominees are . . . Sasha Sol for 'On the Rocks,' Eden Sands for 'Alone,' Tony Marko for 'Life of the Party,' Anna Moss for 'Love Me, Love You,' and Lamar Cruz for 'Tension.'"

Eden's heart thumped against her ribs, and she struggled to keep her breathing even. *Please. Please. Please.* The beady eye of the camera moved closer, poised to catch every nuance of her expression as the winner's name was read.

"And the winner is . . ."

Paris squeezed her hand, and Eden tossed a grateful glance in her direction.

"Sasha Sol for 'On the Rocks'!"

Eden's smile didn't waver. She applauded enthusiastically as Sasha popped to her feet several rows ahead. This was definitely Sasha's night, and although Eden felt a crushing sense of disappointment, she couldn't help but be happy for Sasha too. She deserved the win.

Now Eden just had to keep her game face on until she got home. No one here could know how upset she was. It shouldn't be hard. She'd perfected her stage face early in her career, but she was just so worn down lately. For the first time ever, she was afraid a crack might show.

After the ceremony ended, Eden greeted a seemingly endless stream of people as she made her way out of the arena. She might not have won an award tonight, but everyone was talking about her performance with Anna. Eden had performed at the Grammys many times. Eight? Nine? She wasn't entirely sure, but she had never received a standing ovation before. She owed that to Anna and her brilliant idea for "After Midnight."

"Sorry tonight didn't go your way," Paris said as she guided Eden toward the door. "Ready for the Crescent party?"

For a moment, Eden actually wavered. She was in no mood to attend a flashy after-party, but this was expected of her. She had to at least put in an appearance at her label's party. Have a drink. Be photographed. "I'm ready."

After what felt like hours, she was finally in the car on her way to the after-party. Her feet ached. She was tired and thirsty and couldn't seem to shake the melancholy mood that had settled over her.

"You trended on Twitter earlier tonight," Paris told her as the car pulled away from the curb.

"I did?" Eden reached for a bottle of water in the cooler between the seats.

"Mm-hmm." Paris held up her phone, scrolling through a stream of tweets, many of which contained photos of her performance. "You and Anna had the buzzworthy performance of the night. You'll be in a lot of headlines tomorrow."

Eden settled in her seat and took a long drink of water. "And to think, I didn't want to bring her on."

Paris grinned. "You two really lit up the stage together."

"Hmm." Eden looked out the window. The dress she'd thought would be so comfortable had started to chafe beneath her arms. She couldn't wait to take it off. "Let's make this a relatively short stop, okay?"

Paris nodded, adjusting her glasses as she peered at her phone. "Just give me a signal, and I'll interrupt to let you know it's time to get to your next engagement of the evening."

"Which will be my bed," Eden said with a weary smile. "Thank you."

"You got it, boss."

Eden closed her eyes as the car wound its way slowly through the crowded streets. Tonight's performance had been a rush. Live performances were always exhilarating, and she couldn't wait for her upcoming tour to begin. She'd get the thrill of performing almost every night. Seeing fans singing her lyrics back to her? There was nothing like it in the world.

Maybe tonight's performance would give her ticket sales a boost too. Stella had been hassling her lately about various gimmicks to drum up publicity for the tour. Eden had never had this problem before. Her tours had always sold out as soon as tickets went on sale. Not this time. Just one more way this past year had thrown her off her axis.

"We're here," Paris said a few minutes later.

Eden opened her eyes to see the car pulling up in front of Velvet, the club her record label had rented for the night. Its entrance was lit with a strip of lights that scrolled the colors of the rainbow. Two men in gray suits stood on either side of the door to check guest credentials, and as expected, the paparazzi had already established a heavy presence along the sidewalk, eager for a glimpse of the stars as they arrived.

"Here," Paris said, and when Eden turned toward her, she was holding up a compact. "Let's touch you up for the cameras."

Eden leaned in obediently so Paris could smooth out her foundation and reapply lipstick.

"All right. Let's do this." Paris handed Eden her clutch as Taylor got out of the front of the car and came around to open Eden's door for her.

Eden sucked in a deep breath before she stood. Immediately, the photographers began shouting her name. She waved with a wide smile, pausing halfway up the steps so they could get their shot.

Once they were inside, she helped herself to a glass of champagne. She didn't have much to celebrate tonight, but she'd certainly earned a drink . . . or two. She tended to get quiet and introspective when she drank, so she wasn't worried about making a fool of herself.

Eden greeted the team from her label before she was pulled into conversation with none other than Max Briner, the man her fans had overwhelmingly thought she'd be performing with tonight. From there, it was a blur of people, and then she spotted Anna herself standing just inside the door, looking slightly shell shocked.

Probably, someone at the label had extended an invitation because of her duet with Eden. And she owed Anna a thank-you for how it had turned out. Eden snagged two flutes of champagne from a passing waiter and made her way over to Anna.

"Champagne?" she said in lieu of hello, holding one of the flutes toward Anna.

Anna looked at her in a way that made Eden stand a little taller in her heels, like Eden was the most important person in the room and Anna couldn't quite believe she'd come over to talk to her. Of course, a lot of people looked at Eden that way, but it felt different somehow, coming from Anna.

"Thank you," Anna said as she accepted the flute. "This is some party, huh?"

"They do this every year, if you can believe it," Eden told her. "There's an empty sofa over there, and my feet are killing me. Want to see if we can grab it before someone else does?"

Anna nodded eagerly, leading the way toward the sofa. Her pink dress seemed to glow beneath the slightly exaggerated lighting in the club. "I wasn't sure if you'd be here," she said as she sat, carefully smoothing the bow at the back of her dress.

"I'm not staying much longer," Eden said. "I've schmoozed my way around the room, and now I'm more than ready for pajamas and my bed."

Anna's smile was softer this time. "Same. I've already been to my label's party. I just stopped by to thank Colin Braithwaite for the invitation, and then I'm going to call it a night."

"That's him over there by the window." Eden pointed him out to Anna.

"Thank you," Anna said. "And thanks again for this whole experience. Performing with you tonight has been a career highlight for me. Not sure anything will top it."

"Oh, I'm sure you'll have plenty of bigger moments. You're just getting started." Eden sipped her champagne. This was her second glass, and she could feel the warmth of alcohol in her veins. It soothed her aching feet and the chafed spots from her dress. "I actually wanted to thank *you* for your idea with 'After Midnight.' It went over well with the audience."

"Sounds like it," Anna said with a cheeky smile. "My phone's been blowing up with notifications all night."

"Really?" Eden hadn't even looked at hers since before she left her condo earlier that evening.

"Oh my God, I think everyone I've ever met has messaged me tonight," Anna gushed. "Not to mention my social media."

"I don't have notifications turned on for any of that. It makes my head explode even trying to look at it. Paris will probably send me a few screenshots of the good stuff."

"That sounds like a good strategy." Anna looked down and adjusted the sash of her dress.

Eden was suddenly reminded of their encounter on the steps of the arena before the ceremony, and maybe the alcohol had loosened her tongue after all, because she heard herself saying, "Forgive me if I'm about to ask a really stupid question, but what's a pan flag?"

Anna blinked. "What?"

"Earlier, Camille Dupont said your dress looked like a pan flag. I thought that meant pansexual? But she made it sound like an insult." Eden could feel her face heating. She was probably making a fool of herself, maybe even being insensitive. She wasn't a member of the LGBTQ community, but she did try to be a good ally. "Sorry if that's an inappropriate thing to ask."

Anna shook her head. "Not at all. You're right. I'm pansexual, and the colors of the pan flag are pink, yellow, and cyan." She gestured to her dress.

"Oh." Now Eden wasn't sure what to say.

"Camille was my voice coach. And my ex."

"Sorry."

Anna waved a hand. "You didn't say anything wrong. I had blinders on for a very long time where Camille is concerned."

Eden frowned. "Mentors should lift you up, but she sounded so condescending."

"Making people feel small is a special talent of hers." Anna pressed her lips together, and now she looked vaguely sad.

Eden searched for a change of topic. "Could I ask another possibly insensitive question?"

Anna gave her a somewhat wary look. "Sure."

"It's just . . . I've never quite understood the difference between bisexual and pansexual."

"Oh." Anna's expression brightened. "That's not insensitive at all. In fact, I love when people want to better educate themselves. It shows that you care."

Eden nodded. "I do."

"So, the difference between bisexual and pansexual is fairly nuanced, and some people define it different ways, but to me, bisexual means that you're attracted to more than one gender, and pansexual means that you're attracted to a person regardless of their gender."

Eden smiled, relaxing into the cushion beneath her. That actually made sense. "So for you, attraction is more about a connection with a specific person, not their gender?"

"Exactly."

"Thank you," Eden said. "For explaining, and for not making me feel silly for asking."

Anna's eyes sparkled playfully. "You may be a lot of things, Eden Sands, but silly is not a word I'd use to describe you."

Except, at that moment, Eden did feel rather silly. A laugh built in her chest, but she swallowed it. "Anyway, I think it's awful that Camille was rude about your dress. You've taken colors that have meaning to you and incorporated them into your outfit for an important night. I think that's beautiful."

Anna blinked at her, seemingly lost for words. "Thank you," she said finally.

"You're welcome. And here's my final clueless question of the evening: Did you win tonight? I know we both lost for Record of the Year, but I missed the beginning of the ceremony while I was getting ready for our performance."

Anna scrunched her nose. "Nope. No awards for me tonight."

Eden held up her half-empty champagne flute. "Here's to being two of tonight's biggest losers."

Anna choked out a laugh, then tapped her glass against Eden's. "I'll drink to that, although I'd hardly call you a loser."

Eden made a noncommittal sound. She felt like a loser lately, at least compared to where she was usually. Her career had been on a steady upward climb from her debut at sixteen until last year, and now . . . now she was afraid to see how far she had yet to fall. She looked up and saw Paris watching her from across the room. It was late, and she was tired. "It's time for me to make my escape, I'm afraid," she told Anna.

"Same," Anna said. "Right after I introduce myself to Mr. Braithwaite."

Eden stood. "I'm glad I bumped into you tonight. It was nice talking to you."

"You too." Anna gave her another of those adoring smiles that reminded Eden she'd been Anna's role model. It was flattering, but it also made her feel . . . old. Anna was the future of pop music, but surely Eden hadn't peaked yet. She was just having an off year.

"I'm sure I'll see you around," Eden said. "Good night, Anna."

"Night," Anna said.

Eden caught Paris's eye as she polished off her champagne. In seconds, Paris was at her side, holding out Eden's wrap. Taylor was right behind her.

"Lawrence is pulling the car around now," Paris said.

"Perfect. Thank you."

Minutes later, she was in the car, on the way home . . . finally. Exhaustion settled over her, softened by the alcohol so that she felt relaxed instead of sore from her uncomfortable attire. She pulled out her phone, finding a handful of messages. Most of them were from Stella, who had apparently loved the performance and was outraged that Eden hadn't taken home any awards. The next text was from Zach.

Zach:

Amazing performance tonight!

A smile tugged at her lips. Zach must be the nicest actor in Hollywood. Even their divorce had been friendly. Idly, she remembered the scene she'd witnessed between Anna and Camille earlier. Their exes couldn't be more different.

Eden:

Thank you! And thanks for watching.

The little dots began to bounce, letting her know that he was replying.

Zach:

Hey, are you busy tomorrow? I was wondering if we could grab brunch. I have something to discuss with you.

What in the world did he need to talk to her about? The divorce had been finalized over six months ago. But she wouldn't mind seeing Zach tomorrow. She did miss him, even if she didn't miss sharing a bed with him.

Eden:

Not sure I'll be up for brunch, but I'm around if you want to stop by.

Zach:

I'll bring brunch with me. Around noon?

Eden:

Sounds good. See you then.

As she leaned back in her seat, her mind drifted to Anna. Despite losing tonight, Eden had to admit there had been a few highlights, and they all related to a certain young pop star with an effervescent smile and stars in her eyes.

Eden woke to the sound of the buzzer, blinking groggily into her pillow. What in the . . . ? Brilliant sunlight streamed in the window, and oh shit, the clock beside the bed read 12:05. She'd been so exhausted last night that she'd slept until noon, and now Zach was here. With a groan, she crawled out of bed and walked to the keypad by the door. "Hello?"

"Good afternoon, Ms. Sands," the doorman said. "Mr. Tomlin is here to see you."

"Can you give me five minutes to get ready and then send him up?"

"Absolutely, Ms. Sands."

"Thank you." She dashed to the bathroom to freshen up and brush her teeth and then dressed in jeans and a loose blue top. Her hair was a mess, but it wasn't like Zach had never seen her first thing in the morning before. She'd just turned on the coffee maker when he knocked on the door.

She opened it with a smile.

He took her in with a smile of his own. "You were still in bed when I got here, weren't you?"

"Maybe. I had a late night. What have you brought me?" She motioned him into the condo.

Zach stepped inside, carrying a white paper bag from her favorite café in Santa Monica, where they'd lived when they were married. Where Zach still lived. "Bagel with cream cheese and a large mocha." He held up the cup.

Rachel Lacey

She barely contained a moan. No other place made a mocha quite as good as this one. "Oh my God, I love you." Zach's expression morphed into one of discomfort, and Eden suddenly heard what she'd just said. She winced. "I mean, you know what I mean . . . the mocha. I love the mocha. I just woke up, and caffeine is my love language right now."

He put a hand on her shoulder, steering her into the living room. "We're good, aren't we? You're okay with how things are?"

"I am. I really am." She accepted the insulated cup from him and sank onto the couch.

Zach sat across from her on the love seat. His brown hair was cut a little shorter than she was used to, probably for a movie. He looked good, like over-the-top Hollywood handsome, but she felt nothing more than friendly affection for him. Maybe that was all she'd ever felt for him, if she were being perfectly honest with herself.

"I'm glad." He set the bag on the table between them. "You don't mind if we eat in here, do you?"

"No, go right ahead. I'm just going to have a love affair with this mocha before I get to the bagel."

Zach grinned. "Same old Eden, I see."

"Same old," she echoed, sipping the drink. The rich combination of chocolate and espresso greeted her tongue, and *God*, it was as good as she remembered.

"How are you really?" he asked.

"I'm . . ." "Fine" was on the tip of her tongue, but she'd never lied to Zach. Why start now? "Okay. I'm okay."

"Just okay?" His eyes locked on hers, crinkled with concern.

She shrugged. "Adjusting to the single life. You know how it is."

Something indecipherable passed across his face.

"My last album didn't do well, and I'm in a bit of a creative slump." She closed her eyes as she took another sip. "But I'll bounce back."

"Yes, you will. If I wasn't already sure of it, your Grammy performance left no doubt. You were on *fire* last night, Eden. There was a spark in you I hadn't seen in a while."

"Was there?" She'd felt it, but to hear him say it . . . well, it felt validating. She opened her eyes to find him watching her closely. "I've been looking for that spark, to be honest."

"I think you've found it."

"I hope so." She took another sip of her mocha, watching Zach as the sleepy haze in her brain began to clear. "So what brings you to my condo on a Monday morning?"

"Ah." He straightened, putting down his bagel, and that was the moment she realized he'd come here to tell her something important, something she probably wasn't going to like. "I have some news, and I wanted to make sure you heard it from me first."

She inhaled. "Okay."

"I've met someone."

Her stomach dropped. *Oh.* Of course he had. God, she hadn't prepared herself for this. She forced a smile. "I'm happy for you, and I appreciate you telling me before I read it online."

"I'll always care about you, Eden. You know that, right?"

She nodded. "I feel the same way. So who is she? Do I know her?" *Please say no.*

"I don't think so," he said. "We met on the set of my last movie. She's an assistant director. Hallie Milzovski."

"Not a celebrity? That's new for you."

"It is, and a good change, I think." He held up his phone, showing her a photo of himself with a pretty brunette. He gazed at Hallie with a kind of adoration she wasn't sure she'd ever seen on his face before. He looked like a man in love.

She pushed her shoulders back, fighting the urge to slump in her seat. Zach had moved on, and she hadn't even been on a date since their divorce. She couldn't even remember the last time she'd been kissed.

Had she ever looked at Zach the way Hallie did? "You two look good together."

"Thanks. We're really happy."

He didn't mean it as a jab. She knew he didn't. He didn't have a mean bone in his body. But even so, she felt a stab of pain right in her heart.

CHAPTER SIX

Stella settled herself on the love seat across from Eden—much the way Zach had done earlier that week—and something in Stella's expression made Eden think she wasn't going to like this conversation any more than she'd liked the last one. "I have an idea for you, and I need you to promise to hear me out before you say no."

"No," Eden countered with a coy smile.

Stella threw her hands up in the air. "Oh, come on!"

"You've already told me I'm not going to like it. So . . . whatever it is, my answer is no." Eden was joking. They both knew she was joking, and yet in her heart, she'd never felt more serious. She was tired. She was frustrated. And she was fighting a rising sense of disillusionment, this feeling that the rest of the world was out there living their lives and loving each other while she sat in her condo above the beach she couldn't even walk on, alone in her tower.

Bitter. That's what she was. She was turning into a bitter woman, and she didn't like that at all.

Stella waved a hand. "Wipe that scowl right off your face. I'm going to start the conversation over with a new approach."

"Fine." Eden didn't try to stop her. They both knew she'd probably say yes to whatever Stella was about to propose.

"The internet is still buzzing about your Grammy performance four days after the fact," Stella said. "You and Anna had the most talked about performance of the night."

"I'm glad." Eden *was* glad, but she was tired of talking about it. The Grammys were over. Soon, she'd begin rehearsals for her upcoming tour. She'd rather focus on how to get people buzzing about the tour than rehash her Grammy performance.

"Ticket sales for the tour are still sluggish," Stella said as if she'd read Eden's mind.

Eden didn't respond. She just sipped her coffee, waiting for Stella to continue.

"Part of what made your Grammy performance so captivating was the energy between you and Anna onstage together. She hasn't received much critical acclaim yet, but she has a wildly enthusiastic fan base. Her fans are younger than yours, and some of them have started downloading your music. Your streaming rates are up and trending younger over the last few days, which is great news. Let's jump on this while it's hot, Eden. Bring Anna on board for the tour. Invite her to open for you."

Eden pressed her lips together in frustration. She hadn't had an opening act for either of her last two tours, and she preferred it this way. Opening acts were distracting. It was hard to find the right match. They ate into her profits . . . not that she was hurting for money, but still. Eden liked to be in control when it came to her career, and adding a last-minute opening act would involve compromises she didn't like to make.

The teenage pop sensation who'd had every moment of her day dictated to her while her parents lived large on her millions was still a part of her. They'd micromanaged every aspect of her life—before and after she'd become famous—and it hadn't stopped when she turned eighteen. She'd tried so hard to get them to listen to her and respect her wishes, but she'd finally come to terms with the fact that she'd have to cut her parents out of her life if she wanted to have a career on her own terms.

She sent them enough money to keep them living in luxury and saw them from time to time, but they were less interested in being her parents than in taking credit for her celebrity. She still sent them tickets to all her local concerts and events, but they usually gave them away to impress their friends instead of coming to see her. That made her unspeakably sad, but she'd made her peace with it. Eden had control of her life now, and she wouldn't give it up for anything or anyone.

"If you announce Anna as your opening act, tickets will sell out in a matter of hours. Like it or not, she's hot right now," Stella said.

Eden definitely did *not* like it, no matter how much she reluctantly liked Anna herself. "We didn't factor the cost of an opening act into the ticket price."

"No, but we always build a buffer into the ticket price to accommodate unexpected costs, and I've already put together a plan to recoup some of the cost through merchandising and additional VIP options. If you don't do this, you're either going to have to offer discounted ticket bundles or have unsold seats in every arena, so any way you look at it, you're going to need a way to recoup costs."

Eden clenched her jaw. Why couldn't she sell out her own damn tour? Her *After Midnight* album might not have been her best work, but she was still proud of it. Had that many of her fans really abandoned her so easily?

"I know you're thinking about that girl who opened for you on the Daylight Tour," Stella said. "The one who showed up late and unprepared half the time."

"Harmony Cox," Eden said flatly. "The audience booed her. She made me look bad."

"No, she didn't. People come to see the headliner. Their night won't be ruined if the opening act is mediocre, but my point is . . . Anna is not

Harmony. Her work ethic rivals yours, if what we saw last week is any indication. Plus, she has a great rapport with her fans. She's the perfect choice. Bring her on board."

Eden looked toward the balcony, a sliver of blue water just visible over the railing. She'd been looking forward to this tour for months, the chance to shine, to reclaim her popularity with her fans. Vain or not, she didn't like to share the spotlight.

But Eden respected Anna. She might not even mind having her around on tour.

"Fine," Eden said with a sigh. "Make the call. Invite her on the tour."

Anna wished she could feel the wind in her hair. She twisted the throttle on her Yamaha motorcycle and felt the engine roar beneath her. This was her favorite way to unwind. Behind the protection of her full-face helmet, she had total anonymity as she cruised the streets of LA, but the open roads outside the city were what she truly craved. She loved to ride up the Pacific Coast Highway, taking in the stunning houses and the ocean view.

It was breathtaking, although she did miss the somewhat wilder days of her youth, when she would have worn a less protective helmet that allowed her to feel the wind on her face and blowing through her hair. Safety first, though. And with safety came anonymity.

Anna had grown up outside San Francisco, so the California coastline was ingrained in her DNA. She loved it with a passion and wasn't ashamed to say that one of her top career goals was to be able to afford one of the beachfront houses she cruised past on these rides. She wanted to walk out her back door and put her toes in the sand, to hear the waves and inhale the salt air.

Today, her destination was Point Dume Nature Preserve, about an hour outside of the city. She didn't have time for a hike, but for her, the ride up the coast was the best part anyway. She would spend a few minutes in the parking lot at the scenic overlook atop the cliffs, taking in the view. Then she'd zip back to her house for a meeting with David.

As the park came into view, Anna slowed her bike and guided it into the parking lot. She found an empty spot at the end of the lot, far enough away from the other vehicles that no one would notice her, and then she took off her helmet and shook out her hair. Usually, she was only recognized by people her age or younger, although that would change with her next album, if she had anything to say about it.

And I will.

The need to be taken seriously as an artist was a hunger gnawing inside her, one that grew with each passing day. She was ready—*beyond* ready—to broaden her appeal. There was so much more to her than the bubblegum image the mainstream media focused on.

A contented smile settled on her face as she gazed down the cliffs to the waves crashing below. She was tempted to take a selfie for her social media, but she'd avoided taking pictures here so far. Anything she posted online was fair game for her fans to pick apart, to retrace her steps and recreate her selfies. Nearly every aspect of her life was public.

But she'd kept Point Dume for herself. No one knew this was her spot.

She reached behind herself and pulled a bottle of water and an energy bar out of her bag. As she enjoyed her snack, her mind replayed the moment her earring had snagged on Eden's dress at the end of their performance, anchoring them together. The warmth of Eden's embrace and the rose-petal scent of her skin. Anna's cheeks flushed at the memory.

Would she and Eden have the same rapport the next time they met at an industry event? Anna liked to imagine that they'd share a moment together again someday. Of course, her sapphic heart had fantasized about more than that, but she was a realist. Eden wasn't interested in her like that, and anyway, Anna had learned her lesson when it came to dating her mentors.

Her stomach clenched just thinking about the scene with Camille before the Grammys. She hated that Eden had witnessed it, although she couldn't quite bring herself to regret the way it had played out. The look on Camille's face when Eden brushed her off, only to compliment Anna's dress . . .

Priceless.

Anna polished off her snack and tucked her trash inside the saddlebag. Then she spent a few minutes just gazing out at the sea, soaking it in. This time of year, you could sometimes see gray whales pass by on their migration up the coast, although she hadn't been lucky enough yet to see one.

She was relaxed and invigorated as she headed back down the coast, her muscles tensing slightly as she reentered the congested streets of greater Los Angeles. She skirted past Ernest E. Debs Regional Park on her way to her house in Montecito Heights. When her gray-painted duplex came into view at the end of the block, David's black Durango was in the driveway. Either he was early, or she'd taken longer to get home than she'd anticipated.

She wiggled her bike past his SUV to park in the shed beside the house. "Sorry, I had no idea I was running late," she said as she climbed off the bike and removed her helmet.

He stood from the SUV, wearing a lavender button-down shirt and gray pants. "You're not late. I'm early."

"That's not like you," she teased as she stowed her helmet. She locked the door to the shed and led the way into the house, stretching her legs as she went. They were sore from hugging the bike for several hours.

"I came from another appointment nearby, and rather than pay an exorbitant amount for a coffee at one of the places in your neighborhood, I decided to just drive over and catch up on email while I waited for you to get home."

"The coffee's expensive as hell around here," she agreed. "Want one for free? I could use some caffeine myself."

"I won't say no to coffee." David settled himself at the kitchen table. "Although you might prefer champagne after you hear why I'm here."

Anna froze with one hand on the coffee machine. "What? I thought we were just going over usual stuff."

"We were, until I got a very unexpected phone call this morning." He tapped his well-manicured fingers against the tabletop, watching her intently. He loved dragging things out like this, reeling her in for his big reveal, whatever that might be.

"Okay," she said, knowing by now that it wouldn't do her any good to try to rush him.

"That phone call was from Stella Pascual."

"Eden's manager called you?" A burst of something warm and tingly flooded Anna's system, because whatever David was getting at, if it had anything to do with Eden, she was almost guaranteed to love it. She abandoned the coffee machine and sat across from him. "What did she want?"

David interlaced his fingers and leaned forward. "Eden's going on tour this spring, and they've invited you to open for her."

Anna inhaled, and something went wrong, like she'd inhaled her own spit, which left her coughing and spluttering. Tears leaked out of her eyes while her mind was reeling, because *oh my God*. Opening for Eden Sands on tour? This was beyond anything her fangirl brain had even dared to dream of.

"Don't choke to death before we've had a chance to discuss this," David admonished, grinning at her.

"You'd better not be joking," she managed, jabbing a finger at him.

"I'm dead serious. Eden wasn't planning to have an opening act for this tour, but according to Stella, they loved the vibe between you two on Grammy night so much that they'd like to bring you on board."

"Fuck me," Anna gasped. "That's it. I've died. This must be heaven."

His grin turned slightly devilish. "I thought your idea of heaven might be something a little more romantic than opening for her on tour."

Her face heated. "Pretty sure she's not into women, David."

"Pretty sure you're right, but we're talking about a fantasy anyway, am I right?"

"Right," she agreed, still bouncing in her seat. "But opening for her on tour? Hell yes. Tell me where to sign."

"Ah-ah, not so fast." He waggled a finger. "I knew you'd react this way, but I'm not convinced this is your best move right now."

"Fine," she said. "Be my manager instead of my friend if you insist."

"Oh, I insist. First of all, when Stella says Eden hadn't planned to have an opening act for this tour until she saw how well you two worked together at the Grammys, I don't think that's the whole truth. Ticket sales for Eden's tour have been lackluster at best. You're hot right now—especially after that performance—and she's not. If you ask me, they need you to sell out the damn tour."

"What? No way." The idea that Eden needed Anna to sell out her tour was ludicrous.

"I'm being serious, Anna. Her career's in a slump right now. Her last album didn't sell well. People are saying she's lost her edge, while your star is on the rise. You're moments away from your big break, and

Eden's team damn well knows it. You don't need to open for Eden this summer. You could sell out arenas on your own. You were considering your own tour this year. Let's stick with that plan."

She stared at him for a long moment as she considered his words. He had a point. She could probably sell out arenas on her own—small ones, anyway. And yes, she'd been thinking about a tour. She loved performing live, and her fans had been clamoring for the chance to see her. But . . . "I can't say no to this."

Anna loved to jump at unexpected opportunities, to take a left turn when people expected her to go right. Opening for Eden was a no-brainer, and it might even earn her some of the gravitas she sought by introducing her to Eden's fan base.

"I'm going to insist that you sleep on it and give me an answer tomorrow. Really think about it, Anna. Think with your head, not with certain other parts of your anatomy."

She sat up straighter in her chair. "I'm going to pretend you didn't just insult me by insinuating that if I say yes, it's because I want to get in her pants and not because she's a fucking legend that I'd be honored and lucky to go on tour with."

He held his hands up in front of himself. "You're right. That was uncalled for."

"I'll think about it, but my answer's not going to change. I get what you're saying, but the thing is, touring with Eden would be a career boost for me too. Her fan base is older than mine, which is exactly the demographic where I've been hoping to grow my visibility. This could be the way I finally get people to take me seriously, to see me as more than a teen phenom. Not to mention, I'd get the opportunity to learn from my idol. Imagine what all she can teach me? I could sell out small arenas on my own this summer, but I have a feeling I'll be an even bigger star if I team up with Eden Sands."

David just looked at her for a moment, and then a wide smile broke across his handsome face. "Damn, girl. Okay, you've sold me. I was afraid you were in it for the wrong reasons, but everything you just said is dead on. Even I can't fight your logic."

"Good," she said, and then she lurched out of her seat and did a little dance around the kitchen. "Oh my God. I'm going on tour with Eden Sands!"

CHAPTER SEVEN

Anna's heart tapped a happy—if somewhat frantic—tune against her ribs as she pushed the gold button to summon the elevator. It was as shiny as the rest of the high-rise apartment building where Eden lived. A waterfall trickled over an elaborate rock structure on the far wall of the lobby, and Anna could see the Pacific gleaming on the other side of the glass doors in back.

It had taken three weeks for the tour contract to be signed. Anna's team went back and forth with Eden's team to sort out all the details, and once everything was finalized, Anna received a most unexpected invitation to Eden's home for lunch. A formal "welcome to the team" was how Stella had framed it to David.

Anna intended to treat it as an opportunity to make a more mature impression on Eden. She'd resolved to leave her inner fangirl at home today. David motioned her into the elevator ahead of him, and Anna smoothed her hands over the front of her pants as it whisked them to the fifteenth floor.

There were only two doors on Eden's floor, one on either side of the hall. Unsurprisingly, Eden's door was on the backside of the building. She would have ocean views, and Anna couldn't wait to see them.

David knocked, and the door opened almost immediately. Stella beckoned them inside, looking very springy in a pink-and-orange floral-printed dress that beautifully complemented the bronze tones of her skin. "Come in. We're so glad you could make it."

"Thanks for the invite," Anna told her. "And I love your dress, by the way. Those colors look great on you."

"Thank you," Stella said with a pleased smile. "We thought we'd have lunch on the balcony today since the weather's so nice."

"I love that idea," Anna said. In fact, she was itching to take her bike out for a spin later that afternoon, eager to soak up all the fresh air she could. She paused in the living room to take it in. The space was as fancy and modern as she'd expected, with lots of glass and silver accents. A gray sofa and love seat were the centerpieces of the room. The walls were white and adorned with a tasteful amount of art.

The space had a polished look, as if it had been decorated by an interior designer. Gorgeous but almost too gorgeous? Anna scanned the room and found nothing that said *Eden*. There weren't any personal knickknacks that Anna could see. Then she spotted a Grammy on a shelf by the window and walked over to it before she could stop herself.

"That was her first," Stella said.

"I'm glad she keeps it here where she can see it every day." Anna gazed greedily at the gleaming gold gramophone. She'd never seen one up close before. Her eyes were drawn to the inscription on the base, showing that Eden had won it for her *In the Clouds* album.

Anna remembered watching Eden win this award as a little girl at home on her sofa, dreaming about winning her own Grammy someday. That little girl never could have anticipated this moment. And she still wanted a Grammy of her own so badly.

"She's waiting for you on the balcony," Stella said.

Anna took that as a hint not to snoop. She dutifully stepped away from the Grammy and turned toward an open door she presumed led to the balcony. Sheer white curtains billowed in the breeze, and when Anna pulled one of them back, she saw Eden standing against the railing, her dark hair blowing behind her. She had on a loose knit dress in a pattern of blues and grays. Those seemed to be her favorite colors: blue, gray, and black.

"Hi," Anna said, so as not to startle Eden.

Eden turned her head with a warm smile. "Hi yourself."

Anna walked out to stand beside her at the railing, staring down at the waves lapping against the sand fifteen stories below. "That's quite a view."

"Not gonna lie. I bought this condo for the view."

"I don't blame you." Anna rested her arms on the railing. She could hear Stella and David talking in the living room and was glad for this moment alone with Eden. "You must be down there all the time. I know I would be."

"On the beach?" Eden asked, and damn, her eyes were really blue right now.

"Yes."

"Hardly ever, actually," Eden said. "It's not so relaxing with a million cell phones in my face. I love to watch the waves from up here, though."

Anna frowned. "That sounds awful." It seemed like the worst kind of tease to have that gorgeous beach right there and not be able to use it.

"Just you wait." Eden's lips curved in a small smile. "Your time is coming."

"I guess, yeah . . . or at least, I hope so."

Eden's smile widened. "This tour might help with that."

"It might. Thanks for that, by the way. I probably don't have to tell you how over-the-top honored and excited I am about going on tour with you."

"Why, Anna Moss, do you mean to tell me you're a fan?" Laughter sparked in Eden's eyes.

"Don't make me show you a picture of the poster that hung over my bed when I was a girl," Anna teased, internally chastising herself for slipping back into fangirl mode.

Eden groaned. "You're making me feel ancient."

Anna shook her head. "You're not that much older than I am. You've just been famous a lot longer."

"I'm not?" Eden asked, brows raised.

"You're what, thirty-six?"

Eden nodded.

"And I'm twenty-seven."

Eden stared at her for a moment in obvious surprise.

"You thought I was younger," Anna said.

"Yeah, sorry . . . wow. Twenty-seven?"

Anna winced. "I was twenty-two when I was cast in *Hex High*, playing a sixteen-year-old, and now America can't seem to see me as anything but a teenager."

"That's not necessarily a bad thing," Eden commented. "Things have definitely gotten better, but female celebrities still have a shorter shelf life than our male counterparts. They want us to stay young forever."

"I'd just like to be seen as an adult," Anna admitted.

"That's fair, and I guess I'm guilty of treating you like a kid too. Sorry about that. I thought you were closer to twenty."

"Most people do."

"It was the opposite for me." Eden stared at the waves below. "I released my first single when I was sixteen, but I was seen as an adult from the start. The way the media talked about me, sexualizing everything I did or said or wore . . . it made me so uncomfortable."

"Yikes. I was too young to see that happening to you, I guess. They treated you like a woman when you were a child, and they won't let me grow up."

"This industry can be hell when you're a woman," Eden said.

"Or anyone who's not a cis white man," Anna added.

"That's very true."

There was a noise behind them, and Anna turned to see Stella and David setting platters of sandwiches and other finger foods on the table. Stella motioned to them.

"Lunch is served."

Stella raised her glass with a flourish. "As of noon today, the tour is officially sold out. Congratulations, ladies. You're a winning combination."

Anna fist-pumped the air, her ponytail bouncing. "Yes!"

Eden wished she felt anywhere near that excited. Instead, she felt relief mixed with a healthy dose of resentment that she'd needed Anna's help to sell out the tour. Behind her bitter feelings, fear lurked. This was probably just a bump in her popularity, a dip that would right itself with time, but what if it wasn't? What if she'd lost her spark, as the media kept saying? Or worse, what if she was past her prime in the eyes of an ageist world?

"You're awfully quiet over there, Eden," Stella said.

Eden reached for her glass, pasting on a smile. Regardless of her inner turmoil, she would be gracious and make sure Anna felt properly welcomed onto the tour. "Anna and I make a great team."

Anna's smile in response to that was luminous. She held out her own glass, tapping it against Eden's. "I couldn't possibly be more excited about touring with you."

"But you hide it so well," Eden teased. Anna was fun to talk to, someone Eden had things in common with. Eden didn't have many friends, but maybe Anna could become one.

Anna pressed a hand against her chest. "Fangirl at heart, and I refuse to apologize for it."

Everyone laughed. Eden usually disliked when people were so open with their flattery. From fellow musicians, it often felt like they were trying to suck up, to get in her good graces so she would do them a favor.

Anna didn't give off that vibe. She just seemed to be unapologetically enthusiastic. It was oddly refreshing.

"While we're talking about the tour," Eden said, "I've rented Limelight Studios for the four weeks before opening night as a rehearsal space. I rented the whole studio, so there's more than enough room for you to rehearse there, too, if you'd like."

Anna's eyes widened. "I mean, if you're sure you don't mind, that sounds amazing."

"I don't mind," Eden told her. "It could be helpful for us to be able to bounce ideas around, and I'll have the staging all set up for you to use."

After lunch, Anna and David headed out. Stella lingered to help Eden clean up, using the opportunity to reassure her that she'd made the right decision by bringing Anna on board. Eden's tour was now sold out and receiving more internet chatter than it had since the day it was first announced.

"I just wish . . ." Eden pressed her lips together, not wanting to sound like an ungrateful, arrogant bitch, because she liked Anna. She did.

"You wish you could have sold out the tour on your own," Stella said. "Of course you do. And I know you resent needing Anna to give you a boost, but let me reframe that for you. Have you ever considered that maybe it's not Anna's success that sold out the remaining tickets but rather the appeal of seeing the two of you together?"

Eden grimaced as her feet slammed into the stage. The room tilted, and she probably would have landed on her ass if not for the harness holding her upright.

"Much better," Lora said. "You're starting to get the hang of it."

"Thanks. I hope so." Eden didn't feel like she'd gotten the hang of it. This was the third day of tour rehearsals, and she'd spent much of it in this harness, twirling above the stage for a stunt at the end of her song "Smash."

Opening night was just four weeks away, and she was so excited she wanted to shout it from the rafters, even if this stunt was a lot harder than she'd anticipated. She was exhausted, dizzy, and sore from the harness, but she'd always loved this part of the process, seeing her vision for the show start to come to life in rehearsals.

"Let's stop here for today." Lora unclipped Eden's harness and helped her out of it.

"Thanks. I'll see you in the morning, then."

"Yes, you will." Lora walked over to talk to the stage manager.

Eden swiped a loose strand of hair from her face and turned to look for Paris, who was standing in the back corner of the rehearsal space, talking to Anna. Eden started toward them.

"Ready for me to have Lawrence pull the car around?" Paris asked.

Eden nodded. "Just give me a few minutes to freshen up first."

"You got it." Paris headed for the door, already typing on her phone.

"I hope you don't mind that I stopped by to watch," Anna said.

"Not at all." Eden had spent a few minutes watching Anna rehearse earlier too. She didn't doubt Anna's capability, but she also hadn't been able to escape her need to be sure. She needn't have worried, though. Anna and her dancers had been in the middle of a dance sequence far more complicated than anything Eden herself was capable of.

"Great work in that harness." Anna crossed her arms over her chest, and something beneath them sparkled, drawing Eden's gaze. A belly ring. "That's going to look amazing during the show."

"Thanks." Eden dragged her gaze away from the unexpected bit of jewelry. "It's harder than I expected."

"You'll get it. I have full confidence."

Eden studied Anna, remembering the energy she'd brought to their Grammy performance. The video of that duet had more views than any other performance on Eden's official YouTube channel. An idea had sparked, and it wasn't like her to be impulsive, but . . . "How do you feel about recreating our Grammy duet for the tour?"

"Like, you and me singing 'After Midnight' together every night during your performance?" Anna's voice had crept up in pitch, which Eden took as a good sign.

"That's exactly what I mean."

Anna bounced on her toes. She actually bounced. "Yes! Oh my God, yes, that would be so fun, and awesome, and generally . . . yes. I would love to do that."

"So, that's a yes?" Eden teased.

Anna spun in a circle, singing "Yes" at the top of her lungs.

"Great. Maybe we can find some time to sit down tomorrow and talk through the logistics?"

"Definitely. This will be so fun, and I bet our fans will love it."

Paris popped her head through the door. "Car will be here in five."

"Thanks, Paris," Eden said.

"Plans tonight?" Anna asked.

Eden shrugged. "Figure out something for dinner, and probably a hot date with my Kindle."

"Well, absolutely no pressure, but I'm having a few friends over tonight to hang out. I'm going to do a stir-fry and relax on the back patio to enjoy the weather. It's private, so no paparazzi concerns. Feel free to stop by if you'd like."

Eden slow-blinked. It had been so long since someone invited her to hang out, she didn't even know what to say. What were Anna's friends like? Would Eden have anything in common with them? It might be awkward if they were fans of Eden's music like Anna was. She wasn't sure why she was even considering this, except she seemed to enjoy being around Anna. Well, that, and the lonely evening that awaited her if she stayed at home.

"But I totally understand the allure of a quiet night and a good book. I did that last night." Anna lifted her water bottle for a drink.

"Actually, I'd like to stop by, if you're sure I wouldn't be imposing."

"Positive," Anna said. "And my friends are all in the business, so fangirling will be kept to a minimum."

That was a relief. "All right. What time?"

"Come around seven. I'll text you my address."

"Great. I'll see you then."

CHAPTER EIGHT

Anna wielded the knife with a level of expertise that came from being a chef's daughter. Its polished blade sliced rapidly through a red bell pepper, chopping it into neat, narrow slices. Music played softly through the built-in speakers that were located throughout the first floor of her house, and she hummed along as she chopped.

She still couldn't believe she'd impulsively invited Eden to join her and her friends tonight . . . or that Eden had accepted. But she had, and Anna was pretty damn excited about it. She hoped that tonight would be a chance to get to know each other better before they headed out on the road together.

The more time Anna spent with her, the more enchanted she became. She'd always been drawn to successful women. Competence was sexy as hell as far as Anna was concerned, not that she was thinking about Eden like *that*—or she was trying very hard not to, at least—but she'd be thrilled to call her a friend.

"Knock, knock," Zoe called as she poked her head in through the patio door.

"Come on in and give me a hand," Anna said.

"I left a bucket of beer on the patio, and I've got some lemon meringue bites I picked up on the way home . . . vegan, I checked."

"I love you," Anna told her friend.

"What can I help with?"

Anna paused before picking up the next pepper. She could slice much faster than Zoe. "Would you mind mixing up the marinade? The recipe's open on my phone."

"You got it. So who's coming over?"

"Nicole and her boyfriend, Kyrie, and Eden."

Zoe's eyebrows went up. "Eden's coming?"

"Yeah, I saw her at rehearsal today and asked if she'd like to stop by." Anna shrugged as if it were no big deal, as if she invited superstars to her house all the time. Anna and Zoe were B-list celebs, but Eden . . . she was the kind of celebrity that even fellow celebs got starstruck over.

"My little Anna is moving up in the world," Zoe said. "Just don't get too cool to hang out with me. Promise?"

"That could never happen." Anna elbowed her friend. "Eden's a bit of a diva sometimes, but she also seems, I don't know . . . lonely. I don't think she has a lot of friends."

"She's recently divorced," Zoe said. "That's got to wreak some havoc on her social life."

"Right."

"Well, good for you, hanging out with a superstar. I'm excited to meet her."

"Be cool," Anna said. "I promised her we'd all behave."

Zoe shrugged as she poured soy sauce into a bowl. "You know I'm not really the fangirl type. Eden's just Eden as far as I'm concerned."

If only Anna could turn off her own inner fangirl as easily. She and Zoe chatted as they worked. Anna wanted to have all the ingredients for the stir-fry ready to go before her friends got here. Then she could just toss it in the pan and have it ready quickly whenever people got hungry.

Kyrie was the first to arrive, carrying a brown paper bag. "I stopped for some of those veggie spring rolls we love from the place on Figueroa."

"Oh my God, those are amazing. Thank you." By now, Anna had finished the stir-fry prep, and she joined Zoe and Kyrie on the patio for a beer. Anna loved to be outside this time of year. It had been in the low seventies earlier, but now that the sun had begun to set, it had dipped into the sixties. Perfect hoodie weather.

Unlike San Francisco, where she'd grown up, springtime in LA tended to be crisp and clear, not endlessly gray and damp. Her phone buzzed with a text.

Eden:

I'm here.

Anna popped out of her seat embarrassingly quickly and went inside. She pulled open the front door to see a sleek black sedan idling outside. The back door opened, and Eden stepped out. She had on skinny jeans and a pink patterned top, and Anna's traitorous heart gave a little leap in her chest. "Hi," she said, motioning Eden inside.

"You know, I had been trying to picture where you lived," Eden said as she stepped through the door.

Anna shut it behind her. "And?"

"And this is pretty close to what I had imagined." Eden swept her gaze around the living room. "Colorful, comfortable, and not at all pretentious."

"Is that how you see me?"

"I think you're those things and more." Eden held out a small bottle. "I would have brought wine, but you didn't quite strike me as a wine drinker."

"I do drink wine sometimes, but you're right. It's not my first choice." She accepted the bottle of spiced rum, which looked expensive and elegant, just like Eden. Anna was trying to play it cool, like she wasn't ridiculously touched by Eden's thoughtfulness. Like she wasn't developing a massive crush despite her best efforts not to. "This looks amazing. Thank you."

"You're welcome." Eden smiled at her, and for several beautiful seconds, they were caught in the moment, just watching each other, relaxed and happy and comfortable. Then Eden looked down at her feet.

Anna followed her gaze and saw Nelle sniffing Eden's boots. "This is the actual owner of the house, Nelle. She's currently evaluating whether you get to stay."

"Uh-oh," Eden said. "I hope I make the cut."

"Looks promising, but I wouldn't try to pet her just yet. She's a total asshole sometimes."

"Got it." Eden looked up, her eyes sparkling with humor. "Nelle, hmm?"

"Yeah, she's, um . . . I named her Villanelle because one minute she loves you, the next minute she's drawing blood. A very complicated lady."

"A bit of a psychopath, are you, Nelle?" Eden asked. "Beautiful and lethal, just like your namesake."

Nelle looked up at her and meowed. Behind them, the patio door slid open, and Zoe stepped inside.

"Figured I'd see where you ran off to," she said, looking first at Anna and then Eden. "Zoe Morales. Nice to meet you."

"Hi, Zoe." Eden extended a hand, which Zoe took. "I'm Eden. Anna was just introducing me to Nelle."

"Oh, you want to watch out around that one." Zoe gave the cat an affectionate glance. "She'll slice you open when you least expect it."

"So I hear. Zoe Morales, your name is familiar. How do I know you?" Eden asked.

"Anna and I were on *Hex High* together, and now I'm starring on *The Match*. I live in the other half of the duplex." She jerked a thumb over her shoulder in the direction of her house.

"That's nice, having a friend next door," Eden said.

"It's great," Anna confirmed. "What can I get you to drink? We've got beer, soda, water, sparkling water, and now spiced rum." She held up the bottle.

Eden glanced at it and then at Anna. "What are the rest of you drinking?" There was something in her voice Anna hadn't heard before, hesitation or maybe even the tiniest bit of insecurity, as if Eden was worried she wouldn't fit in. And that was as unexpected as it was adorable. As if Eden Sands could ever possibly not be the coolest person in the room.

"Beer," Zoe said, holding hers up.

"Same," Anna said. "I left mine out back when I came to get the door."

Eden nodded. "Beer sounds great."

Anna set the bottle of rum on the counter and led the way toward the back patio. "Right this way. We're just waiting on two more people, and then we'll eat."

Eden shivered. The temperature had dropped quite a bit since she'd arrived. Before her, flames from the firepit danced, illuminating the patio area behind Anna's and Zoe's homes. After two beers and some delicious stir-fry, Eden was full and relaxed, kicked back in a chaise beside Anna. Her friends Nicole and Tom had asked Eden for a selfie, but other than that, no one seemed to care who she was.

And she was surprised by how easily she'd settled in their presence. Eden was generally wary of letting her guard down around people she didn't know, yet somehow, Anna's friends put her at ease. Maybe that had something to do with Anna herself, who always seemed to find ways to make Eden smile.

"Awfully quiet over there, Ms. Pop Superstar," Anna said in a teasing voice, turning her head to look at Eden.

"Sorry. Alcohol makes me introspective." She rubbed her hands over her arms. If she hadn't been so cold, she'd be content to sit here all night.

"Really?" Zoe asked. "It doesn't make you want to get wild and dance on tables?"

Eden smiled. "No, but I had a full day of tour rehearsal, so I'm probably just tired."

Anna stood and went inside, and Eden fell into conversation with Kyrie, learning that she and Anna had met when Kyrie worked as a production assistant on *Hex High*. The patio door slid open behind her, and Anna was back, carrying something.

"Here. You look like you're freezing." Anna passed her what turned out to be a hoodie.

"Oh, thank you." Eden sat up and tugged it over her head, immediately enveloped in warmth and a faint, vaguely sweet scent that she associated with Anna. It was thick and soft and a pretty lilac color that was subtler than the yellow hoodie Anna herself had on tonight. Eden sank her hands into the front pocket with a happy sigh. "This is perfect."

Anna smiled, the flames from the firepit casting dancing shadows over her face. "No problem."

"Dessert, anyone?" Zoe held up a plate full of small pastries. "Lemon meringue bites, and before you ask, I bought them."

"Phew," Nicole said with an exaggerated look of relief.

"Not much of a cook?" Eden asked Zoe.

"I'm a hazard in the kitchen." Zoe held the plate toward Eden. "So you should definitely be glad I didn't make these."

"I'm no better. Thank you." Eden grabbed one of the pastries. It looked almost like a lemon bar, with a white topping she presumed wasn't actual meringue since she'd learned earlier tonight that Anna was vegan.

The dessert was delicious, and between the six of them, they polished off the entire plate while they chatted. The combination of the borrowed hoodie and the firepit had Eden feeling warm and cozy despite the chilly air. Her balcony had a better view, but the ambiance here was so much friendlier.

"Could you point me toward your restroom?" she asked Anna.

"Of course. It's the door on the right, just past the kitchen."

"Thank you." Eden stood and went inside. She found the bathroom with no problem and freshened up. As she came back out, she was startled to find Nelle sitting on the other side of the door, staring up at her. "Hi," she said to the cat.

Nelle meowed.

"Talkative, hmm? Just like Anna." Eden crouched and extended a hand, wary after the way she'd been introduced to the cat. Nelle looked harmless, but then again, so did her namesake.

Nelle sniffed her fingers and meowed again.

"I bet you wish you could come outside with everyone."

Nelle looked up at her with wide green eyes, then rubbed the side of her head against Eden's hand. Deciding to risk it, Eden gave her chin a quick scratch. She was rewarded by a thin purr.

"I'm starting to think you get a bad rap," Eden whispered.

Nelle looked up and meowed again.

The patio door slid open, and Anna stepped inside. "Oh jeez, be careful, Eden. I'm not kidding."

"No blood has been spilled," Eden said.

Nelle batted at Eden's hand and stalked toward Anna, tail stuck straight up in the air.

"That was a soft paw, for the record." Eden straightened, holding in a groan at the ache in her abs. She'd used some weird muscles today in that harness.

"Well, I'm glad she didn't fillet you. That's not the kind of hospitality I like to show my guests." Anna placed a handful of empty beer bottles into a blue trash can, presumably for recyclables.

"I have no complaints about your hospitality." Eden rested her elbows on the counter. "Need a hand with anything?"

"Nope. Nicole and Tom are getting ready to head out, though. She's got an early call time tomorrow." Anna's friend Nicole had told Eden earlier tonight that she was currently filming a Netflix movie.

Eden enjoyed being around other people in the industry when it was low key like this. Too often, she found herself at events where everyone was trying to schmooze her, the kind of event where she had to put on an expensive dress and walk around in uncomfortable heels. She hadn't minded that kind of event as much when she had Zach at her side, but on her own, they could be excruciating. "I should probably go ahead and call for my ride too."

"Do you ever drive yourself?" Anna asked, glancing up. "Tell me to buzz off if that's none of my business."

"I gave up driving here in LA," Eden told her. "I had a few too many scary run-ins with the paparazzi. They would photograph me through my windows at stoplights, and one time, they actually ran me off the road. It became more stress than it was worth."

"I'm sorry," Anna said. "That sounds like a nightmare."

"It doesn't happen to you?" Eden asked.

Anna gave her a look Eden couldn't quite decipher. "Wicked" was the word that came to mind to describe it. Eden found herself leaning closer to hear what Anna would say. "I ride a motorcycle."

"Oh." Eden could immediately visualize it, Anna on a motorcycle, whizzing down the road with her blonde hair blowing in the breeze behind her. The image sent Eden's pulse racing. She sucked in a breath. What would it feel like to be so free?

"With a full-face helmet on, no one has any idea who I am. I love it."

"Well, now I'm jealous," Eden said. "That sounds way more fun than being chauffeured around town all the time."

"I could take you for a ride sometime, if you'd like," Anna offered.

Eden considered that for a moment. She'd never been on a motorcycle before. It sounded a little bit reckless, a little bit dangerous, two things Eden had never been and wasn't sure she even had in her. "Maybe."

"Cool. No pressure." Anna gave her another of those radiant smiles.

Eden found herself returning it. Smiles felt like work for her sometimes. At a photo shoot. On a red carpet. Those were smiles she had to think about, the kind of smile that hurt her cheeks at the end of the night from holding it in place. Anna inspired the best kind of smile, the kind that just . . . happened.

Something bumped the back of her calves, and Eden looked down to see Nelle turning in circles behind her, rubbing against her legs. "Look."

Anna leaned across the counter to peer down at her cat. "Eden Sands, you didn't tell me you're a cat charmer."

"I *was* voted most likable female celebrity a few years ago."

Anna looked up. Her arm was pressed against Eden's now that she'd leaned over the counter, and Eden felt hyperaware of her proximity and the warmth of her skin where they touched. She moved her arm just as the patio door slid open.

"We were starting to think you left without saying goodbye," Zoe said to Eden as she walked into the kitchen, carrying the empty dessert plate.

"Nope. I just got sidetracked by Nelle."

"And Anna, looks like." Zoe grinned as she set the plate on the counter.

Nicole, Tom, and Kyrie had followed her in, and they all gathered in the kitchen as they prepared to head out. Eden slid her phone out of her back pocket and texted her car service. Hopefully Lawrence was still on. He was polite and friendly but didn't try to make conversation all the way home, and tonight, she was ready to sit with her thoughts for a little while.

When she looked up, Anna was sitting on the counter, talking to Nicole.

"If anyone wants a ticket to the premiere for the new season of *The Match* next weekend, let me know. I can hook you up," Zoe said.

"Me." Anna raised her hand in the air like a student.

"I already saved you one," Zoe told her.

Anna beamed. "Yay."

They talked for a few more minutes, and then Eden's phone buzzed with a text. "My car's here. Thanks so much for having me tonight, Anna."

"Anytime," Anna said. "I'll walk you out."

"Okay," Eden agreed. She didn't need an escort, but she was glad for the chance to spend another moment with Anna. "Night, everyone."

They said their goodbyes, and Eden went out the front door. Anna stood on the porch behind her, watching as Eden walked to the car waiting at the curb.

"Good night," Eden said. "I'll see you tomorrow."

"Can't wait. Good night."

Eden waved before she opened the door and slipped into the back seat of the sedan, relieved to see Lawrence's friendly face in the driver's seat. "Hi, Lawrence."

"Good evening, Ms. Sands."

As the car pulled away from the curb, Eden realized she was still wearing Anna's hoodie.

"Are we going to talk about that moment I walked in on between you and Eden earlier?" Zoe stretched out in her chair, beer in hand. Everyone had gone home, and she and Anna were having one last beer together on the patio before they shut off the firepit and called it a night.

"It wasn't a moment," Anna said. "She was bonding with Nelle, and I was watching."

"That's not what I saw. You were leaned across the counter looking at her like you wanted to kiss her."

"I wasn't going to kiss her," Anna protested, and that part was true, at least. She wouldn't kiss Eden—no matter how much she wanted to—even if they *had* shared a moment in her kitchen. Their arms had touched, and Eden had looked at her in a way that made Anna forget how to breathe.

It didn't change anything. Eden wasn't interested in her that way. Anna wasn't naive.

"Sweetie, you were making heart eyes at her all night," Zoe said. "Don't worry, I don't think anyone but me noticed. I know she's always been your celebrity crush, but you look at her the way you used to look at Camille, and that scared me a little bit."

Anna looked down at the beer in her hands. "I know. It scares me too."

"Gorgeous older women in a position of authority have always been your catnip."

That was an understatement. Anna suspected it came down to the age-old dilemma: *Do I want to be her or be* with *her?* In this case, it was a little of both but mostly the latter. Anna lifted her beer and took a hearty drink. "Eden's not exactly in a position of authority."

"No, but she did hire you to open for her on tour."

Anna took another drink as she absorbed Zoe's words. She'd known this already, but hearing Zoe voice it out loud made it sound a lot more real. "I hear you. I do."

"Good." Zoe reached over and clinked her beer bottle against Anna's. "Because I don't want to sound like an asshole. I'm just trying to be a good friend. I don't want to see you get hurt again, especially not before you're fully healed from all the damage Camille inflicted."

Anna winced. Years of Camille's emotional abuse had taken their toll, especially on her self-esteem. She hadn't been in a serious relationship since. "You're right. I knew this already, but if you could see me fawning over Eden tonight, then I'm obviously more infatuated than I thought, and I've got to stop."

"She's hot. I get it," Zoe said. "And I say that as a woman who couldn't be any more straight. I certainly see why Eden has turned your head."

"Well, I'm pretty sure she's as straight as you are, so . . ."

"All the more reason to keep that big heart of yours under lock and key."

Anna mimed turning a lock over her heart. "Promise."

"That's my girl. In the meantime, maybe you and I should go out one night and try to find ourselves dates?"

"For sure," Anna agreed. "We can do one of our fifty-fifty nights where we hit a queer bar and a straight one."

"You got it."

Anna went to bed that night with Zoe's warning ringing in her mind, but she fell asleep remembering the way Eden had looked in her purple hoodie, the joy in those ocean-blue eyes as she rubbed Nelle, and the sparks that had lit Anna up like a packed arena on opening night when their arms brushed in the kitchen.

The next morning, she gave herself a stern lecture in the bathroom mirror before she headed to the studio for rehearsals. Eden was off limits for so many reasons. It wouldn't be easy to ignore the sparks, but if Anna could move past her crush, there was a good chance they could be friends, and she wanted that. Friendship with Eden sounded amazing, and to be honest, Eden seemed like she could use a friend.

It sounded ludicrous to imagine someone as rich and famous as Eden needing a friend, but Anna had been in the business long enough to realize that sometimes the richest, most successful people were *exactly* the ones most in need of honest, no-strings friendship.

At the studio, Anna checked in with Kyrie. She would be working on choreography again after lunch, but she'd come in early because . . . well, she was enthusiastic about rehearsing for her first tour.

She spotted Eden in the room that had been set up as her rehearsal space, an outline of the stage layout marked on the floor in bright-red tape. Eden stood with her back to the door, wearing what Anna was starting to think of as her rehearsal uniform: black skinny jeans paired with an athletic tank top, neatly tucked in. Today's tank was a soft shade of blue.

Eden's hair was down, landing halfway down her back, and she stood with her feet planted about a foot apart, both hands on the microphone stand. Anna slipped through the door and sat cross-legged in the back corner to watch. Eden was working on the arrangement for "Alone," and for the next fifteen minutes, Anna listened to her belt out those powerful lyrics. Her voice filled the room, making goose bumps rise on Anna's arms.

Eden had tweaked the arrangement for the tour, and it was so beautiful, especially in the more haunting portions of the song when she lamented having no one to warm her bed or hold her when she cried. What kind of place must Eden have been in when she wrote it? Probably a dark one. It had been released not long after her divorce.

"I'm never alone, because I have myself to keep me company," Eden finished, bowing her head before she turned and faced the rear of the stage. Her eyes found Anna, and Anna felt a jolt in the pit of her stomach as their gazes locked.

The ghost of a smile touched Eden's lips before she turned to face her team. "How was that?" she called out. "I think the new inflection at the end of the second chorus really helps to maximize the impact of the strings."

"I agree," a man who'd been sitting in front of the stage said. "Very strong, perhaps a bit more vibrato at the end, but I think you nailed it."

Eden nodded. They spoke for a few more minutes, and Anna wondered if he was Eden's vocal coach. If so, they had a much more respectful relationship than Anna had had with Camille. It had taken her years to realize that Camille's criticisms weren't the constructive kind.

"Lunch is ready in the break room," Paris called from the doorway.

Wow, Eden's people ran a tight ship. Everything was so organized. Anna had thought her team had it together, but lunch so far had involved her and Kyrie heading out to find a nearby vegan-friendly drive-through.

Eden set her microphone in the stand and walked toward Anna. She extended her hands, and Anna gripped them, letting Eden pull her to her feet. "So what did you think?" Eden asked.

"Amazing, and that's not just a blind compliment because I love your music. The changes you've made to the song really elevate it. You gave me shivers." She held up her arms to show Eden the goose bumps that hadn't quite faded.

Eden's smile lit up her whole face. "Thank you. That means a lot. Have lunch with me?"

"Um, sure, but—"

Eden waved a hand. "Paris always orders too much, and there will be something vegan friendly, I'm sure. We can talk about our duet if you want to call it a working lunch."

"I'm happy to call it a casual lunch between friends," Anna said, "but I do want to talk about that duet."

"Great." Eden led the way out of the studio and down the hall to a room Anna hadn't been in yet. It looked more like a boardroom than a break room, with a long oval table taking up most of the space. The counter in back was laden with food. Anna saw platters of various Mediterranean dishes: black bean salad, tabbouleh, stuffed grape leaves, kebobs, rice, and several other things she couldn't identify by sight.

She and Eden filled plates and grabbed bottles of water, and then Eden led her down another hall and out a door. Anna found herself on a small patio overlooking a pond behind the building. There was a glass table ringed by metal chairs at the center and two lounge chairs at the edge of the patio.

"Shh, don't tell anyone, but I kind of pulled a diva move and claimed this space for myself," Eden told her with a smug smile.

"Well, if anyone here is entitled to pull a diva move, it's you."

Eden's smile faltered slightly. "If the media's going to call me a bitch, I might as well act like one, right?"

Anna scoffed as she set her plate on the table. "That's not what I meant. I haven't known you long, but I've never seen you act like a bitch. You are, however, the woman who's footing the bill for all of this, so if you want to sit outside and claim a few minutes of peace and quiet during a demanding day, I'd call that self-care."

"You're good for my self-esteem, you know that?" Eden sat across from her, unscrewed the cap on her water, and took a long drink.

Anna forced herself not to watch Eden's throat as she swallowed. "I'd say I can't imagine how a woman in your position could possibly need a boost to her self-esteem, but this industry can be harsh, especially on unapologetically successful women."

"Tell me about it." Eden set down the bottle, which was now half-empty. "I barely look at social media, but somehow I still see it and internalize it."

"It's hard not to."

"Hey, slightly off topic, but speaking of public image, I was just thinking . . ." Eden hesitated, spinning her water bottle between her fingers.

"Yeah?" Anna prompted.

"Well, you mentioned that you want people to take you more seriously, to see you as an adult, so what if you use the tour to debut a bit of a new look for yourself?"

"A new look?" Anna twisted her lips to the side. She liked her look. It was very authentically *her*, no matter how bubbly and colorful, and her stomach sank to realize Eden didn't understand that.

"Nothing drastic," Eden said. "A new hairstyle, maybe? A little tweak like that can go a long way toward making you look older. And you could upgrade your tour costumes from athletic wear to something a little fancier. I could totally see you rocking a pair of rainbow sequined pants."

Oh. Just like that, Anna's disappointment vanished. She imagined herself onstage with a fresh new haircut, wearing pants that glittered with the colors of the rainbow. It felt more mature, yes, but it still maintained her signature style. "You know what? I love that. I'm going to call my stylist after lunch."

Eden's cheeks pinked just slightly, but it was enough to make Anna's stomach give a dizzying swoop. Eden looked down at her plate. "We can't always control the way the media portrays us, but there are ways to help steer the narrative."

While they ate, they chatted about the tour schedule and which cities they were most looking forward to visiting, and then they moved to the lounge chairs and stretched out. Eden looked relaxed and content. She had a beautiful laugh, which made Anna want to hear it more often.

"Let's take a selfie," she suggested, pulling out her phone. "I can post it and tag you to help keep the excitement for the tour going."

"Sure." Eden slid onto Anna's lounge chair, her body pressed close as Anna held her phone overhead. Her cheek pressed against Anna's, and there was the scent of roses Anna had come to associate with her. Today it was mixed with lemons from her lunch.

Anna took a burst of photos as she and Eden hammed it up for the camera, and then she spun her phone to check them out. "Oh, we're cute."

"Very cute. Pick whichever one you think is cutest and post it. I trust you."

CHAPTER NINE

The first week of rehearsals was always the most difficult. It felt like trying to juggle a hundred balls, all of them different sizes and sometimes moving in unexpected directions. Eden enjoyed the challenge, even on the days when it was hard to imagine things ever coming together to form a cohesive show.

She'd learned to trust the process. It always felt chaotic at first, and it always came together in the end. Today, she and Anna had their first official rehearsal for the "After Midnight" duet. They'd spent the afternoon finding ways to tweak what they'd done at the Grammys to make it fresh and exciting.

"We have to remember that after opening night, our duet won't *really* be a surprise," Anna said after Paris suggested a change to the staging that would better conceal Anna before the big reveal.

Eden frowned. "Won't it?"

"For the casual fans, the people who attend a show without following our social media or interacting with other fans online, sure, yeah, they'll be surprised each night," Anna said. "But our hard-core fans will have heard about the duet and seen pictures online. They'll be anticipating it, so we should lean into that and make sure we give them what they want."

"How so?" Eden asked.

"A way to tease, maybe? What if I rotate between several costumes that reflect your iconic looks? You could do a post on your social media asking fans to name a favorite 'early Eden' look that they'd like me to recreate or even put up a poll for them to try to guess which costume I'll wear each night. We embrace the fact that they're expecting me to appear during the song and still build their anticipation because they want to see what costume I'll be wearing."

"I love that idea," Eden said. "What do you think, Paris?"

"Love it, too, and I'm jotting everything down." Paris held up her phone. "A Twitter poll could be a great way to get the fans hyped."

After they finished rehearsing, Paris showed them a post she'd drafted with a few photos from their rehearsal—photos that hinted at but didn't confirm a duet to start building hype. With their permission, she shared it on Eden's social media and tagged Anna. Then Paris excused herself to make a call.

"Heading out?" Eden asked Anna as they began to pack up their things.

"Yep. I rode my bike today so I could take a ride up the coast before I go home."

"Oh." Eden felt a tug in her chest. It took her a moment to realize it was longing.

"I brought my spare helmet," Anna said, glancing at her. "Just in case."

"In case of what?" Eden asked, even as her heart sped, imagining them whizzing down the road together, leaving the pressures of the world behind.

"In case you wanted to join me."

"Yes," Eden answered before she'd had a chance to second-guess herself.

Anna laughed. "That was easier than I expected. Really?"

Eden nodded. "You thought I'm not the kind of person who impulsively decides to get on a motorcycle, and that's exactly why I want to.

Because you're right, I hardly ever get to be impulsive and go somewhere without a team of people looking after me like I'm a toddler."

"Let's go, then," Anna said, linking her arm through Eden's. "You're going to have so much fun, I promise."

"I just have to . . ." Eden pulled out her phone. She sent a text to Paris to let her know she didn't need the car tonight, which prompted an awkward response from her assistant, who was clearly not comfortable with Eden going off on her own like this but knew she didn't have the authority to tell her not to.

A minute later, a text from Taylor popped up. Taylor wanted permission to follow the motorcycle, which Eden also declined. Just for tonight, Eden wanted to leave her entourage behind. She wanted to be just the tiniest bit reckless.

"Your jeans and boots will be perfect for riding," Anna was saying. "But I do need to find you a jacket."

"There's a bunch of random stuff in the storage room." Eden pocketed her phone. "Leftover costumes and things like that. I bet there's a leather jacket in there somewhere."

"Let's go see."

Fifteen minutes later, they were ready to go. Eden had on a borrowed leather jacket that was a little too big but thankfully didn't smell like whoever had worn it before her. Part of the adventure, she told herself as she accepted a helmet from Anna. They put their helmets on inside the building and then slipped unnoticed to Anna's motorcycle, parked in back.

A few minutes ago, Paris had gone out the main door. She'd told the fans gathered in the parking lot that Eden had already left, and as a result, the lot was nearly empty now.

"I'll get on first, and then you're going to put your right foot here." Anna gestured to a spot on the side of the bike. "And swing on behind me. Then you'll wrap your arms around my waist and hold on for the ride of your life. Ready?"

"Ready," Eden answered breathlessly. Her heart rate hadn't returned to normal since Anna first mentioned the motorcycle, and now that she was standing in front of it, butterflies flapped anxiously in her stomach.

"It may feel like the cars are getting really close to us before we leave the city, but don't worry about it, okay? I promise I won't let anything happen to you."

"Okay."

"And remember, they won't know who you are. You can look in their windows and gawk at them from the privacy of your helmet if you want to." Anna grinned at her.

That kind of freedom sounded . . . amazing.

"One more thing. My favorite spot is about an hour from here. You okay to go that far? I can bring you straight home afterward."

"That's fine." Eden couldn't deny she was curious to see Anna's favorite spot, even if it was farther away than she'd thought they would be going.

"Okay then. Time to blow your mind." Anna mounted the bike, looking as natural as she did onstage or making stir-fry in her kitchen. "Now climb on behind me."

Eden scanned the parking lot to make sure no one had spotted them, but Paris's decoy seemed to have worked. Carefully, she put her foot in the spot Anna had indicated and swung into place. The seat sloped beneath her so that gravity pressed her against Anna's back. She fought it at first, attempting to sit up straight, before she remembered she was supposed to sit close to Anna anyway.

The engine rumbled to life, and Eden's arms flailed, wrapping themselves around Anna's waist almost without her permission, but the bike didn't move. Of course, Anna wasn't going to start before Eden was ready. She rolled her eyes at herself.

They sat like that for a few minutes while the engine warmed up. Then Anna craned her head to look at her. "Ready?"

Eden nodded. She threaded her fingers together in front of Anna's stomach and tightened her thighs around the machine. She could barely hear Anna now and knew she probably wouldn't be able to hear her at all once they started moving.

Anna pressed a hand over Eden's and shouted, "Hold on tight!"

Eden clamped her arms tighter around Anna's body. The engine revved beneath her, and Eden sucked in a breath. Adrenaline spiked through her system, flooding her with a combination of fear and excitement. She was about to do something wild, but as the bike began to move forward, she was almost positive this had been a good decision.

It was slow going at first as Anna guided them through the busy streets near Limelight Studios. Several times, Eden had to close her eyes to keep from panicking about the traffic around her. She felt so *exposed*. There was nothing separating her legs from the bumper of the nearest car, but she remembered Anna's words, and slowly she felt herself begin to relax.

Anna rode this motorcycle all the time, and nothing bad had happened to her. Well, Eden actually hadn't asked that question, but it was too late now. She was on it, and she was going to enjoy herself, dammit. She peeked into a few cars, thrilled by the anonymity provided by her helmet.

And then, Anna turned onto the Pacific Coast Highway, and Eden forgot all her hesitations. They picked up speed as the road opened up before them. Eden's head was sheltered from the wind, but she felt it buffeting her body. Once, she'd gone indoor skydiving, floating on a cushion of air, and this felt a little bit like that.

She wrapped her arms more tightly around Anna so she didn't blow right off the back of the bike. On her left, the Pacific shone a deep navy, glistening beneath the late afternoon sun on the other side of the beachfront houses that lined this stretch of the road. On her right, more homes were nestled into the hills, from small cottages to outrageous mansions.

She'd lived in one of those once. Not one of the enormous ones, but the home she'd shared with Zach was by far the nicest place she'd ever lived. It had a pool in back and stunning views of the ocean. And she'd been almost as lonely there as she was in her new condo. She wasn't lonely now, though, with her arms wrapped around Anna.

Eden gradually realized that the bike had slowed. Anna was pulling into a parking lot to their left. If this was their destination, it hadn't felt like it had taken an hour to get here. Then again, as Eden blinked to clear her mind, she had a feeling she'd zoned out.

Could you get high from the thrill of a ride? Because she felt a little bit high right now. Her body was buzzing like she'd just come off the stage after an exhilarating performance. They were at a scenic overlook that also seemed to be the entrance to a nature park. The coastline had risen, and she could see the ocean crashing against the base of the cliffs.

Anna guided them to the far end of the lot, pulling into a spot without any cars nearby. She rolled the motorcycle to a stop and planted her right foot on the pavement. Then the engine went silent. Eden's ears rang in the absence of its steady roar. Her heart was beating way too fast, and she was breathing hard. *Wow.*

Anna turned her head and gestured for Eden to take her helmet off. She glanced over her shoulder first, trying to make sure no one was paying attention, but it was hard with the helmet blocking her peripheral vision.

Anna shifted in front of her, and Eden was suddenly very aware that her arms were still wrapped tightly around Anna's torso. She could feel Anna's chest rise and fall with each breath, and she seemed to be breathing pretty hard too. Eden felt a burst of warmth through her system, centered low in her stomach.

What was the matter with her? Was she actually getting aroused by a ride on a motorcycle? God, she really did need to get out more often. She needed to get laid, not that sex had ever been all that exciting for her.

Her arms were still around Anna, and now she was thinking about sex. Eden yanked her arms back, doing her best to put a little space between them, but the slant of the bike kept her hips pressed firmly against Anna's.

Still aroused.

Eden took off her helmet and practically leaped off the bike, and then she groaned because, God, her thighs hurt from gripping the motorcycle. She was going to be so sore at rehearsal tomorrow. She really hadn't considered that.

"You okay?" Anna asked. She'd taken her helmet off, too, and was smoothing out her ponytail as she watched Eden.

"Yes." Eden's voice sounded weird. Hoarse. She cleared her throat and tried again. "I'm great. That was amazing."

"Oh good." Anna looked relieved. "I got worried for a second the way you jumped off. Thought maybe you hated it."

"No, not at all." Eden's breath was almost back to normal, although she still felt a bit wobbly on her feet. "I just needed to stretch my legs."

Anna nodded as she swung off the bike herself. "Yeah, I forgot to warn you about that. You'll probably be sore tomorrow."

Eden looked past Anna at the waves crashing at the bottom of the cliff. Her heart felt light. Her whole body felt light. She smiled as she met Anna's eyes. "Totally worth it."

Anna sat on her back patio later that evening, grateful Zoe was out. She wasn't ready to talk about her evening with Eden yet. No, she just wanted to sit here and bask in the memories, because it had been *perfect.* So perfect. Too perfect.

Roaring up the Pacific Coast Highway with Eden's arms around her had been highly arousing, but Anna could keep her hands to herself. There was no way she was going to let her attraction ruin their budding friendship, because she enjoyed every moment she spent with Eden. She couldn't even explain it. They just clicked. They had fun together, whether they were choreographing a performance, sharing lunch on the patio, or riding on Anna's motorcycle.

Eden sometimes seemed melancholy when she wasn't performing, like she was going through the motions. But tonight she'd looked alive in a way Anna hadn't seen before, brimming with energy and joy. Anna would do anything to see that look on her face again.

With a happy sigh, she unlocked her phone and began to scroll through her notifications. There were a lot tonight, and most of them seemed to be coming from Twitter. People were reacting to several black-and-white photos of her and Eden, the pictures Paris had shared from their rehearsal.

They'd been careful not to make it obvious that they were rehearsing a duet together, so in the first photo, Anna was looking on as Eden sang. The second photo showed Anna singing, with Eden visible in the background, and in the final photo, they were hugging. All three filled Anna with warmth and happiness. The black-and-white filter gave the photos an artful touch. Anna wanted to frame them and put them on her wall. Maybe she would.

Her fans had gotten pretty excited when she shared the selfie from their lunch a few days ago, so Anna was curious to see how Eden's fans felt about these, since they'd been posted to her social media accounts.

@QueerCat918: THEY ARE SO CUTE OMG I AM DECEASED
@EdensGarden565: Yasssss queens! Ur gonna slay, can't wait until I see u in Vegas
@HexMeAnna: OMG Anna!! I know #gaypanic when I see it

A close-up of Anna's face was attached from the photo where she was watching Eden perform, and *oof*, the longing on her face was painfully obvious. Her cheeks burned. She kept scrolling, surprised by how many usernames she recognized, her own fans commenting on Eden's post.

An alarming number of them were convinced Anna was swooning over Eden. They'd even dredged up an old YouTube clip from one of Anna's first interviews after she was cast on *Hex High*, in which she gushed about Eden and alluded to Eden being her celebrity crush. Thank God Eden didn't read the comments on her social media, or Anna might never be able to look her in the eye again.

> @peanutonthebutter: I'm calling it. These 2 are 2 cute not to date #Edanna
> @KatieCat1989: #Edanna omg they're so cute eeeeeeeeeeeee
> @adoringanna_x: SCREAMING IN #EDANNA
> @HexMeAnna: The way Anna's gazing at Eden – my heart! #Edanna
> @chelseexxx: I SHIP THEM SO HARD #EDANNA
> @PunkyCutester44: But did anyone notice the way Eden's looking at Anna in that 2nd pic bc omg?!?! #Edanna
> @Daydreamer05: Please! If Eden dated a woman, it would be someone at her level not a child like Anna Moss
> @BriannaLong598: Gah the way these 2 look at each other!! #Edanna

It went on and on, with the fans dissecting every nuance from each of the photos. They'd even given them a celebrity-couple name, mashing Eden and Anna together to create #Edanna, which . . . made Anna's heart flutter for entirely inappropriate reasons.

The majority of the comments were positive, although a few of Eden's fans thought Anna wasn't worthy of dating their idol. That knocked the wind out of Anna's sails, even though she could hardly blame them for feeling that way. Still, she was hardly a *child*.

When Anna looked at the photos again after she'd read hundreds of posts from fans accusing them of making romantic eyes at each other, now she was seeing them in a different way too. Was Eden looking at her that way? No. The soft smile on Eden's face as she watched Anna sing was affectionate, but in a friendly way, not a romantic one.

They did look awfully damn cute together, though. Anna's phone pinged with an incoming text message, and her pulse misfired when she saw Eden's name on the screen. Oh God. Had she seen the hashtag? When Anna clicked on the text, she revealed a selfie of Eden sitting on the gray couch in her condo, wearing Anna's purple hoodie.

Eden:

I keep forgetting to give this back! And I wanted to thank you again for tonight. It was amazing.

She'd attached a motorcycle emoji and several smiley face variations. Anna's heart clenched. Seeing Eden in her hoodie did things to her.

Anna:

Keep it! I didn't wear that one often anyway.

That was a lie. It had been one of Anna's favorite hoodies, but she loved seeing it on Eden more than she liked wearing it. Anna had plenty of hoodies.

Anna:

And I'm happy to take you out again on the bike anytime! I go out on it a few times a week.

Eden:

Might take you up on that 🏍

Anna:

Anytime

Eden:

See you tomorrow

Anna tabbed back to Twitter, and this time, she impulsively saved the photos to her phone. Yeah, she had it bad. And no, she didn't care.

CHAPTER TEN

"You and Anna caused quite a stir on Twitter last night," Paris told Eden as they rode toward the rehearsal studio.

"What? How?" Eden glanced at her in surprise. Surely no one had seen them on the motorcycle. She'd been careful to make sure no one was looking before she took off her helmet . . .

"The photos I shared from your rehearsal. A bunch of fans are speculating you two might be dating. They even gave you a celebrity-couple name: Edanna."

Eden laughed. "Well, that's new. I'm used to the rumors every time I'm photographed with a man, but it hasn't happened with a woman before."

"Maybe because Anna's gay?" Paris asked, tapping at her phone.

"Pan," Eden corrected.

"What?"

"Anna is pansexual."

"Oh, sorry. Anyway, you know what they say. All publicity is good publicity."

"Right." Curious, she pulled out her phone and opened Twitter. She rarely used it and had all the notifications turned off, but she could still view her tweets, or rather, the tweets Paris sent on her behalf. She pulled up the photos in question, looking at them with a critical eye.

Sure, she and Anna looked friendly with each other. She could see the admiration in Anna's eyes as she watched Eden sing. But attraction? Eden wasn't so sure. She pinched her fingers over Anna's face to enlarge it. Maybe she did look a little starry eyed, but Eden had always assumed that stemmed from the way she'd idolized Eden when she was younger.

Was it more than that?

Eden felt a strange thrill at the thought that Anna might *like* her, but that was absurd. Even if Eden hadn't been straight, she and Anna had no business fooling around together, not when they had to see each other every day on tour for the next six months. And Eden was straight. She couldn't forget that part.

She scrolled through the replies, and wow, there were a lot. So many #Edanna hashtags and emoji she didn't understand. A lot of flames. And GIFs of people fainting. And references to ships that made no sense. Then there was a GIF of a woman fanning herself, with the caption #gaypanic. Eden's face was flaming as she lowered her phone.

"Why are they talking about boats?" she blurted.

Paris gave her a blank look. "What?"

"On Twitter. I'm so confused . . . this is why I usually don't look."

"Oh, you mean ships?" Paris asked.

Eden waved a hand. "Ships. Boats. What does that have to do with me and Anna?"

Paris grinned. "It's a fandom term, short for 'relationship.' When you 'ship' two people, it means you want to see them as a couple. The term originated in the nineties from fans of *The X-Files* who wanted Mulder and Scully to be together."

"Oh." Eden's cheeks grew even hotter. "That's . . . how do you know that?"

"It's my job to understand fans," Paris said. "And today, yours are shipping you with Anna."

"Well, they're in for disappointment on that front."

"Not necessarily. You and Anna have great chemistry onstage together, and the fans are going to love seeing that on tour. Who cares if some of them fantasize about you being more than friends? That just adds to the appeal, right?"

Eden cleared her throat. "Right."

At the studio, she spent the morning in a meeting with her tour manager, ironing out final details on the stage, which would soon be installed in the same arena where the Grammys had been held. Eden would open her tour here in LA, and she'd be rehearsing at the arena for the last few days before opening night.

From there, she'd go up the West Coast, then across the center of the country and up into Canada. She had a week off toward the end of the North American leg of the tour before she made her way down the East Coast and then overseas. All told, she'd be on the road until October, and she couldn't wait.

"Knock, knock," Anna's voice called from behind her.

Eden was alone at the table in the break room, looking over paperwork. She smiled, waving Anna into the room. "Hey."

"No rehearsal for you this morning?" Anna had on black athletic pants and a rainbow-striped top.

Eden shook her head. "A production meeting. I'll be rehearsing this afternoon."

"Ah." Anna grabbed a bottle of water and perched on the edge of the table. "This is exciting, you know? Seeing all the details come together."

"We'll be on the road before you know it." Eden studied her, looking for evidence of the "gay panic" Anna's fans were so sure she exuded. Eden didn't see it, but her own heart was racing, and she wasn't sure why. "This is your first tour, right?"

Anna nodded enthusiastically. "Yeah. I mean, I've played shows here and there, but I've only played a full-size arena once . . . with you, at the Grammys."

"You'll be a pro in no time," Eden told her. "I heard we caused a stir on Twitter last night." Oh God, why had she said that? A warm flush spread over her skin.

Anna jumped like Eden had poked her, hopping off the table. She paced to the window. "Yep. We have our own hashtag now. Twitter official." She paused, glancing over her shoulder at Eden. "I thought you didn't look at your social media?"

"I don't. Paris told me about it this morning."

"I had a good laugh when I saw it last night," Anna said with a cheeky smile. "Fans are always wanting me to hook up with the celebrities I'm photographed with. It must happen to you too?"

"God, yes," Eden said with a laugh. "Constantly. First time I've been linked to a woman, though."

"Oh, I get it from all sides." Anna shrugged. "For a while, they thought I was hooking up with Zoe. I've even had questions about Kyrie. And Carlos Alito, the actor my character dated on *Hex High*. Nothing we can do but laugh, right?"

"Exactly," Eden agreed. "At least this is more flattering than when they invent feuds and catfights."

"Also true."

"Anyway, we can hardly blame them for dreaming, right? We *would* make a cute couple." Eden wanted to slap a hand over her own mouth.

Anna's eyebrows went up. "I mean, yeah, sure."

"Except I'm straight, sorry to say." There. She'd finally brought the conversation back to safe ground.

"Your sexuality is never something to apologize for." There was no disappointment on Anna's face, no hint that she harbored feelings for Eden. Which meant the fans on Twitter were off base with their "gay panic" memes.

Eden should feel relieved. Why didn't she?

For a long moment, they just stared at each other. The conversation seemed to have stalled. Then Paris burst through the door, her arms laden with bags of takeout for today's lunch.

"Oh my God." Anna bounced on her toes. "You brought Honeybee!"

"What's that?" Eden asked.

"Burgers," Anna said. "Vegan burgers."

Eden resisted the urge to make a face. Veggie burgers weren't her favorite. Her opinion must have shown on her face anyway, though, because Anna laughed.

"They're delicious, I promise," she said.

"Kyrie convinced me to try them," Paris said with a shrug. "I figured we needed something new in our rotation."

"I'm sure they're great," Eden said, glad to be talking about burgers instead of whether she and Anna would make a cute couple.

"There's one in there with extra pickles," Paris told Anna, who looked elated at this news. "Kyrie said that's your favorite."

"I love you and Kyrie both so much right now." Anna followed Paris to the table in back and rooted through the bags until she found the burger with extra pickles.

Eden joined them and selected a cheeseburger for herself. She and Anna took their burgers outside to the patio, where they often ate lunch together, and to Eden's relief, the conversation flowed easily as they ate. Anna wanted to hear tales from the road, and Eden had plenty of those to share.

After lunch, Eden spent a long afternoon in rehearsal. Her thighs were already sore from yesterday's motorcycle ride, and they were screaming at her by the time she got home that night. She took a couple of ibuprofen and soaked in a hot bath, where she found herself inexplicably wondering if #Edanna was still trending on Twitter.

Had they been trending? She wasn't sure, but she'd definitely seen that hashtag a lot when she looked this morning. And she absolutely shouldn't be thinking about #Edanna while she was in the bathtub. She shouldn't be thinking about Anna at all.

Eden closed her eyes and attempted to clear her head. Except now she was remembering the way she'd felt on the motorcycle yesterday, the arousal that had thrummed through her body while the engine hummed beneath her, her arms wrapped around Anna's body. Was it possible . . . had that been a response to *Anna?*

Her eyes popped open. This water was too hot. *She* was way too hot. What in the world had gotten into her tonight? Of course her response yesterday had been from the excitement of the ride, maybe even from the vibration of the engine. Not Anna. She'd let those fans on Twitter put thoughts in her head.

In a huff, Eden got out of the tub, sloshing water on the floor in the process. She wiped it up, dried off, and dressed in lounge clothes, then went in search of her Kindle. She was halfway through a very suspenseful thriller, and that was exactly what she needed to turn off the chaos in her brain.

Anna didn't see as much of Eden after that day. On the surface, nothing had changed. Eden was just as friendly when Anna rehearsed with her, but they didn't hang out. No more rides on Anna's motorcycle or lunches on the patio. Ostensibly, Taylor had put an end to the patio after she'd caught several fans lurking behind the building, trying to photograph Eden, but it was more than that.

Eden had taken a definitive step back after the #Edanna incident. Either she was giving the hashtag a chance to blow over before she and Anna were photographed together again, or she'd been freaked out by the thought that Anna might have a crush on her. That was the possibility that was keeping Anna up at night.

Either way, Eden had dropped a gauntlet by telling Anna point blank that she was straight. Anna had received the message loud and clear, and she was mortified that she might have inadvertently made Eden uncomfortable.

To compensate, Anna had been extra careful around Eden when she saw her at the studio. She kept her feelings pushed down so deep there was no way anyone could construe the way she looked at Eden as anything other than friendly. Anna had also gone barhopping with Zoe. She'd flirted with a few people and gotten a few numbers—and she'd told Eden all about it just to emphasize how *not* into her she was—but she hadn't followed up with any of her potential dates.

She was about to head out on tour for six months, so now wasn't the time to start anything serious. Anna had never enjoyed random hookups, but she enjoyed them even less now that she was becoming famous. She couldn't stop worrying that the person in her bed was there because of her fame.

Ironically, even though Eden had pulled away in person, she was texting Anna more often. Always about random, safe topics, like what she was reading or a funny thing that had happened during rehearsal.

On this particular evening, Anna was tired and a little bit down after a frustrating day at the studio. In two days, they'd move to the arena for the final rehearsals before opening night, and Anna kept messing up her footwork during the last dance sequence in "Headfirst." She'd gotten in her head about it, and now she was literally tripping herself up.

Her phone dinged with the opening note of "Daydreamer," the sound she'd assigned Eden. Anna's stomach clenched as she reached for her phone.

Eden:

Heard you took a hard fall today! Are you okay?

Anna:

Yep, just a few bruises, mostly to my confidence

Eden:

Those can be the worst kind!

Eden:

Talk me through it. What happened?

Anna:

Frustrated with a piece of choreography, and the harder I try to get it, the more I keep messing up

Anna:

I'm about to open for you on a world tour, and I think it just sunk in 😬

Eden:

Okay, 1st of all, you are ten times the dancer I'll ever be. And 2nd when I get stuck on something like that, I usually just change it.

Eden:

Ask your choreographer to modify the step, and it's like a reset for your brain.

Anna:

That's really good advice. Thank you!

Eden:

Anytime. Whatcha up to tonight?

Anna:

Binging some reality show about ugly houses. You?

Eden:

Reading.

Anna:

You read a lot

Eden:

Guilty.

Anna:

Favorite genre?

Eden:

Tie between suspense and fantasy. I like to escape the real world when I read.

Anna:

I'm a sucker for a good romance novel

Eden:

They're so unreal stic though! I get frustrated.

Anna:

Noooo Eden don't break my heart like that

Eden:

. . .

The dots appeared and disappeared several times, yet no reply came. Anna had gotten so caught up in the conversation that maybe she'd taken it too far. As she was trying to decide how to shift them back on track, Eden's reply finally came through.

Eden:

It's the overdone sex, I think. The way they're all I'LL DIE IF I DON'T HAVE YOU THIS MINUTE.

Anna:

um that's my favorite part

Eden:

It makes me roll my eyes.

Anna didn't know how to respond to that. Was Eden saying she'd never had that "I'll die if I don't have you" feeling with anyone? The thought made Anna want to . . . nope, not even going to finish that thought.

Anna:

if you ever want to try a romance with imho the perfect balance of sexual tension and an engaging plot that won't make you roll your eyes, try On the Flip Side by Brie

Eden:

Hang on . . .

Eden:

Ok bookmarked it but no promises

Anna wondered whether she should mention that it was a sapphic romance, but any way she tried to phrase it seemed to veer into territory they were both trying to ignore. Eden had probably read the description when she bookmarked it anyway.

The next morning, neither of them mentioned it at rehearsal. Anna took Eden's suggestion and asked her choreographer to tweak the step she was messing up, and it worked like a charm. Still, she felt oddly unsettled as she headed into her final days of rehearsal.

Anna stared into the empty arena as nerves gripped her chest, squeezing the air from her lungs. Not quite three months ago, she and Eden had performed together on this very stage. The iconic arena looked even bigger empty than it had the night of the Grammys, filled to the rafters with people in glittering gowns and elegant suits.

She'd just completed her final sound check. In minutes, she'd go backstage to start getting ready. The arena would fill with eager concertgoers here to see Eden. Some for Anna, but mostly Eden. *Opening night.* Nothing she'd rehearsed so far seemed to have prepared her for this moment.

A hand gripped her shoulder. "Breathe, slow and deep."

Anna did as she was told, while sparks filled her belly at the sound of Eden's voice. Anna had barely seen her all week, except for the moments they'd rehearsed together onstage. She missed the friendship that had begun to grow between them.

"Remember at the Grammys when I told you not to look at the audience if you were feeling nervous?" Eden said.

"I remember." Anna turned her head to find Eden standing behind her, dressed all in black.

"It's a good strategy at award shows. The first time I stood on this stage and looked into an audience full of musical legends, I froze. But during a regular concert, I think it helps to look at the audience. Focus on the people right in front. They're usually very enthusiastic, and sometimes it helps to make eye contact with someone. Smile at them. Focus on them instead of how many other people are in the room."

Anna nodded. "Do you still get nervous?"

"God, yes," Eden said with a laugh. "If I ever stop getting nervous before I go onstage in front of thirty thousand people, I should probably get my pulse checked."

"I definitely don't need my pulse checked." Anna pressed a hand against her chest, where her heart thumped frantically.

"You'll be terrified when you first walk out. That's a given, so there's no point fighting it. Look at your dancers, look for those people in the front rows, focus on the music. And remember, if you mess up, most people won't even notice. Just keep going and know that it'll be easier tomorrow night."

"Thank you." Anna turned and grabbed Eden in an impulsive hug. This was a big deal. Anna was about to perform before her first sold-out arena. She was opening for her idol. And that idol was out here giving Anna a pep talk, which she super didn't have to do.

Eden's arms came around her, squeezing Anna tight. "Will it make you more or less nervous if I tell you I'll be watching your performance?"

"More," Anna whispered, lost in the familiar rose-petal scent of Eden's skin. "But also less, because it's nice when a friend has your back."

Eden released her and took a step back. "That's what friends are for."

"It's time, ladies," Paris said, stepping onto the stage behind them. "They're about to open the doors to the public, so you need to clear the stage."

Eden nodded. She turned to leave the stage, and Anna followed. Kyrie was waiting to intercept her, and when she turned to thank Eden again, she was gone. So Anna went into her dressing room, where her hair and makeup team was waiting to work their magic.

It took almost an hour for them to get her ready. When they finished, Kyrie told her, "Fifteen minutes until showtime. Let me know if you need help getting dressed."

"Thanks. I will."

Kyrie left the dressing room, and Anna closed the door behind her, grateful for a few minutes alone to collect herself before she took the stage. She made a quick trip to the bathroom before shimmying into the sequined pants and red top she'd be wearing tonight. The pants clung like leggings and glittered with all the colors of the rainbow.

She'd taken Eden's advice and jazzed up her tour costumes. Plus, she'd had a few inches taken off her hair and would be wearing it down tonight too. It was pinned back on one side with a red clip. As she surveyed herself in the mirror, she decided she liked it. She *did* look more mature this way without feeling inauthentic.

She sipped the tea Kyrie had left for her and ran through her vocal warm-ups. Her dressing room was somewhere deep beneath the stage, isolating her from whatever was going on above. She couldn't hear the crowd, and that was probably for the best. She'd been waiting for this moment her whole life, the chance to perform in front of an arena full of people.

Exhaling slowly, she closed her eyes, doing her best to clear her head and calm her nerves. She pictured Eden's face, the gentle, encouraging smile she'd given Anna right before they parted on the stage. Those blue eyes, as deep as the ocean but so much warmer. Roses. Anna inhaled, imagining she could still smell them.

A knock at the door interrupted the moment. "Yes?" she called.

"Five minutes," Kyrie said.

"Okay. Come in."

The door opened, and Kyrie slipped inside. She spent the next few minutes double-checking Anna's appearance and helping her with her ear monitors and the sound pack that slipped into a pocket sewn onto the waistband of her pants.

"Ready?" Kyrie asked, walking in a slow circle around Anna to give her one last check.

Anna nodded. She reached for the tea and took a final sip, then pursed her lips while Kyrie touched up her lipstick.

"All right, then. Let's do this. And can I just say, I'm so proud to be here with you tonight, Anna. You're going to be amazing." Kyrie gave her a quick hug, careful not to disturb Anna's hair or makeup.

"Thank you" was all Anna could manage as she blinked back tears.

"I'm going to tell them to kill the houselights." Kyrie pulled up the mouthpiece for the headset Anna hadn't even noticed she was wearing and spoke into it in a brisk, professional voice. She'd really stepped up lately. They both had. They were playing in the big leagues now, and Anna was so glad to have a friend like Kyrie at her side on this journey.

A muffled roar came from overhead, the sound of thousands of people clapping and whistling as they realized it was showtime. Zoe would be in the crowd tomorrow night, and Anna found herself suddenly wishing her friend were here tonight, a familiar face in the audience cheering her on.

"Houselights are out. Let's move." Kyrie rested a hand on Anna's elbow, guiding her out of her dressing room and through the maze of hallways that led to the stage.

Anna walked on autopilot, letting Kyrie guide her as she focused on her breathing. Deep and slow. Sweat dampened her skin, and the full-body jitters had hit now. Her sequined pants sparked in her peripheral vision, and she almost stumbled.

"Here we are." Kyrie came to a stop at the bottom of a darkened staircase. She pressed Anna's microphone into her hand. "The stage tech will take you from here. Good luck. Can't wait to celebrate with you later."

Anna smiled. "Thanks."

A man dressed all in black appeared before her, holding a small flashlight pointed at the floor by her feet. "Follow me, Ms. Moss."

"Thanks." She sucked in another breath and stepped forward so her toes met the glow of his flashlight.

He led her up the steps as the opening beats of her latest single, "Headfirst," began to play. Anna synched her steps with the music, the way she'd done in rehearsals, as she walked onstage. The spotlight engulfed her as she lifted the microphone, and her head went fuzzy with nerves. Vaguely she was aware of the dancers joining her onstage and the excited whoops and cheers from the crowd.

"On my feet. Count the beat. I'm dancing for you." Her voice sounded steady and clear as it filled the arena, and her body began to move automatically to the dance steps she'd perfected over the past month. She made her way toward the front of the stage as the dancers fanned out behind her.

Anna looked into the crowd, her gaze landing on a young woman with hot-pink hair and a bright smile singing Anna's lyrics back to her. Warmth filled Anna's heart, and she grinned widely as she sang. When she scanned the arena, she saw plenty of empty seats—she was only the opening act, after all—but she also saw so many excited faces. She could hear the hum of hundreds if not thousands of voices singing along with her, and it was *magic*.

This was why she'd become a singer. This moment.

She turned, following the choreography toward stage left when her gaze caught on a face near the side of the stage, out of sight of the crowd. Eden was swathed in shadow, but Anna saw her clear as day, watching, *singing*—was she singing along to Anna's song?

For a moment, Anna lost the lyrics, but then Eden caught her eye and smiled, giving a faint nod that said, "You got this." With a surge of confidence, Anna turned to face the crowd.

CHAPTER ELEVEN

"Thank you, Los Angeles. It's an honor to open the After Midnight Tour here in my hometown, and you've been an amazing audience. I love you! Good night." Eden lifted a hand overhead, waving to the crowd, which was on its feet and cheering with enough enthusiasm for her to feel the vibrations in her chest.

That energy filled the withered spot in her heart from this awful year. Her fans *did* still love her. And she loved performing for them so damn much. Tears welled in her eyes, and she was grinning so widely that she squinted, causing a few tears to overflow.

She spun, waving to the fans on both sides of the stage, and then she turned and jogged toward the staircase in back, where a tech with a flashlight was waiting to guide her down the darkened stairs. He led her through a curtain-draped doorway and into the well-lit hall beyond.

"Awesome show tonight." Paris handed her a bottle of water and a towel to dab the sweat from her face.

"Thank you." Eden sounded breathless. She *felt* breathless. Her body buzzed with that familiar postshow mixture of adrenaline and exhaustion, and she knew she'd crash soon. Usually, she'd end up back at the hotel after a show, watching mindless TV while she waited for the adrenaline to leave her system so she could sleep.

Tonight, though, she'd be sleeping in her own bed, a luxury of opening the tour in LA. She'd perform here again tomorrow night before heading down to San Diego and then up the West Coast.

Eden wiped the sweat from her face and tossed the towel over her shoulder before taking a hearty drink of water. Tonight, her exhaustion was compounded by opening night jitters and the extra stress of performing her first show after the most lackluster year of her career. She'd barely eaten today, she'd been so nervous, and now her ears were buzzing.

Someone squealed, and she caught a glimpse of Anna barreling toward her a moment before she was engulfed in a tight hug. "Oh my God, you were so amazing tonight. Like, one of the best performances I've ever seen, and I've seen all your tours, so I can say that with authority," Anna babbled as she spun Eden in her excitement.

"Thank you." Eden smiled into the depths of Anna's hair as she hugged her back. "You were pretty awesome tonight too."

Anna made a scoffing sound. "I was fine. You were brilliant. The part where you spin above the stage? I mean, of course I'd seen it in rehearsal, but tonight . . . wow. Just wow. And your voice . . . chills."

Warmth spread through Eden's system, not just from Anna's praise but from her exuberant energy. Whenever Anna was around, Eden felt lighter on her feet. *Happy.* She'd fought this for the last few weeks, trying not to add to the #Edanna hype, but now she realized that had been a mistake, because she missed this. She missed Anna.

Anna pulled back, and for a moment they just grinned at each other.

"Our duet seemed like a hit," Eden said.

"I shared a photo from it earlier," Paris said, reminding Eden of her presence.

She felt a prickle of annoyance. She'd been so caught up in Anna, she'd forgotten she was surrounded by people bustling around in post-show mode. Suddenly, the hallway felt loud and chaotic.

Paris was holding her cell phone in Eden's direction, displaying a photo taken during their duet. Anna wore a red pleated dress almost identical to the one Eden had worn in the video for her single "Take Your Time." In the photo, Eden had an arm over Anna's shoulders, and they were smiling at each other.

"Your hashtag is trending again," Paris said, looking amused.

Eden almost flinched. She wasn't sure why that hashtag made her uncomfortable, but suddenly she didn't care. Somewhere over the past few months, Eden had regained her passion for her music, and Anna was at least partially responsible. She energized Eden, and Eden valued her friendship too much to let a silly hashtag bother her.

"Let's move this along. We're in the way here." Paris waved an arm, herding Eden in the direction of her dressing room.

Eden nodded gratefully. She very much wanted to change and go home. Also, food. And probably another bottle of water. She started walking, flanked by Paris and Anna.

"The new dress was a hit," Anna said, bubbly as ever as they walked. "When I scrolled the comments earlier, it seemed like people had been hoping—if not expecting—that we'd recreate the duet for the tour, but they weren't expecting me to model a different early-Eden look. Now they're tossing theories left and right on what I'll wear next."

"You were right," Eden mused. "The outfits are creating buzz."

Anna bounced on her toes. "I'm so excited that the fans are excited."

"Me too." Eden brushed a strand of hair from her face. Her skin felt sticky from a combination of makeup and sweat. God, she couldn't wait for a shower. "I wasn't sure you'd still be here," she said to Anna.

Paris, who'd been walking a few steps ahead, paused and unlocked the door to Eden's dressing room, motioning her inside.

"Are you kidding?" Anna gave her an incredulous look. "There's no way I'd miss watching you perform, especially on opening night.

But I'll probably—" She cut herself off as if she'd just realized that she'd followed Eden into her dressing room. "Sorry, I'll get out of your hair."

"No," Eden said, surprising even herself. "Stay a minute. We can head out together."

"You sure?" Anna asked.

Eden nodded, tossing her empty water bottle in the trash.

"I'll find Kyrie and coordinate both cars to be ready in about five minutes?" Paris asked.

"Perfect. Thank you." Usually, Eden left the arena faster than this after a show. She would walk off the stage, change, and get straight in the car. But everything moved slower on opening and closing nights.

Paris left, closing the door behind herself, while Anna dropped onto the couch and started reading Eden some of the comments the fans had left about tonight's show. Eden opened her duffel bag and took out the jeans and top she'd brought to wear home.

"Be right back," she told Anna as she opened the door to the bathroom, but before she could go in, there was a knock on the dressing room door. Eden sighed. She felt half-drunk as the adrenaline left her system. All she wanted was to freshen up and go home, not schmooze whoever was at the door.

"I'll get it," Anna said, standing from the couch. "You go change."

But Eden lingered to see who it was. It was her dressing room, after all. When Anna opened the door to reveal Paris standing there, Eden relaxed. Surely the car wasn't here yet? It hadn't even been a minute since Paris left her in her dressing room.

"Eden . . . ," Paris began, sounding apologetic. "Your parents are here, and they'd like to see you before you leave."

"Oh." Eden braced a hand against the wall as her knees forgot their job for a moment. *Oh no.* She hadn't seen her parents in over a year, and while she'd sent them tickets to the show the way she always did, she hadn't expected them to come. Now she was left unprepared for the soul-sucking experience of entertaining them, and she certainly didn't have the energy—physical or mental—for it tonight.

She inhaled, lifting her chin. "Fine. Send them in."

Anna shouldn't be here. She shouldn't have invited herself into Eden's dressing room in the first place, and she definitely should have left before Eden's parents came in. But it had all happened so fast. She'd been caught up in the moment, celebrating with Eden after she came off the stage, and now here she was.

But while Anna had initially thought Eden's parents' visit was an exciting surprise, it hadn't taken her long to realize something wasn't right. Eden wasn't acting like herself. Beneath her stage makeup, she seemed pale, and the look in her eyes . . . well, Anna wasn't sure exactly how to read it, but it made her sad. No one should look like that when faced with their parents.

The well-dressed couple in the doorway weren't giving her warm fuzzies either. Eden's father radiated "self-important white man" energy, and her mother was literally looking down her nose at Anna. Yikes. Anna leaned against the wall and tried to make herself as unobtrusive as possible.

"Mom, Dad, this is a surprise," Eden said, hands clasped tightly in front of herself.

"Why?" her mother asked. "Your manager provided us with tickets. If she didn't tell you she'd sent them, perhaps you should think about new representation. I never have felt she was as good as Peter."

"No, I knew she sent them, I just . . ." Eden trailed off, looking down at her hands. She'd known her parents had tickets to the show tonight, and yet she hadn't expected to *see* them?

Anna swallowed hard. Now that she was experiencing it firsthand, she remembered reading a few vague references to Eden having a fallout with her parents early in her career. Indignation burned in Anna's chest for whatever Eden had been through.

"Richard Sandowski," Eden's father said, extending a hand toward Anna. "Are you Eden's assistant?"

She took it, already anticipating his crushing grip. Anna did her best to match it. "Anna Moss. I'm the opening act. I just stopped in to congratulate Eden on the show, the same as you."

"Good to meet you." He gave her hand several hard pumps, and she refused to flinch. "Regretfully, Cathy and I didn't arrive early enough to see the opening act."

"Oh, that's okay. We're all here to see Eden anyway," Anna said. Richard finally released her hand, and she stepped back against the wall.

Eden glanced at her, then back at her parents. "Thank you for coming."

Her mother nodded. "Honestly, I was surprised to hear that you had an opening act for this tour. I thought you'd moved past the need for that years ago."

Anna blinked at her, suddenly remembering what David had told her, that Eden needed the boost from Anna's name to sell out the tour. She'd thought he was bullshitting her, but it *had* sold out the day Anna's name was announced. Even if it was true, Anna didn't want Eden to have to admit it to her parents.

"An opening act isn't a measure of my success," Eden said. "I'm honored to have Anna on tour with me."

Honored. Now Anna was blushing. If the circumstances hadn't been so otherwise stifling, she would have definitely swooned at this unexpected compliment from her idol. "Thank you," she murmured.

Cathy cleared her throat. "Actually, we stopped by to extend an invitation to lunch tomorrow. Peter will be there. He's certain he could have helped you avoid the drop in sales with your last album. I've heard his plan to get you back on track, and it's a good one. He'd be willing to take you back as a favor to us."

Eden seemed to get taller then, chin up, eyes flashing. "I'm fully booked with tour press tomorrow and perfectly satisfied with my current representation."

"That attitude is unbecoming," Richard snapped. "You'd do well to listen to us. God knows how much more successful you might be if you'd been less headstrong."

A muscle in Eden's jaw clenched, and Anna wondered what she wasn't saying. Her parents hadn't congratulated her or given her a single compliment on her performance tonight. All they'd done was talk to her like she was a petulant child, and Anna felt the irrational urge to call them on it.

"I'm not rehiring Peter." Eden's tone was flat and dull but hard. Like flint. Anna had the impression that if she struck stone, she might spark, and wow, that was unexpectedly sexy.

"You'll reconsider that position after you hear what he has to say," her father said. "Peter and I have always known what's best for your career."

Oh, *hell* no! Anna had had enough. She pushed away from the wall before she could stop herself. "Eden has been the top-earning female performer in America for over a decade. She's the benchmark that the rest of us measure ourselves against, so I'd say she's done an *excellent* job of managing her career, actually."

Just like that, all eyes were on Anna. Eden's lips parted silently, and her wide blue eyes blazed into Anna's, but was that a spark of anger . . . or gratitude? *Please let it be gratitude.* After a beat of shocked silence, Eden's parents spoke almost simultaneously.

"I don't recall anyone asking your opinion," Cathy said, her voice dripping venom, while Richard barked, "That was absolutely uncalled for, young lady."

Anna shrugged helplessly. She didn't regret what she'd said . . . unless she'd upset Eden.

"I'm not going to the meeting with Peter," Eden told her parents, ignoring Anna's outburst. "But thank you for stopping by." Her gaze fixed on someone outside Anna's line of vision, and she gave a faint nod.

Paris stepped into the room. "If you'll follow me, Mr. and Mrs. Sandowski, I'll show you out."

"We aren't finished here," Richard said.

Eden's chin went up. "Actually, we are."

"Tomorrow at noon," her mother said over her shoulder as she turned to leave. "Be there, Eden."

Eden didn't respond. Her parents left the dressing room, and Paris closed the door behind them. Eden stood there for a long moment, just staring at the door. Anna's heart was racing, and oh God, had she really just called out Eden's parents like that? Was Eden mad about it? The dressing room was too quiet. Then Eden exhaled heavily. She pressed a hand against her forehead, swaying slightly.

"Whoa, hey." Anna grabbed Eden's hand. It was cold and clammy. She tugged Eden toward the couch. "Maybe you should sit for a minute. You walked right off the stage into . . . that."

Eden let out a humorless laugh and dropped onto the couch, head back and eyes closed.

"Do you want me to go?" Anna asked.

Eden huffed. "You've already seen . . ." She waved a hand in the direction of the door. "So you might as well stay."

"I'm so sorry." Anna sat beside her. "I didn't mean to go off on your dad like that. I just . . . I couldn't stand the way he was talking to you, and I lost it for a second, but it totally wasn't my place to say anything."

"Don't apologize," Eden said quietly. "You were . . . amazing. Really."

She was staring at Anna now, and there was an intensity in her gaze that Anna didn't dare name, but it knocked the air from her lungs in an audible whoosh. Eden's pupils were wide, and she was breathing so fast, and *oh God*, what was happening right now?

Adrenaline. It was just adrenaline from the scene with her parents. *Don't be silly, Anna. She's told you she's straight!*

Eden leaned forward, resting her elbows on her knees, and now they were sitting way too close. Anna could see a bluish makeup smudge beside Eden's left eye, and she fought the urge to reach out and smooth it away. For a moment, neither of them moved, their gazes locked as powerfully as the spotlight that had lit them on the stage earlier that night.

Abruptly, Eden looked down at her hands, which were shaking. And she was still so pale, alarmingly pale.

Anna straightened. "Eden?"

"I'm okay, just an adrenaline crash and probably low blood sugar. I didn't eat dinner . . . too nervous." She gave Anna a wry smile before she bent forward and fished a protein bar out of her bag.

Anna, you idiot, while you were fantasizing about kissing her, she was sitting here trying not to pass out. She tapped Eden's wrist in gentle reproach. "And you were out there giving *me* a pep talk before the show. You didn't tell me you were nervous too."

"I did, actually," Eden said as she tore open the wrapper. "I told you I still get nervous before every show. I didn't tell you that opening night hits me hardest, because that didn't seem helpful right before you went onstage, or that I was feeling the pressure of my first show after the worst year of my career, but you already heard it from my parents, so . . ."

"I'm sorry." Anna had been so caught up in her own nerves, she'd never stopped to think about how Eden was feeling. She'd just assumed Eden was as cool and calm as she always seemed to be. But they'd never discussed the recent bumps in Eden's career either.

"It is what it is." Eden took a bite of the protein bar. She chewed and swallowed, then darted a glance at Anna. "And my parents are . . .

well, we're mostly estranged. I see them once a year or so, and it usually goes about like that."

"They were so condescending. I just . . . gah! How can they not realize how amazing you are?"

Eden smiled around another bite of the protein bar. "No one will ever convince them I know how to manage my own career, but I did enjoy watching you try." She popped the last bite of the bar into her mouth and stood. "Anyway, I need to change, and then we both need to go home."

"Yes," Anna agreed, casting one last glance over Eden's shimmery gold dress. God, she was beyond hot tonight, and Anna really, *really* had to put a lid on this attraction before it boiled over and ruined everything.

Eden gave her a soft smile that set Anna's heart racing, and then she went into the bathroom, pulling the door shut behind herself.

CHAPTER TWELVE

"Anyone gambling today?" Paris looked up from her plate, sweeping her gaze around the table.

"Not me." Eden reached for her tea. They were a week into the tour now, and it had been a whirlwind so far. The beginning of a tour always involved enough press to make her head spin, in addition to the performances themselves and readjusting to life on the road. Today, they were in Las Vegas. She, Paris, Anna, and Kyrie had gathered for lunch in Eden's suite.

For the first time since opening night, Eden didn't have any press obligations this afternoon. She planned to curl up in bed with her Kindle and spend the afternoon reading and drinking a lot of tea with honey. She'd done entirely too much talking—and singing—this week, and she'd been performing long enough to know she needed to stay ahead of the inevitable strain to her vocal cords.

"I'd like to," Kyrie piped up. "I've never been to Vegas before, and I'd love to go put a few quarters in the slot machines. Want to, Anna?"

Anna pursed her lips, looking thoughtful. "Tempting, but I'm kind of tired. I think I'm going to take it easy until showtime."

"Probably a good idea," Kyrie agreed.

"But you should totally go if you want," Anna said. "I don't need you for anything this afternoon."

"Same for you, Paris," Eden chimed in. "You two should go see some of Vegas."

"Really?" Paris asked. "You're sure you don't need me?"

"Positive," Eden told her. "I'm not planning to leave my suite."

Paris looked at Kyrie. "Want to?"

"Yes," Kyrie agreed, and they began making plans as they cleared the remainders of lunch from the table. Paris was explaining that slot machines didn't actually take quarters anymore. It was all digital now. She was an endless source of random information.

Eden sipped her tea, staring into its amber depths. Her mood had been . . . off ever since the tour began, and she wasn't sure why. It wasn't sadness or even exhaustion. She felt vaguely unsettled, like none of her routines were bringing their usual sense of comfort.

"Want company this afternoon?"

She looked up to see that Anna had slid into the chair beside her. "Company?"

Anna was in her usual athletic gear, a matching purple set today. Her hair was down, and it looked so soft, although Eden had no idea why she was noticing such a thing. "We could watch a movie or something?" Anna suggested.

Eden usually spent her afternoons alone on show days, but right now, the idea of watching a movie with Anna sounded undeniably fun. "Yeah, sure. Stay."

"Really?" Anna asked as one of those infectious smiles stretched her cheeks.

"Yes," Eden said, feeling a smile of her own forming in response. "But who gets to pick the movie?"

"You pick this one, and I pick next time?"

Next time. Yeah, okay, she liked the sound of that. "Deal."

Paris placed a fresh cup of tea in front of Eden. "Are you sure you don't need anything else from me before I go?"

"Positive," Eden told her. "Thanks for the tea. Now go have fun, and don't lose too much money on the slots."

"No worries. Fifty dollars is my gambling limit," Paris told her.

Kyrie's eyes widened. "I'm going to follow her lead."

"Have fun, you two," Anna said, waving them off. "Don't do anything I wouldn't do."

"That doesn't narrow it down much," Kyrie responded, pulling a silly face.

Anna laughed, and it was such a joyous sound. Once Kyrie and Paris had left the suite, she turned to Eden. "This is going to be fun, like the daytime version of a middle school sleepover. Think room service would send us popcorn?"

"I'm sure they would." Eden picked up her tea and took another sip. "Can you drink tea at sleepovers?"

"Not any sleepover I ever attended," Anna told her earnestly. "I think you might be breaking sleepover code."

Eden shrugged. "Would you believe I've never been on a sleepover?"

Anna pressed a hand to her chest. "No! That's tragic. Why not?"

"My parents moved us to LA when I was twelve. After that, I was homeschooled between auditions and music lessons. I didn't really have any friends my age."

Anna's smile faded. "Was that what you wanted? The move to LA?"

"Oh yeah." Eden didn't share this story often. She didn't like the way it had ended, at least not for her relationship with her parents, but Anna had already had a front-row seat to that disaster, so maybe she deserved the backstory too. "Being a pop star is the only thing I've ever wanted since I was a little girl. I was *thrilled* when we moved to LA."

"You and me both," Anna said. "Living our childhood dreams."

"Mm," Eden agreed. "When I got my first record contract at sixteen, it was like wow, I really did it, you know? I was going to hear my song on the radio. That was one of the best days of my life."

"At sixteen." Anna gave her head a quick shake. "I knew that, obviously, but I never really thought about what it meant for your adolescence."

"I don't feel like I had one, to be honest," Eden told her. "Like I mentioned before, the media treated me like an adult from the start. They were constantly critiquing my body and speculating about who I was dating. In reality, I'd never even been kissed, yet they were telling jokes about my sex life on late-night shows."

"That's . . . yikes."

"Yikes" didn't begin to cover it. "It was a weird time. The world saw me as this super-successful singer, but offstage, I had no control over my life whatsoever. I got a monthly allowance from my parents, and not a very generous one. My father hired Peter Roth as my manager, and the two of them made all the decisions about my career. I was just the face, the voice."

"I had no idea," Anna said quietly.

"I was so young that at first, I was glad I had people telling me what to do, because reaching superstardom before you turn eighteen is surreal and overwhelming. But then I *did* turn eighteen, and I still had people making all my decisions for me. They chose which songs I would record and told me what to wear and how to act. I probably let it go on longer than I should have, but they were my parents, and I assumed they knew best."

"Of course you did. Oh, Eden, I had no idea. You've never talked about this in interviews."

"No." She sipped her tea. "It's not a particularly tragic tale. It's just not one I enjoy sharing. Around the time I turned twenty-one, I fired my manager and told my parents I was ready to make my own decisions about my career. It didn't go well. We're . . . well, you saw what things are like between us now. I'm so embarrassed you had to see that."

Anna rested a hand on her arm. "Yeah, and I'm embarrassed that you saw my run-in with Camille at the Grammys, but really, we shouldn't be embarrassed by other people's behavior, right?"

Eden still didn't quite meet her eyes. "I guess not."

"And we've both done the work to cut those people out of our lives, so kudos to us for that."

"Right," Eden agreed. "So you've cut Camille out of your life, then?"

"Pretty much, although it took me a while. We broke up the first time about two years ago, but for a while, every time I'd run into her somewhere, we'd end up in bed together. I think that's what she was expecting at the Grammys, to be honest. Even when we were awful together, we still had this passion, you know? We couldn't keep our hands off each other. Was it like that for you and Zach?"

Eden shook her head. "Zach and I were the opposite of that. We're better as friends than lovers." In fact, Eden wasn't sure she'd ever experienced passion like what Anna was describing.

"Are you guys still friendly?" Anna asked.

"Yeah, we are. He's a great guy. We had a very amicable divorce."

"That must be a Hollywood first," Anna said with a laugh.

"Right? I miss him, but I think I mostly just miss having someone around the house to talk to. It's lonely living by myself, especially when I can't exactly just go out like a regular person."

"Yeah, I love having Zoe next door. We hang out a lot. Hey, speaking of families and things, you know I'm from San Francisco, right?"

Eden turned to look at her. "Yes, and we'll be there tomorrow. Are your parents coming to the show?"

"They are, and they really want to meet you." Anna gave her a bashful smile. "In fact, I'm having lunch at their house tomorrow after we land, and they'd love for you to come. No pressure if you're busy or just want to rest and do your own thing."

Eden chewed her lip, considering. "I'd like to, but I don't want to impose if you'd rather have that time alone with your parents. We're going to be on the road for a while, after all."

"I see them plenty, and they've heard me fangirl over you for a very long time, so they're pretty thrilled that you might actually come to their house." Anna's cheeks were bright pink now.

"So you need me to show up and prove that our friendship is real and you're not secretly my stalker?" Eden teased, rewarded when Anna's blush grew even brighter.

"Sure, yeah, basically," she said with a silly laugh.

"Well, I guess I'll have to come, then." She stood and gestured toward the bedroom of her suite. "Time to rest our voices and rent that movie. Slumber parties involve lying in bed, yes?"

"Absolutely." Anna bounced out of her seat. "You're really getting the hang of this sleepover thing."

Eden lifted the microphone from its stand as she turned to face Anna. The spotlight engulfed them, making Anna's eye shadow sparkle. Tonight, she wore a deep-blue princess-style gown, modeled after a dress Eden had worn for one of her first live performances, and she looked so beautiful. Eden's gaze traced her face to the delicate curve of her neck and down to the swell of her breasts.

"I kick off my heels," Anna sang, kicking one of her feet up in the air.

That was Eden's cue. She began to sing, stepping in front of Anna to illustrate her struggle with her younger self. The lights shifted, partially illuminating the audience. Vegas crowds weren't her favorite. The seats in the first few rows were generally reserved by the casino to give out as freebies to the high rollers, so she tended to see a lot of bored people up front who had no real interest in her music.

Tonight, she glimpsed a lot of senior citizens in the first few rows, and while some of them were actively watching the show, most of them were focused on snacks or even their phones. Behind them, several younger fans held up a hot-pink sign, and Eden shielded her eyes with her hand to read it.

#EDANNA4EVER

Oh. Eden turned away as Anna stepped beside her to begin the next chorus. She caught Eden's eye with another one of those radiant smiles, and Eden's stomach fizzed with something strange, like electricity surging through her, like . . . *sparks.* Oh God, was this what people meant when they said they felt sparks?

Heat swept through her body. Anna twirled, and Eden's stomach sparked again. She pressed a hand against it reflexively. Her gaze focused on Anna's calves as the skirt flared, and drifted up to the curve of her waist. Then she was staring at Anna's breasts again. Everywhere she looked, she was noticing Anna's body. What was happening to her? Eden had never . . . she didn't . . .

Anna was in front of her now, giving Eden a funny look, and oh God, she'd missed her cue. What was her next line? She spun, desperately searching for something, anything to orient herself, and then Anna's hand was on her arm. Eden remembered earlier that evening, watching *Captain Marvel* together in her bed, the way Anna's hair had tickled her arm.

Anna was singing Eden's line, covering for her. Her hand was so warm, and . . .

Eden sucked in a breath, closing her eyes for a moment as she pulled herself together. Then she gave Anna a grateful smile as she took over, singing the next line. Eden turned to face the audience, fixing her gaze on an empty seat several rows back, a safe focal point as she channeled herself into the music. To her relief, the rest of the song passed smoothly.

She gave Anna a quick hug the way she always did at the end of "After Midnight," trying not to notice the little flutter in her belly as they touched. She couldn't think about it or about Anna, not until she was back at the hotel, alone in her room.

Eden threw herself into the next song, relieved to feel her equilibrium return. She finished the show without another misstep, walking off the stage to thundering applause. Anna was waiting for her backstage, as had become her habit, and she, Eden, Kyrie, Paris, and Taylor rode to the hotel together. No one mentioned Eden's fumble. To them, it was just a missed line. These things happened all the time during live shows.

How could anyone know the world had shifted beneath her feet on that stage tonight? That she was currently questioning everything she'd thought she understood about herself? Her brain was tuned to existential crisis, but she was reasonably confident that her expression was as cool and collected as ever.

At the hotel, she and Anna paused to sign autographs for a group of fans clustered outside. Well, "fans" might have been a generous term, as the majority of them asked her not to personalize their photos, which meant they were actually autograph hounds looking to sell photos of her online, but at least they weren't asking her about #Edanna.

Taylor kept them in order until all the photos had been signed and then ushered Eden into the lobby of the hotel, with Anna and the rest of their group in tow. They all got into the elevator together.

"See you in the morning," Anna said as she exited on her floor.

"Night, Anna."

Kyrie and Paris got off at the next floor.

"I'll pick you up at seven to head to the airport," Paris said.

Eden nodded. "I'll be ready."

The elevator finally reached Eden's floor, and Taylor walked her to her door, making sure Eden got inside safely. She said good night, and

Eden was finally alone. Thank God. She headed straight for the bathroom, stripped off her clothes, and stepped into the shower.

She let out a sigh of relief as she scrubbed the stage makeup from her face. Beneath the shower's hot spray, her mind wandered, reliving that moment with Anna, the moment she'd lost her place in the song because she was . . . what? What had that been? A reaction to the #EDANNA sign?

Eden couldn't think about it right now, not while she was naked in the shower, hands on her body as she washed away sweat and makeup. Especially not while her body was reminding her how long it had been since she'd taken care of certain needs. She was too unsettled to take care of them tonight, too confused about why she was feeling this way, maybe too afraid of whose face she might see in her fantasies.

Get a grip, Eden.

She finished her shower and dressed in pajamas, then sat in bed with her phone and a bottle of water to wind down with her usual postshow ritual so she could sleep. But tonight, sleep didn't seem to be anywhere in her future. She kept replaying the scene onstage. Had it started when she saw the #EDANNA sign, or had she been looking at Anna first?

Surely it had started with the sign. She saw the sign, and it reminded her how some of the fans wanted her and Anna to be a couple. Obviously, that was why she'd felt those sparks or whatever they were when she looked at Anna afterward.

Because Eden was thirty-six years old, and she'd never been attracted to a woman before. Then again, had she ever *really* been attracted to a man? She shook her head at herself. She was being ridiculous. Surely, if she wasn't straight, she would already know.

After she'd finally rid herself of her first manager and the team of overbearing men he'd hired, Eden had made a point to surround herself with capable women. She'd always been around women. And she'd always appreciated women. Of course Eden admired the female form.

Women were beautiful. So many curves, a softness that belied their underlying strength. But that didn't mean . . .

Eden felt an uncomfortable tug in her stomach. She'd always been drawn to women. When she watched movies or TV shows, she inevitably ended up talking about the actresses while her friends gushed about which actors they thought were the hottest. Did that . . . mean something?

She unlocked her phone and opened Twitter. Her fingers searched #Edanna before she could stop herself, and *God*, there were a lot of posts. Hundreds from tonight alone. She saw photos of herself and Anna onstage together, photos of Eden staring at Anna with a dazed look as she lost track of the song.

> @ChaiLatte999: Did anyone else notice the way Eden totally forgot the words to her own song tonight while she was gazing at Anna?! Girl has it so bad, and I LOVE IT SO MUCH. #Edanna
> @EdensGarden565: OMG I need to see video of this!!! #Edanna4ever
> @PinkCookiesxx: Y'all are in luck because I GOT IT ON VIDEO #Edanna4ever

Eden's thumb hovered over the play button on the attached video, but at the last moment she closed Twitter instead. She blinked, and tears spilled over her cheeks. It was bad enough she'd questioned her sexuality onstage in front of thirty thousand people, but someone had gotten it on video.

Story of her fucking life.

CHAPTER THIRTEEN

"Mom!" Anna squealed as she launched herself into her mother's arms. Earlier that morning, she'd flown from Las Vegas to San Francisco with Eden and the rest of their entourage. From there, everyone else had gone to the hotel, but Anna had come straight to her parents' house. She'd be staying here tonight after the show.

"Look at you, my budding superstar," her mom murmured, hugging Anna tightly. "You're glowing."

"I'm really happy, Mom." She pulled back to grin at her mom before the sound of her dad clearing his throat interrupted them.

"Still waiting for my hug," he said.

She released her mom and turned to let her dad wrap her in one of his bear hugs. "I missed you, Dad. Let's do the crossword together tomorrow morning like old times."

"I'm going to hold you to that." He patted her back before releasing her.

"But first, we want to hear all about your big tour," her mom said, guiding Anna into the kitchen, which Anna had always thought of as the heart of their home. She and her mom had spent countless hours here while she was growing up, cooking and bonding.

It was a chef's kitchen, with gleaming double ovens in back and a large gas cooktop, everything finished in warm earth tones. Today, it smelled like a combination of lemons and mint, courtesy of the pitcher of freshly made lemonade on the island.

Anna's mouth watered. Her mom's mint lemonade was legendary. "For a glass of lemonade, I'll tell you everything."

"Are you hungry?" her mom asked as she picked up the pitcher and began to fill a glass. "And is Eden still joining us for lunch?"

"A little hungry, and yeah, she is. She'll be here in an hour or so. She had to get checked in to the hotel. Did you take today off from work?" Her mom owned Terrace Bistro, a popular restaurant in downtown San Francisco.

"I did. Couldn't miss the chance to spend some time with you. John's coming with us to the show tonight, by the way."

"Yay." Anna accepted the glass of lemonade her mom handed her. She hadn't seen her brother in months. He was two years older than she was and worked in Silicon Valley doing some sort of techy thing that went right over her head but earned him a lot of money.

Her mom produced a bag of homemade granola for Anna to snack on, and they brought everything into the living room to relax and catch up until Eden arrived.

"Since she's not here yet, tell us all about what it's like to be on tour with Eden." Her mom gave Anna a knowing smile as she settled into the chair across from her. Her parents probably knew better than anyone how much Anna had idolized Eden while she was growing up, and Anna would have to tread carefully here or they would easily realize just how desperately infatuated Anna had become with the real-life Eden.

"Well, I've decided that whoever coined the phrase about never meeting your idols must have idolized terrible people, because Eden's wonderful. She can be a little standoffish at times, but not in a rude way. More like she's the most famous person in the room and feels the pressure to watch everything she says and does because of that."

"I can see that," her mom said thoughtfully.

"And when she performs, it's like . . . I literally get goose bumps. She's that amazing."

"Wow." Her dad exchanged a look with her mom. "I'm certainly looking forward to meeting the woman who can put stars in your eyes like that."

"More like hearts in her eyes," her mom said. "Anna, hon, it sounds like your adolescent crush has turned into something more?"

Anna covered her face with her hands. Well, that had taken all of two minutes for them to figure out. "Am I that obvious?"

"Only because we know you so well." There was laughter in her dad's voice. "We know how you look when you're smitten with someone."

"It's a harmless crush," Anna said. "I'm not going to act on it. Not only do we have to work together for the next six months, but she's straight."

"I'm relieved to hear that," her mom said, "because the dynamic between you does remind me a little too much of your relationship with Camille."

Anna flinched.

"I didn't want to say it, but I thought so too," her dad said with an apologetic smile. "You used to gush about her just like this."

"I know, I know, I see it too," Anna said. "But for the record, even though I'm absolutely not going there with Eden, she's nothing like Camille."

"I'm glad," her mom said. "Manipulative people are toxic to be around, whether you're romantically involved with them or not."

Anna nodded. "Eden's been nothing but kind. You'll see when you meet her."

Eden hesitated on Anna's parents' front porch as anxiety churned in her stomach. Standing here left her feeling exposed, though. She always felt vulnerable when she was outside in a public place, just waiting for an overzealous fan or paparazzo to pounce. The car she'd arrived in still idled at the curb, with Taylor watching from the passenger seat to make sure Eden made it inside safely. And that meant Taylor was watching her freeze on the porch.

Eden lifted her hand and knocked. Footsteps approached from the other side, and then the door swung open to reveal Anna's smiling face. *Sparks.* Eden's whole system lit up like an arena full of fans illuminating their cell phones.

She immediately tamped it down. She would *not* feel anything other than friendship for Anna while she was in her parents' house. "Hi," she said, pleased that her voice sounded unaffected.

"Hi yourself." Anna gestured with her hand. "Come on in and meet my parents. My mom hasn't told me what she's making for lunch, but it'll definitely be amazing."

"I'm sure it will." Eden stepped into the house. It was fancier than she'd expected, but then again, Anna had mentioned that her mom owned a restaurant. Eden couldn't name the architectural style, but it felt modern, with plenty of decorative touches in the woodwork. The paint was a warm beige, and she saw lots of family photos on the walls.

She stepped closer to one of them, smiling at the adorable blonde girl in the photo, striking a silly pose in red overalls. Anna had been colorful even as a child. There was a blond boy next to her, a little bit older, sticking out his tongue at the camera. "You and your brother?"

"Yep," Anna confirmed. "That's John. He's coming to the show tonight."

"Oh, that's fun."

"I can't wait to see him." Anna chattered happily as she pointed out various photos, and Eden was thrilled for this peek at her childhood.

"There you are," a woman's voice said.

Eden turned to see an older version of Anna walking toward her. Anna's mother was tall and slim, with an air of authority about her, but her smile was warm and welcoming. Eden extended her hand. "You must be Mrs. Moss. I'm Eden."

"Please call me Bev. It's a pleasure to meet you, Eden. Anna left to answer the door, but then she didn't come back." Bev gave Anna a slightly reproachful look, but there was no malice behind it, only affection, at least as far as Eden could see.

"Sorry, Mom. That's your fault for putting all these family photos just inside the door. Eden got sidetracked looking at them."

"It's true," Eden said apologetically as she followed Bev toward the living room. "Little Anna was very cute."

In the living room, she met Anna's father, George. He was a tall but unimposing man in jeans and a well-worn Metallica T-shirt who immediately set Eden at ease by asking questions about the tour. She sat on the sofa beside Anna and accepted a glass of lemonade from Bev.

"So what do you get up to while you're on the road?" George asked, sipping his own lemonade. "Sightseeing? A chance to visit out-of-town friends and family?"

"A lot less than you'd imagine, honestly," Eden told him. "Sometimes—like today—we're only in town for a day, and we need to be at the arena by six for sound checks, so I usually don't see much of the city except the view from my hotel room."

"Well, we're glad you made it out today," Bev said.

"So am I," Eden said, and she meant it. She almost never visited someone's home when it wasn't for an industry event or an interview. It was nice to spend time with Anna's family and talk about regular things.

After a few minutes, Bev left to prepare lunch, refusing Eden's offer to help. "No one's allowed in the kitchen with me when I'm cooking."

"She takes her kitchen very seriously," Anna told Eden.

"That she does," George chimed in. He was leaned back in his chair, one foot propped against the opposite knee.

"I guess that comes from being a chef," Eden said. "And what do you do, George?"

"Oh, a little of this and that," he told her. "These days, I mostly enjoy puttering around the house."

"He builds model ships," Anna said, pride gleaming in her eyes. "They're so detailed, it's incredible."

"I'd love to see them," Eden said, and that was how she found herself in the basement a few minutes later, walking around George's workshop as she admired the ships he'd built. Most were about two feet long, made from real wood, and the level of detail on everything from the sails to the rigging blew her mind. "These are amazing, George. I've never seen anything like them before."

"Just a hobby." He shrugged, but she saw the way he seemed to come alive here in his workshop, the twinkle in his eye and the affectionate way he spoke about the ships. She knew that feeling. It was the way she felt when she sang.

And to an extent, it was the way she felt when she was around Anna. She'd never had a connection like this with another person before, and while it was somewhat confusing, she felt happy and energized when she was with Anna.

She didn't trust anything she was feeling beyond that basic knowledge. Probably, all the #Edanna talk was causing her to question herself, when that warm, tingly feeling she felt around Anna was just the joy of being around a new friend. Truthfully, it had been a long time since Eden had had a real friend.

After they looked at George's model ships, Bev called them to the kitchen table for crispy sweet-and-sour tofu served with a side of kale salad.

"Are you both vegan as well?" Eden asked as she took her seat.

"Goodness, no," Bev told her. "I didn't learn to cook many meat-free recipes in culinary school that I actually liked, but vegan cuisine has come such a long way since then. I look forward to the challenge when Anna visits, cooking something we can all enjoy."

"I'd say you've done it," Eden told her as she sampled the tofu. "This is delicious."

"Thank you. Now," Bev said, looking from Eden to Anna and back. "I want to hear more about the tour."

Anna tugged at the baseball cap on her head. Tonight, she was going to watch Eden's performance from the audience for the first time. Well, she'd get to watch the first hour or so from her seat before she ducked backstage to get ready for their duet.

She would wait until the houselights went out and then sneak into the empty seat waiting for her, hoping she could go unnoticed for long enough to enjoy Eden's performance. It was also a welcome chance to spend more time with her family. To help conceal her identity, she'd had Kyrie buy her one of the hats from Eden's merchandise stand.

When the time came, she left her dressing room to meet Kyrie, who was waiting to show her to her seat. She knew the moment the houselights dropped because the crowd went wild, screaming for Eden. Anna could relate.

As she made her way into the audience, excitement spread through her system. She'd been attending concerts in this arena since she was a little girl. In fact, she'd seen Eden for the first time here when she was ten. And now, here she was, touring with Eden, performing in her hometown arena.

It was another *moment*.

She kept her head down as she walked, not that it mattered. No one was looking at her. All eyes were on the stage, where a musical sequence had begun. Anna had about thirty seconds to find her seat before Eden stepped onstage.

Her family was seated in the section directly to the left of the stage, close enough that Anna had been able to easily spot them during her opening set. Seeing the pride and joy on their faces was a memory she'd carry with her forever. She was so lucky to have them.

Briefly, she thought of Eden's parents. Had it been hard for her today, being around Anna's family when her own was so stifling and unsupportive? Anna hoped not. Eden had certainly looked happy all afternoon, but Anna knew by now that Eden was exceptionally good at hiding her true emotions when she felt like she needed to put on a performance for someone.

Ahead, Anna spotted her parents and John, and she slid into the empty seat between John and her mom without drawing any undue attention to herself. "Hi," she said, wrapping an arm around John.

He grinned, leaning in so she could hear him over the music. "You were so great tonight. It freaked me out a little bit, to be honest. You look like a star, not my little sister."

"Can't I be both?" she asked playfully, nudging him with her elbow.

"Oh yeah, and also—" His voice was drowned out by the roar of the crowd.

Eden appeared through a trapdoor in the middle of the stage, wearing a pink miniskirt and matching top, looking like the kind of superstar Anna hoped to be someday. Eden began to sing, moving with her dancers in a way that made it seem like she was doing a lot more dancing than she actually was. Anna hadn't really noticed how much Eden let the dancers accentuate her moves until she'd watched her in rehearsals.

It was so well choreographed. Flawless but not *too* polished. Eden added her own flair, making eye contact with the crowd when she got to the edge of the stage, smiling and waving to her fans. She was a pro. And her voice had the hairs on Anna's arms standing on end all over again.

Eden made her way to the left side of the stage, standing about ten feet in front of Anna and her family, and she was brimming with energy, like someone had turned her inner spotlight back on since Anna first met her before the Grammys. She was *radiant*.

She caught Anna's eye and winked. Anna grinned, dancing and singing Eden's words back to her like the fangirl she was. The look Eden gave her made Anna want to melt into a happy puddle. Eden was looking at her like Anna had made her day, like she loved seeing Anna in the audience as much as Anna loved being here.

Anna pressed a hand against her heart, which was about to pound out of her chest. God, she was in over her head when it came to this woman. Eden moved back to the center of the stage, staring into the depths of the arena as she sang, showing the audience exactly what they wanted to see.

Anna had glimpsed Eden without her professional mask in place, though: moments when she let her guard down around Anna, when she felt comfortable to just be herself. Those were the moments Anna treasured most.

Eden's real smiles—the genuine ones, like the one Anna had just received from the stage—felt like a gift, like something private given only to Anna.

She danced around in her row, thrilled for this chance to enjoy the show from the audience. She and her mom hooked elbows and swayed to the music together, and when she looked past Bev, her dad was on his feet, grooving to the beat too.

About thirty minutes into the show, Eden reappeared onstage in a billowing blue skirt. She stood at the microphone stand to sing "Alone." As Eden sang the lyrics, Anna's heart ached. Eden might wear a mask when she spoke, but she showed her heart when she sang. The raw emotion in her voice made Anna's eyes well with tears.

After "Alone," Eden segued into one of her more upbeat songs, moving her hips to the beat as that blue skirt swirled around her feet. One of the dancers unclipped her skirt and whisked it away, drawing screams from the crowd as her blue mini shorts were revealed. Anna realized belatedly that she'd screamed, too, drawing a look from her mother. Oops.

At the end of the song, the dancers clipped Eden onto a line that had descended from the rigging above the stage, connecting to the harness sewn into her costume. Then she rose into the air, spinning like a tornado in the move Anna had watched her struggle with so much during rehearsals. Tonight, she was flawless, twirling effortlessly through the air before she returned to the stage to deliver the last line of the song.

Now it was Anna who felt dizzy, her mind—and her heart—whirling with the power of her feelings for Eden.

CHAPTER FOURTEEN

Anna:

Plans today?

Eden:

The usual. Tea. Movie. Want to join me?

Anna:

I'm on my way to your room.

Eden sat up in bed, glancing at herself to make sure she was ready for company. She swallowed down that familiar yet confusing burst of fluttery excitement she felt every time she saw Anna, but especially when they were going to hang out together in her room.

They'd been on the road for a month now, and Eden had settled into all her usual tour habits. Paris would bring her a protein smoothie every morning for breakfast, and then Eden would have a private session in the hotel's gym. She had to keep up her fitness on the road, since she rarely left her hotel room except when she was doing press or onstage.

After a shower and lunch, Eden would spend the rest of the afternoon relaxing in her suite, reading or watching TV until it was time to get ready for the show. Sometimes Anna came to her room to watch a movie with her, and those afternoons were Eden's favorite.

There was a knock at her door, and Eden slid out of bed. She walked to the door and checked the peephole. Even though she was expecting Anna, she could never be too careful. It hadn't happened yet on this tour, but inevitably a few overzealous fans would correctly guess which hotel she was staying at and knock on all the doors on the VIP level, hoping she would open the door so they could, what . . . hang out?

It would never happen. She always checked the peephole, and when she didn't recognize the person on the other side, she called Taylor.

But today, it was Anna's face she glimpsed through the rounded portal. She looked sunny as ever in a yellow top, her hair in a ponytail. Eden was already smiling as she unlocked the door and pulled it open.

Anna held up an orange plastic bag that looked like it had come from the gift shop downstairs. "How do you feel about going on an adventure?"

"What kind of adventure?" Eden shut the door behind her and reengaged the dead bolt.

"The 'let's leave the hotel' kind." Anna led the way into Eden's suite. She set the bag on the table in the living room and pulled out two baseball caps. One was hot pink, the other purple. Both of them had some sort of touristy slogan printed on the front.

Eden was starting to get an idea of where this was going, and she didn't like it. Anna often went out with Kyrie during their tour stops, exploring the cities they were in, but Eden couldn't do that. The very idea of going out in public made her want to pull her arms and legs inside her oversize sweatshirt, just curl up in a ball and stay there for the rest of the day.

"Have you ever seen the San Antonio River Walk?" Anna asked.

"No." Eden turned away so she wouldn't see the hopeful gleam in Anna's eyes.

"Want to? Because I've brought everything you need for the perfect disguise."

"I don't want to wear a disguise," Eden protested. It sounded uncomfortable, and going out in public already made her uncomfortable enough.

"It's not the kind of disguise you're thinking of," Anna said. "It's super simple. We go undercover as tourists." Anna produced oversize, brightly colored T-shirts from the bag, with SAN ANTONIO printed on the front beside an outline of Texas.

"Anna, I can't."

"Don't you get a little stir crazy cooped up in your room all the time?"

Eden sighed, crossing her arms over her chest. "Of course I do, but it's just part of life on the road. I love my fans, but I hate being mobbed on the street. I've accepted that I can't do things like walk around in public or go sightseeing without causing a scene."

"Don't you miss it?" Anna asked, her voice quieter now. "Walking down the street without anyone recognizing you?"

"I guess? To be honest, I don't really remember what that was like. I've been famous since I was a teen."

Anna put on one of the hats and grinned at her. "Listen, I know I'm not as famous as you are, but I've been using the tourist disguise for weeks now, and no one has recognized me. People expect celebrities on the street to look like celebrities. They're looking for glamorous clothes and an entourage, not tacky tourists. Come on. Let's go for a walk along the river, eat some tacos, maybe have an ice cream? What's the worst that can happen?"

"I get mobbed, and Taylor's not there to help?" Eden raised her eyebrows. "I'm sorry, Anna, but it scares me. I'd rather stay in my room."

"Let's bring Taylor, then," Anna said. "She can hang out with us, or maybe she can just hang out nearby, so you could text her if you need her. Would that make you feel more comfortable?"

Eden sat on the sofa, staring at the T-shirts Anna had brought. Despite her protests, she couldn't help picturing the scene Anna had described: the two of them out for a casual walk without anyone giving them a second glance. She felt a tug of longing. Could it really be as simple as Anna described?

Anna sat beside her, resting a hand on Eden's thigh. "If you really don't want to, then I'd love to stay in and watch a movie. Mostly, I just want to spend the afternoon with you."

Eden felt warm where Anna's hand touched her. "I want to spend the afternoon with you too. And I'm not saying no to going out, necessarily. I'm just hesitant."

"How about this? Let's try on our disguises and see how you feel. Then if you want to give sightseeing a try, we'll ask Taylor to come with us. If no one notices you, maybe Taylor can do some sightseeing of her own while still being nearby if you need her."

Eden sucked in a deep breath and blew it out. Was she seriously considering this? "Tacos and ice cream?"

"Or whatever you want," Anna said with a grin. "I'd suggest margaritas, but we have a show tonight."

"I haven't walked down the street with an ice-cream cone since I was a kid."

"Then you should do it today," Anna said. "Come on, Eden. Say yes."

She met Anna's eyes, immediately lost in their chestnut depths. In that moment, she'd have said yes to almost anything. "Okay."

"Really?" Anna asked, and was she closer now than she had been a moment before?

Eden had gone from staring into her eyes to looking at her lips, which were glossy and pink. They looked so soft. Would they feel as soft as they looked? Anna leaned forward, and oh God, was she going to kiss her? Eden felt a surge of something hot and urgent between her thighs. But wait, she didn't actually want—

Then Anna's arms were around her, and they were hugging, and Eden was trying very hard not to sound like she'd forgotten how to breathe. Anna pulled back, beaming at her. "We're going to have so much fun!"

"Are you sure you want vanilla?" Anna asked.

Beside her, Eden looked adorably ordinary in a purple baseball cap and sunglasses, paired with an oversize lime-green T-shirt, black shorts, and sneakers. For the first ten minutes or so after they'd arrived at the river walk, she'd been so visibly uncomfortable that Anna almost gave in and took her back to the hotel. Every time someone even glanced in their direction, Eden's entire body tensed.

But now, she seemed to be realizing that her disguise worked. No one—except Anna—was paying her any attention, and as they approached an ice cream stand, Anna wanted to celebrate the moment, even if Eden had picked a boring flavor. If vanilla was truly her favorite, Anna would happily buy her a vanilla cone, but she wondered if Eden was just playing it safe, which seemed to be her default setting.

"Vanilla's fine." Eden shrugged, eyeing the ice cream stand like it was filled with overzealous paparazzi who were about to leap out and accost her.

"Of course vanilla is *fine*, but at least look at all the flavors before you pick."

"What are you having?" Eden asked.

"I'm having lemon sorbet because it's the only vegan option, but you have like twenty flavors to choose from. Come see." Anna gestured for Eden to follow as she walked closer to the stand.

Eden positioned herself slightly behind Anna in a reversal of the way they'd stand onstage together later tonight. Anna was enchanted by this somewhat shy version of her. She couldn't have even pictured it until this moment. For the first time since they'd met, Anna was in charge, which was a heady feeling.

"Okay, actually I want to try the mint chocolate chip," Eden said. "I remember loving that when I was a little girl."

Anna gave her an incredulous look. "Eden, when is the last time you had ice cream?"

"From a stand like this? Probably when I was about ten. I love dessert, but ice cream isn't really something I seek out, other than a scoop on top of a piece of pie or something, you know?"

"I know you've been deprived of the joy of ice-cream cones for entirely too long, and I'm very happy to remedy that for you." Anna gave her a playful nudge. "Okay, so mint chocolate chip. And how do you feel about waffle cones?"

Eden looked sheepish. "They sound interesting?"

"All right, Ms. Snooty Celebrity, let me reintroduce you to the simple pleasure of ice cream. Be right back." Anna headed toward the stand, half expecting Eden to follow. She'd been glued to Anna's side ever since she finally gave Taylor permission to go off on her own here on the waterfront. Anna wasn't sure where Taylor was now, but she'd promised to stay nearby in case Eden needed her. Anna was glad that so far, she hadn't.

She approached the stand and ordered a cup of lemon sorbet for herself and Eden's mint-chocolate-chip cone, grateful not to see any hint of recognition from the employee behind the counter. The girl scooping the ice cream looked to be in her late teens, which was Anna's core fan demographic.

Anna paid with cash and turned around to look for Eden, who was nowhere in sight. Where had she gone? Anna felt a flicker of panic. She

Rachel Lacey

wanted this outing to be casual and fun, a chance for Eden to escape the confines of her life for a few hours. If anything happened to her . . .

But there she was, standing at the edge of the river with her back to Anna. Eden's hands were clasped behind herself, and from a distance at least, she appeared at ease. Anna exhaled as she hurried toward her.

"One mint-chocolate-chip cone for the lady by the river," Anna said.

Eden turned toward her with a smile. Their hands brushed as she accepted her cone, and Anna felt a happy tingle travel up her arm. "Thanks," Eden said.

"See that bridge ahead?" Anna asked. "We could stand up there and people watch while we eat our ice cream if you like."

"I think I'd like that a lot." Eden licked her cone, distracting Anna with the sight of her tongue as it swirled over the ice cream.

"When I was in high school, my best friend and I used to play this game where we'd watch the people around us when we were out somewhere and make up stories for them."

"What kind of stories?" Eden asked as they began to walk.

"The more outlandish, the better," Anna said. "Want to try?"

"Sure." Eden licked her cone again. "You're right. This is better than vanilla."

"Are you having fun?" Anna had never visited the San Antonio River Walk before. She'd only seen it in pictures, but so far it was living up to her expectations. The San Antonio River ran through the heart of the city, bordered on each side by a walkway lined with shops and restaurants. Here and there, tourist boats glided past. It was hectic enough for them to blend in but not so crowded that they couldn't enjoy themselves.

"Yeah," Eden said, giving Anna a smile that looked a hundred times more relaxed than she had a little while ago. "I am."

"I'm glad." Anna led the way onto the concrete bridge that spanned the river. From here, they had a decent view in either direction. Many of the storefronts were brightly colored, which felt cheerful and suited Anna's mood. It was the last week of May, and San Antonio was unexpectedly hot. They'd probably both need showers before the show tonight.

Anna held up her phone and took several photos of the river, then spun to take a selfie, gesturing for Eden to step in beside her. "A selfie just for us. I won't share it."

"Why won't you share it?" Eden asked as she moved closer.

"In case we do this again in another city. Our undercover ruse will be blown if the fans start looking for us along the tour route, dressed as tourists." Anna held her phone out and snapped several photos as they grinned for the camera.

"Send me the good ones?" Eden asked.

"You bet." Anna scrolled through the pictures and sent several of them to Eden, who had transferred her attention to the ice-cream cone in her hand. They ate for a few minutes in silence, just watching the people walk by around them.

"I'm surprised there aren't any barriers to keep people from falling in," Eden commented as they watched a couple of children skip along the sidewalk. She was right. The sidewalk ran along the edge of the river without any sort of railing.

"I'm guessing the water isn't very deep, but I actually don't know," Anna said.

"I wonder how many people have one too many margaritas and go for an unexpected swim?" Eden's tone sounded light and happy, and that made Anna feel the same way.

"I'm sure it's happened," Anna agreed.

"Uh-oh." Eden looked down at her sneakers, which were splattered with green ice cream. "I'm melting."

"Better eat faster, then."

"I'm trying," Eden mumbled around a mouthful of waffle cone. She had a dot of green on the tip of her nose, and Anna yearned to reach out and dab it away with her finger. If she hadn't been so over-the-top attracted to her, she probably would have, but as it was, she was hyperaware of her every move around Eden, being extra careful not to cross any lines.

Anna was glad she'd tucked some napkins in her pocket to give Eden instead. She munched through the last few bites of her cone and then wiped her hands and face with the napkins Anna handed her before stooping to clean her sneakers.

"Okay, that was extremely worth it, even if I have to spend the rest of the afternoon with sticky hands," Eden declared. "Now demonstrate this people-watching game you told me about. You just make up stories about people?"

"Yep. See those women over there?" Anna nodded toward a table she'd been watching at one of the nearby restaurants. The three women at the table had leaned in close and were having what looked like an intense conversation. "They've just found out that they were all dating the same guy, and now they're plotting his demise."

"Oh!" Eden laughed, looking at the table in question.

"Your turn," Anna said.

Eden watched the table for a few seconds in silence. "The one in the blue shirt just suggested they dump their cheating ex right here in the river."

"And the woman in red? She's a private investigator, so she knows a few things about how to get away with a crime. She thinks they should put him in an incinerator."

Eden glanced at her, lips twitching. "Remind me not to piss you off."

"Listen, I've watched *How to Get Away with Murder*. I have endless useful information about the topic at hand."

"There's a show called *How to Get Away with Murder*?" Eden asked. "How is that legal?"

"It's a drama, not a how-to show. The characters do get caught up in a lot of murder, though. The lead, Annalise Keating, is an absolute badass, plus she likes the ladies, which is always a bonus for me. She's played by Viola Davis. You should check it out. Great show to binge in your hotel room."

"Maybe we can watch it together," Eden said, and was she blushing?

"Sure." Anna turned her gaze back to the table, where the women were high-fiving each other. "The incinerator plan is a go."

Eden giggled. "Oh, look, the woman in the floral dress is commemorating the moment with a selfie."

"So she is," Anna said. "Ballsy of her."

She and Eden crossed to the other side of the bridge to throw away their ice cream trash, and then they walked past the table of women as they continued on their way down the river walk, both of them laughing quietly as they passed.

"You're right," Eden said. "The disguise works, and this is so much more fun than spending the afternoon in my hotel room."

"Oh, I don't know. We've had a lot of fun in your bed too." Okay, she hadn't thought that through before she said it, and now Eden was definitely blushing. Anna searched desperately for a change of topic, deciding to return to their game. "See that man over there in the huge hat? He's an actor in town filming a movie. He obviously got the memo I sent out that today was undercover-celebrity day here on the river walk."

Eden threw her head back and laughed. "Oh, but I already knew that. He taught me the secret handshake while you were buying our ice cream."

Eden couldn't stop smiling. Not that she was generally an unhappy person, but her usual happy place was the stage . . . not the San Antonio

River Walk. She hated going out in public, and yet this was the most fun she'd had in ages.

Then again, she and Anna always seemed to have fun together, whether they were sightseeing or rehearsing or watching a movie together in bed. Maybe that explained why she couldn't seem to get Anna out of her head, but deep down, she was starting to have her doubts. Straight women didn't fantasize about kissing their female friends, and lately, Eden couldn't seem to stop thinking about kissing Anna.

She wasn't ready to acknowledge those thoughts yet, though. Maybe she never would be. She and Anna were friends, and Eden wasn't about to ruin the dynamic between them, especially not when she was so confused about her sexuality.

"Penny for your thoughts," Anna said.

Eden blinked, yanking herself out of her spiraling thoughts, none of which she'd share with Anna for any amount of money. *God.* Her cheeks felt too hot. "Just thinking that this is the most fun I've had in a while. Thanks for pushing me to come, although I still can't quite believe no one's recognized us." She dropped her voice on that last part.

She and Anna were seated at an outdoor table at one of the restaurants that lined the river walk, having an early dinner before they went back to the hotel to get ready for the show.

"Just out of curiosity, the last time you went out in public, did you and Zach take a stroll down Rodeo Drive looking like the ultimate celebrity 'it' couple?" Anna's eyes twinkled with humor.

"Not Rodeo Drive, but I guess most of my negative experiences were in LA." Eden sighed. "I've been missing out, haven't I?"

"I can't answer that question for you," Anna said. "But if today was any indicator, we should do this more often. Think of all the cities we can explore together!"

"Yes," Eden agreed. "I'd like to do this again, although not in every city. We need to rest when we can. You won't believe how exhausted you'll be after a few months on the road."

"Oh, I'm sure you're right. Right now, I'm so giddy about being on tour for the first time that I feel invincible."

"Maybe you are," Eden countered with a wink, and she caught herself staring at Anna's lips again. "I had a lot more energy in my twenties too."

"Stop that right there." Anna pointed an accusatory finger at her. "We've already been over this, and you're only nine years older than me."

Nine years felt like a lot when Eden thought about kissing her, especially when she remembered the way Anna used to idolize her. Their meals arrived, saving Eden from that line of thought. Her stomach growled as she surveyed her enchiladas. They looked incredible. The chips and salsa they'd munched on while they waited for their entrées had been wonderful too. Honestly, the whole afternoon had been perfect. Eden had barely even wondered where Taylor was, although she'd texted with her several times to check in.

"Zoe would be so jealous right now," Anna said as she picked up one of her tacos. "She grew up here in San Antonio."

"Oh, really?"

Anna nodded. "Her parents emigrated from Mexico when she was a baby and settled here. I'm sure she would have taken us to a more authentic restaurant well away from the river walk, but I've really enjoyed being a tourist today."

"Me too," Eden said. "In fact, if we have time after dinner, maybe we should pop into one of the stores and buy a souvenir?"

And that was how she found herself in her hotel room several hours later holding a lollipop that contained a scorpion. She doubted she'd ever find the courage to eat it, but in the meantime, she was being spontaneous, the way she imagined Anna would in this situation. Eden took a silly selfie with the lollipop and posted it to her social media all by herself, which prompted an immediate text from Paris.

Paris:

What in the world? You're eating SCORPIONS and posting on your own?!?!?!

Eden:

Had a fun afternoon and this seemed safe! I didn't mess up, did I?

Paris:

Nope. Just surprised me, that's all.

Eden had surprised herself more times than she could count since she'd met Anna. She was confused as hell about her feelings, but it boiled down to this: she felt *good* when she was with Anna. And while she'd worried that she would be tired after her sightseeing afternoon, when she stepped onto the stage that night, she'd never felt lighter on her feet.

CHAPTER FIFTEEN

"This is amazing." Anna settled beside Eden on a large rock overlooking Clear Creek, just outside Denver. This was their fourth sightseeing excursion since they'd explored the San Antonio River Walk together three weeks ago. Today, they'd decided to go on a short hike to take advantage of Colorado's stunning scenery. Taylor was somewhere behind them on the trail, but in their hats and sunglasses, no one had paid them any attention.

"It's so peaceful." Eden stretched her legs out in front of herself on the rock. Their resting spot overlooked Clear Creek Canyon, although the creek looked more like a river to Anna. It rushed over the rocks below, water churning. "I've always loved hiking."

"So this is something you've done more recently than that ice-cream cone when you were ten?" Anna teased.

Eden scoffed. "I *have* had fun as an adult, you know."

Anna raised her eyebrows. "Do tell."

"I own a house in Vermont. It's on about seventy acres, so I can hike right on my own property."

"Okay, that's amazing, and also, how many houses do you own, lady?"

"One," Eden said with a laugh. "I own condos in LA and New York and the house in Vermont. It's my sanctuary. I stayed there for two months after my divorce, just hiding from the world. I love it there."

"It sounds wonderful." Anna was glad Eden had a place like that, somewhere she could be off the radar and go outside without fearing she'd be photographed.

"One of my favorite places in the world." Eden wrapped her arms around her knees, and for a few minutes, they both watched the water rushing through the canyon below. There was something so peaceful about sitting here, surrounded by trees, just taking it all in.

Even the air felt fresher here in the woods. It was mid-June now, but the air was crisp and cool in Colorado, nothing like San Antonio's sticky heat. Being on tour was exposing Anna to so many parts of the country she'd never seen before, and she was loving every minute.

Her feelings for Eden were growing, though. It was getting harder for Anna to hide how much she wanted and cared about her. In her more optimistic moments, she still hoped she'd wake up one day and miraculously have moved on. And then there were the moments when she feared Eden was acting weird or reserved around her, like she'd noticed Anna's crush.

But surely that was just Anna's overactive imagination . . .

Eden pulled her phone out of the back pocket of her shorts and began typing rapidly on the screen. "Just had a thought for one of the new songs I'm working on," she explained after she'd finished.

"Ah," Anna said. "Have you been doing a lot of songwriting?"

Eden nodded. "I'd love to go into the studio after the tour's finished."

"I've been working on a few new songs too," Anna told her.

"Yeah? How's it coming?"

Anna shrugged. "Slower than I'd like."

Eden sighed. "Same. I think I'm a little gun shy after my last album did so poorly."

"Sales might have been disappointing by your usual standard, but it didn't do that badly. Eden. I think you're being too hard on yourself."

Eden looked down at her hands. "Not according to my label. They were extremely disappointed and made sure I knew it."

"I'm sorry. That sounds like a lot of pressure."

Eden laughed bitterly. "This industry is nothing *but* pressure once you've reached a certain level. Honestly, it's exhausting, and it sucks some of the joy out of doing the job you love, constantly being told you didn't smile enough, didn't sell enough, didn't promote hard enough."

"Have you considered taking a break?" Anna asked.

Eden shook her head. "I don't want a break. What else would I do? Music is pretty much my whole life, but songwriting's been slow for me lately. I'm not exactly inspired to write love songs at the moment, but I'm not heartbroken either. I'm just . . . meh."

"Have you ever tried using books or movies as inspiration?" Anna asked. "Not to plagiarize or anything, obviously, but just to get in the right emotional mood, like watching a romantic movie to inspire a love song."

"I haven't, but that's not a bad idea."

"I do it a lot. Our current show might inspire some weird songs," Anna said with a laugh. She and Eden had started watching *How to Get Away with Murder* together last week. "But maybe we should watch a romantic movie together tomorrow before the show and try to get some good songwriting in afterward?"

Eden smiled. "I'd love that."

Eden sat cross-legged in the middle of the bed. Tonight, she'd give her second performance in Denver before continuing to Minneapolis. She tapped lyrics into the document on her phone, her mind spinning with music. She'd unlocked something as she sat on that rock by the river yesterday.

"Turbulent" was the title that had come to mind as she watched the water surging through Clear Creek. It described so much of her life recently. She couldn't write a decent love song, but she was pouring her heart into this song about her personal crisis.

She opened the app she used to record herself and sang a rough verse before she lost the melody in her head. In this way, songwriting was so much easier now than it used to be. Her phone allowed her to compose and record her ideas on the go. It was much more efficient than the notebook she'd relied on at the beginning of her career.

As she finished recording, her phone dinged with an incoming text message.

Anna:

Want to watch a romcom with me? And write love songs after? 🎶 💜

Eden:

Yes!

Anna:

Should I come to your room? I've got snacks!

Eden:

I'll come to you this time. See you in a few.

Eden set down her phone and pressed a hand over her racing heart. Somehow it didn't seem like a good idea to have Anna in her bed this afternoon—no matter how innocent the context—not that being in Anna's bed was much better. Eden's head was an absolute mess when it came to Anna lately. She was doing her best to embrace the joy of being around her and ignore the rest. It was the only way to keep herself even semirational these days.

She texted Taylor and asked her to escort her to Anna's room. Eden had gotten so used to having Taylor accompany her everywhere that she hadn't realized how dependent on her she'd become until she saw Anna going about her life, unconcerned with the consequences of being recognized.

Eden envied her that freedom, but she'd been cornered by paparazzi or overzealous fans too many times to risk it. It was a helpless feeling to be mobbed by people who had no respect for her personal space or her safety, who ignored her attempts to flee, who wouldn't hesitate to photograph her in an embarrassing or vulnerable moment.

She loved to interact with her fans, but she needed the sense of security that came with having Taylor nearby, the knowledge that if anyone got too pushy, Taylor would intervene. Eden had so little control over her life sometimes, but she had this.

A knock at the door signaled Taylor's arrival. Eden picked up her phone and walked to the door, checking the peephole before she opened it.

"You two watching another movie together this afternoon?" Taylor asked with a smile as Eden stepped into the hall.

"Yeah."

"Glad you've found a friend on tour." Taylor scanned the hallway as she led the way to the elevator.

"Me too." Eden heard what Taylor wasn't saying. She'd accompanied Eden on her last three tours, so she knew better than anyone that Eden was usually a hermit. Sightseeing afternoons or even watching movies with a friend wasn't something Eden usually did, and unsurprisingly, she was having more fun on this tour than she could ever remember having.

The elevator was thankfully empty when it arrived. Taylor pushed the button for the thirty-ninth floor, five floors down from Eden's suite. Two floors into their journey, the elevator slid to a stop and four women got on, chatting excitedly among themselves.

Eden watched as Taylor discreetly pressed the button for the fortieth floor, giving them a decoy exit if they were spotted. The last thing they wanted was to lead anyone to Anna's door or to spark any rumors about why Eden was on her way to Anna's room.

Sure enough, as the elevator dinged its arrival on the fortieth floor, one of the women met Eden's eyes in the mirrored wall and let out a shriek. "Oh my God!" she squealed. "It's you. I mean, it *is* you, right? We're going to your show tonight, and oh my *God!*"

"It's me," Eden confirmed as the doors to the elevator opened, and just like that, all eyes were on her, four women gaping as they realized they were in the elevator with a celebrity.

Taylor placed a hand against her back, ushering her into the hallway.

One of the women stuck her hand out, holding the door open. "This is so surreal. We're such big fans, and maybe we hoped you were staying at the Four Seasons, too, but we never imagined we'd actually *see* you."

Eden smiled. "Surprise! Thanks so much for coming to the show. I appreciate it."

"Could we . . . ," another woman asked hesitantly, holding up her phone.

"Sure." Eden waved them over. The request for photos had been inevitable, and she didn't mind, not with Taylor here to keep things civilized.

The women clustered around her, talking over each other in their excitement. Eden answered their questions as she posed for selfies. She hadn't realized until she saw herself reflected on one of their phone screens that she was wearing Anna's purple hoodie.

"Could you sign this for me?" one of them asked, handing her cell phone to Eden.

"If you have a pen," Eden told her, and they all started rummaging through their bags until one of them came up with a marker. "What's your name?" Eden asked.

"Nancy," the woman told her breathlessly.

Eden scrawled, "To Nancy. Love, Eden Sands" on the back of the phone case. They all managed to come up with something for her to sign and then asked for a group photo with her, which Taylor took.

"Which outfit will Anna be wearing for your duet tonight?" someone asked after Taylor had snapped several quick photos. "Can you give us a hint?"

"It's purple," Eden told her.

"The dress you wore to accept your first Grammy!" Nancy squealed. "I *love* that one."

Eden shrugged as if she could neither confirm nor deny, but she also winked, letting them know they'd guessed correctly. Taylor politely ushered them back to the elevator now that they'd gotten their photos and autographs, and then she guided Eden down the hall to the stairwell, since they'd gotten off on the floor above Anna's.

Taylor paused, listening to make sure no one had followed them into the stairwell before they descended to the thirty-ninth floor. Finally, they arrived at Anna's door, and Eden knocked.

"Just text me when you're ready to go back to your room," Taylor told her.

"I will. Thank you."

Anna opened the door in a loose blue T-shirt that hung off one shoulder, and Eden's stomach fizzed at the sight of that bare skin. "Hey, you," Anna said. "I've narrowed down our movie choices and ordered popcorn from room service."

"Perfect," Eden said as she waved goodbye to Taylor.

Anna closed the door behind her and led the way to her bed, where a bowl of popcorn waited. "So, if you want a modern rom-com, we've got *Marry Me*, which is a celebrity marriage of convenience with Jennifer Lopez. I haven't seen it yet, but it's supposed to be good. Then there's *To All the Boys I've Loved Before*, which is a teen rom-com that's super cute. Or we could do a classic like *One Fine Day* or *Sleepless in Seattle*."

"I think all your emotions are amplified when you're a teenager, so if we're using this as songwriting inspiration, let's go with the teen movie," Eden said. "Plus I've heard a lot about that one, but I haven't seen it yet."

"Perfect," Anna said.

To keep from staring at her, or worse . . . kissing her, Eden walked to the window and looked out at downtown Denver. Her own room overlooked the mountains on the other side of the hotel. Behind her, Anna tabbed through screens on the TV.

"Okay," Anna said after a minute, patting the bed beside her. "Get ready for cuteness overload."

"I'm ready." Eden walked to the bed and sat to take off her shoes.

They propped pillows behind themselves and leaned against the headboard with the bowl of popcorn between them as the movie began to play. Two hours later, she was indeed on cuteness overload. She felt light and silly and just overall happy.

Anna pulled out her phone. "Now let's capture these emotions in song."

"Pressure's on." Eden settled beside her. She'd taken off the hoodie earlier when she got warm, and now she was in a tank top and leggings, trying not to notice the way Anna's tee kept sliding off her shoulder, highlighting the fact that she didn't seem to be wearing a bra. Her skin was so tan and looked so soft, and Eden couldn't remember what her life had been like before she became consumed by thoughts of Anna.

"To all the girls I've loved before . . . ," Anna sing-songed as she pretended to type into her phone.

Eden giggled. "I know there are a lot of you, but you're all special to me in different ways . . ."

"Hey!" Anna bumped her shoulder into Eden's. "There aren't that many, I'll have you know."

"Sure," Eden teased. "I've listened to enough of your songs to doubt that."

"How do you know they aren't all about the same person?" Anna countered. "Also . . . I didn't really know you'd listened to my music." Her cheeks were pink, and something in her expression reminded Eden of the way she'd looked the first time they met. She hadn't seen the starstruck version of Anna in a while.

"Of course I have," Eden said. "You didn't think I'd invite you on tour without doing my homework, did you? Besides, I already knew your hits. They're pretty hard to avoid these days."

"So you were trying to avoid them . . ."

"I can't help it, babe." Eden sang the chorus of "Obsessed," one of Anna's most popular songs. "You're everywhere I look, everywhere I turn. One look from you makes me burn."

"Oh my God." Anna tackled her, rolling Eden to the bed. "I can't believe you know my songs and never told me!"

"Where did you get the impression I didn't know your songs? You know I watch your performance every night." Eden was staring at Anna's bare shoulder again. Her heart was beating too fast. She tried to sit up, but Anna moved at the same time. They collided, and somehow Eden wound up sprawled on top of her.

Her lips were on Anna's, and she didn't even know how they'd gotten there, who'd made the move, but they were kissing, and Eden was on fire. Anna's lips were so soft, so warm, and they felt better than anything Eden had ever known. Her pulse thrummed in her ears and between her thighs, where an overwhelming ache grew, making her feel frenzied and wild.

"Oh my God," Anna whispered as her arms came around Eden, drawing her closer.

Eden whimpered, clinging to her as she kissed her with a sort of desperation she'd never felt before. One of her hands was on Anna's bare shoulder, the other fisted in her shirt. Her knees were straddling Anna's hips. *Holy shit.* This . . . this need, this pleasure. It was wonderful. It was so wonderful! Why hadn't she known a kiss could feel like this? Why hadn't she . . .

Her head swam. She felt almost drunk. Out of control. Oh God, what was she doing? She broke the kiss, blinking at Anna in a foggy haze. Her body felt like someone else's. Every inch of her skin felt hypersensitive. She was gasping for air. Her nipples were tight, and *oh*, the need throbbing in her core . . .

This was the spark she'd been missing her whole life. This was what it was supposed to feel like. She'd had no idea what she was missing, and now . . . now her world had tilted off its axis.

Anna stared up at her, her expression equally dazed. Eden had kissed her. Or maybe Anna had kissed her first. Eden wasn't sure, but she'd kissed a woman, and it had been the hottest kiss of her life, and now nothing made sense, and she didn't know what to do.

Eden dragged herself backward, sitting on her heels as tears flooded her eyes. She was breathing too fast. Way too fast. Oh God. She'd kissed Anna.

"Whoa, hey, are you okay?" Anna crouched in front of her, eyes crinkled in concern.

Eden shook her head. Tears spilled over her cheeks. She swiped at them, but the next thing she knew, she was full-on sobbing in the middle of Anna's bed. Anna. Who she'd just kissed. Eden was spinning out of control, and that was the one thing she'd never been able to handle. "I'm sorry," she whispered. "I just . . . I need to go."

She scooted backward off the bed and ran for the door as Anna called after her. Eden could hardly hear her over the roaring in her ears. She yanked the door open and stumbled into the hall, wiping frantically at her tears. She'd forgotten to call Taylor, and now she was alone in the hall, completely unprotected and looking like an absolute mess.

Desperate, she swept her gaze up and down the hallway, and at least there was no one here to see her like this. She couldn't risk the elevator, and she couldn't face Anna, so Eden ran for the stairwell, already breathless as she began the five-flight climb to the safety of her room.

CHAPTER SIXTEEN

Anna stared at the door Eden had just fled through. She pressed a finger against her lips, which were swollen from Eden's kisses. Eden had kissed her and blown Anna's mind in the process. She hadn't kissed Anna like a straight woman satisfying a curiosity either. She'd kissed like she was drowning and Anna was her only source of air, like she couldn't *not* kiss her.

And then she'd burst into tears and run before Anna could even process what had happened. She turned, staring blankly at the bed. The bed where she and Eden had kissed. The bed where Eden's phone lay, forgotten in her mad dash from the room, next to the purple hoodie that used to be Anna's but that she now thought of as Eden's.

Eden hadn't called Taylor. She never went anywhere without Taylor, except for that one perfect time when Anna had taken her on the back of her motorcycle.

Eden kissed me.

Anna wanted to shout it from the rooftops. She wanted to dance and sing and celebrate and . . . cry, because Eden had run away, distraught. Anna had to go after her. She needed to make sure Eden was okay. She needed to know Eden had made it to her room safely and return her phone, at the very least.

What would she say when she got to Eden's room? Anna's head was spinning. Hopefully the right words would come to her once she was there.

Anna picked up Eden's phone and the hoodie and tucked a room key in her pocket. She drew in a steadying breath and left her room. She was too jumpy to wait for the elevator and also wary of being recognized. When she'd ridden down to the lobby earlier to buy snacks, she'd ended up taking selfies with several people, which had been an awesome feeling at the time, but she wasn't in the mood for greeting fans now. She had to get to Eden.

Anna turned right and headed for the stairwell. Had Eden taken the elevator? She was so paranoid about being recognized. Anna hoped she hadn't run into anyone, especially in the state she'd been in when she left Anna's room. That would have been super traumatic for her. Anna jogged up the first two flights of stairs and walked the remaining three. She was gasping for breath when she exited on the forty-fourth floor.

As she approached Eden's door, Anna's breathing grew even more ragged. Why had Eden kissed her? And why had she been so upset afterward? Was she questioning her sexuality?

Only one way to find out. Anna lifted her hand and knocked. Silence greeted her from the other side of the door, but somehow she knew Eden was there, watching her through the peephole. Or maybe Anna just hoped she was.

"I brought your phone," Anna said, loudly enough for her voice to carry through the door. She didn't want to say anything else while she was standing in the hall. Who knew who was listening? And she'd thought Eden was the paranoid one.

The door swung open, and Eden gestured for her to come in. Anna stepped through the door, and Eden closed it firmly behind her. They faced each other in loaded silence. Eden's eyes were puffy but dry. She was still in the tank top and leggings she'd worn when she left Anna's room, and her chest was mottled with red patches. Embarrassment? Nerves? Exertion from five sets of stairs?

Anna held out the phone and hoodie. "Eden . . ."

Eden took the phone, her hand visibly shaking. "Thank you. The hoodie's yours, you know."

"I think of it as yours now. Keep it. I've got too many."

Eden took it and turned, walking farther into her suite to place it on the sofa.

"We need to talk about that kiss," Anna blurted before she lost her nerve.

Eden froze with her back to Anna. "Can we . . . not? At least, not right now? It's almost time to get ready for the show, and I . . ." She huffed a shaky breath, and wow, Anna had never seen her anywhere near this rattled, not even after her awful parents stormed her dressing room on opening night.

"I think we have to, at least a little bit." Anna gentled her tone. "I couldn't bear it if things got awkward between us, and I don't think either of us planned that kiss. Please, let's not let it ruin anything. You're too important to me."

Eden spun to face her then, her eyes shimmering with fresh tears. "I couldn't either. You're . . . this might sound pathetic because we haven't known each other that long, but I think you're my best friend."

Anna felt like her chest had been inflated with helium, like she might float up through the ceiling of this fancy penthouse suite and drift away. "That could only be pathetic if I'm pathetic, and I think I'm pretty awesome, so . . ."

It had the desired effect. Eden smiled. "We both know you're the opposite of pathetic. You've kept me on my toes since we met, and I mean that in the best possible way."

"So we're both awesome," Anna said. "Now that we've gotten that out of the way, do you want to talk about the kiss?"

Tears splashed over Eden's cheeks. Her bottom lip trembled, and it was all Anna could do not to pull her into her arms. An hour ago, it's exactly what she would have done, but after that kiss . . . well, Anna was trying desperately to get them back onto solid ground.

She wanted to fling herself into Eden's arms and kiss her again, kiss her until those tears were gone and Eden was moaning beneath her as Anna showed her exactly how wonderful it was to be with a woman. But none of that was going to happen, at least, not today.

"I know we have to talk about it." Eden's voice was barely more than a whisper. "But can it wait? I'm just . . ." She shoved both hands into her hair, pushing it back from her face. "My head's a mess right now, and I need to focus on the show."

"Yeah, that's fine, as long as you're okay," Anna told her. "I just need to know that before I leave. Are you okay, Eden?"

"Honestly? No," Eden said, and the haunted look in her eyes corroborated her words. "I'm not okay. I don't think I've been okay for a long time."

"Wow." Anna blinked at her, desperate to know what that meant. Had Eden realized she wasn't straight after all? Or had she already known when she told Anna she was? Had she said it to keep Anna at a distance? Or was this just an experiment that had confirmed for Eden that she *was* straight? So many questions, and this was obviously not the time to ask them.

Still, Anna remembered the urgent way Eden had kissed her, the way her body had pressed against Anna's as if she couldn't get enough, that little whimper she'd made, as if she were every bit as turned on as Anna had been. Surely that meant . . .

"I need some time to sort myself out," Eden said. "But we're okay, you and I. Our friendship. I mean, we are, right?" Her voice rose at the end, doubt creeping in, and her vulnerability broke Anna's heart.

"Of course we are." Anna stepped forward and flung her arms around Eden, relieved when Eden squeezed her back, clinging to Anna as if she needed this hug as badly as Anna did. "And if you want to talk anything through, I'm here. I can't promise to be a totally impartial ear, because I was involved in that kiss, too, but I'm here for you, anything you need, and no judgment, no matter what you're feeling."

"Thank you," Eden whispered, her breath gusting warm against Anna's neck. "I appreciate that."

Anna gave her another squeeze and then released her, because her body was overheating the longer she stayed in Eden's arms, memories of that kiss flooding her senses. And no matter how much she'd enjoyed it, she couldn't do it again, at least not until Eden had sorted out whatever she needed to sort.

Because Anna's crush was so much more than that now. Real feelings were involved. She could fall for Eden so easily, if she hadn't already. Eden had the power to break her heart the way no one had since Camille. Eden could have her kicked off this tour if things between them went south. Eden had the power to destroy her, even if right now, she was the one who looked destroyed, staring at Anna out of eyes brimming with a mixture of affection and panic.

They'd destroy each other if they weren't careful.

Anna took a step toward the door, suddenly as eager to escape as Eden had been earlier. Where would they go from here? Could they really stay friends after that kiss? Anna couldn't imagine watching TV in bed with her ever again without reliving their kiss, and yet she couldn't really imagine dating her either. She'd filed Eden in her brain as straight and off limits, and now she was at a loss. "I'm just going to . . ."

Eden nodded. "See you in a little while for the show."

"Yep." Anna's voice was too high pitched. Could Eden see her spiraling emotions? "So . . . bye."

"Bye."

Anna managed to walk to the door when her feet were itching to run. This time, it was her turn to flee.

Eden wished she weren't such a creature of habit, but here she was. It would cause too many questions from her team if she deviated from her usual preshow routine, so a mere hour after the kiss that rocked her world, she sat beside Paris in the car bound for the arena while Anna rode in the seat behind her. They were both trying to act like nothing was wrong, like they hadn't just shared the world's most unexpected kiss in the middle of a Thursday afternoon.

At the arena, Eden was ushered to the stage for her sound check. She felt like she was on autopilot, going through the motions as she stared blankly into the empty arena. Afterward, she headed to her dressing room for a light dinner. Tonight, Paris had gotten her a protein-packed salad, loaded with eggs and chicken to fuel her through the show. Her stomach was so tight, she could barely eat, but she knew she'd regret it later if she didn't force at least some of it down.

Desperate for a distraction from her chaotic thoughts, she turned on the TV in her dressing room and watched a business-makeover reality show where the host was renovating a failing bar. The bar owner was a pretty blonde who reminded her of Anna, and *God*, Eden's head was a mess.

At 7:30, Paris knocked on her door. Eden always watched the first thirty minutes of Anna's performance before she started getting ready for her own. Why did all her routines for this tour involve Anna? She could feign a headache, but honestly, the best thing she could probably do right now was to stick to her schedule.

The quickest way to regain control was to act like tonight was any other night. So she let Paris lead her to the darkened area beside the stage where she could watch without being seen.

There in the shadows, she watched Anna take the stage in shimmering silver pants and a rainbow-striped tank top. The rainbow was made of sequins, causing Anna to sparkle from head to foot beneath the spotlight. Her hair was down, tumbling over her shoulders in messy waves.

Gone were her high ponytail and athletic wear. Anna had tweaked her appearance for the tour to help shed her teen-star image, and it was working, in Eden's opinion, anyway. Anna looked more mature, all right, and God, she was beautiful.

Eden's heart sped at the sight of her. That tank top clung to her chest, outlining the shape of her breasts. What would they feel like in Eden's hands? Her gaze dropped to the swell of Anna's hips as she swayed to the beat of the song. Eden remembered the feel of Anna beneath her, those soft curves pressed against her body.

Just thinking about it flooded her with heat. What did that mean? Eden's breath hitched. She'd finally felt all-consuming passion for the first time in her life, and she'd felt it for a woman. What else could it possibly mean? But she couldn't . . . she just couldn't wrap her head around it yet.

Anna was a glittery rainbow up there onstage. She embodied pride. She knew all the terminology and had a diverse fan base that represented every color in that rainbow. She was secure in her identity, confident about who she was.

Eden didn't feel comfortable even *thinking* she might not be straight. It wasn't that she was homophobic. No, her discomfort stemmed from somewhere else, and while she wasn't ready to look too hard at herself yet, she suspected it was good old-fashioned impostor syndrome.

She felt deeply uncomfortable at the thought of claiming a label or wearing a pride flag on her clothing. She didn't fit in with the queer community the way Anna did. Eden wasn't even comfortable using the word "queer," no matter how many times she'd heard Anna say it.

She was so clueless she'd apparently gone thirty-six years without experiencing the kind of passion most people enjoyed all the time. They were writing books and movies and songs about it, and she'd been trying to imitate them, unaware she was even missing out.

How could she have misunderstood herself so completely? Heat flooded her system again, and this time it was embarrassment. Discomfort. She wanted to crawl out of her own skin. She wanted to curl up in her bed and stay there until she'd figured herself out. The last thing she wanted tonight was to get on that stage and perform for twenty thousand people.

Onstage, Anna was singing "Love Me, Love You," a powerful ballad about self-love. Eden's ears rang with the thousands of voices singing along with her, the fans reacting to Anna's music. Eden had never had an opening act who was so popular, who got the fans in their seats right at 7:30 to see her. She had no doubt she was witnessing a star in the making.

Had Anna wanted to kiss Eden? Was she attracted to her, or had she just reacted to the moment? Eden knew that Anna still idolized her, at least on some level, despite their friendship. But was it more than that? Were the fans onto something with #Edanna?

Eden wished she had someone she could talk this through with. But while she was friendly with Paris and the rest of her team, she couldn't confide in them about something like this. They were her employees, after all. She considered Stella a friend, but she was straight and happily married, and while she wasn't Eden's employee, she was her manager, which still felt awkward. Calling Zach felt even more awkward.

Eden's only real friend at the moment was Anna, and despite what she'd said earlier, Eden couldn't talk to her about this. She couldn't dissect that kiss with the woman she'd kissed, the woman she wanted more than she'd known it was possible to want someone. No, like it or not, Eden was going to have to process this on her own.

She squeezed her eyes shut and exhaled. Paris would be here any minute to take her backstage, and she had to get herself together. She'd performed on difficult days before—days when she had a headache or cramps, days when she'd had a horrible fight with her parents or read something awful about herself online. This was no different.

"Ready?" Paris said, touching Eden's arm to get her attention. Eden squared her shoulders with a nod. "Yes."

When she took the stage that night, Eden felt her world shift into balance for the first time since the kiss. The music poured through her, centering her. As always, onstage she was in control. Here, she belonged. Eden worked her way through the choreography of her opening number, feeling like she was supercharged, like the emotional energy she'd been suppressing since that afternoon had finally found an outlet.

Before her, the crowd was on their feet, dancing and singing. Eden smiled for the first time in hours, relaxing into the familiar comfort of the stage. This was her happy place, surrounded by thousands of people who loved her. There was nothing like it in the world.

But when she blinked, she was remembering other happy moments. Sightseeing with Anna. Quiet afternoons watching TV together in bed. Anna made her happy. Eden blinked again, clearing the thoughts away.

As the song ended, she waved to the crowd. "Good evening, Denver! I hope you're ready to dance, because we've got a fun night ahead. I think you might recognize this next song." She winked as the opening beat of "Daydreamer" began to play.

The crowd screamed, smiling faces as far as she could see. Sometimes she resented having to sing this song night after night. She'd recorded it when she was sixteen, back when she'd had little say over the type of music she made. She'd been singing it for twenty years now, at least a decade since she'd gotten sick of it, but seeing the excitement on the fans' faces, she'd happily perform it for twenty more.

She'd sing this song every night for the rest of her life if it meant she got to do *this*.

"I love you, Eden!" someone screamed.

She grinned. "I love you too."

The show passed in a blur of choreography and costume changes, and before she knew it, Anna had joined her onstage for their "After Midnight" duet. Anna wore the purple dress tonight, reminding Eden how she'd told those fans in the elevator about it.

Had that really only been a few hours ago? It felt like a lifetime. Everything in Eden seemed to sparkle as she faced Anna, like her emotions had taken on the qualities of the sequins on her costume. Her brain short-circuited when Anna's arm brushed against hers, and for a moment, she feared she'd lose the song the way she had that night in Vegas.

Worse, she feared she'd ruined their friendship with that kiss. But then Anna smiled at her, and everything inside Eden calmed. They'd be okay. There was no other option.

The connection between them—platonic or not—was too important to lose.

She and Anna danced around each other as the crowd cheered and sang along, as #EDANNA posters were thrust in the air and cell phones snapped photos that would be all over the internet in minutes. If they only knew she and Anna had actually kissed . . .

Anna left, and Eden finished the show, feeling more like herself with each song. When she left the stage that night, her spirits were high. As usual, Anna greeted her in the hallway backstage with a hug and excited ramblings about her favorite parts of the night. This was familiar, comfortable, good.

"You were on fire tonight, Eden," Paris told her as they rode back to the hotel. "I can't remember the last time I saw you pour so much of yourself into a show."

"Really?" Eden asked, hyperaware that Anna was sitting behind her, hearing every word and knowing exactly where Eden's energy had come from.

Paris nodded. "You lost a bit of your spark last year, with the divorce and everything, but ever since your Grammy performance, it's like I've been watching you come alive a little bit more each night."

The Grammy performance. The first night she'd performed with Anna. Eden's skin prickled uncomfortably at Paris's observation, but she forced a gracious smile. "Thank you."

Eden slept fitfully that night. Her dreams were frantic, a repetitive sequence where she was trying to get to the arena and just couldn't make it. She was rushing through a mazelike building, unable to find the stage. She woke, heart racing, anxiety prickling through her system.

She'd had this dream before. When she'd googled what it meant, she'd found that this kind of dream generally meant you were feeling, well . . . lost. As she blinked into her darkened bedroom, hands fisted in the sheet beneath her, that had never felt more true.

CHAPTER SEVENTEEN

Anna tugged Eden's hand, urging her down the sidewalk. For a week, Eden had declined Anna's attempts to hang out, obviously doing her best to put some distance between them, but Anna had finally won her over. They were in Chicago. It was Anna's first time in the Windy City, and she was determined to do some sightseeing.

So here they were, strolling through Millennium Park like a couple of tourists. Neither of them had mentioned the kiss since right after it happened. Eden seemed to still be processing her feelings—or *ignoring* her feelings—and maybe that was for the best.

Dating a mentor? Anna had been there, done that, and had the emotional scars to prove it. She needed to protect her heart. If only she could convince her body not to react every time she was near Eden, every time she thought about her or remembered the all-consuming heat of that kiss. God, an ill-advised kiss had no right to be so *hot*.

"It's so hot today," Eden said.

Anna startled, because it felt like Eden had read her mind, but of course she meant the weather. And yeah, she had a point. Chicago in June was a lot hotter than Anna had expected. "Feels like we brought San Antonio's weather with us."

"Less humid," Eden commented.

"Have you been here before?" Anna asked. "And by 'been here,' I mean, have you left your hotel room and explored the city?"

Eden smirked. "Yes, I've been here *and* explored the city. I'm not a total hermit."

"Only a partial hermit, then?"

Eden cocked her head, looking down the path ahead, where the infamous "bean" sculpture had come into view, gleaming a shiny silver beneath the midday sun. "I stayed here for a month while Zach was filming a movie, and we went out together a lot."

"Oh." Anna bristled. The last thing she wanted to talk about right now was Eden's ex-husband. "So you don't mind going out in public with a big, strong man to protect you?"

"You know that's not true." Eden sounded faintly offended. "My protection detail is headed by a woman, after all."

"Right. Sorry." Anna wasn't sure why she'd said that in the first place. Misplaced jealousy, if she had to guess.

"Anyway, Zach gets a thrill out of being recognized, so he loved the attention we got when we went out together."

"And it didn't bother him that that kind of attention bothered you?"

Eden sighed. "It wasn't like that. He didn't drag me against my will. That was just how we lived. I didn't mind it at first, but somewhere along the way, I got tired of being photographed everywhere I went. I started to dread it, and so, after the divorce, I did what I could to lower my public profile. I'm fine being photographed at events or anywhere I'm putting in an official appearance, but I don't like it anymore when I'm just trying to go about my life."

"I think that's totally fair, and I'm glad you've set boundaries for yourself that way."

"And I'm glad you've shown me a way to have my cake and eat it, too, so to speak," Eden said. "With Zach, we were almost trying to create a scene when we went out. I hadn't really tried to be incognito.

I guess I just assumed I couldn't. To be honest, I'm still a little anxious being in a big park full of people like this. What if someone recognized me and everyone mobbed us? We're so outnumbered."

Anna glanced around them, seeing the park with new eyes. It was true that they could create a mob scene if Eden was recognized. Anna had never really experienced that. She still got a thrill from being recognized, but she wanted Eden to feel comfortable. "Let's take our picture with the bean and then find a less crowded part of the park."

Eden nodded. "It's called Cloud Gate, you know."

"What?"

Eden pointed toward the bean-shaped sculpture before them, the one Anna had seen in a million photos but never in person. "That thing is called Cloud Gate."

"You're pulling my leg."

"No, I'm not. Google it." Eden led the way toward the bean, which was heavily surrounded by tourists.

Anna pulled out her phone and did just that. "Holy shit. You're right!"

Eden raised an eyebrow as if to say, "Aren't I usually?"

"How did you know that?"

"I did some press while I was here with Zach. One of the radio hosts corrected me when I called it the bean. He was being a smart-ass, but he was right."

"Huh." Anna squinted at the sculpture. "I don't get it. Cloud Gate?"

"I think it has to do with how you see the reflection of the clouds on it." Eden shrugged.

"I guess. Okay, this looks like it's as close as we're going to get without being caught up in that crowd. Selfie?"

Eden nodded. She raised her right arm as if to wrap it around Anna's shoulders, then froze and dropped it, and just like that, their tentative return to the friend zone shattered. Now they were both thinking about the kiss, both eyeing each other warily. Anna's pulse picked up speed, and she wondered if Eden's had too.

Anna wanted to groan in frustration. She hated when things got awkward. It wasn't like her to fumble around with someone like this, not talking about the elephant in the room. She hadn't felt this powerless since she'd been with Camille. At the thought, she flung a hand onto Eden's shoulder, effectively crumbling the wall Eden had thrust between them.

"Just friends posing for a picture," Anna said unnecessarily as she held her phone up in front of them.

Eden smiled for the camera, looking as easy-breezy as ever, as if she hadn't just made things weird by refusing to touch Anna.

Anna snapped several photos, then pocketed her phone and led the way toward what she hoped was an exit. "The lake's nearby, right? Lake Michigan?"

Eden nodded. "It is. There are some nice walking paths along the waterfront. Want to?"

"Yes." That sounded perfect.

They made their way through the park and onto the paved walkway that led along the waterfront. Lake Michigan spread before them, so vast it might as well have been the ocean, except that it lacked the salty scent of the sea. Anna stared out at it as her hair whipped around her face.

"Nice, hmm?" Eden said.

"Yeah." Anna glanced at her. They were both trying so hard to pretend everything was normal between them, but it wasn't. Maybe it would never be normal again after that kiss. How could it? Anna was dying to know what Eden was thinking, what she was feeling. Had it been a fluke or something more? Unfortunately for her, Eden's expression was as hard to read as ever.

Wordlessly, they started walking. The path was busy, bustling with people out walking and jogging. Eden looked tense, staring at her feet to avoid making eye contact with anyone to the point where Anna wondered if she was even taking in their scenery. Maybe coming here today had been a mistake.

"Ready to call it a day?" Anna asked.

"Yes." Eden's relief was palpable. "Sorry. There are just too many people, and I swear that group over there is watching us."

Anna looked where she'd indicated, spotting a group of young people who *did* seem to be paying close attention. One woman held her cell phone in front of herself as if she was videoing them. Had they been recognized? "You're right. Let's get out of here."

Anna led Eden briskly in the opposite direction. Beside her, Eden pulled out her phone, presumably to text Taylor. When Anna glanced over her shoulder, the group was following them. One of them was wearing a T-shirt with Anna's face on it. Definitely fans. She pursed her lips. Why was she running away from her fans? She *loved* her fans.

But she'd promised Eden that she'd do everything she could to keep these outings under wraps. Eden feared being mobbed—plus she seemed to need to be in control of her situation, and they definitely weren't in control here.

"The car's pulling around to get us, and Taylor's headed this way just in case." Eden sounded vaguely out of breath. They weren't walking that fast. She must be more anxious than Anna had realized.

"Okay. Worst case, we have to pose for some pictures." That sentence didn't feel right in Anna's mouth. Posing for pictures was something she enjoyed. Once she'd gotten Eden safely to the car, maybe she'd come back and greet her fans on her own.

After Camille, Anna had promised herself that she wouldn't compromise herself for anyone again. She wouldn't go against her gut. And yet here she was, avoiding a difficult but necessary conversation about that kiss and rushing out of the park to avoid her fans. Anna didn't like the way she felt about either.

They kept walking. The group of fans was still following them, and while Anna was trying not to be obvious about checking over her shoulder, she was pretty sure there were more of them now. The woman in front was definitely filming them on her phone. She wasn't even trying to be subtle about it now.

"I have a bad feeling about this," Eden muttered.

"We're fine," Anna said, increasingly annoyed that she couldn't just turn around and greet her fans. "Taylor will be here any minute."

Eden didn't respond. They walked for a few moments in strained silence, and then all hell broke loose. With a shriek, several people ran toward them from the path ahead. Eden froze, and when Anna glanced at her, she wore her stage smile, but it was tense at the edges. The group from behind caught up to them, and everyone was talking at once, cell phones held overhead.

"Oh my God!" someone screamed.

"Eden! Eden, over here!"

"Anna! I love you so much, can I—"

Anna didn't hear the rest because someone grabbed her arm, spinning her sideways.

"Say hi, Anna." The woman who'd been filming them held her phone in Anna's face. "You're live on Instagram!"

"Hi, everyone," Anna said cheerfully. She waved for the camera and then turned to look for Eden, who was several feet away, completely surrounded by fans. They were all waving phones in her face and vying for her attention.

"Can I have a selfie?" someone asked.

"Sure," Anna agreed, leaning in to pose for a quick photo.

"You were my role model when I came out," the girl, who didn't look more than sixteen, told Anna. "I can't believe I'm meeting you right now. This is so wild!"

Anna gave her a hug, touched by the girl's words. Moments like this were the reason she'd always been so open about her sexuality. She'd been lucky to have a supportive family behind her every step of the way, but not everyone had that, so if she could make it even a tiny bit easier for her queer fans, she was honored to do so. "Thank you. That means a lot."

More phones were shoved in Anna's face, along with various photos and other items people wanted her to sign. Someone grabbed the back of her shirt, and she felt a tug on her ponytail. That wasn't cool. She'd almost lost sight of Eden now, and seriously, where had all these people come from?

Anna posed for selfies and signed shirts, photos, and cell phone cases, trying to work her way closer to Eden, but Eden kept drifting past her reach. No matter how hard Anna tried, Eden kept getting farther away.

Anna's stomach clenched uncomfortably. She was crushed by fans on all sides now. People were touching her and jostling her and yelling in her face. This was out of control, even a little bit scary. With a sinking feeling, she realized Eden had been right all along.

"You two were so cute together walking through the park," someone said. "Do you always go sightseeing together before a show?"

"Um, not that often, but I'd never been to Chicago before." Anna managed not to flinch when someone stomped on her foot.

"Is it true that you're dating?" someone asked.

"Yeah! We need answers about Edanna!" someone else shouted.

"My private life is private for a reason," Anna told them. "But I'm not dating anyone at the moment, sorry to disappoint."

"Oh, come on . . ."

"Tell us the truth, Anna!"

The shouting intensified, and she really couldn't breathe with so many bodies pressed against her. *Where is Eden?* Anna couldn't see her. Panic clawed at her throat. As she desperately scanned the crowd for Eden, she felt like a naive asshole for not taking Eden's concerns seriously.

Shouting Eden's name felt like a bad idea. For whatever reason, she didn't think she should let the crowd know she was afraid. She needed to play it cool until Taylor got here. What was taking her so long, anyway?

"Anna! Oh my God, Anna . . . ," someone screeched in her ear, and she was pulled in for another photo.

When she looked around, all she could see were arms and cell phones. Several people had mentioned a live stream, which might explain why the number of fans seemed to keep multiplying exponentially.

"All right, everyone. I'm going to need you all to take three big steps back." Taylor's voice boomed above the din, and Anna exhaled in relief.

The crush of bodies around her lessened slightly, but Taylor didn't come to her rescue. She headed in the other direction, hopefully to find Eden and get her the hell out of here. Anna kept smiling and posing for photos, wondering in desperation if Taylor was going to leave her here. Anna wasn't her responsibility, after all.

Maybe it was time for Anna to hire a security person of her own. Then she felt a firm hand on her shoulder. "Come with me."

She turned to find Eden's driver standing beside her. She'd never been so grateful to see someone as she allowed him to lead her through the throng of fans. Ahead, she could see Taylor with Eden, and relief flooded her all over again. Anna didn't say anything as they walked. Eden kept her head up, the picture of nonchalance, when Anna knew she must be anything but.

Taylor hustled them through the park and into the waiting car. Anna flopped against the seat, breathing hard. She was sweaty and frazzled and felt a sudden need for a shower after having so many hands and bodies touching her.

She twisted to face Eden. "You can say it."

Eden's hair was somewhat disheveled, and her neck was splotchy, but overall she looked more composed than Anna would have expected. Then again, that was Eden. She was always composed. That was why it had thrown Anna so much when she broke down in tears after they kissed. She looked at Anna. "Say what?"

"You told me so," Anna said. "Because you did. You *so* did."

Eden nodded and turned away, staring out the window as the car pulled away from the curb. And she wasn't okay. Anna could see that now. Her hands, which were clenched in her lap, shook, and she was breathing funny, like she was trying not to hyperventilate. Of course, Eden would panic quietly when she was in public. She must have been terrified out there, and it was all Anna's fault.

"I'm so sorry," she whispered.

Eden didn't respond. She swallowed, and Anna heard the click of her dry throat. She reached for a bottle of water from the center console and handed it to Eden.

"Some fans spotted you while you were taking selfies in front of the bean," Taylor said from the front seat. "They started following you, live streaming on Instagram, and every fan in the area—which there are a lot of, because of the show tonight—flooded into the park to try to spot you. I apologize. I should have stayed closer."

"It's all right." Eden sounded hoarse. She cleared her throat and then took a drink from the bottle Anna had given her. "I guess it was bound to happen sooner or later."

"I had no idea." Anna clutched her seat belt. "I'd never experienced . . . I mean, there were so many, and they were so pushy . . ."

Eden just nodded. She didn't say anything else for the rest of the drive.

That was the end of their sightseeing excursions. For the next few days, Anna barely saw Eden, except when they were at the arena. But she missed her. She missed hanging out with her, even if it meant staying in one of their hotel rooms. They had watched half of the first season of *How to Get Away with Murder* together before everything got weird, so on Friday morning, she texted Eden.

Anna:

We need to catch up with our favorite murderers!

Eden:

Yes, we do.

Anna:

This afternoon?

Eden:

Sure. Come to my room after lunch.

It was all so polite, but Anna's pulse was already racing. Sure, she was looking forward to watching a few more episodes of *How to Get Away with Murder* with Eden, but mostly, she was excited to hang out with her. It was time to put that kiss behind them.

Eden obviously didn't want to talk about it. Anna could imagine that it would be shocking for a control freak like Eden to realize she was attracted to a woman after having only been attracted to men up until now . . . assuming that was what she felt, because honestly Anna had no idea what was going on in her head at this point.

But if Eden was going to keep throwing up walls, Anna would bridge them by doing everything in her power to repair their friendship. It seemed like the safest option, for both of their sakes.

Anna messed around in her room, ordered room service, and enjoyed a delicious pasta dish she'd never heard of—bucatini, who knew? It was like spaghetti that was hollow inside, served in a yummy veggie sauce.

Then she headed to Eden's room, briefly wondering if she should still be walking the halls by herself after what had happened in Chicago. Maybe she'd gotten too comfortable in her anonymity, because her celebrity had definitely risen since she'd been on tour. David said her overall streaming stats were up—like, *way* up.

#Edanna mentions online were also way up. The video of Anna and Eden in Millennium Park had gone viral, as had fan speculation about their relationship. Were they friends or more than friends? Their fans couldn't stop talking about it.

Some of their most dedicated fans were now visiting popular tourist spots on show days, hoping to bump into them. Unfortunately for them, Anna and Eden's sightseeing days were over.

She made it to Eden's room without being spotted and knocked, butterflies dancing in her stomach. They hadn't been alone in a hotel room together since . . . well, since the day of the kiss.

The door opened, and Eden stood there in the purple hoodie and black leggings. She waved Anna into the room. "Want me to order popcorn?"

"I just ate a big lunch, so I'm fine without it, but totally order some if you want."

Eden shrugged. "I'm pretty full too. And tired. Definitely reached that part of the tour where exhaustion hits."

"Yeah, I hear you." Anna followed her into the bedroom.

Eden walked around to the far side of the bed and perched on the edge. "Thank goodness the break's coming up."

Anna toed out of her shoes, then sat cross-legged, facing Eden. It was a king-size bed; plenty of room between them. They used to just flop onto the bed together without a care in the world, but they were both clearly overthinking it now. "You were smart to put that in the schedule."

"I learned from past experience. After two months of shows almost every night, I'm always ready for a week off, a chance to rest and stay in one place for more than a night or two. I'm so sick of packing up every morning."

"Is that your plan for the break, then?" Anna asked, trying not to notice how weird it was, the two of them on opposite sides of the bed. "Just rest?"

"Pretty much. I'm going to my house in Vermont, so there will be hiking too."

"Jealous," Anna said. "That sounds awesome."

"What are your plans?" Eden asked.

Anna shrugged. "Headed home, I guess. I'm sure Nelle is in dire need of some spoiling."

Eden smiled. "Who's watching her while you're on tour?"

"Zoe. I have a built-in cat sitter with her living next door. It's so easy for her to pop by and check on Nelle."

"Makes sense." Eden reached for the remote control to the TV. "You were right about this show. I've been dying to get back to it and find out who killed Lila."

"Let's do it, then." Anna was still sitting cross-legged on her side of the bed, but now she scooted back to lean against the headboard.

Eden started the show and settled in. There was a lot more space between them than there used to be, but just being here, watching TV together, felt like they were taking an important step back toward normalcy.

The show began, and Anna relaxed against the headboard. She'd seen the whole series before, but there was so much going on plot-wise that she was picking up on lots of things she'd missed the first time. On the other side of the bed, Eden had leaned forward, watching the TV with a look of intense concentration.

Watching her watch the show was distracting.

"Oh my God," Eden exclaimed during an intense moment. "I can't believe he—" She cut herself off as the scene took another dramatic turn. "Shit!"

Anna loved seeing her reactions. She remembered being just as shocked when she'd watched the first time. Eventually, Anna quit watching her and got sucked into the show. She lay on her belly, facing the TV. Eden moved to lie beside her, bumping into Anna in the process. Anna had just registered the warmth of her body before Eden lurched to the far side of the bed. It was such an overreaction that Anna wanted to scream in frustration.

On the TV, someone *did* scream, a loud shriek that filled the room, making them both jump. Anna looked at Eden, who stared back, eyes wide and wary.

"Not talking about it isn't working," Anna blurted. "Not if you're going to keep acting like this. Come on, Eden. This is ridiculous."

"I—" Eden's gaze darted to the TV and back to Anna.

"Maybe I should just go." Anna slid off the bed and stood. So many conflicting emotions swirled inside her. She wanted things to go back to normal between them, but it just wasn't happening. It had been over a week now since their kiss, and they still couldn't be around each other without making things weird.

"Don't go." Eden scrambled across the bed and grabbed Anna's hand. She gave a gentle tug at the same time Anna tried to pull her hand free. The combined effort caused them to stumble into each other, bodies flush, breasts pressed together. Eden exhaled, but it sounded more like a whimper.

Anna couldn't breathe. Arousal swamped her senses, hijacking her brain so that instead of running for the door, she leaned in to smell the rose-petal scent of Eden's skin, close enough that she felt the warmth of Eden's breath on her cheek, and then . . .

Eden's lips met hers for a desperate kiss, the kind of kiss that had Anna's hands fisting in the soft cotton of Eden's hoodie as she pulled her closer. Eden's eyes were squeezed shut as if she couldn't face what she was doing, and . . . this wasn't right.

Anna pushed backward out of Eden's arms. Tears rose hot and furious in her eyes. "I can't do this. We can't keep doing this!"

Eden blinked at her, cheeks pink and chest heaving.

Anna took another step back. "This isn't fair, Eden. You told me you're straight, and then you . . . then you kiss me . . . *twice*. I think it's pretty obvious at this point that I'm attracted to you, but you can't keep yanking me around like this."

Eden's eyes widened, glossy with tears. "I'm not . . . that's not . . ." She gulped. "I'm so sorry, Anna." Her voice was nothing but a whisper now. Tears spilled over her cheeks, and when she pushed a hand into her hair, it was shaking. "I never meant to do . . . anything you just said."

Anna blew out a breath. "Okay. It's time. It's *past* time. We need to talk."

CHAPTER EIGHTEEN

Eden sat in the middle of the bed, knees drawn against her chest and arms wrapped tightly around them. She couldn't meet Anna's eyes, so she looked down at herself instead. She was wearing the purple hoodie. Anna's hoodie. Of course she was.

Anna had shut off the TV, and now the room was so quiet, Eden's ears rang with it.

"Talk to me." Anna's voice was so gentle, with none of the hurt or anger she'd expressed after they kissed a few minutes ago.

Eden felt like she was in one of those fun houses where the furniture was mounted to the ceiling so you felt like you were upside down. Her equilibrium was way off. She felt like she might topple over, like she had no idea which way was up.

Anna was right to insist they talk, and yet . . . Eden had never felt more vulnerable. She was terrified to speak these words out loud. Once she said them, there was no taking them back, and she still wasn't sure if she could trust what she was feeling.

"I don't know where to start," she whispered.

"Wherever feels easiest," Anna said. "Just say something—anything—and we'll go from there."

"I wasn't lying . . . when I told you I was straight. I am, or I was, or . . . I thought I was." She'd barely started, and already she wasn't making sense.

"Okay." Anna sounded unfazed by this confession.

Eden, by contrast, was starting to hyperventilate. Her head spun, and she couldn't catch her breath. "I don't know . . ."

"It's okay." Anna slid closer so her shoulder bumped against Eden's. "You don't have to label yourself before you're ready . . . or ever, if you don't want to. How you identify is so personal, and you're under no obligation to share it with anyone."

"I feel like . . . like I don't know myself anymore," Eden whispered. Talking about this made it feel so much more real, like Eden was being yanked out of her own self-denial. Despite the thick hoodie, she felt naked. Exposed.

"You know it's not unusual for people to come out later in life, right? So many people in their thirties or forties—or even older than that—realize they're bi or gay or trans or nonbinary or whatever. Gender and sexuality can be fluid, and the older we get, the better we understand ourselves anyway. So if you're going through something like that now, you should know that it happens literally all the time."

"Really?" Eden peeked at Anna over her knees. She hadn't known that. She'd assumed that if you were gay, you just knew—that she should have known in her teens. Didn't most people?

"Totally," Anna told her. "And you had such a sheltered upbringing in a way. You spent your teens rocketing to superstardom. You told me you'd never been kissed when you signed your first contract and that you had people controlling every aspect of your life, so you probably didn't have a chance to experiment. If you assumed you were straight, and now you've realized you're not . . . that's really not so surprising, when you think about it."

"Wow." Eden blinked rapidly, looking at her knees. Everything Anna had just said rang so true . . . terrifyingly true.

Anna wrapped an arm around her shoulders and squeezed. "There's no right or wrong answer here, only what feels right to you. And that can change with time. That's okay too."

Eden's lungs hurt. She was breathing too fast, and her muscles were so tight. Why was this so hard? Anna was being so gentle and patient, and still Eden wanted to crawl out of her own skin.

I think it's pretty obvious at this point that I'm attracted to you.

Anna's words drifted back to her, and something in Eden settled at the memory. Anna was attracted to her. Eden was attracted to Anna. Maybe . . . maybe it was as simple as that.

"I don't think I'm straight," she whispered, and just like that, the pressure in her chest eased. She gulped in a breath and met Anna's eyes. "In fact, I know I'm not."

"Congratulations." Anna beamed at her, and that was the last thing Eden would have expected her to say. "I'm so happy for you that you've learned this about yourself, and I'm honored that you felt comfortable enough to tell me."

"Well, kissing you was probably a clue." Eden's cheeks burned.

Anna laughed, giving Eden's shoulders another squeeze. "Not necessarily. A lot of straight women want to try kissing a woman just to see what it's like or for a dare or whatever. But to be honest, you don't kiss like a straight woman."

"God." Eden squeezed her eyes shut, torn between mortification and curiosity. In the end, curiosity won out. "What does that mean?"

"It means you kissed me like you enjoyed it, like you were trying not to but couldn't stop yourself."

"Oh," she managed. That was pretty damn accurate, but she felt oddly vulnerable for Anna to have read her so easily.

"Hey." Anna nudged her shoulder. "Look at me."

Eden opened her eyes, meeting Anna's steady gaze.

"I told you after that first kiss that I'm here for you, and I meant it. I'd love to help you work through this, but if you don't want to talk anymore right now, that's okay too."

"Thank you," Eden said. "And I'm truly sorry . . . for kissing you and making you feel awkward. I never meant to do that."

"Hey, it's okay. Neither of those kisses was one sided. I was very much involved. I just needed to have this conversation with you before anything else happened." Anna paused. "I have my own hesitations about getting involved with you, because . . . well, Camille really messed with my head, but maybe that's a conversation for another day."

Eden nodded. She felt overwhelmed and just *exhausted*. This conversation had come at the tail end of a grueling few months. "Do you think we could just watch TV together for a little longer, but not hiding on opposite sides of the bed this time?"

"Yeah," Anna said with a gentle smile. "I'd like that."

They restarted the episode they'd been watching earlier since they'd both gotten distracted and missed a good part of it. This time, they snuggled together in the middle of the bed, and Eden felt her world right itself. In Anna's arms, her equilibrium returned. Her pulse was still a little faster than it should be, but she didn't think it had anything to do with fear or stress. That was her reaction to Anna, the reaction she finally felt comfortable acknowledging.

She rested her head on Anna's chest. It felt so good, so *comfortable*. Even though Eden felt like she'd fumbled the entire conversation and hadn't really said anything she needed to say, she felt closer to Anna than ever.

When the credits rolled at the end of the episode, Anna reached over and stopped it before the next episode began to play. They didn't have time to watch another one before they had to leave for the arena. Eden was so relaxed right now, so tired, she had no idea where she'd find the energy to perform.

Anna rolled to face her, trailing a hand through Eden's hair. "Okay?"

Eden nodded as a shiver of excitement raced through her. She moved closer, resting a hand on Anna's hip. It felt unfamiliar, touching a woman this way, but at the same time, it felt like the most natural thing in the world. They smiled at each other, and Eden felt the last of her tension drain away.

"Can I kiss you?" she whispered. "On purpose this time?"

"Yes," Anna murmured, her gaze dropping to Eden's lips.

Eden closed the gap between them, brushing her lips against Anna's. Everything about this kiss was different from its predecessors. Those had been clumsy, unplanned, and frantic. This one was . . . soft. It was warm and sensual and made Eden's toes curl against the duvet. She'd thought that was another myth, another thing people said but didn't really mean.

Anna's hand brushed against the bare skin on Eden's lower back. The hoodie must have ridden up, and Anna's fingers on her skin felt like heaven. They also lit her on fire. Eden whimpered, pressing closer. Her heart was racing, and she felt the most exquisite ache in her core. It was so intense that she trembled in Anna's arms.

"Mm," Anna murmured as her fingers traced patterns on Eden's lower back. "Now this is more like it."

"Anna . . ." Eden heard the catch in her voice. She sounded breathless and needy, completely unlike herself.

"Yeah?" Anna's fingers traced the waistband of her leggings, and Eden almost lost her mind. She ached to feel those fingers in other places, even though she knew she wasn't ready. But God, her body was *begging* to be touched.

"I didn't know," she whispered. "I didn't know it could be like this."

Anna pulled back to give her a wicked smile. "Now you know."

Anna had been on cloud nine when she left Eden's suite, but by the time she climbed into bed that night, doubt had begun to creep in. Eden had been all business at the arena tonight, her mask as impenetrable as ever. Was she having second thoughts about the things she'd shared, or was she just being her usual guarded self while they had an audience?

Anna was about to shut off the light when her phone chimed with an incoming text.

Eden:

Thanks for this afternoon 💜

Anna:

my pleasure xx

Anna clutched her phone to her chest. Those four words—plus the heart emoji—dissipated all her insecurities. She was so happy that Eden had texted her, that she seemed comfortable with this latest development in their relationship. She had come out to Anna today, and that was such a big deal. It was a *huge* step for Eden.

This famously private person had trusted Anna with one of her most vulnerable moments, and Anna didn't really have words for how much it meant to her. Eden hadn't explicitly said so, but Anna suspected she was the first person Eden had told, and that was such an honor.

Anna fell asleep with a smile on her face.

The next day was a travel day, which meant a chartered flight on one of the private jets Anna had seen in movies but never ridden on before the start of the tour. This plane had single seats facing each other on either side of the aisle. Eden sat on one side facing Paris, and Anna and Kyrie sat on the other. As they jetted toward Toronto, Eden read on her Kindle while Anna stared out the window, lost in her own thoughts.

"I booked our flight for Sunday," Kyrie told her. "I couldn't get us a nonstop flight during the day, but since I know how much you hate the red-eye, I booked a midmorning flight with a layover in Dallas."

"I'll take a layover over a red-eye anytime," Anna told her. "Thank you."

"Yep," Kyrie said. "I don't know about you, but I'm ready to sleep in my own bed for a few days."

"Yeah. Same." Anna could use a week at home to catch her breath. At the same time, though, she was having such an amazingly fun time on tour, she didn't want it to end. And she was a little worried about what would happen for her and Eden during the break. Would a week alone in Vermont cause Eden to overthink things and pull away from Anna, just when they were starting to explore the possibility of being more than friends?

It seemed like the worst time to spend a week on opposite sides of the country. Well, maybe not quite as bad as if the break had happened right after that first kiss. At least they'd begun to talk now, but still . . . Anna worried.

They landed in Toronto and breezed through a VIP version of customs that Anna hadn't known existed. Once they were checked in at their hotel, Eden and Anna were whisked to a local television station for a scheduled interview. They didn't have a show tonight since the staging components were still on the road from Detroit.

At the station, they were sent to separate dressing rooms, where Anna paced impatiently as she waited for hair and makeup to arrive. Yesterday had been somewhat monumental for Eden, coming out to Anna and then sharing what Anna assumed had been her first real make-out session with a woman. How was she feeling about things today?

They'd seen each other almost constantly since the kiss, but they hadn't had a moment alone, which meant all their interactions had been . . . polite. Other than that text last night, Anna had no idea how Eden was feeling about things.

Before she could stop herself, Anna slipped out of her dressing room. The studio around her bustled with activity, people rushing past carrying tablets and wearing headsets, and a burst of nerves filled her stomach. Live interviews were intimidating. So was sneaking into Eden's dressing room.

She wandered down the hall until she found the door with Eden's name on it. Already breathless, she knocked. The door opened, and Eden smiled at her in a way that immediately smoothed over Anna's nerves. Eden looked relaxed, happy even. Not like a woman with regrets.

"Hi," Anna said. "I just, um, wanted to steal a few minutes with you before things get hectic."

"I love the way you think." Eden pushed the door shut behind Anna and then stepped in close. "May I?" she asked, dropping her gaze to Anna's lips.

"Yes," Anna managed as her heart leaped for joy. This was really happening. *They* were really happening.

Eden's lips brushed against Anna's, and Anna could feel her smiling even before she'd pulled away. "Can't seem to stop doing that."

"Me either." Anna gripped Eden's shirt and hauled her in for another kiss.

Eden gasped, her back arching so that her breasts pressed more firmly against Anna's. She was wearing that hoodie again. Did she wear it every day? As much as Anna loved seeing her in it, she also couldn't help wishing Eden had on fewer clothes.

Anna ducked her head and pressed her lips to Eden's neck, feeling her pulse pounding hard and fast beneath her skin. "You always smell like roses," Anna murmured against Eden's neck. "Drives me crazy."

"It's my lotion." Eden's voice sounded hoarse. Goose bumps had risen beneath Anna's lips, and there was no way Eden was cold under that hoodie. "Anna . . ."

"Yeah?" Anna swirled her tongue over a spot below Eden's ear that was one of Anna's personal favorite places to be kissed, and Eden's gasp seemed to indicate she liked it just as much.

"I can't . . . even remember what I was going to say." Eden gripped Anna's hips, pulling her closer.

Anna was so turned on she could hardly think straight, and . . . it was time to slow things down before they got carried away. She lifted her head to grin at Eden. "Hi."

Eden slow-blinked the way she did when Anna had surprised her. Her pupils nearly eclipsed the blue of her eyes, and there was a lovely flush on her cheeks. "You expect me to be able to speak coherently after you kiss me like that?"

"You're cute." Anna tapped Eden's cheek with her finger, then walked farther into her dressing room, amused to discover that it was a lot bigger and fancier than the one Anna had been assigned. "But we only have a few minutes before someone comes looking for us."

"Maybe you could come to my hotel room later for more of that kissing?" Eden lingered in the middle of the room, something uncertain in her expression.

"I'd love to watch TV and make out with you later." Anna walked to her and pressed another kiss against Eden's lips. "But I also don't want to move too fast while you're still figuring things out."

"Thank you," Eden whispered. "I'm working on that."

"Yeah?" Anna led the way to the couch.

Eden nodded. "I guess I'm still . . . sorting."

"And like I told you before, I'm here for you if there's anything you want to talk through." Anna paused, then pulled Eden in for another hug. "I also just wanted to say congrats again for coming out to yourself and to me. It's such a huge step, and I hope it helps you embrace your authentic self."

"I never thought of it like that," Eden murmured. "Coming out to myself, that is, but that part was really hard."

"It's a big deal, and I'm so proud of you."

Footsteps echoed down the hall outside, and Eden pulled back, casting an anxious glance toward the door. They both exhaled in relief when whoever it was kept walking, but there was a lingering tension in Eden now, the fear of getting caught.

If only they could take some time together away from the frantic pace of the tour. Time to explore what was happening between them. Time they didn't have.

Anna searched for a change of topic, something to lighten the mood. "I have an important question for you before we watch another episode of *How to Get Away with Murder* later."

Eden gave her an inquiring look.

"Do you have a crush on anyone on the show? Like, do you swoon for the ladies in your favorite TV shows the way I do?"

Eden's cheeks immediately darkened, which was an answer in and of itself. She ducked her head. "I, um, I always prefer the female characters. I just didn't know why."

Anna grinned. "So who? Annalise? Laurel? Eve? Just wait until you meet Tegan . . ."

"Annalise for sure," Eden said. "I mean, Viola Davis is impossible to look away from whenever she's on my screen."

"Agreed," Anna said.

"But also . . . Bonnie." Eden looked somewhere between embarrassed and euphoric to be sharing her TV crushes with Anna.

"Ooh, Bonnie," Anna said. "Interesting choice. If you ask me, she gets even hotter in later seasons . . . and also more complicated."

"Guess I'd better keep watching, then." Eden turned to face her, her gaze searching Anna's face. "The break's soon."

"Yeah." Anna swallowed at the reminder that they were about to spend an entire week apart. "I'm really going to miss this . . . you . . . us."

"Come to Vermont with me," Eden said in a rush.

"What?"

"Come with me for the break." Eden's fingers gripped Anna's and squeezed. "My house has two guest rooms, unless . . . well, we can figure it out when we get there, right? But we'll have time to relax and figure things out away from the chaos of the tour."

Anna couldn't stop smiling, because this was the answer to everything she hadn't known how to ask for. "Yes. God, yes."

CHAPTER NINETEEN

"Can't quite get used to seeing you drive a car."

Eden smirked. "You'll see me do a lot of things you're not used to while we're in Vermont."

Anna made a choking noise, and Eden realized belatedly how that sounded. Heat spread over her chest and onto her cheeks. She reached over to swat at Anna where she sat in the passenger seat of their rental car. "Get your mind out of the gutter. I meant hiking and cooking and normal-people things."

"Looking forward to that too," Anna told her with a goofy smile. "Should we stop for groceries before we get to the house?"

Eden gave her an exasperated look. "Have you even met me? Paris already had the basics stocked, but we can put together a list for whatever else we need to have delivered."

"Grocery delivery," Anna said with a laugh. "Got it."

"Good."

"So you don't go out, even here?" Anna asked after a few seconds of silence.

"You're not actually surprised, are you? After what happened in Chicago?"

"Well . . . no, but we're a long way from Chicago." Anna gestured to the farmland passing by outside the window.

She had a point here. This part of Vermont was a world away from the hustle and bustle of the city, and that was exactly why Eden had bought a house here. She loved the old-fashioned farmhouses and roadside produce stands and endless wooded hills.

Eden could drive here. She could sit on her porch with her morning coffee and listen to the birds. She didn't have to adhere to anyone's schedule or expectations. No one was going to take her picture. She could just . . . be.

The radio played a cheerful pop playlist that Anna had carefully curated not to include either of their music. When she was in Vermont, Eden didn't want to hear her own voice. She wanted to sing along to other people's songs.

She and Anna were belting out a Sasha Sol tune when Eden pulled the car into her driveway an hour later. She paused at the gate to input the code. On the other side, the driveway curved, disappearing into the trees. Eden's house was completely hidden from the road, just the way she liked it.

"Prepare me," Anna said. "Do you live in a mansion out here?"

"You'll see," Eden told her, deciding to let Anna wait in suspense a bit longer. In truth, she hoped Anna would like her vacation home. She'd had it custom built and loved every inch. This house was her sanctuary.

She pulled through the gate, and it swung shut behind them. Now she could truly relax. There were only two people inside this fence: she and Anna. Eden's body fizzed with anticipation to spend the week here alone with her. Even if they slept in separate bedrooms, Eden was glad she was here.

Gravel crunched under the tires as she rounded the corner on the driveway and the house came into view. It was a two-story log cabin–style home with plenty of modern accents and amenities inside.

"Oh," Anna said quietly. "It's not what I expected."

"Two thousand square feet," Eden told her. "Not a mansion."

"A cabin." Anna clapped her hands together. "A real log cabin! I'm so excited."

"I'm glad." Eden pulled the car under the carport beside the house. She didn't have a garage, nor did she need one. She didn't often visit in the wintertime, but when she did, she'd hire a car service to drop her at the house, and then she'd stay here the entire time, enjoying the views while she sat in front of a crackling fire.

"Come on," Eden said as she shut off the car. "Let me show you around."

"Yes, please."

They grabbed their bags and lugged them to the side door. Eden unlocked it, and they stepped into the mudroom, where she kept boots, coats, and all the other gear she used to hike on her property throughout the year.

"It's beautiful," Anna said as she rolled her suitcase into the living room. The walls were wood paneled, with exposed beams overhead. A woodstove was the centerpiece of the far wall, facing the sofa. Eden had decorated the walls with paintings from local artists. She'd always been a fan of landscape paintings and loved to bring a bit of the local area into her home.

The main floor was open concept, with the living room, dining area, and kitchen all sharing the space. "There are three bedrooms upstairs," Eden told her. "And that's it. The real star of the house is the view."

"Yeah?" Anna looked at her, smiling happily.

"Mm. We'll go out on the patio later, but first, you can leave your bags in one of the guest rooms . . . at least for now."

"I like the 'at least for now.'" Anna leaned in to give Eden a quick kiss.

Eden's body flushed hot in an instant, and she was grabbing at Anna's hips, pulling her closer. She'd never felt this uncontrollable urge to kiss someone before, the need to touch her and be near her every minute of every day. And that was why she'd brought Anna with her to Vermont . . . to tell her these things, and hopefully more. Hopefully a lot more.

She was thrilled and terrified and dying of anticipation. A confusing cocktail of emotions that left her feeling jumpy as hell. Hopefully, by the end of the week, she'd be settled, because she couldn't take much more of this emotional roller coaster.

Reluctantly, Eden broke the kiss. Already, she felt the ache of arousal burning inside her. Now she understood why people became so obsessed with the person they were dating. She got it now. Oh boy, did she. "Come on," she said, giving Anna's hand a tug. "Let me show you the rooms upstairs."

Anna sat on the sofa in Eden's living room, feet curled beneath herself and a glass of wine in hand. She didn't often drink wine, but it seemed to suit the aesthetic of this romantic Vermont cabin. They'd placed a large grocery order earlier, and Anna was thrilled for the opportunity to cook for Eden this week.

But first, they needed a rest . . . and a conversation. They'd flown in from Toronto that morning, and after two months on the road, they were both exhausted. Anna took another sip of her wine. Eden sat beside her with her head against the cushion, eyes closed and a peaceful look on her face.

Anna couldn't resist the opportunity to lean in and kiss her cheek. "I love being here with you."

Eden's cheek lifted under Anna's lips as she smiled. Then she reached out and tugged Anna closer. Anna snuggled against her with her head on Eden's shoulder. She was contemplating whether to put her wine down and take a nap using Eden as her pillow when she realized Eden was watching her, looking rather serious.

"Okay?" Anna asked.

Eden nodded. "I just . . . can't quite believe you're here, or really . . . *why* you're here."

"The 'why' doesn't have to be important," Anna said, turning so she could meet Eden's eyes. "There's no pressure, I promise."

"It's important to *me*." Eden closed her eyes and blew out a breath, then stared right into Anna's eyes. "I need to say it out loud. I need you to know what's going on in my head, because it's been pretty chaotic in here these last few weeks." Eden tapped her forehead.

"Okay." Anna put down her wine and took one of Eden's hands, offering quiet support.

"Remember when we were texting, way back in LA, and I told you I didn't like romance in books and movies, because it was so unrealistic?"

"Yeah." That wasn't even remotely where she'd expected Eden to begin this conversation.

"I believed that," Eden said quietly. "Because I . . . I'd never felt that before."

"Oh," Anna said, still not entirely sure where this was going.

"I was twenty when I had my first kiss," Eden said. "And it was . . . fine. All the kisses after that were okay, but I didn't really understand why people got so excited about kissing. Or sex." She shrugged, but the movement was stiff.

Anna was starting to catch on now, and if Eden was saying what she thought she was saying . . . *oh wow*. Anna hadn't expected this. She'd assumed Eden was bi or pan, that she'd just never realized she was attracted to women too.

"I didn't get the hype," Eden said. "Sex wasn't bad, but it wasn't great either. I thought the way romance books portrayed sex was made up. People don't really feel that uncontrollable urge to rip each other's clothes off. They don't really feel like they'll *die* if they don't kiss someone."

"Oh, Eden . . ."

Eden trailed a finger down Anna's arm. "A touch can't light you on fire."

Anna's breath hitched.

When Eden lifted her head to meet Anna's eyes, her pupils were blown. She was breathing hard, and *God*, her nipples had tightened beneath her shirt. "I was wrong." Her voice was hoarse. "Anna, I was so wrong."

Anna rested a hand on Eden's knee, leaning closer but not kissing her, just offering support.

"And then you came along," Eden said. "You turned my life upside down, and I didn't understand what was happening. I felt like I was spiraling out of control every time I was around you, and if you've learned anything about me by now, you know I hate to lose control."

"I do know that," Anna breathed.

"At first, I thought we were just really good friends. It's been a while since I've had a real friend, someone I enjoy being around this much. But . . . it was more than that. Obviously." Eden huffed a frustrated laugh. "I finally felt it . . . the need to kiss someone more than I needed air. I felt that. For you."

Anna gulped. "Me too. I felt that for you too."

"But you knew." Eden's tone was anguished. "You knew you were attracted to women. I didn't know I could be attracted to *anyone*, not like this."

Anna could hardly breathe. "What are you saying?"

"I'm saying . . . I'm saying . . ." Eden blinked, and tears spilled over her cheeks. "I don't think I'm bi or pan, like you. I think I'm *only* attracted to women."

"Oh, Eden." Anna lunged forward to kiss her. "God, I can't imagine how you must feel right now, to finally understand yourself like this."

Eden made a frustrated sound. "I feel angry, in a way."

"Why?" Anna slid into her lap, sitting across Eden's thighs so they were facing each other.

Eden's hands slid down Anna's back, settling at her waist. "I feel like I've been lied to, or that I've lied to myself, to be honest. I wasted so many years just . . . not understanding myself, not knowing what I was missing, and I hate that."

"No, no, no. You haven't wasted anything. Oh, Eden. No."

"What if we hadn't met?" Eden asked. Tears were streaming down her cheeks now. "What if I spent my whole life walking around with these blinders on?"

"If it hadn't been me, you would have met someone else. You're just starting to figure yourself out, and that's okay. There's no timetable on coming out, and Eden, even if you had *never* realized you were gay . . . you're more than your sexuality. So much more." She wiped the tears from Eden's face, feeling the way she trembled beneath Anna's touch. "Now tell me more about this 'I'll die if I don't kiss you' feeling."

In response, Eden gripped Anna's leggings, yanking her closer. "Every time I'm around you," she whispered as she brought her mouth to Anna's, kissing her with the kind of desperation she'd described.

"Can I confess a secret now?" Anna asked between kisses. Her hips were flush against Eden's, and already, it was all Anna could do to keep herself still, not to rock into her, but she would never rush Eden before she was ready.

"Please." Eden squirmed beneath her as if it was every bit as hard for her to hold back as it was for Anna.

"I might have realized I liked girls while I was watching your 'Smash' music video."

Eden's eyes widened. "Oh my God, really?"

Anna nodded. "Since we're confessing our deepest secrets today, I've had a crush on you since I was about sixteen."

"That's . . . that's . . ." Eden blinked at her. "I'm not sure what that is."

"Flattering?" Anna suggested hopefully.

Eden laughed. "Yeah, I guess it is. Wait. Did Camille know that? When we met outside the Grammys?"

"No! Oh God, I would never have joked about a celebrity crush when I was with her."

"Why not?" Eden asked.

"Because . . ." Anna slid over so she was sitting beside Eden instead of in her lap. "She was so jealous. She would have freaked out."

"What was it like with Camille?" Eden asked, turning sideways so her legs rested over Anna's. "Since we're sharing. I mean, if it's not too hard to talk about."

"It's hard, but . . . I don't mind telling you about her. In fact, I think I *need* to tell you about her so you can understand where my head is when I worry about repeating past mistakes." Anna blew out a breath.

"I had a crush on her almost as soon as I started training with her, but I never dreamed she would feel the same way. She's older than me and so sophisticated. In my eyes, she could have anyone she wanted."

"In my eyes, why would anyone *not* choose you?" Eden said.

Anna pressed a hand against her chest, giggling. "Stop! You're going to give me a complex. Anyway, one night after my session, she kissed me, and before I knew it, we were dating. She took me to all these fancy places, and I was so in awe of being with her, but in hindsight, that was part of the problem."

"An imbalance of power?" Eden asked. "Because she was your teacher?"

"Yes, and because I idolized her. I never felt like her equal, and she took advantage of that. She would tell me what to wear and decide where we were going when we went out. I was dazzled by it all . . . until I wasn't."

Eden gripped her fingers and squeezed.

"She was controlling," Anna said. "And so jealous. It bothered her that I'm pansexual. I think she was afraid I'd leave her for a man or some bullshit like that. Anytime she saw me talking to someone else, she was convinced I was flirting, and she'd get so angry."

"Oh, Anna . . ." Eden's brows were pinched in concern.

"She'd demand that I stay by her side if we went to a party together, and for a while, I just went along with it. She's a very hard woman to say no to."

"I'm so sorry."

"Eventually, my rose-colored glasses came off, and I started to realize that I wasn't happy, that this wasn't a healthy relationship. Zoe helped me see that she was being emotionally abusive, that our whole relationship was toxic. So I broke it off."

"Good for you," Eden said. "That must have been so hard to do."

Anna flinched at the memory. "Camille didn't take it well. She got really mean and acted like she'd been doing me a favor by dating me, like I meant nothing to her at all. That was about two years ago. But then, we'd see each other at events or whatnot, and God, that chemistry was still there. She still had this hold over me when she came into a room. I went home with her a few times, and twice it lasted longer than a night. It took me a long time to finally get her out of my system. I'm so ashamed when I think about how many times I went back to her."

Eden's eyes were sympathetic. "I can't really relate, since I'm just figuring out why I've never felt that kind of physical pull toward someone before, but I think you owe yourself some grace. You were doing the best you could. When did things end for good?"

"About a year ago. We had an awful fight. I don't think I've ever been that angry in my life. It was like someone turned on the light, and I could finally see her for who she was. That was it. I still see her around—like at the Grammys—but there's no spark for me anymore. I just try to be polite."

"Your politeness is probably more than she deserves," Eden said.

"Probably, but it's not worth getting into another fight with her." Anna looked at Eden, pondering whether to say this next part, but deep down, she knew it needed to be said. "That's why I was so skittish about getting involved with you. There were too many parallels to my relationship with Camille. The power imbalance. You're older. I idolized you. You elevated my career by bringing me on board for your tour, and you could snatch that away. You could fire me from the tour if things between us went south."

Eden opened her mouth and then snapped it shut. She withdrew her legs from Anna's lap, drawing her knees against her chest. "I . . . well, I hadn't really thought about that, to be honest, other than the age difference. I guess I was too caught up in my own head. But when it comes to our careers, I see you as a peer, Anna."

"Yeah, I feel that way around you now too. I just . . . I'm gun shy after Camille."

"Okay, then let me see if I can set your mind at ease." Eden quit hugging her knees and sat up straight, taking Anna's hands in hers. "My relationship with my parents was controlling, and after going through it, I would never try to do that to someone else. But also, I'm not a manipulative person." Eden's gaze was steady and unflinching. "I'm reserved. I'm inclined to play it safe, sometimes to my own detriment. I like to be in control of my own situation, but I've always tried to lift up other women, not tear them down. I would never intentionally hurt you or misuse my power against you, and if you ever feel that I have, *please* tell me."

Anna's chest felt warm and fuzzy, and her eyes were watery. "Thank you."

"In the interest of total, brutal truth here, you should know that Stella suggested bringing you on board because *I* needed *you* to sell out the tour. You were having an amazing year, and I . . . was not. And I wasn't very happy about it either."

"I . . . you . . . what?"

Eden's eyes twinkled with amusement. "I resented needing you to sell out the tour."

"You certainly never showed it."

"Of course not." Eden flicked a hand as if the idea were ridiculous. "I'm a professional. So have I helped set your mind at ease?" She drew her bottom lip between her teeth. "And if not . . . it's totally fine. You're right that it could be tricky, trying a relationship when we're on tour together. I promise I won't be upset if you just want to be friends."

Anna's brain was still tripping over the words "trying a relationship" because she hadn't known what to expect when she came to Vermont with Eden, but starting a relationship with her had seemed almost too much to hope for. "Are you sure you're ready for that . . . for a relationship with a woman?"

"You mean, coming out?" Eden flinched. "Sorry, that still sounds weird to say. And I don't know how I feel about it, to be honest. I'm obviously not ready to talk about it publicly before I'm comfortable saying the words, but I'm going to get comfortable with it, for my own sake. So long term, no, I'm not worried about coming out. Our fans obviously already love the idea of us dating. For me, the biggest hurdle has just been . . . coming out to myself." Her tone changed on that last part, becoming quieter, more hesitant.

Anna flung her arms around her. She'd never expected Eden to start talking about publicly coming out so soon. That was just . . . wow. Eden never ceased to amaze her. "And I'm so proud of you for it."

Eden hugged her back, her heart thumping against Anna's breast. "I never told the world I was straight, so I guess I don't see why I need to tell them I'm not. I think, if we reach that point, I'd just announce our relationship and let that speak for itself."

"I love that approach," Anna told her. She loved everything about this conversation, and for the first time, she could see a real future for them . . . the kind of future where they lived happily ever after. Anna knew she was getting *way* ahead of herself, but then again, she'd never been afraid to dream big.

"Oh my God." Eden sat up straight, staring at Anna with wide eyes.

"What?"

"I just realized . . . you just told me you figured out you were attracted to women while you were watching me on TV, and I . . . I realized the same thing from my reaction to you. That means . . ."

"It means we were each other's sexual awakenings." Anna pressed a hand against her heart. This felt monumental somehow. It felt fated, like a moment in a romance novel.

"That's . . ." Eden seemed to be at an uncharacteristic loss for words.

"It feels like we were meant to be."

CHAPTER TWENTY

Eden leaned back in her chair, comfortably full and relaxed. Anna had cooked stuffed bell peppers for dinner, and they were delicious, almost as wonderful as spending this kind of quietly domestic evening together. "I'm so glad you're here."

Anna smiled. "Me too. Do you usually come to Vermont alone?"

"Usually. Zach came with me sometimes, but he'd rather be in the city than out in the mountains any day, so even while we were married, I tended to come here alone."

"No staff?"

Eden shook her head. "Paris handles the logistics, getting the place ready for me when I visit, and if I'm going to be here longer than a week, I have a cleaner who comes, but other than that, no. The whole reason I come here is to get away from the Hollywood life. This is my place to rest and relax."

"I love this place for you," Anna said. "It made me a little sad to see you trapped in your LA condo, where you couldn't even go outside for a walk on the beach."

"I do love it here, and thanks for dinner. It was delicious," Eden said. "Do you enjoy cooking?"

"I do," Anna told her. "It's something my mom and I did together when I was growing up. I have so many fond memories of being in the kitchen with her."

"What does your dad do?"

Anna grinned. "He raised John and me."

"Really? He was a stay-at-home dad?"

"Yep. Mom worked a lot of nights and weekends, so he was pretty much a full-time dad while we were growing up. The coolest dad too." Anna's expression was fond. "He took us to our after-school activities and went to all our games. My friends loved him because he was the dad who'd bring ice cream cups and drink pouches for the whole team."

"Aww, I love that." Eden tried to imagine her own dad doing anything similar and failed to form a believable mental image. When she thought of Anna's dad, though, she could easily picture it.

"After we were out of the house, he worked a few odd jobs, but by then, my mom was making more than enough money at the restaurant, so eventually he declared himself retired and started building model ships."

"Your family is really great." Eden glanced out the window to her left, where golden sunlight bathed the treetops as the sun settled low in the sky. "Let's clean up the kitchen, and then there's something I want to show you."

"Okay," Anna agreed easily.

Together, they cleared the table and loaded the dishwasher. Eden enjoyed these everyday tasks when she was in Vermont. As someone who lived a pampered life most of the time, she'd always found something soothing about the reminder that she could take care of herself when she needed to.

"This is really nice, you know," she said. "You and me, working together in the kitchen."

Anna bumped into her as she reached for the cutting board she'd used earlier. Eden dropped her towel and turned to wrap her arms around Anna. It was amazing how natural it felt now to hold a woman in her arms and kiss her. The heat she felt no longer frightened her, although it was starting to overwhelm her, after the amount of kissing she and Anna had done today. If she was already this aroused from a simple kiss, Eden could hardly fathom what it would be like if they took the next step together.

At the same time, she couldn't imagine *not* taking that step. She wanted Anna. She wanted to experience sex with someone she was actually attracted to, even if it also terrified her, because she liked to be in control, and she felt increasingly out of control when she kissed Anna. She had no idea what to expect once their clothes came off, but it was a risk she really, *really* wanted to take.

"Come upstairs with me," she murmured against Anna's lips.

"Um . . . really?" Anna's eyes went wide.

Eden chuckled. "I mean, yeah, I was definitely thinking about sex just now, but first, I want to show you the balcony off my bedroom. We'll have a perfect view of the sunset."

"Oh." Anna laughed, giving Eden a squeeze before she released her. "I won't say no to sunset views . . . or whatever happens after."

Eden swallowed, her throat gone dry. "Let's start with the sunset and take it from there."

"Okay, I love it here." Anna sipped her wine as she watched the sun settle against the treetops. Her right hand was loosely clasped in Eden's. Despite it being late June, the air was pleasantly warm and crisp, not overbearingly hot. It reminded her of LA.

"Mm," Eden murmured in agreement.

Anna tore her gaze from the sunset to look at her. Eden wore a sapphire-blue sleeveless top paired with black skinny jeans. Her hair was down. She wore minimal makeup, and she looked . . . "peaceful" was the best word Anna could think of to describe the expression on Eden's face. The sunset had cast a golden glow over her skin.

Birds chattered in the nearby woods. Nelle would love to sit out here with them if she were here. She loved bird-watching from the windows at home. Anna missed her. She'd never been away from her cat for this long before, but as much as she'd been looking forward to seeing Nelle this week, she was more glad to be here with Eden.

"Are there trails out there?" Anna gestured to the woods behind the house.

"Yes. They lead up that hillside you see there." Eden pointed. "There's a stream that runs through the middle of the property, and one of the trails leads along it. I put a little gazebo up there where I can sit and read while I listen to the babbling water. It's *bliss*."

"Wow, you know how to do your relaxation right. I definitely want to see that."

"Good, because I was hoping to take you there after breakfast." Eden slid a glance in her direction, a satisfied smile on her face.

Impulsively, Anna leaned over and kissed her, immediately lost in the warmth of Eden's lips. They'd kissed more today than they ever had before, and Anna had been low-key aroused all day. Based on the slightly dazed look on Eden's face, she might be feeling the same way. She tasted rich and spicy, like the wine they were drinking, her lips hungrily moving against Anna's.

It was almost hard to believe this was real, that Anna was here in Vermont with Eden, kissing her like she couldn't get enough, *feeling* like she couldn't get enough. Eden had acknowledged her sexuality and her interest in a relationship. They'd talked through all their stumbling blocks. There was nothing stopping them from going into the bedroom and taking this all the way . . . if Eden was ready for that.

"Oh," Anna gasped as she looked up and saw the orange blaze over the mountaintops. "Oh wow . . . I almost missed it."

"Gorgeous, right?" Eden sounded breathless, but when Anna looked over, she was watching Anna, not the sunset.

"So pretty," Anna agreed, and she wasn't watching the sunset anymore either. She could see it reflected in Eden's eyes, like flames in her pupils. Anna felt those same flames blazing inside her as their gazes locked, and she was fairly sure the heat in Eden's eyes wasn't solely an optical illusion caused by the sunset.

"Come here," Eden said.

Anna put down her nearly empty wineglass. She spared one more glance at the sunset, because it really was stunning. She'd pay more attention tomorrow . . . probably. Then she straddled Eden's knees so she could kiss her properly. She heard Eden's wineglass hit the table beside them with a clink of glass against glass, and then Eden's hands were on her ass, dragging her closer.

They kissed until the orange glow had faded from Eden's eyes and the evening had begun to darken around them, until Anna's body was flushed, her pulse racing out of control. When she lifted her head for some much-needed oxygen, Eden's lips were swollen, her eyes dazed, her chest heaving for breath.

"Anna . . ." Eden looked up at her with a kind of desperation that mirrored the arousal blazing inside Anna.

"Yeah?"

"Want to move this to the bedroom?" Something flickered in Eden's expression as she spoke. Not hesitation exactly, but something vaguely insecure. This was a huge deal for her: not only her first time with a woman but her first time since realizing she was gay. Her first time having sex with someone she was physically attracted to. Anna couldn't even imagine what that must feel like.

"Are you sure?" Anna asked. "Because I don't want to do anything you're not ready for."

"I'm sure," Eden said. "I'm also terrified and excited and dying of anticipation. It's going to be all those things for me and probably a lot more I haven't even thought of yet."

Anna grinned at her. "We'll go slow, okay?"

Eden nodded. "Yeah."

"Remember, we can stop anytime you want, and talk me through everything you're feeling so I can help." Anna scooted backward off Eden's lap and stood, extending a hand to tug her to her feet.

"I'll try." Eden entwined her fingers with Anna's as they walked through the doorway into the bedroom.

Anna's gaze fell on the king-size bed. It looked comfortable, not overly fancy or frilly, with a dark-brown quilt covering it. She sat on the edge, tugging Eden down beside her. It'd been a long time since she'd been someone's first, and the idea of being Eden's filled her with a heady combination of heat and clarity, the knowledge that she needed to follow Eden's lead tonight while also guiding her when necessary.

Anna needed to be patient and thorough, making sure she left no doubt how mind-blowing sapphic sex could be. She wanted to show Eden what it was like to be with someone who understood her body, someone who wanted to please her, and oh, how Anna wanted to please her. She wanted tonight to be *perfect*.

"Just so you know, I was tested around the beginning of the year, and I haven't been with anyone since," she told Eden.

Eden sat up a little straighter. "Right, um, the safe sex convo is a little different with a woman, isn't it?"

Anna grinned. "No need for condoms."

"I'm on the pill anyway to keep my cycle regular, but . . ." Eden looked uncharacteristically flustered for a moment. "That's not relevant, is it?"

"I can't get you pregnant." Anna's grin grew even wider at Eden's flushed cheeks.

"I've been tested since my divorce, too, and there hasn't been anyone since Zach."

"Then it sounds like we're good to go." She offered Eden a reassuring smile.

Eden returned it, and for a moment, they just grinned at each other like lust-struck fools. It was warm and comfortable and so freaking wonderful.

"Can I?" Eden placed a hand on Anna's lower back, lingering just beneath the hem of her shirt. Her eyes met Anna's as she sought permission, their blue depths ablaze with desire and something else that Anna interpreted as an eagerness to find out how it felt to touch a woman.

"Yes," Anna said, because *yes*, she wanted to be touched by Eden.

Eden's hand slid up her back until she encountered Anna's bra strap. She paused there for a moment as her gaze dipped to Anna's breasts. Then she popped the clasp on Anna's bra like a pro, gasping as she slid her hand around to cup one of Anna's breasts. "Oh," she whispered.

"Oh," Anna echoed with a groan as Eden's warm fingers explored her breast. The next thing she knew, she was on her back with Eden straddling her thighs as she pushed Anna's shirt and bra up to expose her chest.

"You're so beautiful." Eden sounded awed as she took in the sight of Anna's bare breasts. Her hips rocked slightly, as if she were so turned on that she couldn't *not* get a little friction right now, and *oh*, Anna could relate. Then Eden froze, staring down at Anna with wild eyes.

"Okay?" Anna asked.

"I don't know what . . . comes next." Eden closed her eyes at the admission, her cheeks flushing pink. She hated feeling out of control, Anna remembered belatedly. She needed Anna to take the lead tonight.

"There's no rule book," Anna said as she put her hands on Eden's shoulders and guided her to lie beside her. "But I'd like to do some exploring of my own, if that's okay with you."

"More than okay." Eden's voice was low and raspy.

"Perfect," Anna responded as she gave in to what she'd wanted to do all day and slid her hands beneath Eden's top.

Eden hadn't known it could feel like this. Anna's hands were on her breasts, and *God*, it was all she could do not to grind her hips against Anna's thigh to relieve the almost overwhelming need building between her thighs. They were still fully clothed, and already Eden was so turned on, she was about to come out of her own skin.

How had she gone so many years without experiencing this kind of pleasure?

Anna pushed Eden's shirt up and then dipped her head, swirling her tongue over one of Eden's nipples. It shot a bolt of need through her so sharp, her whole body jolted with it. A startled whimper escaped her throat. Anna lifted her head, meeting her gaze. "Okay?"

Tears flooded Eden's eyes, and she didn't even know why. "Yes," she managed, arching her hips forward until they met Anna's. Every nerve ending tingled as if her body were literally begging to be touched. *This* was the feeling she'd rolled her eyes at when she read about it in romance novels. If she'd only known . . .

Anna's expression turned a bit wicked as she seemed to read Eden's desperation. "You like that, hmm?" And then she brought her mouth back to Eden's breast, nipping gently. At the same time, she pushed one of her thighs between Eden's, threading their legs together so Eden finally had some friction where she needed it.

"God," she moaned as her hips began to move. "Anna . . ."

"I've got you." Anna swept her hands up and down Eden's sides, her fingernails scratching lightly at her skin.

Eden moaned again. She couldn't seem to stop making noise. Somewhere in the back of her mind, she remembered being in bed with Zach, trying to sound enthusiastic enough that he'd be satisfied he'd gotten her off. She'd had to remind herself to moan for his benefit. She didn't have that problem tonight . . .

Anna's mouth left a hot, wet trail as she worked her way down to the waistband of Eden's jeans. Her tongue swirled around Eden's navel, and Eden yelped, her back arching as she pressed herself more firmly against Anna's tongue.

"Good?" Anna asked, and Eden felt the damp gust of her breath against her skin.

"Good is not a strong enough word for what I'm feeling." Eden squirmed. Anna's hips had left hers when she scooted down Eden's body, and she missed the contact immensely.

Anna gripped the button on Eden's jeans, and then she looked up, catching Eden's gaze. "Okay?"

"Yes. *Please.*" Her arousal spiked in anticipation of Anna's touch.

Anna popped the button, and Eden gasped at the sound, and then she gasped again as Anna slowly lowered the zipper. Her knuckles grazed Eden's skin, leaving heat in their wake. Eden felt the silky brush of Anna's hair on the exposed skin at her waist, and *oh*, that was nice.

Anna kissed the front of Eden's underwear, and another whimper tore from her throat. God, was she even going to last until Anna had finished undressing her? The ache in her core had grown almost unbearable.

This is what it's supposed to feel like.

Tears slipped past her eyelids and trailed into her hair, and she was glad Anna wasn't looking at her face. Anna was gently tugging the jeans down her legs, and Eden lifted her hips to help her out. There was no graceful way to take off skinny jeans, but Eden was beyond caring at this point. She writhed and kicked until she was free of them.

As the air hit her exposed legs, Eden realized she was soaked. Her underwear was drenched in her own desire, probably visibly so, and she tensed, embarrassed for Anna to see it. She wrenched her eyes open to find Anna watching her with a gentle smile.

"Still okay?" Anna asked.

Eden could only nod, not trusting herself to speak.

Anna bent down and gripped Eden's shirt and bra, which had been bunched beneath her arms. She helped Eden slide them over her head, leaving her in only her panties. Anna was still fully dressed.

"Your turn," Eden managed, reaching for Anna's top.

Anna gripped her shirt, pulling it and her bra over her head in one graceful movement, aided by the fact that Eden had unhooked her bra earlier. Then she shimmied out of her leggings, exposing yellow bikinis.

Eden's gaze fell on the pink jewel glinting from Anna's belly button. This time, Eden could stare openly. She didn't have to hide her interest. This time, she could touch. She reached out, brushing a thumb over Anna's stomach to her belly ring, loving the way Anna's muscles tensed beneath her touch and the hunger in her eyes when Eden looked up to meet her gaze.

"This is so sexy," Eden murmured.

"I'm glad you like it." Anna settled herself against Eden, rocking their hips together, and when Eden moaned that time, she wasn't alone. Anna threw her head back, letting out a groan of pleasure. Her nipples had hardened into tight buds, her breasts bouncing as she moved against Eden. Anna's breasts were larger than hers, rounder, fuller, and before Eden had even realized what she was doing, her hands were on them, cupping them, drawing another moan from Anna.

"Do you have any idea how beautiful you are right now?" Anna asked, her voice breathless. She paused her movements, dragging her gaze from Eden's face to the juncture of her thighs, and Eden felt a surge of heat there. "You're so wet for me, Eden. I *love* it."

"You do?" Eden sounded just as breathless. She resisted the urge to press her thighs together, shocked to discover that she liked letting Anna see her this way. The heat in Anna's gaze only fueled Eden's own desire.

This is what it's supposed to feel like.

This time, no tears came at the realization. Only more heat.

"Yes." Anna brought a hand down to cup Eden over her underwear. She jolted at the contact, releasing another needy sound she didn't even recognize as her own voice. The heel of Anna's hand pressed firmly against Eden's clit, and she almost came on the spot. "I'm just as wet," Anna whispered.

"Show me," Eden said. *Show me?* She didn't even know who she was at this point. Her body felt like something new to her, every sensation, every urge a surprise.

Anna hooked a finger beneath the waistband of her panties and dragged them down her hips, kicking them to the floor. Eden had just processed the wave of desire that surged through her at the sight of the neatly trimmed hair between Anna's thighs, the wetness glistening there, before Anna had seized her hand and pressed it firmly against the evidence of her desire.

"Oh," Eden gasped as her fingers met Anna's hot, wet skin. She felt a jolt to her clit so sharp that she thought she might come without even being touched.

"Now you," Anna said as she reached for Eden's seamless panties.

"Yes." Eden fumbled with them, her movements clumsy, hands shaking.

Then her underwear was gone, and Anna's fingers were on her, slipping through her folds, and Eden couldn't breathe. She made a wheezing sound, arching helplessly against Anna's hand.

"Shh," Anna whispered, stilling her fingers to give Eden a moment to gather herself. "Take a deep breath, Eden. We've got all night."

"No," Eden gasped, hips moving without her permission. "I can't wait that long."

"Just another minute, babe," Anna practically purred as she removed her hand. "I want to make it so good for you. Do you trust me?"

"Yes," Eden whispered. She trusted Anna more than she'd ever trusted anyone in her bed. She sucked air into her lungs, breathing through the arousal blazing inside her. Anna was right. Eden didn't want to rush this. She wanted to savor every moment. Anna's fingers brushed against her again, and she tensed. "Wait . . ."

Anna froze. "Yeah?"

"I'm so close, and . . ." She gulped. "You're right. I don't want it to be over this quickly."

"Want to know a secret?" Anna's breath warmed her ear as she leaned in. Her fingers pressed against Eden's clit, covering her, holding her on the edge.

Eden nodded desperately, clinging to what remained of her self-control to keep from grinding against those fingers and ending this right here and now.

"One of the most beautiful things about sapphic sex is that we can go over and over, as many times as you need until you're satisfied. Okay?" Anna's fingers were moving before she could respond, thrusting against her hard and fast.

"Fuck!" Eden practically shouted. She gasped as Anna's fingers slid past her entrance before retreating to circle her clit, now wet with Eden's arousal. Tension coiled deep inside her. She was shaking. Begging. Writhing.

And then she was coming. "Anna," she cried, grinding herself against Anna's hand. "Oh, yes. Oh!"

Her entire body caught fire, filling her with several seconds of the most wonderful feeling in the world, and then she collapsed against the quilt beneath her, shuddering with the aftershocks of what might have been the most powerful orgasm of her life. Anna swirled her fingers, and Eden twitched, letting out a long, low moan.

"Holy *fuck*," she gasped, her voice hoarse.

Her body trembled. She was covered in sweat and so wet beneath Anna's fingers, she was afraid it might have dripped onto the quilt beneath her. "Fuck" indeed. For the first time in her life, Eden felt well and truly fucked.

CHAPTER TWENTY-ONE

Eden couldn't catch her breath. Not with Anna's body pressed against hers, Anna's tongue in her mouth, Anna's fingers digging into her hips, rocking them together. Eden had barely recovered from her first orgasm, and already she was on fire all over again.

Anna had unleashed something in her tonight. She'd shown Eden what it felt like to be so turned on, so needy, so *desperate*, she forgot everything but pleasure.

Eden had always been somewhat self-conscious during sex. She'd been so aware of where her hands were and what expression she was making, usually wondering if she'd actually come or have to fake it. Tonight, she felt primal. She was all instinct, as if her body had been waiting a lifetime for this very moment.

She slid her hands over Anna's hips to cup her ass, pressing her closer. "I finally get what the fuss is all about."

Anna's smile turned slightly smug. "You know just what to say to a girl."

"Maybe I was only ninety-nine percent sure earlier today, but I'm definitely a lesbian." Eden wasn't sure she'd ever said the word out loud before, but now she couldn't hold it back. As her hips moved against Anna's, desire blazing inside her with a force that threatened to overwhelm her, there was no denying the undeniable. She was gay. A lesbian. A woman who loved women . . . and maybe one woman in particular.

"I am so freaking proud of you, babe." Anna kissed her, deep and hot and hungry. Her thigh pressed between Eden's, moving with a steady rhythm that had Eden on the edge, even though it couldn't have been ten minutes since she came the first time. Had she ever come twice during sex before? She didn't think so, but her brain was a haze of arousal at the moment.

Dimly, she realized she'd barely touched Anna yet. She wanted to. She wanted to explore her body and give her as much pleasure as she'd given Eden, even if she was slightly intimidated about her ability to do so. Before she could spiral into the land of performance anxiety, Anna planted a wet kiss against that spot below her ear that made Eden's brain misfire.

Her hips jerked, but Anna's thigh was no longer pressed between them. Eden groaned, shocked to feel her own fingers against her clit, to realize she'd been so aroused that she'd touched herself during sex. She'd never done that before. She saw Anna watching and immediately yanked her hand away, cheeks burning.

"Don't be embarrassed," Anna said, her tone gentle. "Do whatever feels good, but don't come yet. I want you to come in my mouth this time."

"Oh," Eden gasped, pressing her thighs together as her core clenched in anticipation. Anna was so commanding during sex, so *confident*, and it was unbelievably sexy.

"If that's what you want?" Anna cocked her head, searching Eden's face.

"Yes. Please." She hardly recognized the pleading tone of her voice, but despite what Anna had said, she didn't touch herself again. She was already so close, and she didn't want to come the moment Anna's mouth touched her.

Instead, she writhed and begged, nearly overcome with pleasure as Anna kissed her way down Eden's body. She located so many erogenous places Eden had never known about as her tongue and lips explored Eden's neck and then her collarbone before moving on to her breasts.

She closed her eyes, reveling in the way it felt to be this aroused. The ache in her core was almost overpowering, throbbing in time with her runaway pulse. As Anna's hair tickled her rib cage and her tongue flicked against her nipple, Eden marveled at each new sensation.

Anna ventured lower, kissing her way down Eden's stomach. She could hear herself panting and the wet sound of Anna's mouth against her skin. Anna's tongue circled her navel, and Eden arched off the bed, her hips automatically seeking Anna's mouth.

"You are so fucking sexy," Anna murmured before pressing a kiss against Eden's hip.

Eden could only whimper in response.

"I can't wait to taste you." Anna's hair brushed against Eden's thighs as she settled between them. She guided Eden's legs over her shoulders, and if Eden had thought she was dying of anticipation before, she was in agony now.

Anna brushed her lips against Eden's inner thigh, and she trembled. Her fists clenched in the quilt beneath her, and she wished briefly that she'd pulled the covers down before they started because the quilt was too stiff for her to get a good grip. She longed to clench her fingers in the cool fabric of her sheets. And then Anna pressed a kiss to the crease where Eden's thigh met her body, and she forgot everything but Anna's lips.

"Anna, please . . . ," she gasped, hips shifting restlessly against the mattress.

"Seeing you this worked up is so fucking hot." Anna looked up, and their gazes locked. She looked so comfortable, lying on her stomach between Eden's thighs, with Eden's legs draped over her shoulders, eyes gleaming with hunger.

Eden seared the image into her brain, never wanting to forget it. Anna grinned at her, and then she leaned in, parting Eden with her tongue, setting her body ablaze with one long, slow lick.

"Oh," she gasped as her legs shook and her clit throbbed. *"Oh . . ."*

Anna seemed entirely unhurried as she explored Eden's body, periodically swirling her tongue over Eden's clit but never lingering there, probably realizing Eden would come as soon as she did. And as desperate as Eden was to come, she was also completely enraptured by what Anna was doing. Unable to hold still, she moved her hips, thrusting against Anna's mouth as pleasure swept through her veins.

"Is this okay?" Anna murmured as she circled Eden's opening with a finger, and Eden realized with a jolt that in everything they'd done together so far, Anna hadn't been inside her, and that was so, *so* different from her prior experience. Even more surprising, she hadn't missed it in the slightest.

"Yes," she answered Anna's question, and that finger slid inside her, followed by a second. Eden had expected her to thrust her fingers, mimicking a penis, but instead she crooked them forward, hitting a spot that made Eden's body tense and an outrageous cry of pleasure escape her lips. Oh God *God . . .*

She panted and shook. Spots danced across her vision. That felt so good, she couldn't . . .

"Hey," Anna said, resting a hand on Eden's thigh. "Take a deep breath."

Eden realized she'd been gasping for air, breathing so fast she was making herself dizzy. She took several slow, steadying breaths, relieved when the buzzing receded from her ears and her vision cleared.

"Ready?" Anna asked.

Eden nodded. Her hands were in Anna's hair, and it was all she could do not to drag her closer, because if she didn't come soon, she really might lose her mind. Anna seemed to know this, though, because she leaned in, focusing the full attention of her mouth on Eden's clit this time. She swirled her tongue against it and then sucked.

Eden ground her hips helplessly against her as she felt herself tipping over the precipice, past the point of no return. Release ignited beneath Anna's tongue, tearing through Eden with such force, she screamed with pleasure. She'd never been this uninhibited during sex before.

She'd never been this *anything* before.

Anna stared at Eden in awe. She lay sprawled beneath her, gazing up at Anna out of glazed eyes, looking like someone who'd just been thoroughly debauched. Eden had begged and writhed and trembled, and *God*, when she came, the sight of her pleasure was almost enough to take Anna with her.

She lowered herself to lie beside Eden, then wrapped an arm around her waist and drew her in for a kiss. Eden kissed her back eagerly, still breathless from her orgasm, her skin damp beneath Anna's fingers.

"That was so . . ." Eden lifted a shaky hand and mimed her head exploding.

"You're really good for my ego," Anna told her with a cheeky grin.

"And you're really good at, well . . . sex." Eden trailed a hand down Anna's spine, making her shiver with pleasure.

"I didn't want your first time with a woman to be disappointing."

Eden scoffed. "You could have just laid here and let me look at you, and it wouldn't have been disappointing. But this . . . this was amazing."

"I'm glad."

"Now can I . . . ?" Eden slid her hand to Anna's hip, her expression turning hesitant.

"God, yes." Anna had been trying to ignore her own need while she focused on Eden, but she was so worked up at this point, it wouldn't take much.

Eden's fingers trailed across Anna's stomach. She toyed with Anna's belly ring and then dipped lower, brushing against Anna's soaked flesh. Now it was Anna's turn to groan, her hips jerking toward Eden.

"Wow." Eden sounded awed. "You're so wet."

"What can I say? Getting you off is pretty arousing."

Eden grinned. "Roll onto your back."

Anna complied, feeling a rush of arousal at the authoritative tone of Eden's voice. She'd enjoyed taking control earlier, but now she was more than happy to let Eden take over. Eden sat up, straddling one of Anna's thighs as her gaze roamed over Anna's body.

"I've been looking forward to this." Eden leaned in, kissing Anna on the mouth before venturing down to kiss her breasts, her mouth hot and wet against Anna's sensitive skin. She slipped a hand between Anna's thighs.

"Yes," Anna gasped, moving against Eden's hand.

She felt Eden smile around the nipple she'd been kissing. Eden's fingers moved hesitantly at first. When Anna looked down, Eden's brow was wrinkled in concentration. Her fingers were gentle as they explored Anna's body, gradually becoming firmer as Eden's confidence grew.

Eden found her clit, and at Anna's cry of pleasure, she looked up. "Yes?"

"Right there," Anna confirmed. "You can take your time with me later. Right now, just keep doing what you're doing."

Eden's fingers resumed their movements, circling Anna's clit as she nipped at Anna's breast, and she arched her back, pressing herself more firmly into Eden's touch. Anna thrust her hips to Eden's rhythm, and within minutes, she felt herself losing control, moaning as Eden took her over the edge.

"Yes," Anna cried as she came. She clutched Eden against herself as she rode out her orgasm, and the next thing she knew, Eden was grinding against her thigh as she came again too.

"My *God*," she gasped as she collapsed against Anna on the bed. "You weren't kidding when you said women could just keep going."

Anna grinned, sucking in deep breaths as she recovered. "Multiple orgasms are a fun perk, that's for sure."

"I love this," Eden murmured, nuzzling closer so that her head rested in the crook of Anna's neck. "I love being with you."

Anna's heart clenched happily at that *L* word on Eden's lips. Of course, it was too soon to say it for real, but Anna knew she was well on her way to falling for Eden, and she hoped Eden might feel the same way. As she lay with Eden cradled in her arms, aftershocks of pleasure still fizzing in her veins, Anna couldn't imagine anything more perfect. "I love being with you too."

She stroked a hand through Eden's hair, and Eden sighed, sounding at peace with the world. The door to the balcony was still open, and Anna could barely see the trees through the gathering dark. A ceiling fan circled overhead, and the hum of crickets filtered through the room.

This was bliss. But after a minute, she realized the dampness she felt on her neck wasn't sweat but Eden's tears. A slight hitch in her breathing was the only other warning sign.

Anna tightened her arm around her. "Hey. You okay?"

Eden nodded, not lifting her head. "Good tears. Happy tears. Maybe relief? Like so many things finally make sense. I finally understand why . . ." A little sob escaped her. "But at the same time, I can't help feeling frustrated that it took me *so* long."

"None of that." She gave Eden's hair a gentle tug, drawing a gasp from her. "Don't question your journey, Eden. You're here now, but nothing about you was any less valid a few months ago, when you still thought you were straight."

Eden looked up with a smile on her lips despite the tears on her cheeks. "You're right. No more beating myself up about things that are outside my control."

"That's right." Anna dipped her head to kiss her, tasting salt on Eden's lips.

"Can't seem to get enough of you," Eden whispered.

"Same."

They kissed and touched, and Eden used her newfound skills to give Anna another shattering orgasm before they took a much-needed shower and ventured downstairs for some equally needed water. And then, exhausted, they went to bed . . . together.

CHAPTER TWENTY-TWO

"Almost there," Eden huffed as she led the way up the path. Sunlight filtered through the canopy of leaves overhead, casting dappled patches over the ground around them. Ahead, she could hear the babble and splash of water.

"This path is a great workout." Anna sounded as breathless as Eden. After coffee and a light breakfast at the house, they'd prepared a picnic lunch and set out on a hike to Eden's favorite spot on her property. She could hardly wait to share it with Anna.

"It's the only working out I do when I'm here," Eden said.

"That sounds good to me," Anna said. "Oh!"

The gazebo had come into sight ahead, its white paint a stark contrast to the rich browns and greens of the forest around it.

"Isn't it adorable?" Eden asked.

"So cute," Anna agreed.

As they approached the gazebo, the stream meandered over to run alongside the path. The melodic sound of water rushing over rocks combined with the chatter of birds and the whisper of the breeze through the trees to create the world's most relaxing soundtrack. Eden had tried to capture it on her phone, but the recorded version wasn't the same. So far, she had only achieved this feeling of contentment when she was here in person.

They entered the gazebo, which had a wooden bench that ran the perimeter of the structure. On one side, she could sit and watch the stream babbling past. Eden sat there now, setting her backpack at her feet.

"This is the perfect spot for a picnic," Anna said.

"I bring lunch up here a lot."

"I can see why." Anna pressed closer, bringing their lips together.

"Mm-hmm," Eden murmured into the kiss, marveling at the way her body awoke at the simple press of Anna's lips to hers. Already, she felt a warm flush of arousal. She dug her fingers into Anna's ass, urging her closer so their hips pressed together. She moaned as Anna began to rock against her.

Anna reached for the waistband of Eden's leggings, then paused. "How likely is it that someone will come by and see us?"

"No chance of that happening," Eden answered, hips automatically arching toward Anna's hand. "The property has a seven-foot fence, and it's nowhere near this gazebo."

Anna tsked. "Still in your cage, Eden, even here. I'm going to get you out of that cage before the end of the week, but first . . ." Her hand slid down the front of Eden's pants.

Eden gasped, startled to realize how wet she already was as Anna's fingers reached her. Then Anna was brushing circles over her clit, and Eden couldn't think. She could only feel as pleasure overtook her senses. She threw her head back, her whimpers and rasping breaths mingling with the sounds of nature around them.

Here in the light of day, sober and rested, Eden's mind was blown all over again by the way her body responded to Anna. Arousal built steadily inside her, strong and urgent. Her hips thrust against Anna's hand, and when she broke, her cry echoed through the treetops.

"Beautiful," Anna said, watching her. Then she brought her fingers to her lips and sucked. "And delicious."

Eden groaned again, pleasure still sparking through her system. "I don't know why that's so hot, but it is." She brought a hand between them, brushing against the warm, firm skin of Anna's stomach. She couldn't resist toying with Anna's belly ring, twirling it between her fingers before she slipped them into Anna's pants.

She could hardly wrap her mind around how natural this felt for her already. She marveled at the way Anna felt beneath her fingers, how hot, how wet. Anna's hazel eyes gleamed with all the colors of the forest as a ray of sunshine passed over her face. *Beautiful.* There was a song in those verdant depths. Eden was sure of it.

Already, she was starting to discover what Anna liked, and she couldn't wait to spend the rest of the week learning all the ins and outs of her body. For someone who'd never been very interested in sex, it was all Eden could think about now.

She was already getting aroused again, just watching Anna grow closer to her release. A warm ache grew in Eden's core as Anna ground herself against Eden's hand. She rubbed her thumb against Anna's clit, and Anna gasped, biting her lower lip. Her inner walls tightened around Eden's fingers as she came, and Eden felt an answering clench inside her own body.

"God, you're beautiful when you come." She could hear the awe in her voice.

Anna grinned, cheeks flushed, panting for breath. "Not as beautiful as you."

They sat for several minutes like that, Anna straddling Eden's lap, kissing and cuddling. Eventually, they got up to rinse their hands in the stream. Anna took her shoes off and waded in, squeaking in surprise at how cold the water was. Unable to resist, Eden took off her own shoes and followed her in.

They laughed and splashed in the stream, careful not to get their clothes wet. This property had always been Eden's refuge. She'd come here to relax and unwind. She hadn't come here for fun, but that's what she was having today. She and Anna had fun anywhere they went together, so of course they'd have fun here too. Eden's heart felt light.

As she looked down at the water rushing over her feet, she thought of the song she'd been working on for the last few weeks, the song she'd titled "Turbulent" as she watched the churning rapids in Colorado. Now she was thinking about how rushing water could also bring peace and tranquility.

She waded toward the gazebo to jot down the thought before it evaporated.

"Too cold already?" Anna asked, flicking water at her.

"No. I just had a thought for the song I'm working on, and I need to write it down."

Eden gripped a nearby tree branch to steady herself as she climbed cautiously over the slippery rocks at the edge of the stream. Her toes were semi-numb, not that she minded. She sat on the bench in the gazebo and pulled up the lyrics she'd stored on her phone. There, she added a few new lines to what she already had. It was still missing something, though.

"Will you sing it for me?" Anna asked as she sat beside her. She'd rolled up her green leggings above her knees, and her bare calves glistened with water.

"Yeah." Eden didn't always like to share unfinished songs with people, but she wanted to sing this one for Anna. "It's called 'Turbulent.' It's about the way I've been feeling the last few weeks."

"I'm intrigued." Anna wrapped her arms around her knees and gazed at Eden with an expectant expression.

Eden held her phone in front of herself and hummed a few notes of what she imagined the opening bars of the song would sound like. And then she began to sing. The first verse was about her raging emotions, feeling like she was out of control, culminating with the chorus, where she tied all the water imagery together with the title.

She stopped singing and looked at Anna. "The second verse will be about reclaiming control. That's what just sparked for me in the stream, how the water can be calming and purposeful, even when it's turbulent."

"I love it," Anna said. "I really do. The lyrics are so personal and meaningful, and the tune is so melodic, like water in a way."

"Thank you." Eden ducked her head with a smile.

"I mean it." Anna's voice was thick with emotion. "This is the kind of song that made me fall in love with your music way back when. You always pour so much passion into your music. It makes me feel things when I listen."

"Really?" Eden looked up, surprised to see the tears shimmering in Anna's eyes.

She nodded, taking one of Eden's hands in hers. "Can I be brutally honest for a minute?"

"Of course." Eden sat up a little straighter, unsure what Anna was about to say.

"I didn't feel that passion in your last album, except for 'Alone.' That song brought me to tears the first time I listened, even though I wondered how someone like you could ever feel alone." She held up a hand before Eden could speak. "Now that I know you, I totally get it. I do."

Eden nodded, something uncomfortable twisting in her gut at Anna's words.

"I guess the point I'm trying to make is that the *After Midnight* album kind of felt like you were trying too hard to write a hit, instead of writing from your heart. Like, we all know you don't really turn into a wild woman after midnight, you know? I think that's why it didn't sell as well as your others. Your usual spark was missing."

"It was missing from my life too." Eden looked down at the phone in her hands.

"Exactly. You were in a weird place, and your music fell a little flat, but *damn*, when I say you're back . . ." Anna squeezed her hand.

"Watching you perform on this tour . . . I've never seen you so passionate. Even the songs that felt lacking for me on the album come to life when you perform them every night. You're back, Eden. All this to say, I think this is what your new song, 'Turbulent,' is about, and I'm just so happy to see you blossom like this and so honored to hear your new music and just . . . a lot of emotions."

Tears spilled over Anna's cheeks, and for a moment, Eden just stared. She hadn't seen Anna cry before, and to see her tears now, to know that Anna was so moved by her music, it made Eden's own eyes well up.

"Thank you," she said, her voice hoarse.

"I mean it," Anna said. "Your talent is just so, *so* beautiful." She leaned forward, wrapping her arms around Eden.

Eden's tears fell as she hugged her back. "Look at us crying over pretty words."

Anna laughed, pulling back to grin at Eden with tear-streaked cheeks. "But words are so pretty! And powerful. They can change lives. Actually, I was working on a song yesterday about looking for validation in the right places, wanting to be taken seriously and not just seen as a silly, bubbly girl."

"Can I see?" Eden asked, her mind already drawing parallels between Anna's idea and the song Eden had just sung for her.

"Sure." Anna picked up her phone, tapped the screen a few times, and then held it out to her. "It doesn't have a tune or anything, just a few random ideas."

Eden looked at the lyrics. They were so earnest and hopeful, just like Anna. "What if we combined them? My song and yours?"

Anna's smile widened. "Like a duet?"

Eden hadn't thought past a songwriting collaboration, but as soon as the word "duet" left Anna's lips, she was nodding. "Yes. I love that idea. A duet about female empowerment, about being true to ourselves in a world that wants us to fit a certain mold or sees us as nothing more than a pretty face."

"Oh my God, yes! Let's do it."

They spent the next hour jotting notes, merging their lyrics, humming lines and melodies as they worked. This was the missing piece Eden had been searching for, the thing that might give this song the push from good to *great*.

It was amazing how quickly it came together too. In what felt like no time at all, Eden had recorded them singing a full run-through of the completed song. When she played it back, they both leaned in close to her phone to listen.

"We sound good together," Eden said.

"We do." Anna looked up, and there were fresh tears on her cheeks. "This song is really powerful, and I know I'm not objective because I'm part of it, but it's got the magic that made you a superstar, Eden."

"You have it, too, you know," Eden said. "That magic has you already nipping at my heels after only two years in the business."

"Maybe, but part of the magic is *us*."

Anna stepped behind Eden on the balcony off the master bedroom. She wrapped her arms around her, peering over Eden's shoulder into the woods. "Hear me out."

"Always," Eden responded, relaxing into Anna's embrace.

They'd spent the last two days on Eden's property, going for daily hikes and picnics at the gazebo, followed by lazy afternoons binging *How to Get Away with Murder* and even more songwriting. Anna was having one of the best vacations of her life, but she also wanted to venture outside this haven Eden had built for herself.

"Let's go somewhere," Anna said. "Have a little adventure here in Vermont."

"Sure." Eden spun in Anna's arms to face her. "I love driving around the area. There's a really nice overlook not far from the house."

"And I definitely want to see it, but I also want to go shopping or something, maybe explore that cute little town we drove through on our way here?"

Immediately, Eden tensed. "I don't—"

Anna pressed a finger against her lips. "Hear me out, remember?"

Eden nodded.

"It's not a secret that you own this house, right? I mean, the locals know you're here."

"Yeah, I'm pretty sure they do," Eden said. "Although I haven't met enough of them to confirm whatever suspicions they may have about the reclusive pop star who lives here."

"And do they line up at your gate, trying to get a glimpse of you?"

Eden shook her head. "I've never seen anyone at the gate unless they're making a delivery. It's part of the reason I like it here. So much less nosy than the tourists in LA who buy those maps with the stars' houses on them."

"How do you think they'd react if you walked into a store?" Anna asked.

"I don't know. I just . . . you know how I feel about going out in public without Taylor for backup." Right now, Taylor was at home in LA, thousands of miles away. Eden was truly on her own here in Vermont with Anna, a fact that was etched into the worry lines on her face.

"Here's what I think would happen if you walked into a store here," Anna said. "I think a lot of people won't even recognize you. Some will, especially if you're with me. We've gotten a fair amount of press together this year, and two celebrities are always more recognizable than one."

"Always," Eden echoed.

"But even if a few people ask for autographs or pictures, that's not a big deal, is it?"

"No," Eden said, but she still looked uncomfortable.

"What happened in Chicago won't happen here. There aren't that many people, for one thing. We were in one of the most popular tourist spots in the country when we got mobbed in Millennium Park. I'm thinking the local country store will be a much quieter experience."

"I guess you're right."

"Are you worried about being seen in public with me?" Anna asked. "About people thinking we're a couple?"

Eden shook her head. "No. According to Paris, that hashtag is mostly circulating among our fans on Twitter. The mainstream press sees us as colleagues, maybe friends."

"I agree. Being seen together in public might feed the Edanna furor on Twitter, but where's the harm in that? The fans love it. They'll be thrilled. And the media will think it's nice that we're such good friends."

Eden nodded, and was that a smile lurking around the corner of her lips?

"Then, if you're comfortable with it, I see no downside to us doing a little exploring together," Anna said. "You might even find out that the locals are completely unimpressed by having a celebrity in their midst. Maybe you've been hiding up here in your castle for no reason."

"Cabin," Eden corrected, leaning in to kiss Anna's cheek. "It's not a castle, but it *is* my fortress. I feel safe here."

"What if we stay near the car so we can bolt if anything starts to look sketchy? In fact, we can start by driving to the scenic overlook you mentioned and take it from there."

And that was how, later that afternoon, Anna found herself strolling through a little shop full of maple products. In front of her, Eden carried a basket of gifts for her staff while the owner of the store gave her an in-depth explanation of the process to tap the trees, which he apparently did right here on the property.

If the man had any idea who Eden was, he'd given no indication. "See here." He guided her to the window at the rear of the store. "The tall tree right by the driveway? That's a sugar maple."

"So this syrup came from that tree?" Eden asked, holding up her basket.

"Not likely," he told her. "I do tap that one sometimes for demonstrations, but I have a network of trees throughout the woods back there where I get most of it from. Got a network of tubing that runs between the trees, emptying into that shed back there."

He went on for a few more minutes, explaining the process to Eden while Anna did some shopping of her own. She loved playing tourist, and she'd never actually had maple sugar candy before. She picked out a nice gift set to send Zoe as a thank-you for watching Nelle, plus some smaller gifts for the rest of her team.

The owner of the store was in his fifties, dressed in jeans and a flannel shirt despite the warm weather, and boy, did he love to talk about maple syrup. By the time they made it back to their rental car, they both knew an awful lot about syrup production.

"Oh, look, the post office is right across the street," Anna commented. "Mind if I stop in there and mail this basket to Zoe?"

"Sure, that's fine," Eden said. "And thanks for not saying 'I told you so.'"

Anna grinned. "I would never, but I do enjoy helping you get out and experience a bit more of the world. Just let me know if I ever push too hard." She touched Eden's arm.

"I will," Eden said. "I've lived in LA so long, I guess I forget that there are places where I can still go out and not get mobbed. It's nice being ordinary sometimes."

"So nice," Anna agreed. "And good for our egos too."

"Definitely."

They went into the post office, where an employee helped Anna purchase a box and packing materials for Zoe's gift. As they walked back outside, two teenage girls were passing by on the sidewalk, and it was comically obvious the moment they recognized Eden and Anna.

"Oh my God!" one of them squealed while the other reached for her phone as if to share the moment with her friends rather than interact with them in person.

Anna felt Eden tense, so she stepped forward, eager to seize control of the situation. Two teenagers were manageable. She'd been prepared for something like this to happen. "Hi," she said to the teens.

"Hi," the taller teen said, gawking at her. "You're Anna Moss."

"I am," she confirmed with a smile.

The teen looked past Anna. "And you're Eden Sands. Oh my God, this can't really be happening to me right now. Two of my favorite singers walking down the street here in Bumfuck, Vermont?"

"I wouldn't call your town 'Bumfuck,'" Anna joked. "We're here taking a little break between tour dates, really loving the area so far. Got any recommendations for us?"

"Um." The shorter girl blinked at her in obvious surprise. "There's a good place to hike just outside town. I've gone with my family a few times. I think it's called White Rocks."

"Cool. We were hoping to do some hiking. Weren't we, Eden?" Anna turned to her.

Eden had her stage smile in place, the one that revealed nothing. "We were."

"Yeah, White Rocks is great," the first girl piped up. "And Rosa's is the best place to eat for, like, a fancier meal."

"Perfect." Anna fought a smile at the girl's obvious attempt to recommend things that adults would like instead of whatever pizza joint was the local teen hangout.

"Could we, um . . . could we take a selfie with you?" the shorter girl asked, holding up her phone. Its case looked like it had been dipped in glitter, sparkling in the afternoon sun.

"Of course," Anna responded, stepping in for a selfie. She posed for photos with each girl individually and then one with them both, while Eden did the same.

Soon, the teens were on their way, and Anna and Eden got into their rental car.

"Okay?" Anna asked as she put her bag of maple goodies on the back seat.

"Yes," Eden said. "That was fine, not a mob scene at all."

"I don't think we're likely to get mobbed here in Bumfuck, Vermont," Anna joked.

Eden rolled her eyes at her. "Should we push our luck and try dinner at Rosa's? The girl wasn't wrong, from what I've heard. My housekeeper recommended that restaurant too."

"I would *love* to have dinner with you at Rosa's," Anna gushed, not even trying to hide her excitement. "I would have suggested it, but I didn't want to push you too far out of your comfort zone."

"Well, I've had dinner with plenty of female friends before," Eden said, looking suddenly less certain. "It doesn't have to look like a date, does it?"

"No, it doesn't, and because the world generally perceives you as straight, they'll probably jump to the 'gal pal' conclusion if anyone were to photograph us at dinner, but just in case they don't, make sure you're okay with headlines questioning our relationship and your sexuality."

Eden was silent for a moment, drumming her fingers against the steering wheel. Her eyes were hidden behind her sunglasses, so Anna couldn't be sure what she was feeling. "I honestly don't care about headlines questioning my sexuality," she said finally. "My hesitation is that I don't like to share my relationships publicly when they're this new. Trust me, trying to date someone while the world is watching is a kind of pressure you don't want."

"I do trust you," Anna said. "My gut says we could go to dinner at Rosa's and not have it end up on the gossip sites, but obviously I can't say for sure. I don't have much experience dating publicly, since I wasn't famous enough when I was with Camille for anyone to care, so I'll defer to your expertise here. Whatever you're comfortable with."

"I want to go to dinner with you," Eden said with a nod. "I'm certain Stella would have a fit if I ran this past her, but for once in my life, I want to be impulsive and go to dinner with my girlfriend. What do you say?"

"Girlfriend." Anna's heart leaped for joy to hear that word on Eden's lips. "I say yes . . . to dinner and to being your girlfriend."

Eden's eyes widened. "Oh, was that . . . was I being presumptuous by calling you my girlfriend?"

"No." Anna leaned over and kissed her cheek. "I mean, technically we've only been together for a few days, but we were dancing around each other for weeks before that while we were on tour. Plus, we're sharing a house this week, which definitely feels like girlfriend material to me."

Eden exhaled; then she reached for one of Anna's hands. "I guess I was so busy having a crisis about my sexuality that we never talked about our intentions, but this isn't a vacation fling for me or anything like that. I'm pretty damned smitten with you, Anna, and I'm serious about dating you."

"That's music to my ears, because in case you hadn't noticed, I'm pretty damned smitten with you too."

CHAPTER TWENTY-THREE

"This is nice." Eden smiled across the table at Anna. After their conversation in the car, Anna had called ahead to the restaurant and requested a private table. Consequently, they were seated in Rosa's upstairs loft area, overlooking the main dining room below. Since the restaurant was relatively uncrowded, they were currently the only occupants of the loft.

"If the food is anywhere near as good as the ambiance, it'll be a win, but honestly, I feel like we're already winning just being here." Anna beamed at her. Her blonde hair was somewhat windblown from their adventurous afternoon, but Eden loved that they were here in jeans with messy hair, enjoying a romantic dinner like any other couple.

"Ladies, your wine." Their waitress appeared beside the table, holding out the bottle of wine they'd ordered. She poured a taste for each of them, waiting for their approval before she filled their glasses. "Your appetizer will be right out."

"Thank you." Eden had seen the gleam of recognition in the waitress's eyes, but so far, she hadn't said anything or attempted to take any photos, at least not that Eden had seen. Maybe she really could just . . . go out to dinner with her girlfriend here in rural Vermont. The idea was mind boggling in its simplicity.

"To new beginnings," Anna said, holding up her glass. She seemed to glow with happiness tonight, and maybe it was contagious, because Eden felt pretty damn happy too.

She tapped her glass against Anna's before taking a sip. "Our relationship signifies several new beginnings for me, and I'm grateful for all of them."

If it was possible, Anna's expression grew even more dazzling. She was beaming brighter than the candle on the table between them at this point. "Me too."

Eden's gaze dropped to the main dining room below, where the teens they'd encountered earlier had entered with several of their friends. "Uh-oh."

Anna followed her gaze. "Dammit. I'm sorry. I shouldn't have suggested we come here right after they recommended it. I should have expected them to come looking for us."

"You didn't suggest coming here. I did." She drew in a breath and blew it out. "And . . . it's okay. They might not even see us up here, and if they do? We'll survive a few more photos."

"Yeah, but I wanted tonight to be perfect." Anna's expression fell. "I feel like every time I encourage you to take a risk, something like this happens, and it backfires. I think I still underestimate what life is like for someone as famous as you."

"Even when our plans have backfired, I still don't regret them."

"Not even Chicago?"

Eden shook her head. "I was upset at the time, partly because I was so tied up in knots about my feelings for you. Being mobbed like that while I was feeling emotionally vulnerable was . . . a lot. But I don't regret it."

"I do," Anna admitted. "I've been kicking myself ever since for taking you to such a public place and for not noticing sooner that those fans were live streaming us. It could have been a much bigger disaster than it was."

"It could have, but what I'm trying to say is that I felt like I was sleepwalking through my life before I met you, Anna. I was—as you so eloquently put it—living in a cage. I'd lost my way, and my career slump reflected that. Now . . . I'm living again, *really* living."

"You're trying to make me cry in the restaurant now." Anna swiped at her eyes before reaching for Eden's hands.

"Just being honest. You've shown me that sometimes I have to risk *that*"—she nodded toward the group of teens, who had been escorted to a table downstairs but were looking around the restaurant, phones up and clearly on a celebrity hunt—"in order to be happy."

The waitress approached with their salads, setting a plate in front of each of them.

"Is there anything else I can get for you?" she asked.

Eden decided to take the bull by the horns, so to speak. "You know who we are, right?"

The woman's eyes widened comically, and then she nodded, her expression somewhat sheepish, as if she'd been busted doing something she shouldn't. "Yes, ma'am."

"See that group of teens downstairs?" Eden gestured subtly toward them. "We ran into them earlier today, and while they were very sweet, they're obviously here looking for us, and we're just trying to enjoy our dinner. Do you think you could keep them from coming up here?"

The waitress nodded again, looking more assertive now. "Yes, ma'am. I can put up the rope that we use to block the stairs when the loft is closed, and I could also move you to that table over there, where you can't be seen from the restaurant below?"

"That would be perfect," Eden told her. "Thank you so much."

So they moved to a different table. Eden had taken control of the situation in a way that allowed her to stay in the restaurant. She drew in a deep breath and exhaled, relaxing her shoulders as she settled in to enjoy the rest of her dinner.

"Tomorrow, we head to Boston." Anna stroked a hand through Eden's hair as they lay together, naked and satisfied, after several sizzling hours in bed. They hadn't really talked about what would happen once the tour resumed, and now it was time. This week had been magical, but what would their relationship look like once they were back on the road?

"Mm." Eden snuggled closer against her, eyes closed.

"I'll miss waking up beside you every morning." Anna's heart pinched at the thought.

Eden peeked at her through her eyelashes. "Who says you can't still do that?"

"Well, I mean . . . if I spend the night in your room, our teams would know."

Eden shrugged. "I made peace with my team knowing every intimate detail of my life a long time ago. They're discreet."

"You're really taking this whole 'coming out' thing a lot better than I'd expected," Anna admitted. "It doesn't bother you for them to know?"

"Why would it? They adore you, and I'm pretty sure they're going to be thrilled for us. I can't imagine why they wouldn't be."

Anna sat up, hugging her knees against her chest. She hadn't really thought about it, but she certainly hadn't anticipated telling her team right away.

"Is that okay?" Eden sat up, giving Anna a shrewd look. "Because we don't have to tell anyone, if you'd rather keep it between us for now."

"I . . ." Anna gave her head a quick shake. "I don't know. I just assumed you would want to keep things private."

"I do, but keeping it private will be a lot easier with Paris and Taylor's help. They keep all my dirty secrets for me." She stuck her tongue out playfully.

What other dirty secrets were they keeping for her? Anna's stomach squirmed at the thought. "Um . . . okay."

"*Are* you okay?" Eden asked. "Because you look a little freaked out."

"You caught me off guard. That's all. How do you think your team will react?"

"They'll be shocked, probably," Eden said, looking thoughtful. "I mean, *I* had no idea I was gay, so how could they?"

How was she so nonchalant about this? Anna hugged her knees tighter against her chest. "Do they do this for you a lot?" she blurted, realizing the source of her discomfort as she said the words. "Like . . . they're used to covering for your lovers? Helping you sneak them into your room?"

Eden gave her an incredulous look before her expression shuttered the way it did when she was speaking to the press. "Is that a serious question?"

"No." Anna shook her head. "You're right. It's none of my business."

"That's not what I meant." Eden looked toward the window. "More like . . . how many lovers do you think I've had? Honestly?"

Anna waved her hands in front of her face. "I feel like I've stumbled into a trick question."

"Three," Eden said quietly. "There have been three before you, and one of them was my husband. So no, I haven't asked my team to help me sneak someone into my room on tour since I was first dating Zach almost ten years ago. When I said they kept my dirty secrets, I was thinking about how they covered for me during my divorce . . . and how long it had been before that since my husband shared my bed."

Anna didn't know how to respond to that, and now she felt like an ass for her own insecurities. "I'm sorry. My mind spiraled for a minute. I don't even know where that came from."

Eden scoffed. "Trust me when I say you have nothing to feel insecure about when it comes to our sex life. I thought I was clear about all the ways you'd blown my mind on that front."

"You were." Anna leaned in for a kiss.

Eden slid her hands around Anna's waist and peered deeply into her eyes. "So, are you okay with telling our teams so they can help us sneak into each other's rooms?"

"Yeah, I am."

They arrived in Boston at noon on Saturday, where they were whisked to their respective rooms by their respective entourages. Because they'd been away for a week, they would both be expected at the arena by early afternoon to do a full run-through of the show before doors opened to the public.

Eden sat in the living room of her suite as Paris went over the agenda for the afternoon. Everything felt the same as it had for the last two months of the tour—business as usual—except it wasn't the same. *She* wasn't the same.

Usually, her thoughts would be consumed with the upcoming show. She would be impatient to get to the arena, anticipating the thrill of stepping onstage. She'd always felt more comfortable onstage than she did anywhere else. But, while nothing would ever dampen her love of performing, she'd found that same sense of belonging in Anna's arms.

Was that love? Her heart said *yes*.

". . . don't you think?" Paris's voice filtered through her thoughts.

Eden had totally zoned out on their conversation. She focused on her assistant. "Sorry. What was that?"

"Lunch before your *Boston Globe* interview tomorrow?" Paris gave her a funny look. "The reporter will be here at one."

Eden nodded. "Yes, lunch before sounds good."

"Okay." Paris typed rapidly on her tablet, then leaned back in her chair. "So how was Vermont?"

"Wonderful." Eden could feel the dreamy smile on her face.

"I saw some photos of you and Anna out and about together. That was a surprise."

"She convinces me to do a lot of surprising things."

"Are you—"

"Yes," Eden blurted. She didn't even know what Paris had been about to ask, but she couldn't hold this news inside herself for another moment. "We're together."

"Oh." Paris gaped at her. "Wow. I didn't . . . I mean, I *did* wonder, but . . ."

Eden felt herself blushing like crazy. Coming out to her assistant was both easier and harder than she'd expected. She'd been desperate to get it off her chest, but now she felt oddly vulnerable. She cleared her throat, looking down at her hands. "Obviously, we aren't sharing our relationship publicly yet, but I wanted you to know, since you'll probably see Anna hanging around my suite a lot." Her cheeks were about to catch fire at this point.

"Well, you are full of surprises today."

"It's been a surprising month for me." Unable to sit still, Eden stood and paced to the window. She looked out at Boston Harbor, glistening a deep blue beneath the afternoon sun.

"Good surprises?" Paris asked from behind her.

"Yes."

Then it was Paris's turn to surprise Eden as she crossed the room and gave her a hug. "I'm glad. You've seemed happier since you met Anna. We all noticed it. I assumed it was because you'd found a new friend. I mean, I had no idea you were even into women, but I'm really happy for you."

"Thank you," Eden said as she hugged her back. "And for the record, I didn't know either until very recently."

"I guess that was another good surprise then," Paris said. "Well, thank you for telling me. I'll make sure you two get all the discreet time together that you need."

"Thank you. I appreciate it. You can tell Taylor and Stella, too, but I'd like to keep it there for now."

"You got it, boss."

And that was that. Eden was so grateful to have people in her life that made coming out a positive experience. Not everyone was as lucky. She'd chosen the people she surrounded herself with after she cut herself off from her family, and apparently, she'd chosen well.

With that out of the way, Eden could turn her full attention to tonight's performance . . . her first performance with her *girlfriend*. Eden grinned. She couldn't wait.

CHAPTER TWENTY-FOUR

The day had been a whirlwind. Anna had barely seen Eden since their arrival in Boston, other than a few rushed moments during rehearsal. Eden had kept her stage face in place, and Anna hoped that didn't mean she was having second thoughts. Surely things would be hard for Eden, adjusting to her first relationship with a woman while under such intense scrutiny from everyone around her.

When Anna joined her onstage for their duet, wearing the purple dress—the one she'd worn the night of their first kiss—she caught a brief flash of fire in Eden's eyes when they settled on Anna. It warmed her from her head to her toes and made her wonder whose hotel room she'd be sleeping in tonight . . . hers or Eden's?

Just as quickly, the look was gone, and Eden was purely professional for the remainder of their duet. They hugged at the end of the song, the way they did every night, and the crowd roared its approval. Anna waved to the crowd and left the stage. She went to her dressing room to change and then hurried to the side of the stage to watch the rest of Eden's performance.

Eden was so hard to read sometimes. How did she feel about things now that they were back on the road? Anna should have texted her this afternoon to check in. Why hadn't she?

A hand landed on her shoulder, and Anna turned, surprised to find Paris standing there. Eden's assistant didn't usually seek her out. "Hey, Paris."

Paris gave her a warm smile, then leaned in to whisper in her ear. "I just wanted to say congratulations. I'm really happy for you and Eden." And just like that, she was gone, leaving Anna with her mouth hanging open in surprise.

How did Paris know about them? Eden had said she planned to tell her team, but Anna had never expected her to do it this quickly. In fact, she'd been prepared for it to take weeks or even months. But here they were, only hours after their return to the road, and Eden had apparently already kept her word.

Anna's heart leaped. It really did. There was no other explanation for the flutter she felt inside her chest. God, she was so in love with this woman, and there was no use denying it, at least not to herself. How could she be this emotionally invested so soon? She'd meant to take this slow, for both of their sakes.

Anna watched in a lovesick daze as Eden performed the final songs of her set, briefly leaving the stage before returning for the encore in a glittering gold dress. As she wrapped up the final song, Anna moved to the hallway behind the stage, ready to greet her.

Eden came into the hallway, accepting a towel and bottle of water from Paris before she walked straight to Anna and wrapped her arms around her. Anna breathed her in, detecting the faintest hint of Eden's rose-petal lotion beneath the clashing scents of makeup, hair products, and sweat.

After a moment, Eden pulled back, but she didn't let her go. She kept one of Anna's hands in hers as she led the way to her dressing room with Paris at their heels.

"The car will be here in ten," Paris said, then stepped back and closed the door behind herself.

It latched with a solid click, and Anna immediately twisted the bolt to lock it. She spun Eden, pressing her against the door as she brought their lips together. "Did you tell her about us?" she asked as she lost herself in the pleasure of Eden's kiss.

"Mm," Eden responded, hands on Anna's hips, pulling her closer. "I did."

"Wow." Anna nipped hungrily at Eden's lower lip, making her whimper. Eden's hips arched forward to press against Anna's.

"That was okay, right?" Eden asked, pausing their kiss to meet Anna's eyes.

"God, yes. I just didn't think you'd do it so quickly. That was a big deal for you, coming out to your staff. I'm really proud of you."

"Thank you." Eden exhaled, resting her forehead against Anna's. "It was a little scary, but mostly, it felt good, and Paris was great. Did she say something to you?"

"She congratulated me."

Eden smiled as she freed herself from Anna's embrace. "I'm glad, but speaking of Paris, I need to change before she's back to tell us the car is here."

"Fine." Anna fake pouted.

Eden lifted her eyebrows as she began to strip right there in front of Anna, and Anna wasn't pouting anymore. She watched hungrily as Eden shimmied out of that gold dress and hung it carefully on the rack by the door. She put on leggings and an oversize T-shirt and then went into the bathroom to freshen up.

Anna pulled out her phone and started looking at fan photos from tonight's show, but when Eden came out of the bathroom, they were on each other again in a heartbeat. This time, it was Anna who wound up pressed against the wall as Eden kissed her greedily. Anna slid her hands beneath Eden's T-shirt, cupping her over her bra. She wedged a thigh between Eden's, and Eden immediately began to move against her.

They kissed and groped, completely lost in the pleasure of each other's bodies. Anna was so turned on, she was seriously considering whether she had time to finish what she'd started. Eden was grinding against her thigh, eyes shut, and based on her increasingly desperate whimpers, she was just as worked up. Anna reached for the waistband of her leggings.

And then Paris knocked.

Eden let out a low groan. "Dammit."

"Hold that thought," Anna said as she disentangled herself from Eden. "Your room or mine?"

"Mine," Eden answered, cheeks pink as she took several deep breaths and smoothed out her clothes. "I need a shower, but I also need *you*."

"Joint shower?" Anna suggested hopefully.

"I love the way you think." Eden gave her another quick kiss and then led the way out of her dressing room. It was like flipping a switch, the way she was able to slide her stage face into place. Other than her flushed cheeks, there was no indication she'd been close to coming in Anna's arms a minute ago.

If Paris suspected, she didn't give any indication. She looked as professional as her boss as she led them down a hallway to the car, where Kyrie and Taylor were waiting for them. They got into the car like they had every night of the tour, with Taylor sitting in front beside the driver, Paris and Eden in the middle row of seats, and Kyrie and Anna in back.

Anna looked at her assistant, realizing she hadn't told her own team about her relationship with Eden yet. She hadn't expected Eden to beat her to it, but this wasn't the moment. She'd do it tomorrow. As they drove, Kyrie and Paris gave them a rundown of tomorrow's schedule, and a few minutes later, they pulled up to the hotel.

Taylor escorted them both to Eden's door, her expression betraying nothing. She wished them good night and then closed the door to the room behind them.

"Does she know too?" Anna asked as she threw the dead bolt on the door.

"I don't honestly know," Eden said. "But if she doesn't know yet, she will by tomorrow. I gave Paris permission to tell her and Stella."

"You are really the coolest newly minted lesbian ever, you know that?" Anna backed her across the room, loving the way Eden's breath caught as Anna cupped her over her pants. She could feel Eden's heat through the thin fabric.

"God, Anna." Eden's voice was hoarse as she tugged her shirt over her head. "You have no idea how close I was in the dressing room. I need you *now.*"

"How serious are you about that shower?" Anna asked as she began to strip out of her own clothes.

"How much do you care if I'm sweaty and gross from two and a half hours onstage?" Eden cocked an eyebrow, already down to her bra and panties. Indeed, Anna could see the sweat dampening her skin, but she thought it looked delicious.

"I don't care in the slightest, but shower sex does sound fun."

"Solid point." Eden popped the clasp on her bra and tossed it to the side, then tugged her panties down her legs, and Anna couldn't help herself. She tugged Eden against her, sliding a hand between her thighs. "Fuck," Eden moaned, her hips jerking against Anna's hand. She was so wet.

Anna's core clenched in anticipation. She stroked Eden as she stepped her backward toward the bathroom. Eden stumbled, and they were both giggling by the time they staggered into the bathroom, drunk off their need for each other.

Eden started the shower while Anna discarded her underwear, and they stepped inside, kissing and touching, both of them clumsy with desire. Anna's gaze settled on the detachable showerhead.

"Want to play?" she asked as she reached for it.

"Hmm?" Eden looked up, pausing with one hand on Anna's breast, the other on her hip. "Oh."

Anna held the nozzle over their heads, wetting their hair and bodies. Eden slicked her hands with soap and ran them over Anna's body, paying special attention to her breasts. Once they were soaking wet, Anna turned the nozzle so that it cascaded over Eden's breasts, running down her stomach, which visibly tensed beneath the spray.

Eden threw her head back with a cry. "Please."

God, Anna loved it when she begged. She loved watching Eden get so worked up that she lost control. Anna directed the spray lower, and Eden's hips bucked. She whimpered, eyes sliding shut in pleasure. Anna couldn't wait to watch her come.

And then, before she'd realized what was happening, Eden had snatched the showerhead from Anna's hand. She pressed Anna's back against the cold tile, her eyes gleaming with intention as she aimed the nozzle at Anna's breasts, teasing her until it was Anna's turn to beg.

"Please," she gasped, her hips arching forward.

The look on Eden's face could only be described as feral as she dropped her gaze between Anna's legs. Anna almost came on the spot. Eden brushed her free hand over Anna, toying with her before she finally took mercy on her and directed the showerhead so that it beat directly against Anna's clit.

"Fuck!" Anna shrieked, her hips rocking into the spray. It felt so good, so good . . . she clutched at Eden's hips to keep herself upright. Anna felt herself clench as she reached her breaking point. With a groan, she was coming, grinding against Eden as the shower's hot spray massaged every bit of pleasure from her body.

When she opened her eyes, Eden was watching her, bottom lip pinched between her teeth, eyes dazed with desire. "You are so hot," she whispered before claiming Anna's mouth for a searing kiss.

With trembling fingers, Anna took the nozzle from her and aimed it so that it hit Eden right where she needed it. She cried out, gripping

Anna's shoulders as she ground herself against her until she'd followed Anna over the edge with a long, low moan. Once she'd dropped her head against Anna's shoulder, body limp and trembling, Anna replaced the showerhead in its bracket overhead and held Eden close.

"I love that," Eden murmured against Anna's wet skin. "I love *you*." Almost immediately, she tensed, lifting her head to stare at Anna with wide eyes. "I'm sorry. It's too soon to say that, isn't it?"

"No," Anna whispered, her throat tight with tears. "No, it's not, because I love you too."

It was too soon, though. Anna didn't regret telling Eden she loved her, because she meant those words with all her heart. She only wished they hadn't fallen so fast. As she woke next to Eden the following morning, Anna felt vaguely unsettled. Eden, by contrast, looked blissfully happy. Apparently, once she made up her mind about something, she was all in.

And . . . well, maybe Anna was the one who had needed to ease into this relationship. She hadn't been in love with anyone since Camille. Already, Anna's feelings for Eden were stronger than what she'd felt for Camille. Eden had more power than Camille. Eden had more power than almost anyone in this industry. She had the power to break Anna's heart in a spectacularly devastating way. She might not mean to do it, but that didn't mean Anna wouldn't get hurt.

"Paris is on her way up with smoothies," Eden murmured. She looked so *soft* first thing in the morning, so sweet and tender. It was hard to remember this sleep-rumpled woman was Eden Sands, one of the richest and most successful women in the American music business.

"I need to head out after breakfast," Anna told her. "I've got a meeting with Kyrie."

"And Paris has me booked upstairs in the gym. Will you come back this afternoon to watch some TV together?" Eden asked. Tonight was their second sold-out show in Boston. Tomorrow, they'd travel to New York for back-to-back shows at Madison Square Garden, where Anna would get the chance to see Eden's Manhattan condo.

"That sounds good," she agreed.

Eden gave her a gentle smile, reaching out to tuck a strand of hair behind Anna's ear, and warmth flooded Anna's system. Why was she second-guessing this? Had Camille really damaged her so badly that she'd question every relationship after her?

There was a knock at the door, and Eden slid out of bed, donning a robe before she went to answer it. She returned a minute later with two breakfast smoothies, one of which she passed to Anna.

"This is good," Anna said as she took her first sip. "I see why you like them so much."

"Right? Such a good way to start the day. I'd probably give up on them if I had to make them myself every morning, but, well . . . there are perks to being me."

They drank their smoothies together, and then Anna got dressed. She gave Eden a quick kiss before letting herself into the hallway to head down to her room. As she got off the elevator on her floor, she walked straight into a group of fans.

"Oh my God, Anna Moss! I love you!" one of them squealed.

"Thank you." Anna said, painfully aware she was wearing the clothes she'd left the arena in last night, no makeup, her hair an unruly mess from going straight to bed after her adventurous shower with Eden.

"Could I get a selfie with you?" a young woman with short black hair asked.

Anna had no desire to take selfies looking like this, but she couldn't see a way to politely refuse, so she leaned in and smiled. The fans were talking over each other now, clamoring for more selfies while asking what dress she'd be wearing for the duet that night, if she and Eden

266

were dating, what Anna's next single would be: question after question until her head was spinning.

The elevator doors opened, and several more people joined the fray. Had this group texted their friends? Anna kept smiling and posing for pictures, wondering peripherally what to do. She couldn't go to her room without leading the fans right to it, but she couldn't stay by the elevators either. Things were rapidly getting out of hand.

Before she could panic, the elevator opened again. This time, Kyrie stepped out. She took one look at the scene before her and took charge. "Come with me," she said, pulling Anna into the elevator she'd just stepped out of. She put out a firm hand and shook her head when several fans tried to follow them in.

The doors slid shut, and Anna sagged against the wall of the elevator in relief. Was this her life now? She gave Kyrie a grateful smile. "Thank you."

"No problem." Kyrie pushed the button for the floor below, and when the doors opened, she checked the hallway before leading Anna out of the elevator. Kyrie stayed close as she took Anna down the hall to the stairwell and up a flight of stairs to arrive on her floor anew, this time without fanfare.

Kyrie acted as if this were no big deal, and Anna wondered when she'd become such a pro, because she'd handled this as efficiently as Paris or Taylor would have. Not that Anna had found her inefficient before, but Anna and Kyrie had both been inexperienced newcomers when Anna hired her, and now, it seemed, they had both grown up.

"Here we are," Kyrie said as they arrived at Anna's room.

"You're a lifesaver." Anna pulled out her key card and swiped it, then led the way into the room she'd barely set foot inside of yet. She'd dropped off her bags here yesterday before heading to the arena and hadn't been back. The bed was still made, a fact Kyrie took in with subtly raised eyebrows.

"You've gotten a lot more popular since the tour started," Kyrie commented as she headed for the table near the window. "David and I had a conversation about it last week, about what new precautions we should take. I think a good first step is for you not to walk around the hotel unaccompanied anymore."

Anna sighed as she sat at the table across from Kyrie. "You're probably right."

"We can talk about hiring security for you like Eden has, but in the meantime, I'm happy to be your escort," Kyrie said. "I'm always here at the hotel when you are, anyway."

"That would be great," Anna said. "Speaking of Eden . . ." She felt a step behind since Eden's staff already knew about their relationship. Anna and Kyrie were friends, which made the omission feel even worse, especially now that Kyrie had obviously seen that Anna hadn't slept in her own room last night. "We're seeing each other."

Kyrie grinned. "Well, I didn't want to be presumptuous, but I had a feeling that was the case when you headed to Vermont with her last week. That's great, Anna. I'm thrilled for you."

"Thanks." Anna blew out a breath. "It's amazing. *She's* amazing, but . . ."

"But?" Kyrie cocked her head to the side.

"It's just a lot while we're on tour. There's no breathing room, and she . . . she was my idol, you know? It's a lot of pressure to put on a new relationship."

"You do have a habit of falling for your mentors." Kyrie sounded thoughtful. "Are you worried about the parallels with Camille?"

Anna slumped against the table. "That's exactly what I'm afraid of."

"Eden is nothing like Camille," Kyrie said. "I haven't seen you two together as a couple, but Eden has always seemed like she wants to see you succeed, where Camille looked for any opportunity to yank the rug out from under you. She wanted you to be dependent on her, thinking you weren't worthy of anything better."

"You're right," Anna said, blowing out a breath. "But if you see me starting to put my relationship blinders on again like I did with Camille, please tell me, okay?"

"I will." Kyrie fiddled with her tablet, and when she looked up at Anna, her cheeks were unmistakably pink. "I actually met someone during the break too."

"Oh my God, you did?" Anna practically bounced in her seat. "I need details."

"Their name is Tate." Kyrie's cheeks got even pinker. "We'd been chatting online for a few weeks, and we met for drinks while I was home last week. It went really well."

"This is the best news." Anna scooted around the table so she could give Kyrie a hug. She knew Kyrie had been hesitant about dating since she transitioned, so this was a big deal. "Tate uses they/them pronouns?"

Kyrie nodded. "They're a camera operator for that new legal show on HBO. We just really seemed to click once we met in person, you know?"

Anna thought of Eden. "Yeah, I do know, and I'm so happy that you've found someone you click with too. How did you and Tate leave things after your date?"

"We're going to keep calling and texting until I'm back in LA after the tour. I think . . ." Kyrie looked down at her hands. "I think being long distance might be good for us while we get our bearings. I'm going to need to take things slow, so this works for me."

"I'm so glad." Anna had wished for a way to slow things down with Eden, but at the same time, she couldn't bear the thought of being away from her. "Here's to new beginnings for both of us."

The next few weeks were some of the best weeks of Eden's life. She felt relaxed and comfortable with herself in a way she hadn't before. She was energized. She was happy. She was—quite simply—a woman in love.

As the tour made its way down the East Coast, she and Anna fell into a new kind of routine, one where Anna often spent more time in Eden's room than her own. They watched TV together in the afternoons, and Anna almost always spent the night in Eden's bed.

Maybe Eden had expected her first relationship with a woman to take some getting used to, but what was that saying? When you knew, you just *knew*. And Eden knew. She was all in with Anna. But as she sat in her hotel room in Atlanta on this July afternoon, she faced her first real challenge to the happy bubble she'd been living in since Vermont.

Anna had wanted to tell her parents and Zoe about their relationship, which Eden had readily agreed to, but she'd decided to use that as a catalyst to tell her own parents, too, and it had . . . not gone well. Eden had stopped seeking their approval a long time ago, so she surprised herself when she hung up the phone and burst into tears.

Her dad's words rang in her ears. "This will be the end of your career as you know it, once people find out. Honestly, Eden, what are you thinking?"

Of course, he'd been more concerned about what people would think than whether she was happy. Why couldn't he see her as a person—his *daughter*—and not a product to be marketed, just this once?

Now, she had another potentially upsetting phone call to make. She dabbed her eyes and took a cleansing breath, and then she dialed.

Zach answered on the second ring. "Eden, this is a surprise. How are you?"

"Good. I'm good. And you? How are you . . . and . . . and Hallie?" For a horrifying moment, she'd forgotten his new girlfriend's name.

"We're really happy. I didn't expect to fall in love again so quickly, but here we are."

She smiled. His words would have hurt a few months ago, when she was alone and miserable, but now she felt nothing but genuine happiness for him. "I'm glad."

"I've missed talking to you, though," he said. "We said we'd stay friends, and then we sort of fell out of touch. I guess that's partly my fault, because I felt guilty for gushing about Hallie when you didn't . . . well, you hadn't found someone yet."

"I think that's why I pulled away, too . . . so I wouldn't have to hear about her. Not because I'm jealous, but because it made me feel lonely."

"I'm sorry." He sounded pained.

"You have nothing to apologize for, and actually . . . I was calling today to tell you that I'm seeing someone." Now her heart was pounding. She was pretty sure he'd take it well, but on the heels of her conversation with her parents, her emotions were raw.

"That's fantastic," Zach exclaimed, and she could hear the smile in his voice. "Tell me about him."

"Her," Eden whispered as her skin flushed hot. "I'm seeing Anna Moss. I'm . . . in love with her, actually."

There was a beat of silence that seemed to last a lifetime.

"Well, wow . . . I'm . . . you know, I'm not as surprised by that as I probably should be," he said, and she flinched, unsure how to take his words. "That's wonderful, Eden. I'm happy for you, and you're in love with her? That's great. Really great."

"Yeah?" She blew out a breath and unclenched her fists, realizing suddenly how tense she'd been while she waited for his response.

"Isn't this the same woman who's opening for you on tour right now?"

She let out a shaky laugh. "Yes."

"Guess you've been having a wild time on the road." He chuckled. "Good for you. You deserve it. I did wonder sometimes . . ."

"Wondered what?"

"Sometimes we'd be at a party together, and I felt like we were both appreciating the beautiful women in the room, that's all."

She gasped. "No!"

"It's not a judgment, Eden, just an observation. Love is love and all that. I just want you to be happy."

"Why didn't you say anything?" she whispered, dumbfounded that he'd known—or suspected—before she had.

"Say what, 'Hey, gorgeous bride of mine, do you prefer women?' No, I figured you'd tell me if you wanted me to know, and honestly, it wasn't something I really thought about, more of a hazy idea at the back of my mind."

"I didn't know," she told him in a rush. "I didn't know I was gay when we were married."

"Well, I'm glad you figured it out now, and hey, I get it. Women are sexy as hell." He laughed, and she felt her cheeks go hot, but she was laughing too. "Would it be weird for me to invite you and Anna to dinner with Hallie and me once you're back in LA?"

"No, and I'd love that. *We'd* love that."

She hung up the phone a few minutes later with a smile on her face. Coming out was exhausting and stressful, and yet . . . it felt validating even when it was hard. She felt settled in her relationship with Anna now, confident that they were in it for the long haul. Was it time for them to go public?

Certainly she'd face some backlash when she did, but the media had always looked for negative things to say about her, and she'd never let it deter her from being true to herself in the past. Maybe she'd even help some of her fans who were looking for the courage to come out.

#Edanna chatter online continued to increase. Eden had peeked at the hashtag a few times, and she felt a secret thrill to know that so many of their fans wanted to see her and Anna as a couple. She could only imagine their excitement once they learned they were right.

Tomorrow, Eden and Anna would fly to Miami for the final performances on the US leg of the tour. Tomorrow night, Eden was throwing a party at their hotel for the crew and other VIP guests to celebrate the end of this leg of the tour. And maybe it was time for her and Anna to walk in together and announce their relationship to the world. Eden wanted that. She wanted to kiss Anna onstage and watch the crowd go wild. She wanted to stop sneaking Anna into her room and officially share accommodations on the European leg of the tour.

Eden was ready, but was Anna?

Paris knocked at the door. Eden had back-to-back interviews scheduled for the rest of the day, and so did Anna, so they wouldn't see each other today. She had a lot to discuss with Anna during the flight tomorrow. Her stomach fizzed with anticipation as she walked to the door.

CHAPTER TWENTY-FIVE

On Thursday morning, hours before they were scheduled to fly to Miami for the last two performances of the American leg of the tour, Kyrie stopped by Anna's room with coffee. "I heard you and Eden might be sharing a room once we get to Europe?"

"Where did you hear that?" Anna sipped her coffee and frowned.

"Paris said Eden mentioned it."

"Mentioned what? Me not having my own room in Europe?" For some reason, that got Anna's hackles up. Sure, she didn't spend much time here, but she liked having her own space. They were still keeping their relationship under wraps, so she couldn't exactly schedule interviews in Eden's suite.

And Anna had been giving a lot of interviews lately, with magazines and publications she'd only dreamed of before now. She'd signed on for this tour to elevate her status, to be taken seriously as an artist, and it seemed like she'd accomplished that. She hadn't won a major award—yet—but the press David sent her was increasingly high profile.

Kyrie shrugged. "That's what Paris said."

"Well, Paris doesn't work for me. You do, and I want my own room."

"Then you'll have it," Kyrie said with a nod.

Anna took another sip of her coffee. Why would Eden tell Paris that Anna didn't need her own room while they were in Europe? It felt uncomfortably close to the way Camille used to make decisions for her. She'd have a talk with Eden about it later.

"So, for the party tonight . . ." Kyrie paused, a hesitant look on her face.

"Yeah?"

"Well, I received a request from Camille for an invitation. Apparently she's attending the show tomorrow night."

"Camille?" Anna's spine straightened. What in the world was Camille doing in Miami this week? She lived in LA and had rarely left the city when she and Anna were together. She wanted to be wherever the shiniest stars were. Camille loved to be seen and photographed and talked about. LA was made for someone like her. "No way. She's not invited to the party. No."

"I'm in full agreement with you, but I feel like I should point out that if you refuse her request, she might show up tonight and make a scene regardless."

"Ugh." Anna put down her coffee and scrubbed her hands over her face. That was exactly Camille's style, but giving in to her demands felt like Anna was losing all the progress she'd made where Camille was concerned. Still, Anna didn't want her to cause a scene tonight. "Fine. Send her an invite. What's the worst that can happen?"

"She ruins the party for you," Kyrie said sympathetically.

"That's a given," Anna said. "And I can't even flaunt my relationship with Eden in her face since we aren't public yet. Dammit, I was looking forward to tonight too!"

She was still fuming about it when she boarded the plane that afternoon. Eden, by contrast, was beaming as she climbed the steps to the jet, looking glamorous in skinny jeans, a blue silk shirt, and oversize sunglasses. She removed the glasses once they were on board, gesturing for Anna to sit with her.

"What do you think if—"

"Camille is coming to the party tonight."

They spoke at the same time, and then Eden's mouth dropped open.

"Oh," she said after a moment of awkward silence. "Did you invite her?"

Anna groaned. "Under duress."

"Well, that's unfortunate." Eden looked out the window, even though the plane wasn't moving yet.

"Obviously, I don't want her there," Anna said. "She's been bothering Kyrie for an invitation, and apparently she's coming to the show tomorrow, so I'm going to have to see her one way or another."

"She won't cause trouble tonight, will she?"

"I hope not" was all Anna could say.

"Me too," Eden echoed, her expression blank.

"Just let me handle her tonight, okay? If she's being inappropriate, I'll ask her to leave."

Eden's chin went up. "Fine."

"Fine."

The plane began to roll forward, and Anna wished they were on their way back to Vermont. Anywhere but Miami. She'd been involuntarily comparing Eden to Camille since they met, and she couldn't help feeling like tonight was going to be an unmitigated disaster.

Eden had had such high hopes for tonight. Now she was alone in her suite in Miami, wearing a slinky black dress, glaring at herself in the mirror. She couldn't explain the feelings that had arisen in her after she learned Camille would be at the party tonight. Disappointment. Frustration. And something dark and possessive that she could only explain as jealousy.

Anna had told her once that she and Camille had the kind of chemistry that made them fall back into bed together every time they saw each other, even after they'd broken up. Would that happen tonight? Would Eden have to watch them smolder at each other?

No. She knew Anna wouldn't cheat on her, but would she be tempted? Was she still attracted to Camille?

Eden glared at herself even harder. She didn't recognize that seething feeling in her chest, and she didn't like it. She'd never been a jealous person. She hadn't felt this way when other actresses looked at Zach, not even when one of them was his ex.

There was a knock at the door, and Eden schooled her expression, giving herself a polite smile in the mirror. Then she answered the door, affecting her coolest demeanor to hide the ugly things still swirling beneath the surface. Paris and Taylor were there, waiting to escort her downstairs to the party.

As they approached the ballroom, Eden could hear music already playing from within, somewhat muted by the buzz of conversation. Outside the windows on the far side of the room, the Miami harbor beckoned. Several large cruise ships were lined up to the right of the hotel, brightly lit against the rapidly darkening sky. Beautiful.

She wondered what it would be like at some point in the future, entering a party like this with Anna on her arm. Honestly, she couldn't wait. She'd hoped tonight might be that night, but Anna had dropped her bombshell about Camille before Eden had a chance to bring it up.

Obviously, they couldn't announce their relationship while Anna's ex was here, not after everything Anna had told her about how jealous and theatrical Camille was. So Eden had said nothing.

And now here she was, alone as usual, despite being the center of attention. Taylor and Paris both stayed close as the party guests crowded in to greet her, smothering her in praise and requests for photos. In addition to various crew members, she'd invited local press and influencers who were all eager for a sound bite. When she blinked, she saw bursts of light behind her lids, the result of too many camera flashes.

"Want something to drink?" Paris asked.

"Please," Eden said.

"Champagne?"

Eden nodded before she turned to greet several local newscasters. She never drank on a show night, but tonight she could have a glass or two, as long as she remembered to hydrate. The last few months had taken a toll on her, not that she was complaining. Tours were exhausting, but she also loved them more than anything.

More than *almost* anything. Because she had someone now whom she loved even more than a concert performance. How had she gotten so lucky? And where *was* Anna? She darted a quick glance around the room as she was drawn into conversation with the newscasters, but she couldn't see Anna anywhere.

Eden smiled and greeted and posed for photos, barely managing a sip of the champagne Paris had gotten her, but eventually—*finally*—the crowd around her began to thin. Perhaps she'd literally greeted everyone in the room.

"Have you seen Anna?" she asked Paris.

Paris nodded toward the windows.

Eden followed her gaze and immediately wished she hadn't. There was Anna . . . with Camille. They were leaned in close, and Camille's hand rested possessively against Anna's lower back. Eden learned in that moment that it wasn't possible to literally see red. But she *felt* red. Something fiery and hot pumped through her system as she strode in their direction.

Anna looked up to see Eden sweeping toward her in an absurdly sexy black dress, looking every inch the superstar. Her hair and makeup were done to the nines. To anyone else in the room, Eden's expression probably looked polite, but Anna could see the fire in her eyes. Eden was pissed.

And Anna wasn't sure how she felt about that. She was having a perfectly polite conversation with Camille. Surprisingly enough, Camille had been on her best behavior tonight, full of praise for Anna's recent success. Anna couldn't honestly remember a time when Camille had bestowed so many compliments on her. It felt surprisingly good.

As Eden stopped beside her, Anna was reminded of the scene outside the Grammys when Eden had put Camille in her place. She hadn't seen *that* Eden since then, but haughty Eden was back in full force.

"Camille Dupont," she said, and the frost in her tone sent a shiver down Anna's spine. "I wasn't aware your name was on the guest list tonight." That was obviously a lie, but Eden delivered it with a kind of smooth conviction that left Anna breathless.

"No?" Camille's eyes twinkled. "Anna was kind enough to extend an invitation once she learned I was in town tonight."

"That was awfully nice of Anna," Eden said, and whether she realized it or not, she was standing too close to Anna for any platonic purpose. Possessively close.

Anna took a subtle step toward the window, putting some space between herself and the two women who were eyeing each other like competitors in a boxing ring. This was so ridiculous. She and Camille had been having the most cordial conversation they'd had in years before Eden had swooped in and made everything tense.

Camille didn't know about Anna's relationship with Eden, but she'd definitely picked up on Eden's territorial attitude. There was a predatory gleam in Camille's eyes now, the look of a woman who'd just unsheathed her metaphorical claws in the face of a rival. "I was just telling Anna how thrilled I am for her success. She studied under me for years, you know. You could say I launched her career."

"I'm aware of your history." Eden's look was pointed. She knew everything, and she wanted Camille to know she knew.

"Then you must know how special Anna is to me." Camille rested a hand on Anna's arm, and for a moment, Anna feared Eden might actually push Camille's hand away. Eden's eyes snapped dangerously.

"Not really," Eden said. "You haven't even spoken to Anna since you insulted her dress at the Grammys, have you?"

"Anna knows I always keep tabs on her career." Camille's gaze was laser sharp as she looked from Eden to Anna and back. "And a little criticism where it's warranted can only help Anna improve in the future." She swept that assessing gaze over the red-and-black printed dress Anna wore tonight, making an appreciative sound.

"Anna doesn't need your criticism . . . or your approval," Eden snapped.

Anna wanted to leave. She didn't like this side of Eden . . . or Camille, whose earlier friendliness had evaporated. She'd taken Eden's bait, and now they were sniping at each other as if Anna wasn't even here.

"Anna's really come into her own this year. So mature, so lovely to see," Camille said. "She might outpace you in sales soon, Eden."

"Enough." Anna held her hands out in front of herself. "Stop it. Both of you." Horrified to feel tears welling in her eyes, she turned and fled toward the nearest exit, hoping she could sneak out of the party without causing a scene.

No such luck.

A wall of fans waited outside the ballroom, phones up and screaming her name. Anna froze, suddenly aware that her cheeks were wet with tears. She was gasping for breath and could only hope she looked like less of an emotional mess than she felt.

"This way." Kyrie appeared at her side. She led Anna back into the ballroom and steered her toward a different doorway.

"Anna, wait!" Eden called from behind her.

Anna walked faster, hurrying toward what she could now see was a staff entrance. Kyrie ushered her through the doorway into a hallway that was blissfully empty, except for two waiters filling trays with flutes of champagne.

"Anna . . ." Eden sounded closer now, breathless, as if she'd run to catch up with her.

"Not here, ladies," Kyrie said, keeping a hand on Anna's shoulder.

Anna finally turned to face Eden, who was flanked by Paris and Taylor, and wasn't this fun? They couldn't even have their first fight without involving their entire entourage. Anna swiped beneath her eyes, relieved the tears had stopped. Eden's cheeks were pink, but she looked as obnoxiously composed as ever.

Kyrie, Paris, and Taylor escorted them into the staff elevator, and they began a painfully silent ride up to their rooms. Anna glanced at the panel and saw the button for the fiftieth floor was lit. Someone— probably Paris—had selected Eden's floor as their destination, and that made Anna even angrier. She reached out and stabbed the button for the forty-seventh floor, because she was going to her own damn room tonight.

When the elevator stopped on her floor, she stormed out of it. To her annoyance, Eden followed with Taylor, Paris, and Kyrie in her wake. What a ridiculous procession! Anna had never hated being a celebrity more than she did at that moment.

She keyed into her room, unsurprised as Eden slipped in behind her. Anna closed the door as hard as she could, somewhat pleased by the solid *thump* it made as it slammed shut. Then she whirled on Eden. "What the fuck was that?"

"Why are you so mad?" Eden asked, arms clasped over her chest. Her stage face had gone the moment the door closed, and now she looked as upset as Anna felt.

"Because you . . . you acted like Camille down there!" Anna shouted, hoping no one was in the hallway to hear them, although she had a sneaking suspicion Taylor was still there, waiting to escort Eden out of here after their fight.

"What?" Eden had the audacity to look offended. "I am *nothing* like Camille."

"Not usually," Anna said. "But Camille was on her best behavior tonight. We were having a polite conversation, and you just stormed in like an alpha male in a pissing contest and ruined everything."

Eden scoffed. "I was trying to help you."

"I didn't need your help!" Anna was yelling, and she almost never yelled. Her throat hurt, and her eyes stung with fresh tears.

"Why do you think Camille was being so nice tonight, hmm? Why do you think she's here in Miami in the first place?" Eden sounded infuriatingly calm, almost condescending, and Anna couldn't take it, not tonight.

"To see me!" Her face was hot, tears streaming over her flushed cheeks. "Maybe she wanted to be supportive for once. I'm sorry if that made you jealous."

"She was trying to win you back," Eden said. "Your star has risen this year, Anna. Camille sees it, and she *wants* it. She wants to parade you around and tell everyone how she launched your career. She wants to take credit for your success. She's a leech. Trust me, I did you a favor by interrupting."

Trust me, Anna. I was doing you a favor.

Anna's vision went hazy as Eden tossed out one of Camille's favorite, most patronizing lines. Anna had heard it too many times. Her fists clenched against her sides. "You did me a favor? Are you serious right now?"

"Yes, I'm serious." Eden hugged herself tighter, blinking rapidly. "But I'm sorry if I overstepped. I was only trying to help."

"I had things under control with Camille, just like I told you I would. Now you've made a scene, and who knows how many people saw it?"

"I didn't make a scene." Eden's neck was splotched with red, and her voice was higher than Anna had ever heard it. Maybe this was the closest Eden came to yelling.

Anna had the irrational urge to scream in her face, just to see if she could break Eden's control. "Yes, you did. You were territorial and possessive, and Camille can probably guess why. She may be a lot of things, but stupid is not one of them. If she suspects we're seeing each other, she'll start rumors. Did you think about that?"

"I . . . well . . . ," Eden stammered, clenching her arms tighter across her chest. "You know what? I don't care. I was going to ask you to attend the party tonight as my date, because I was ready to make things public, and then you invited Camille and ruined everything."

"You wanted to tell people about us?" That stopped Anna in her tracks.

Eden sucked in a ragged breath. "Yes. I love you, and I want the world to know. I wanted to walk into that party tonight with you on my arm. I wanted to kiss you onstage tomorrow night and let the Edanna fans go crazy for us."

"And I just wanted someone to listen to *me* for a change!" Anna was still yelling. Tears burned her eyes, and she couldn't catch her breath. She wasn't even sure why she was so upset, because she loved Eden just as much, but suddenly Eden was making decisions for her the way Camille had, and Anna couldn't go through that again.

She *wouldn't*.

"I listened!" Eden cried. "I didn't say anything to anyone about us tonight without your permission. I just . . . I couldn't stand seeing you with her."

"But you aren't listening. You told Paris I wouldn't need my own hotel room anymore without even talking to me about it, and then— despite me asking you to let me handle Camille tonight—you just blasted in there and made a scene that will probably make headlines tomorrow."

"I'm sorry about making a scene with Camille." Eden pressed her hands over her face, and when she took them away, her cheeks were streaked with tears. "But I didn't tell Paris you don't need a hotel room. I just mentioned to her that you might not, that I wanted to ask you about it since you were spending almost every night in mine. It seemed pointless to have two."

"Then why didn't you ask me?"

"Yet, Anna." Eden sounded frustratingly calm despite the tears on her cheeks. "I hadn't asked you *yet*. There were a lot of things I wanted to talk about during our flight today, and then you brought up Camille and derailed the conversation."

But Anna's mind had spun ahead to Europe, to the fact that Eden *could* cancel Anna's hotel reservation if she wanted to. She had that power. She got to make all the decisions about the tour because she was the star. What if they broke up? Would Eden use the tour to punish her, to sabotage Anna's newfound success?

That's what Camille would do.

Anna pressed her hands over her eyes. "I feel so powerless right now."

"What? Why?"

"Because you're *you*." Anna forced herself to look at Eden. "This is your tour. I'm just the opening act. I'm . . . replaceable."

Eden made a sound like she'd been kicked in the stomach. "You are *not*."

"But I am. You could get someone else to open for you in Europe if we . . . if we broke up or whatever." Anna swallowed painfully.

"Stop it." Eden stepped forward and took Anna's hands in hers. "We aren't breaking up, and even if we did, I would never replace you as my opening act. Anna, I'm so sorry for how I acted downstairs, but you're just being ridiculous now."

Don't be ridiculous, Anna. You're overreacting.

Camille's words echoed in her head, and when Anna exhaled, she half expected to see smoke escaping from her nostrils. She certainly felt like she was on fire. "Don't *ever* call me ridiculous. I never thought you'd act like Camille. I don't even know who you are right now."

"That makes two of us, then." Eden's voice trembled, and more tears splashed over her cheeks. "Because I can't believe you'd accuse me of being anything like her."

Anna pulled her hands free from Eden's. "I just . . . I need some space."

"Oh." Eden blinked. "You mean . . ."

"I want you to leave. I need to be alone tonight."

"Okay," Eden whispered. "But . . . we're okay, right?"

"I don't know. I just . . . I need time to think." And she needed a woman who respected her request for space. Camille had never been that person. She'd push and smother Anna when she asked for room to think.

But Eden nodded. "Okay, I'll be . . . I'll be in my room. Please call if you want to talk more, okay? Or just come up?"

"Not tonight." Anna told her. "I'll talk to you in the morning."

"Okay," Eden murmured, eyes downcast. Her cheeks were wet with tears. "I just, um, need to text Taylor."

"Yep." Anna turned toward the window. Even upset, she didn't want Eden to go out there without her bodyguard for backup. She heard Eden typing on her phone and several heartbreaking sniffles. And then . . .

"Bye, Anna."

"Bye." Anna flinched as the door closed behind Eden. Unlike Anna, she'd closed it gently, leaving with a whimper instead of a bang.

CHAPTER TWENTY-SIX

"And then . . . then she said I was being ridiculous," Anna sobbed into the phone.

"Well, that's total bullshit." Zoe sounded outraged.

"I just feel . . . I don't know. Overwhelmed." Anna wiped her face with the already wet sleeve of her dress. She hadn't been able to stop crying since Eden left. They'd said some awful, hurtful things, and Anna felt sick. Her mind was a whirlwind, blurring her fight with Eden into every fight she'd ever had with Camille until she was dizzy with the parallels. Why did she keep falling for women more powerful than she was? She *hated* this feeling.

"Well, you're basically living and working with her right now, and that's a lot for any new relationship. Is there any way you can take a break from the tour, come home for a few days to catch your breath?"

"No," Anna said miserably. "We're about to fly to London, and then we'll be nonstop across Europe, and I . . . maybe I *do* need a break."

"Then come home," Zoe said. "Fuck the tour. Eden's behavior tonight makes me so uncomfortable after everything you went through with Camille. If she truly loves you, she'll understand you need a break."

Anna wiped more tears from her cheeks, remembering what Kyrie had told her about her new relationship with Tate. *I think being long distance might be good for us while we get our bearings. I'm going to need to take things slow, so this works for me.*

"I'd have to break my contract," Anna told Zoe.

"And I repeat: if she loves you, she'll understand." Zoe's voice was firm.

If Anna left the tour, Eden could sue her. And maybe that was exactly why Anna had to do this. If Eden wanted to pull her strings, Anna would cut them. She wouldn't be controlled, not ever again.

"I'm going to call David," she whispered.

"Good luck," Zoe said. "Call me back after."

"Okay." Anna felt hysteria bubbling up as she disconnected the call and dialed David's number. She was still crying as she told him everything that had happened that night. "I need a break, David. I want out of the European leg of the tour."

"Whoa, now. Let's not be hasty," David said in her ear. "If you back out, you'll be in breach of contract. Eden's team can force your hand, threaten to sue if you don't fulfill your contracted performances. Or they can take your pay." He paused. "For the whole tour. You'll earn nothing. In fact, you'll lose money, because you still have to pay your staff and dancers."

"And that's why I have to do it." Anna's voice shook. "I can't be with her while she has this much control over my life. I need to do this for the sake of our relationship."

"Okay," David said quietly. "But sleep on it first. Decisions like this should never be made when you're this upset."

"No, I have to do it now *because* I'm upset, before I forget how she made me feel tonight. Please, David. Promise me you'll do it tonight."

"Anna, no."

"Yes." She put every ounce of her strength into that word.

He sighed heavily into the phone. "Fine. If you're absolutely sure."

"I am. Thank you."

"I'll call with an update when I have one." He disconnected the call.

Anna set down her phone, tears streaming over her face. She was overreacting. She knew she was. But she also knew she had to do this to protect herself. Once she was no longer contractually obligated to Eden, hopefully they'd be able to continue their relationship on even ground. But that depended on how Eden reacted to what Anna had just done. She wiped more tears from her cheeks, then stripped out of her party dress and headed for the shower.

If Eden sued her for breach of contract, that would be the end of their relationship. And even if she didn't, she might be so angry that she never wanted to see Anna again. But as Anna sobbed against the shower tiles, she knew it was a chance she had to take. Seeing Camille tonight had been a timely reminder of what Anna had left behind. She was stronger now. She'd worked so hard to get this strong.

By the time she got out of the shower, her phone was ringing. David's name gleamed on the screen. Suddenly, her decision felt a lot more real. She'd breached her contract, and now she had to deal with the fallout. She started to shake.

"Well, it's done," he said as she connected the call.

"Oh." Her knees went out from under her, and she sat heavily on the bed, wrapped in a towel, her hair dripping down her back. The events of the last hour felt like some sort of drunken nightmare, even though she'd barely had anything to drink. Tonight's bender had been the emotional kind, and now she'd sobered up and realized what she'd done. Anna felt sick.

"She let you out of your contract, no penalties. You get to keep your salary for the shows you've already performed, which is honestly more than you deserve for pulling a stunt like this." David tsked. "So that's that. I asked Kyrie to schedule a flight back to LA for you both on Sunday morning."

"Oh." Anna's throat constricted painfully. That was that. She was done. She was out.

Camille would have sued her. Camille would have made threats and done everything in her power to force Anna to go to Europe with her. Eden hadn't even tried to fight her. She hadn't tried to control Anna. Eden had respected her decision, no questions asked.

Eden wasn't Camille, not by a long shot.

Oh God. What have I done?

"I'll have Kyrie check in with you in the morning, okay?"

"Mm-hmm," she managed through her tears. "Thank you."

"Yep. Sorry it didn't work out. I'll talk to you soon."

"Thanks. Bye." She hung up the phone. The screen glistened with a combination of tears and water from the shower. As she wiped the moisture from the glass, she saw Eden's name gleaming on the screen.

Eden:

Jesus, Anna!

Eden:

How did we get here?

Eden:

I'm sorry. I'm so sorry.

Eden:

Please call me? Or let me see you?

Eden:

Please.

The first text had been sent not long after Anna got off the phone with David the first time. She sobbed harder, having the sudden crushing realization that she'd fucked up. Seeing Camille tonight had sent her spiraling into a bad headspace. Now she'd ruined *everything*.

Eden wasn't pulling Anna's strings. No, that was still Camille. After all this time, Anna was *still* letting Camille control the way she reacted to certain situations, and now it might have cost her the woman she loved. Well, no more.

Without pausing to consider what she was doing, Anna typed in the number she still knew by heart, despite having deleted Camille from her address book years ago. It connected almost before it had begun to ring.

"Anna? What a lovely surprise." Camille's voice was like velvet, it was so smooth. Anna could hear the thorns underneath, though, and she was tired of repairing the damage they caused.

"I'm just calling to say I'm done, Camille. If you ever ask for another party invite, it will be declined. If we bump into each other at an awards show, I will say a polite hello and keep walking. We. Are. Finished."

"I guess you've managed to latch yourself on to Eden Sands after all, hmm?" Camille purred. "Well, darling, that won't last. It never does with women like her."

"You're not listening to me." Anna's voice rose. Her throat was still raw from shouting at Eden. Performing tomorrow would be rough, except . . . she wouldn't be. She was off the tour. Because she'd let Camille get in her head. Again. Fresh tears broke free. "You're toxic, Camille. Your criticisms don't help me improve. They cut me down. Honestly, I could spend hours explaining how badly you've hurt me over the years, but I don't have the energy, and you'd never listen anyway. I've let you poison my life for way too long, but it ends tonight."

"How dare you speak to me like that, you ungrateful little—"

"Do us both a favor and don't finish that sentence. I'm finished. I don't know how to be any more clear about it. Goodbye, Camille. Don't contact me or my staff again."

She wrenched the phone away from her ear and stabbed the red button to end the call. Then she curled up on her bed and sobbed. A heavy feeling settled over her, and she shivered, realizing suddenly she was still wrapped in a towel from the shower. She'd finally said the things she should have told Camille years ago, but had she said them too late?

With shaking fingers, she lifted her phone and clicked on Eden's name. "I'm so sorry," she gasped the moment she heard the call connect.

Eden had thought a broken heart was another of those romance clichés. It hadn't hurt *that* much when Zach asked for a divorce. She'd been disappointed, sad, but also—deep down—relieved.

But now . . . she had a physical ache in her chest, throbbing with each beat of her heart. "Why?" she whispered into the phone, because she had no idea how they'd gotten from her moment of jealousy at the party to Anna backing out of the tour.

It made no sense. And it hurt. God, it hurt *so much*.

"I messed up," Anna said just as quietly. "Can I see you?"

"Yes. Come to my room . . . or I'll come to yours."

"I'll come to you." Then Anna was gone.

Eden sat there in her pajamas, face scrubbed clean from the makeup she'd worn earlier. Luckily, she'd already schmoozed everyone she needed to schmooze before she left the party, so she'd been able to retreat to her room after she left Anna's. She'd been in the middle of a good cry when Stella called with the news that rocked Eden's world.

Maybe now she would at least find out why Anna had done it. Ten agonizing minutes passed before Eden heard a knock at the door. When she opened it, Anna stood there in leggings and a hoodie, her hair wet and uncombed, hanging messily around her face.

"Sorry, I had to get dressed, and I . . ." She gestured to Kyrie, who stood beside her with a sheepish expression. "I can't walk the halls alone anymore."

Eden nodded, gesturing Anna inside. She was relieved when Kyrie didn't try to follow her in. Eden closed and locked the door, then turned to face Anna, not even trying to keep the hurt or the anger out of her expression. "What the fuck, Anna?"

"I panicked." Anna's voice shook, and tears streamed over her cheeks. "I'm so sorry."

"Well." Eden didn't know what to say. Mostly, she was sad. So devastatingly sad. She'd been looking forward to traveling Europe with Anna so much. The idea of her not being there . . . Eden felt her own tears begin to fall. "Are you breaking up with me? Or did you just not want to tour with me anymore?"

"Neither." A sob escaped Anna's throat. "I'd never seen you act the way you did with Camille earlier. It scared me, and I just . . . lost it."

Eden exhaled, clenching her fists at her sides. "I'm sorry for causing a scene downstairs. I didn't mean to get jealous or possessive. I just . . . I hate that woman. I hate the way she treats you, and I wanted her to leave you alone."

"I know," Anna gasped through her tears. "I still think you escalated things with her tonight instead of helping, but that's no excuse for the way I reacted."

"We both fucked up tonight," Eden agreed.

Anna nodded. "We did, but I made the biggest fuckup of all by breaking my contract. I thought you'd fight me. I think I *wanted* you to fight me. I wanted to see if you'd wield your power and try to control me the way Camille did."

"I told you I'd never do that." Eden couldn't believe Anna had thought she would . . . even for an irrational moment. That hurt so fucking much.

"You did, and I should have trusted you. If I could take it back . . ."

"You probably could," Eden said with a shrug. "I mean, if you really wanted to."

Anna swiped at her tears. "What?"

"If you want to unbreak your contract, I won't fight you on that either, but . . . we need to talk first. Obviously. Because this is a lot, and I'm really upset. And hurt."

Anna looked at her hopefully. "Do you think I could?"

"I don't know. I'm not a lawyer. Talk to me, Anna."

Anna dropped onto the bed and covered her face with her hands. "I panicked. Did I say that already? David tried to make me sleep on it, and I overrode him. I'm going to call him back and tell him to never let me do that again."

"Sounds like a good idea." Eden sat beside her, keeping some space between them.

"Did you mean what you said about walking into the party together? About kissing me onstage? You're ready for that?"

"I *was* ready for that." Eden's eyes stung, and her stomach felt sick. "Then you backed out of your contract without even talking to me first, and now . . . I don't know what to think. You broke my heart tonight."

Anna's expression crumpled, and her shoulders slumped. "I'm so sorry. I've told you what it was like with Camille, the ways she would control me and undermine me. And today, Kyrie told me that you wanted me to give up my hotel room, and then you got in a pissing match with Camille, and I'd . . . I'd never seen you act like that before."

"*I'd* never seen me act that way before either," Eden admitted. "I don't intend to make a habit of it, because I didn't like myself very much, either, but I'm new at this. I've never loved anyone the way I love you. I'm protective of you, but that's not the same thing as being manipulative or possessive. I didn't think you were going to run off with Camille. I just didn't want her to hurt you, and I'm sorry that *I* ended up hurting you instead."

"Thank you," Anna whispered. "See? You're amazing, and I overreacted. Can I call David back right now and tell him to undo it?"

"I don't think we're there yet, to be honest." Eden looked up at the ceiling, trying to gather her thoughts. "Because I still don't understand why you backed out of the tour. I understand why you were upset with me, but why didn't you just talk to me? Why go behind my back like this? I felt so blindsided when Stella called . . . like I'd misread our entire relationship."

"I just . . . I felt like we could never be on equal footing when you had this power over me. If I wanted to walk away, you could sue me, and that's terrifying."

Eden exhaled. "Okay. Wow. I would never use our tour contract against you because we had a fight, and if you were worried about that . . . Anna, you should have *told* me. If you'd asked, we could have voided your contract and drafted up a new one."

"Really? You would do that for me?"

"Of course. I'd be happy to work out a new contract that gives you flexibility to walk at any point with no penalty . . . or whatever it takes to give you equal footing in our relationship. I care so much less about the tour than I do about you, Anna."

"And those are the words Camille never said," Anna breathed.

"I'm not her. You have to stop comparing us if this is going to work."

"I know." Anna sucked in a deep breath and blew it out, facing Eden. "You're right, and I'll do my best to stop if you'll give me another chance. Please forgive me for overreacting tonight. I couldn't bear it if this was the end for us, Eden. You're the love of my life."

Eden's eyes overflowed, tears blazing hot trails over her cheeks, washing away the last of her hurt feelings. "And you are mine. Of course I forgive you. Couples fight. And I meant everything I just said about that new contract. I'll give you whatever you need to feel like an equal in our relationship."

Anna nodded, grinning and sobbing at the same time. "I want that new contract. I want to go to Europe with you, and I want to kiss you onstage tomorrow night in front of everyone."

"Even Camille?" Eden asked. "You said she'll be at the show, right?"

"I doubt it, actually. I called her just now and basically told her to fuck off. But even if she still comes tomorrow . . . I'm finished giving her power over my life."

Eden reached for her, clenching Anna's hands in hers. "Then let's do it."

Anna smoothed a hand over the embroidered green skirt of her dress. It was the same dress she'd worn during their Grammy performance, the performance—and the dress—that had started it all. And now, she'd wear it for another new beginning.

She slipped into place behind the barrier onstage as Eden began to sing "After Midnight." Happy tears filled Anna's eyes as she listened to Eden sing. This morning, she and Eden had had a conference call with David and Stella. They'd hammered out the details for a new contract for Anna, one that gave her the flexibility she needed to have control of her situation.

As Eden had cheekily informed her, she no longer needed Anna to boost her own popularity. Eden was back on top of the charts and breaking her own records. Anna's numbers were better than they'd ever been too. Together, they'd lifted each other up, boosting each other to their best year yet.

Camille had contacted Kyrie to say she wouldn't be attending tonight's show. She was currently on a plane, headed back to LA. Perhaps, after Anna had unleashed on her last night, she'd finally gotten the message that they were finished.

"But after midnight . . ."

On her cue, Anna stepped out from behind Eden. She turned to face her, and for just a moment, Eden's stage face broke. She grinned at Anna with unbridled happiness before returning to character. They sang, moving around each other with the practiced ease of two people who'd done this almost every night for the past three months.

When the song ended, Eden pulled her into her arms the way she did every night. Then they turned to face the crowd. The fans were on their feet and screaming with enthusiasm. Anna saw at least three **EDANNA4EVER** signs. She and Eden waved to the crowd before turning toward each other.

Eden lowered her microphone, staring into Anna's eyes. "Sure you want to do this?" she mouthed.

Anna nodded, breathless with anticipation.

Eden leaned in, pressing her lips to Anna's, and the resulting roar from the crowd almost knocked her off her feet. What started as a peck on the lips soon turned into a real kiss, both of them spurred on by the electricity of the crowd, which was now chanting "E-dann-ah! E-dann-ah!"

Eden's hands rested on Anna's hips as she kissed her slowly and thoroughly, and Anna was melting in the very best way. Her eardrums throbbed with the noise of the crowd. She was so happy. So alive. So in love.

Finally, Eden lifted her head, giving Anna a somewhat dazed grin. "I love you."

Anna could barely hear her over the screams from the audience. "Love you more."

She turned to the crowd and gave them a dramatic bow, which drew even louder shrieks in response. EDANNA signs bounced energetically over people's heads. Anna saw tears on several women's smiling faces.

Anna felt tears of joy on her own cheeks. Then she spun to give Eden another kiss before she left the stage. She could hardly wait to kiss her again after the encore . . . and for the rest of their lives.

EPILOGUE

Six Months Later

After weeks of careful planning, Eden was thwarted by a cat. She sat cross-legged in the middle of Anna's bed, staring at Nelle, who stared right back, emerald eyes daring Eden to find out what would happen if she tried to move her. Tentatively, Eden reached toward her. Nelle raised a paw, claws extended.

Eden sighed. She couldn't risk a cat scratch today. In a matter of hours, Anna's home would be filled with people—stylists and makeup artists, assistants and publicists—here to get Eden and Anna ready for tonight's Grammy ceremony.

There would be endless photos on the red carpet, and if Eden won—if *they* won—those photos would include close-ups of her hands holding the award. So no, she couldn't risk Nelle's wrath today.

"C'mere, Nelle." Eden snapped her fingers in an attempt to lure the cat toward her.

Nelle narrowed her eyes, curling herself more tightly over her prize.

Eden leaned forward, twirling the drawstring on her purple hoodie. She and Nelle constantly disagreed over whether this string was a toy. Nelle considered it her life's purpose to wrestle the draw-string out of the hoodie, while Eden maintained that strings on cloth-ing were off limits. But today, she would sacrifice her favorite hoodie to get Nelle to move.

But Nelle, perhaps sensing Eden's mounting desperation, only tucked her front paws beneath herself, settling in for the long haul.

Of course, Anna chose that moment to walk into the bedroom, carrying a box of her own. "My parents sent us a gift. Dad says it's a good luck gift for tonight, and knowing him, it's bound to be some-thing quirky." She sat on the edge of the bed, looking at Eden and then Nelle. "Are you in a standoff with my cat?"

Eden's skin flushed hot. This wasn't how she'd planned it, dammit. "Um . . ."

Nelle sat up, revealing the black velvet box she'd been sitting on. She nudged it with a paw as if presenting it to Anna herself.

Anna squeaked, pressing a hand to her mouth.

To hell with scratch-free hands for the Grammy red carpet. Eden grabbed the box, but when Nelle swatted her hand in retribution, it was a soft paw. Eden's heart was racing, and a jittery feeling had taken hold of her body, because . . . there was no going back now. Ring box clutched in one hand, she slid off the bed to kneel on the floor at Anna's feet.

Anna still had a hand pressed to her mouth, tears glistening in her eyelashes.

For a moment, Eden could only smile at her. She loved this woman with her whole heart. Then she cleared her throat. *Here goes nothing . . .*

"Anna, before I met you, I thought I knew what love was. I thought I was happy. I thought the only place I'd ever truly feel like myself was onstage in front of an arena full of people, but I was so wrong. You turned my world upside down and showed me all the beautiful, wonderful, passionate things I was missing. You were there for me while I figured out my sexuality, always knowing just what to say. You're my best friend and the love of my life, and nothing in the world would make me happier than if you'd agree to be my wife."

Tears spilled over her cheeks as she opened the box, revealing the ring inside. She'd chosen a simple platinum band with a round diamond encircled by tiny pavé diamonds that created a glittering ring around it. The ring had reminded her of Anna, so bright and beautiful as she surrounded Eden with love.

"Yes," Anna gasped, sliding down to join Eden on the floor. She took Eden's face in her hands and kissed her soundly, tears mixing on their cheeks. "A million times yes. Eden, I love you so, so much . . . even if you did just basically let my cat propose to me because you were too afraid to move her after she claimed the ring."

"Hey," Eden protested. "What if she scratched up my hands right before the Grammy red carpet?"

Anna gave her an adoring smile before her gaze dropped to the ring. "It's so beautiful. I can't believe you just proposed! Oh my God, this is the best day ever."

Eden took the ring out of the box and slid it onto Anna's finger, and for a moment they both just stared at the way it sparkled against Anna's tanned skin. "I feel like I was waiting for you, even before we met," she whispered. "I waited my whole life for you."

"And I spent my life dreaming about a fantasized version of you," Anna said. "I love the real you so much more."

Eden's heart overflowed with joy and anticipation for the future. "Last year this time, I never would have thought I'd be marrying a woman." She ran a thumb over the diamond on Anna's finger. "Or that I would be proposing to anyone, for that matter."

"I love everything about this moment," Anna said dreamily. "Even Nelle's interference."

Eden scoffed, looking up to see the cat watching them from the bed. "I put the ring down for *one minute*, and she sat on it like she was nesting."

Anna laughed, reaching up to rub her cat affectionately under the chin. "She keeps things interesting."

"I love you." Eden leaned in for a kiss, and before she knew it, Anna was in her lap, kissing her with a kind of intensity that hadn't lessened in the months they'd been together. Eden hoped their passion never dimmed.

They scrambled onto the bed, pushing the box from Anna's parents to the side as they stripped out of their clothes, bodies moving together in practiced ease as they quickly brought each other to climax.

"Wish I could stay here with you all afternoon." Anna lifted her hand, moving it this way and that to admire how the diamond reflected the sunlight spilling across the bed. It cast rainbow patterns over Eden's bare chest.

"But alas, the cavalry will be here soon, which means we'd better rinse off before they arrive." Eden stroked a hand through Anna's hair, making no attempt to move.

"If we shower together, we can lie here another ten minutes."

"I love the way you think." Eden reached for Anna's hand, obsessed with the way the ring looked on her finger and how it felt against her own fingers as she clasped them with Anna's.

"Do you want me to wear it tonight?" Anna asked, following her gaze. "Should we make it red carpet official?"

"That's up to you, but I vote yes. I want the whole world to know we're getting married." Overall, coming out for Eden had been a non-event. The media had been more interested in her relationship with Anna than in discussing her sexuality, which was exactly what she had wanted. She'd received a few hurtful comments—as was to be expected—but for the most part, everyone loved that #Edanna was real, so Eden saw no reason to delay sharing their news.

"Me too. Let's do it." Anna rolled to the side, reaching for the box she'd brought into the bedroom, the gift from her parents. "You didn't tell them about this ahead of time, did you?"

"No. As much as I love your parents, I didn't ask for your hand in marriage. I've never understood that tradition."

"Me either. So this isn't our first engagement gift, then. Let's see what it is." She sat up and slid a finger under the flap to loosen the tape. Inside the shipping box was another box, this one white and unmarked. Anna opened it to reveal one of her father's model boats. "Oh," she said, lifting the boat out of the box.

It was a sleek sailboat with a white hull, and Eden's heart warmed to think that Anna's dad had made it for them. Now that they were engaged, her mind had already started spinning ahead to buying a house together, because neither Anna's duplex nor her condo really suited them as a couple. They needed their own home, and this would be perfect on the mantel.

Anna had told her once that she'd always wanted to own one of the beachfront houses that ran up the California coastline, and Eden couldn't think of anything more perfect, especially if they managed to find a house on a private beach where Eden could dip her toes in the ocean without being mobbed by paparazzi.

"Look." Anna turned the boat to the side so that its name was visible, printed in blocky blue letters. **EDANNA.**

"Oh my God." Eden started to laugh. "That's amazing."

Anna grinned. "It's a ship. *Our* ship. Did my dad just use the fandom term correctly?"

"I think he did. Your dad is legendary."

"He is indeed."

Anna was about to burst out of her skin. Beside her, Eden looked as serene as ever in a sleek white dress, although Anna knew by now that she was likely freaking out on the inside. On the stage before them, the announcer had begun to read the nominees for Best Pop Duo / Group Performance. This was both Anna's and Eden's only nomination of the night, as neither of them had put out a new album last year, having spent most of it on tour.

But they'd released one single together last September . . . their duet. "Turbulent" had become an instant hit, rocketing to the top of the charts and inspiring an outpouring of love and support from their fans, who were enamored with its empowering message.

Anna looked down at her hand, which was clasped in Eden's. The diamonds winked in the glare of the camera hovering in front of them. They hadn't even made it off the red carpet before #Edanna is engaged! was trending on social media, accompanied by a photo of Eden kissing her as she held Anna's hand toward the cameras.

"And the Grammy goes to . . ."

Anna's breath caught. No matter what happened tonight, they were both winners. Anna had won several Billboard Music Awards last fall and was about to release a new album that promised to cement her status as an adult artist. But she still didn't have a Grammy . . .

"Eden Sands and Anna Moss for 'Turbulent'!"

The camera moved in for a close-up as Eden leaned over to give her a quick kiss, beaming at Anna before she tugged her to her feet. Anna couldn't *feel* her feet. She felt like she was walking on air as Eden guided her down the aisle and onto the stage, where a shiny gold gramophone was pressed into her hands.

Anna's vision went hazy, and she looked desperately to Eden for guidance. Eden was gazing at her with so much love, so much *pride*, it took Anna's breath away. When she looked down at the Grammy cradled in her arms, the diamond ring on her finger shone brightly beside it. *What a day* . . .

Eden stepped up to the podium, as composed as Anna was speechless. "Thank you so much to everyone who helped make this award possible for us tonight, especially Stella Pascual, Paris Kemsley, and the rest of my team. It's an honor to be recognized for a song that's so deeply personal to me, a song I wrote with the woman I love. This one's for everyone out there who's been through turbulent times."

She turned, kissing Anna on the cheek as she nudged her toward the podium. Anna stepped beside her, staring out into the arena full of peers and legends, a group she hadn't felt worthy of standing before last year. Tonight, she did.

"Thank you," she spoke, her voice trembling. "Thank you for believing in the queer pop star who wears rainbows on her clothes and makes rainbows with her music. I've dreamed of this moment my whole life and can't quite believe I'm standing here now, let alone accepting my first Grammy beside the woman who inspired me to chase my dreams. Eden, you're my idol and my everything, and I'm stunned that I get to share this moment with you."

She turned to smile at Eden, her vision sparkling with the tears in her lashes. Then she faced the crowd again. "Mom, Dad, John, thank you for always believing in me. Kyrie and David, I couldn't have done it without you. To all the fans, I love you more than you could possibly know." She held the Grammy over her head, grinning. "Edanna forever!"

Music began to play, ushering them off the stage, and Anna flung her arms around Eden, spinning her in a giddy circle. Today really was the best day ever. They walked offstage, where an usher waited to take them to the pressroom.

Anna gazed down at her award as she walked, stumbling into Eden in her distraction. Eden snaked an arm around her waist to steady her.

The rhinestone accent on Anna's dress snagged in the chiffon on Eden's, anchoring them together, just like that moment at the Grammys last year. Anna's brain sparked. "I think I just titled our next duet."

Eden smiled at her. "Oh yeah?"

Anna nodded breathlessly. "Stars collide."

ACKNOWLEDGMENTS

If you've read my bio or followed me on social media, you may know I'm a lifelong fangirl. It started when I was about four years old and sent a fan letter to Olivia Newton-John (it was the '80s, after all). I received an autographed photo back in the mail. Little Rachel was completely dazzled, and I've had stars in my eyes ever since!

Over the years, I've been involved in a lot of fandoms, from musicians to actors and TV shows, but for me, there's always been something extra magical about pop stars. There's nothing like the thrill of a live show. That moment when the houselights drop, the crowd roars, and you see your idol on the stage for the first time? Pure magic! I've attended countless concerts over the years, from the front row to the nosebleed section. I've been backstage. I've worked as event security. You could say I'm a bit of a concert junkie!

So you can imagine that celebrity romance has always been a favorite trope of mine. I love the glitz and the glamour. I love the moment when the superstar gives a real smile to her love interest, instead of her professional smile. I love watching someone fall for their celebrity crush. For all these reasons and more, writing this book was an absolute joy, and I couldn't be any more in love with Eden and Anna (and no, neither of them is based on an actual pop star—they are 100 percent themselves).

As always, it takes a village to bring a book to fruition. Thank you so much to the amazing team at Montlake! I couldn't be more thrilled for the opportunity to create another book together. Lauren Plude, thank you for being so amazingly enthusiastic about my books and for your guidance to help make them shine.

Thank you to my awesome agent, Sarah Younger, for helping to make my author dreams come true. By the time this book releases, we will have been working together for ten years. How's that for a milestone?!

Annie Rains, critique partner extraordinaire! Thank you for always guiding me in the right direction with your notes. I've said it before, but I can't imagine doing this without you.

I often let readers choose and name the animals in my books. This time around, I owe thanks to the lovely Jude Silberfeld, who named Villanelle the cat.

A huge thank you to everyone who's read, reviewed, recommended, or otherwise supported my books. It truly means the world to me!

xoxo
Rachel

ABOUT THE AUTHOR

Photo © 2013 Kristi Kruse Photography

Rachel Lacey is an award-winning contemporary romance author and semi-reformed travel junkie. She's been climbed by a monkey on a mountain in Japan, gone scuba diving on the Great Barrier Reef, and camped out overnight in New York City for a chance to be an extra in a movie. These days, the majority of her adventures take place on the pages of the books she writes. She lives in the mountains of Vermont with her family and a variety of rescue pets.

Rachel loves to keep in touch with her readers! You can find her at www.RachelLacey.com, or say hi on Twitter (@rachelslacey) or at www.facebook.com/RachelLaceyAuthor.

Subscribe to her e-newsletter for exclusive news and giveaways: www.subscribepage.com/rachellaceyauthor.